This book is a work of fiction. References to real people, events, establishments, organizations, or locales are intended only to provide a sense of authenticity, and are used fictitiously. All other characters, and all incidents and dialogue, are drawn from the author's imagination and are not to be construed as real.

Cover illustration by Đức Lương.
Edited by Tiffani Gardner and Kari Cobham.

www.douthebook.com

DO U.

MARK S. LUCKIE

For black boys everywhere

JASON

The mirror lied. In its reflection stood a confident and presumably straight young man ready for a night of hard partying. In reality, I was a somewhat shy college student frightened to make his third journey to a gay club. My logic and reason implored me not to go. I wasn't "out," as they called it. To be seen again in a public space frequented by gay men would dissolve whatever secrecy I built for myself. My roommate Tyree was one of a very small number of people who knew about my struggle with my sexuality.

I wiped away the remaining steam clouding my reflection. A rinse of winterfresh toothpaste would give me a clearer perspective on my life.

"Jason, can you pass me that after you're done?" Tyree

asked. I obliged, slapping the narrow white tube into his hand.

Tyree went through his beauty regimen, slathering on lotion and twirling moisturizer in his loose curly hair. He would settle for nothing less than perfection before he would set foot out of our apartment. His golden brown complexion and plump pink lips were a dangerous combination he proclaimed "made all the boys weak."

The black shirt I wore did a decent job of covering the belly I carried around. My body wasn't svelte like Tyree's, but I was slim enough to take my shirt off in public and not offend anyone. To some people I might be handsome, but I considered myself to be a mélange of ordinary: short black hair, full lips and nose, and cocoa brown skin dotted with the occasional pockmark.

"Jason, I wanna go to the gay club with you guys tonight," came a voice from the living room.

What? My toothbrush dropped to the bathroom floor. Darn it, that was brand new. Tyree stood at the sink next to me with a mouthful of toothpaste. Unless he had become a master of ventriloquism, he couldn't have said it. Besides, Tyree was the one who suggested we go to the club tonight. I poked my head out of the bathroom door. Our other roommate Cole sat calmly on the living room couch as if he hadn't just made an unprecedented request.

"What did you say?" I asked.

"You heard me. I wanna go to the club too. See what you boys do when I'm not around," he said without flinching. "Is that cool?"

Tyree couldn't contain his shock. He slammed his bare toothbrush down to the counter and charged into the living room with me close at his heels.

"Bitch, you know this a *gay* club we goin' to? Hot guys, disco balls, lesbians, all that jazz?"

"Stop callin' me bitch and yeah, I know," Cole said. "Y'all my boys, right? I figured we should hang on your turf sometimes."

Tyree, Cole and I attended Morrison State University, a historically black college in Tampa, Florida. Cole was in his third year at the school and Tyree and I were sophomores. Cole had an athletic build from years of running track and ebony skin that was kissed by the sun. The bald head he shaved meticulously was complimented by a mid-sized beard that other male students from his hometown of Philadelphia also seemed to favor.

We were in our second semester as roommates and in the time I'd known Cole, he *never* wanted to go to a gay club with us. He wore his heterosexuality like a badge of honor. I'm sure we joked around at some point and extended the invitation to him, but I never thought he'd say yes.

"Okay, what are you gonna wear?" Tyree eyed him suspiciously.

"I dunno, a T-shirt and shorts?" Cole shrugged. Wrong answer.

Tyree's closet was a haven of designer clothing that bested the wardrobe of most other college students. His passion for sartorial excellence meant his roommates were held to an equally high standard. Tyree was more surprised by Cole's plan for a pedestrian outfit than his decision to accompany us for the night.

"I'm gonna have to stop you there," Tyree said. "You are not walkin' outta this apartment wearin' the clothes you found at the bottom of your gym bag! That is *not* cute."

"What's wrong with my clothes?" Cole shrugged.

"It's not that there's anything wrong with them—," I scratched my head.

"If you like that straight thug thing," Tyree interjected. "Please go find somethin' decent to put on and let us check you out first."

Cole dutifully ran off to his room to make a more appropriate selection. The three-bedroom, off-campus apartment we shared was not extravagant by any means, but it was enough for us to have our own space. It was also an upgrade from the shoebox dorm rooms we occupied last year. We populated our cozy living room with personal items and IKEA furniture. A paper lantern lamp and $10 plants in terra cotta pots accompanied a tomato-red couch that made for a restful study space.

We split the utilities and rent three ways, except for Tyree, who paid more because he had the larger room. He opted for it because it had the most impressive closet space. We wouldn't have dared to challenge him for it. Tyree and I stayed out of Cole's room, mostly because it always had the pungent aroma of a recently opened bag of corn chips.

"I don't know what you want me to wear!" Cole yelled from across the apartment.

"Get that red shirt outta my closet!" Tyree shouted back.

"It's too small!"

"Fool, put it on!"

Cole brought the V-neck shirt with him. He poked his head through the opening and tugged it over his broad shoulders. When Tyree wore the shirt, it hit him at the waist. Cole was shorter than both of us, so it held snugly to his hips. Cole was right. He was way too built for this one. It clung to his skin like Saran Wrap.

"Perfect!" Tyree said. Cole and I glared at him in confusion.

"Man, I can't breathe in this shit," he protested.

"Boy, you run track. You're used to pushin' your body, right?

Beauty knows no pain! Think of this as the gay Olympics and you're about to get a gold medal in *fierce!*" Tyree said with a snap. "Hold on is that Old Spice? You tryin' to smell like somebody's daddy? Wash that mess off and get the Tom Ford off the nightstand in my room."

Cole returned with the forest-green bottle and doused himself in sweet cologne. The aromatic blend of woodsy and fruity scents suffocated the room.

"Damn, we goin' to the club, not attractin' a mate on the Serengeti!" Tyree admonished him. He tossed a damp washcloth to Cole. "You s'posed to use a splash, not the entire bottle."

"I'm goin' to kick it with you guys, not get laid, remember?" Cole said as he scrubbed off the offending scent.

"Gay club, straight club, you not goin' out with us until we get you right."

"Whatever man. Jason, does this look okay?" Cole asked me.

"You're good to go," I smiled. "Consider this an act of love. We only want you to look your best."

Tyree unlocked the doors to the older model Camry his father gave him as a high school graduation present. Tyree named his prized possession "Candy" after a well-known promiscuous woman in his hometown. They both got around, he explained. Since I enrolled in college, I learned that having a friend with a car was more essential than textbooks. The three of us had many adventures in the city with Candy as our escort.

Tyree jumped in the driver's seat and I settled in the back. Cole situated himself in the front and turned the dial on the AC to its highest setting. It was a humid night in Tampa, which was par for the course. We turned off Fowler Avenue and drove south toward the club through the residential neighborhood we called home.

Our apartment was near the University Mall in an area of Tampa called Suitcase City. It was so named because supposedly everyone lived out of suitcases. However, contrary to the name, our neighborhood consisted of mostly families and other students living off campus. Suitcase City wasn't an ideal area, but the rent was affordable.

The best part of living here was that anything we could want was a short walk away. On Fletcher Avenue, there was a virtual buffet of fast food: McDonald's, Arby's, Krystal, you name it. The avenue stretched far across the city from the condos of Temple Terrace to the tree-lined roads of residential Carrollwood.

When I first moved to Tampa, I looked forward to going to Busch Gardens and Adventure Island theme park. I discovered upon arrival that most people who lived here didn't go to either of those places unless school was out. Instead, my roommates and I spent most of our time at the apartment or on campus. Cole saw more of Florida than any of us because he often traveled to meets with the track team.

My first time meeting Cole was at the Freshmen Beach Party during orientation week last year. The school arranged barbecue pits on the shore and played upbeat music to create a welcoming atmosphere for the new students. I walked by myself along the cool water when I saw a muscular male student in yellow board shorts splashing around in the tide. The sparkling water dripped with entrapment from his polished charcoal skin. I found myself captivated by the sizeable print in his shorts.

I never acknowledged until that moment that I was attracted to guys. I convinced myself that the right woman hadn't come along. The realization that I was lusting after someone of the same sex brought on dual feelings of euphoria and trepidation.

I paused my mental undressing of his figure when he sauntered toward me to say hello.

"Hi, how are you? I'm Jason," I said, extending my hand to shake his. I denied myself the pleasure of viewing his prominent bulge in such proximity.

"Hey, I'm Colin. Like Colin Powell. But my friends call me Cole," he said, firmly shaking my hand. "It's some fiyah ass females at this party, yeah?"

If there were a stampede of bikini-clad women around us, I wouldn't have noticed. I couldn't restrain myself from ogling his masculine form as he spoke. I shook off my wonder long enough to acknowledge the freshman girls in swimsuits relaxing on the sand. I mulled a decent reply to Cole's statement when the reality of what he said hit me. This guy was straight. So was I, but apparently not as much I previously believed.

"Yeah, they're pretty," I managed to say.

It was barely my first week in college. This was not the time or the place to conduct a haphazard confessional. I dulled the moment with small talk, sharing what Morrison was like for a newly minted incoming student. He nodded as I told him about my family and welcomed me to the school.

I asked if he was a freshman too. No, he was a sophomore, he said. He was a friend of the caterer and helped set up for the event. We exchanged small talk before he made his way back to the day's entertainment.

I continued my stroll down the beach, stunned by my confirmed attraction to men. It took a guy who was nearly nude, save for a thin sheath of nylon, to awaken the hibernating animal inside of me. It was this visceral reaction that I hoped I would feel for a girl but never seemed to happen.

Cole and I ran into each other the next day when I was on

my way to class. As luck would have it, he lived in the same dormitory as I did, in a room across the hall from the one Tyree and I shared. He had on significantly more clothes than he did on the beach. It helped my lust simmer down to a fraction of our first encounter. I expected that because of my drooling on the beach and Tyree's flamboyant ways that Cole would automatically distance himself from us, but he took it in stride.

Cole, Tyree and I became fast friends. We got along great because we may have had different personalities, but our sense of humor was similar. On one end of the scale, there was Tyree, who dabbled in irreverence. On the other, there was Cole whose subtle wisecracks flew under the radar if we weren't listening closely. I was in a safe spot somewhere in the middle. The next fall, we all moved off campus to save money on the pricey cost of dormitory living.

Despite our easygoing friendship, Cole's declaration that he would join us tonight was no less of a surprise. Most straight guys would never consider setting foot in a gay club. I wasn't totally comfortable heading there and I had visited with Tyree twice previously.

"Did you let April know you were coming?" I asked Cole. I worried that his girlfriend would accuse Tyree and I of forcing him to tag along.

"Hell naw, man," he scowled. "What I look like tellin' my girl I'm goin' to a gay club? You know she's touched in the head."

"Did you call that girl touched?" Tyree wailed. "Oh my God, Cole. You can't say that about your girl, boo! She is a wild one, though. But that's the Bonnie to your Clyde."

"Yeah, I can't front. She's good to me," he admitted. "So what's the club like anyway?"

"Why? You nervous?" Tyree asked playfully. "Big, strapping

man like yourself? You ain't got nothin' to worry about."

"No, nothing like that," Cole shifted in his seat. "I wanna know what I'm gettin' myself into."

"It's like every other place," Tyree explained. "Except instead of girls dancing on boys, it's boys dancing on boys, girls dancing on girls and those whose gender ain't none of your concern dance with whoever they want."

"Sounds complicated."

"Not as much as you would think it is. Let's lay down three ground rules," Tyree continued. "Rule number one: don't embarrass me. Rule number two: don't embarrass yourself."

"And what's the third rule?" Cole asked.

"If you see somebody cute, give him my number, my class schedule and the spare key to our apartment."

We followed the yellow lines of Nebraska Avenue, past other late-night revelers to Ybor City, a nightlife district no more than fifteen minutes from our home. There were clubs in our neighborhood that didn't require a drive, but I wouldn't chance being seen at a gay establishment so close to campus. I hadn't planned to issue a declaration of my sexual preferences. A fellow student discovering me in a gay club would be exactly that.

Tyree didn't care if the party was one minute or one hour away from Morrison, but he understood my hesitation. I didn't go out much before I met him, to his delight. He was eager to usher me into a new experience I had never been exposed to. I agreed to the venture because after meeting Cole, I was tantalized by the prospect of a room full of men attracted to other men. The most excitement I experienced before my arrival to college was in church, a far cry from a vibrant nightclub.

I grew up in Athens — an hour's drive east of Atlanta —

with my mom, Deborah Lila Cooper, and my big sister Jamie. We lived in a small, two-bedroom house in Five Points, near Athens Medical Center. My mother worked there as a nurse, so she cherished the convenience. The area I called home since elementary school was cleaner and safer than some of the other places in Athens, most likely because it was so close to the University of Georgia.

Our street was separated from the school by the university's mecca of a football field. Jamie and I knew to stay indoors on game nights. The lights from the stadium that shone like a beacon over the city attracted fans from across the state. Having one of the best schools in the South for a neighbor kept my sights on college as my next step after high school. UGA was truly a major influence on me, but in my senior year I declined to apply there. I wanted my college experience to take place somewhere other than the area where I'd lived for most of my life.

My mother was reluctant for me to leave her care. She had always been protective of her only son. I couldn't say the same for my dad whom I'd never met. All I knew of him was that his name was Jim, and he lived somewhere in Tallahassee. My mom never talked about him much except for when she was on the phone with my grandmother who had retired to Tuscaloosa. Even then, she spoke with her mouth pressed against the phone so Jamie and I couldn't hear her. I'd catch brief snippets of her describing what "that man" did to the family.

Many of my classmates' fathers weren't in their lives either, so it wasn't as much of a disruption as one would think. With my mother, Jamie and I in the house, I never felt at a loss for family. I did always wonder who my dad was and what he did to be excommunicated by my mother. From what I gathered, he asked to visit us several times in the past but my mom always flat out refused. A part of me wanted to catch a bus to Tallahassee or search the internet to find out more about the man from whose loins I sprung.

I yearned to know where he and my mother met or if he missed his son and daughter. To my credit, I had the self-awareness to not be felled by my curiosity. I wouldn't be satisfied with one tidbit of information about him. I likely wouldn't stop until I uncovered everything there was to know about "Jim". It was better to know nothing than only a portion of the truth.

My mom's love for me was unwavering, and I returned it many times over. She was in her 50s, with skin the color of maple syrup and gray strands poking out of her straight black hair. My mother was a registered nurse in her younger days. She decided early in her career that a life surrounded by sick and dying people wasn't what she had in mind for herself.

She left the profession to become the secretary at our church. She wanted to do the Lord's work, she said. We spent a great deal of time in the sanctuary growing up: service on Sundays, Bible study on Tuesdays and revivals on Fridays. I could recite the Bible as if it were my ABCs. There wasn't a scripture or verse that wasn't a part of my lexicon.

After I graduated from junior high, our family needed more money to satisfy the needs of two growing children. My mom quit her job at the church office to return to the hospital. She didn't want to leave what became our second home, but she was steadfast in maintaining an unburdened life for Jamie and I.

My mother endured the re-certification process and with help from her children, we brought her up to speed on how to expertly navigate a computer. The hospital started her off in the records department and eventually moved her to the front desk of the maternity ward. There, she admitted pregnant women and their families.

When there were no births occurring on her floor it gave my mother had her own semi-private space where she could read her pocket Bible in peace. She sent the occasional text to me asking how her precious son was doing. I didn't have to hear her voice to know that she loved me. I felt it with every message I received.

My sister Jamie was five years older than I, resilient, and like my mother took me under her wing to nurture me. Many times we visited Lay Park in Athens where I would watch her play basketball. With an assortment of impressive layups and three-pointers, she would easily outscore the men whom she competed against.

Becoming a pro ball player was the aspiration of everyone on the court, except for Jamie. Her ambitions extended beyond landing a game-ending jump shot. She joined the Army my first year of high school and was eventually dispatched to Germany where she worked as a fire support specialist. With Jamie overseas and my mom working at the hospital, I was often the only person in our house.

I spent most of my time in solitude completing my homework and reading every book that Jamie left behind. I pored through the candy-colored Dr. Seuss tales, then moved on to aged copies of the "Lion, the Witch and the Wardrobe," "Fahrenheit 451," "Their Eyes Were Watching God," and every science fiction tale written by Octavia Butler, my favorite author. No matter what book I found myself engrossed in, my mom always made sure I read the Bible too.

Toward the end of high school, I bloomed into more of a social butterfly. I became involved in school clubs and frequented varsity basketball games to cheer on my friends whose athleticism far outpaced my own. The cheerleaders always sat adjacent to us doing their routines. Among them was a girl named Lisa who developed an intense crush on me.

While the squad performed their rousing moves, Lisa would attempt to catch my eye. Rather than root on the team, she channeled her praise my way. One day, as I left a game with friends, she pulled me to the side and asked if I'd ever consider going on a date with her. Lisa had waited for to me approach her first, but I never returned her advances.

I agreed without hesitation because it seemed like the natural thing to do at the time. My other classmates had girlfriends too. I went along with the status quo as I had done so often in my life. I spent time with Lisa, but I knew that something was off about our chemistry.

At the time, I didn't know what being gay meant and hadn't labeled myself as such. I was taught since I could remember that succumbing to homosexuality meant turning away from God's word and was a sure path to eternal damnation. The gay men that I could clearly identify in my neighborhood had feminine mannerisms and wore flamboyant clothing. That wasn't me. I had no reason to be concerned, I told myself. Yet, I had to know more.

When my mom worked the night shift, I would sneak and watch television shows that featured the occasional gay Black character. I could conduct my investigation from my living room without being judged. I was just curious after all. In my research, I found that some of the actors were feminine but a lot of them were no different from any straight guy on the street. They interacted with other men as if it was completely normal. Their smiles in each other's company beamed from the screen. I didn't understand how anyone could be so content living in sin.

I thought I was careful in my analysis until one evening my mom came home early from work. On her television were two men with their lips locked in unrepentant hunger. She nearly dove to turn it off and scolded me in the form of a barrage of questions about my sexuality. I had no answers for her.

My mother forced me to sit in an uncomfortable chair and read the Bible to me for three hours. Her hands were weighted with sadness as she carefully turned the pages. She spoke slowly so I could absorb every mournful word. I was terrified that she wouldn't love me anymore. Would I still be her son?

We never talked about her disappointment in me after that night. My mom either believed that the marathon scripture reading drove away the demons that tempted her son or she completely shut out the reality of what occurred. She couldn't bring herself to admit that her son might be gay.

I prayed to God many nights for Him to shift my devotion to girls as He intended for me. I didn't want my mom to think that she failed a test of motherhood because her son had possibly fallen victim to homosexuality. I wanted to rid myself of the thoughts that permeated my every being, but I couldn't. My devotion to Lisa waned and fleeting daydreams about my male classmates increased.

Tyree was the reason I was less conflicted about my internal struggles. Before we became roommates our freshman year, I had never met anyone so secure in who he was. Tyree's personality was magnetic. He brought joy to the people around him and sparked conversations where others fell short. He was always the life of the party even when he made no attempt to be.

I never told Tyree outright that I liked guys, though he

suspected I did when we were paired as roommates. The truth was exposed when we watched the movie "Any Given Sunday" on cable one late Friday night. Halfway through the film there was a jaw-dropping scene where a locker room of football players clothed in nothing but air taunted us with the thick ropes between their legs. I practically salivated at the explicit display of manhood. I gawked at the screen, then turned to Tyree.

"We have to rewind that!" we both exclaimed.

We grew closer as the truth emerged, but it took time for me to be seen with Tyree around campus. He was undoubtedly gay and it would arouse suspicion about my sexuality. I didn't want our fellow students to label me with the "G" word.

Tyree didn't attempt to pull me out of the closet, but he did persuade me to explore the gay dating app Grindr. I could indulge in my infatuation with the same sex from behind the veil of my cell phone. I created an account sans photos or personal information that would reveal my identity. Despite my bleak profile, several guys from the Tampa area pinged me to talk. I browsed the sexually charged photos that they posted of themselves. Sometimes we had small conversations that never went anywhere. The meat market was appealing, but I had no interest in connecting with anyone in person.

It took one man to change my perspective. I idled on Grindr for the fifth night in a row, prepared for the same merry-go-round of online conversation. I received a message from "Vaughn." His photos were marked as private, so I had nothing more to go on besides his description of himself. The language in his profile was nothing like the hookup-centric autobiographies that populated the site, so I accepted his chat.

I was enraptured by his personality without ever seeing the

face behind the photos. We exchanged messages for an hour before Vaughn unlocked his pictures for me. In them was a caramel-skinned stallion with lips the color of bubble gum, a shaved head, and a smile brighter than a Georgia sunrise. His toned, but not overtly muscular, figure was similar to the models whose photos hung in the windows of Abercrombie & Fitch clothing stores.

We talked online for hours about our families, our favorite music, and life at Morrison. Vaughn was a freshman English major hoping to become a professor one day. He kept his images private to weed out those who may have pursued him solely based on his physique. Who could blame them? His extraordinary beauty and wit were unlike anything I encountered before. I couldn't stop thinking about him after our conversation. I was enthralled when we talked on the phone the next night and every night after that.

Before I knew it, we were in each other's company nearly every day. I was open to new experiences with him, sometimes literally. I melted whenever I was in his presence. Vaughn was the first person other than my mom and sister that I truly cared for. It was unnerving for me to be so close to another guy, but he made me forget the endless run of scripture and sermons that forbade homosexuality. He was worth it. I prayed my mother could forgive me.

As time went on, I spent many nights in Vaughn's dorm room when his roommate was out of town. We discreetly dead-bolted the door to prevent any surprises. We didn't want anyone coming in and seeing us making love on every available surface. Our time with each other wasn't solely dedicated to quenching our sexual thirst. Among my most cherished moments with Vaughn was when he propped his pillows against his cold dormitory wall so we could watch the anime series I liked. He wasn't a fan, but he lay with me in his bed because he was keen to share my interests.

The one rift that remained between us was that he was more open about his sexuality than I was. If someone were to ask, he would tell them he was gay. "Coming out" was an antiquated notion in a world that assumed everyone was straight, he said. His sexual preference didn't require an announcement. I wasn't immediately put off by his stance because most people never questioned him.

Vaughn wanted me to be less reserved about my feelings, but I wasn't fearless like he was. I could never present him as a romantic interest to anyone, especially my mom. She didn't need to know about Vaughn, Tyree, or any trips to the Alibi, which she would consider to be a black hole of perdition.

As the car turned onto 7th Avenue, the parade of rambunctious college students that were a mainstay of the area alerted us to what lay ahead. During the day, Ybor City was an innocuous collection of classic storefronts with wrought iron balconies. At night, it turned into Mardi Gras. The street was populated by outrageously drunk revelers and the people who came to watch their tomfoolery. There was entertainment to be had on every corner of the street.

"Let's make some magic," Tyree said as we pulled into the gravelly parking lot of the Alibi. He double-checked his eyebrows and hair in the rear-view mirror.

"Yeah, let's do this," Cole said. He didn't sound as sure as he did when we left the apartment. I kept a close eye on him to make sure he didn't leap back into the car and drive off.

From the outside, the Alibi looked harmless. It was a concrete building with a lacquered red door and its name spelled out in a lightbox sign. The only indications that it was a gay club were the guys at the entrance mingling like bees in a hive looking for their potential honey.

A security guard stood fastidiously at the door. His grizzled face would have been threatening if I didn't know of the gaiety that awaited us inside. "Have your IDs out!" he shouted as we approached.

The guard stamped Cole's hand with a purple smiley face because he was 21, barely meeting the legal drinking age. I was only 19, but I wouldn't let a stamp stop me from enjoying a drink or three. I needed the liquid courage.

"Arms out," the guard commanded me.

I spread my arms and legs for the routine pat down that was required for every partygoer. He skillfully ran his hands over my torso and down each leg. The search ended with a lustful grab of my crotch. That was thorough! If I had a stick of gum hidden in my underwear he would've found it. I wondered if he was straight or gay. His review suggested the latter, but who could be sure?

"You good," he finally waved me away.

The thundering bass of hip-hop music invited us inside. The club was so packed it would have left a fire marshal speechless. There was a crowd of wallflowers lined against the perimeter downing mixed drinks from plastic cups. Behind them were a hundred more writhing bodies bathed in artificial smoke and neon lights. A long bar stretched through most of the impossibly warm room. Every wall was covered in mirrors, most notably behind the stage they used for drag shows.

When I first became aware of the existence of gay clubs back in high school, I thought they would be populated by shirtless white guys with jacked bodies that sipped daintily on apple martinis. The men would vogue excessively to the gay pop anthems of Cher or Madonna. The Alibi was the opposite of the glittering paradise of Anglo-Saxon sodomy I imagined. The room was full of young men with varying shades of brown skin swerving to the irresistible baselines of hip-hop, R&B and reggae music.

At first glance, one would think the Alibi was a collection of streetwise thugs posturing from under their tilted caps. It was an easy assumption to make were it not for the details that took a trained eye to detect. Their lips were eagerly coated with sticky balm and their chests were shaved with precise detail. Layers of jewelry were strategically placed to create an effortless look.

In their attempt to separate themselves from gay stereotypes, some of the guys became an unintentional parody of the braggadocious rappers in the music videos on YouTube.

Cole was wide-eyed as he soaked in our environment. "What kind of trap y'all got me in?" he asked anxiously.

"Calm down, baby boy. The night hasn't even begun," Tyree said.

We did our best to shuffle through the gauntlet of patrons. A trip from one end of the club to the other that should have taken sixty seconds or less required ten minutes of pushing past an unending stream of gay men with raging hormones. A few of them took advantage of the closeness. They "accidentally" pressed their crotch against the lower half of my body or ran their hands along my waist as I squeezed by.

"Oh, my bad, wassup shawty?" they'd say with a flirtatious

smile. I was always polite but kept moving.

"Remember, Cole," Tyree said, "If you see somebody from school, say a quick hello if you want, but don't go back to campus tomorrow talkin' 'bout who or what you saw."

"Why not? They're here…" Cole was confused, but to be fair, I asked the same question the first time I came.

"Everybody who's in the club ain't out," Tyree nodded my way. "They might not want their story on the yard. Morrison is a small school so let's not give the kids more to talk about, m'kay?"

"Gotcha," Cole said. "Ay yo, check out that girl over there. I thought it was gonna be all dudes in here."

Sure enough, there was a gorgeous woman not far from us. Her lovely features were accentuated by a healthy dose of makeup. The gazelle wore hip-hugging blue jeans, a vintage Lil' Kim tee and her hair pulled back from her face. Her sway was arousingly feminine as she approached us.

"That's not a girl," I whispered.

"What?" Cole turned his head.

Upon closer inspection, the "woman" was anything but. It was Tyree's friend, Derrick, whom he affectionately called Day Day. Derrick graduated from Morrison two years ago and became the assistant student activities director for the school. He was one of the overtly feminine gay men I tried to avoid on campus. In the dim lights of the club, it was easy to mistake the 6 foot 1 inch tall drag queen for a biological woman.

"Hey, gurrrl!" Day Day delivered a loving peck on Tyree's cheek. "What's good? What's the business?"

"Ain't nothin' goin' on but the rent. You look exquisite!" Tyree fawned over him.

"And you're looking like a platinum mine," Derrick replied.

"Who is this chocolate wonder with you?"

"Day Day, this is my roommate, Cole." Tyree ushered him over.

"Wassup, how you doin'?" Cole shook his hand politely. I expected Cole to be taken aback by the sight of Derrick, the female illusionist, but he took the introduction in stride. Cole seemed more amused than anything.

"Ooh trade *and* good-looking! I'm loving it!" Derrick placed his hand in Cole's. "Pleasure to make your acquaintance! Hello Jason, good to see you again."

I pulled back as Derrick attempted to kiss me on the cheek. To start, I didn't want my face marred with makeup. Also, I didn't want a kiss from a man who was more confused about his sexuality than I was.

"Chile, why you always acting so scared around me? Like I killed your puppy or something. Relax! It's only CoverGirl and a Malaysian silky weave," Day Day teased. "We're family within these walls. No shade. Ain't that right Tyree?"

"Yes, ma'am!"

Derrick flipped his ponytail forward and stroked it tenderly like a pet. The Black Rapunzel was deeply in love with himself. I forced a respectful smile. While Derrick and Tyree conversed, I pulled Cole toward the bar. "We're off to get drinks," I said as we walked away.

I came to understand some of the complexities of being gay, but I couldn't wrap my head around men who altered their appearance to look like women. Why would anyone want to wear dresses and heels when God made them a man? I could handle Tyree's eccentricity because he never crossed that line. Derrick pranced around like a girl every time I saw him. Just because he was Tyree's friend didn't mean he had to be mine too.

I let Cole jostle his way to the bar so he could order for us.

I rarely saw any of the staff other than security check for the smiley face stamp, but I didn't want to tempt fate.

"Can I get two Jack and Cokes!" he yelled over the din to the bartender. We were swiftly equipped with our introductory drinks. Cups in hand, we edged toward the seats facing the dance floor. Cole immediately tossed the stirrer resting among his ice cubes and gulped his drink. He squinted his eyes from the burn of the alcohol. Cole was not ready for the strength of the liquor the Alibi so generously provided to its guests. It was their way of loosening people up and ensuring they visited again.

"There is NO Coke in this whiskey and Coke," he inspected the cup.

"I should've warned you," I smiled. "So what do you think?"

"About the club? It's cool. How often do you boys come here?"

"Tyree has been here many times, but I'm still a rookie. I came back again because it's nice to be in the company of guys with the same interests."

"Sexual interests?" he joked.

"You know what I mean," I said. "So you don't wish you were at a straight club right now?"

"Would you be mad if I said yeah? The music is on point, though," he reclined in his chair. "I'm doin' the same thing I'd be doing at any other place, minus the females. You good?"

"I'm excellent," I said.

My eyes followed the gyrating frames in front of us silhouetted by strobe lights. The music the Alibi played was enchanting for both participants and observers. A group of guys at the table next to us nodded, their chins mirroring the rhythm of the dancers.

Cole caught me admiring them. "Jason, what kind of guys do you like?" he asked.

I resisted the urge to tell him about Vaughn, who I was still trying to figure out for myself. I wasn't ready to expose him to my roommates just yet. Cole had seen Vaughn before, but he didn't know how close we were. Instead, I pointed to a clean-cut guy that was attractive enough to satisfy Cole's curiosity. "Him."

"Why don't you go holla? Get you some booty," he nudged me. "I wanna see what you can do."

"Cole, I could never approach someone in a bar. Not even someone as good-looking as he is."

"How do you hit on dudes then? Do y'all have a secret gay handshake or somethin'?"

"And what would that look like?" I laughed. "The real secret is most guys use social media or apps on their phones to connect with each other. I prefer it too. Meeting a guy on the internet first ensures I'll know something more about him than whether he's cute or not."

"Like if he's crazy?"

"I can handle a dash of insanity. After all, you and I are friends," I winked. "You've given me lots of practice."

TYREE

"Yasssss girl, go in! You givin' 'em fever tonight, Miss Day!" I wagged my finger.

"Thank you, darling! It is my moral obligation to bring beauty into the world," Day Day gushed.

My ace boon coon had eyelashes bigger than eagles' wings and her face was beat for the *gods*. Day was sample-size thin with hair that had other girls holdin' on to their edges for dear life. She swung that weave from side to side for extra drama.

Everybody knew Day Day as Derrick when he was on campus. In the sacred halls of the Alibi, she was Dayneisha Divine, the fiercest queen in all of Tampa. Day Day hosted the drag show they put on every Friday night before most people got here to dance. For about an hour or so, somewhere between two to five girls got on stage and lip synced to their favorite songs. Occasionally they went in on dance and pop tunes, but mostly they performed to classic soul records or R&B hits that moved the club to its feet.

Day Day was one kick-ass performer. The other girls did enough lip syncin' to snatch a dollar or two. But Miss Day gave you acrobatics that made Cirque du Soleil look like a preschool musical. She was Diana Ross, Mariah Carey and Miss Whitney all rolled into one.

I first met Day Day in the Student Activities office when she was giving the campus boy, no makeup. I wanted to get the details about an event the next week. He gave me the info and complimented me on my leather Michael Kors satchel. I told him I lived for the turquoise, mandarin collar shirt he wore. Nothing like impeccable style to bring two people together.

We talked for an hour about our favorite stores in Tampa, places outside the city we wanted to visit, gossip, et cetera, et cetera. Students came in and out of the office with nary an acknowledgment from either of us. Day Day became my road dog after that. I loved that boy like a sister. I did my best to never miss any of her shows.

Day Day placed her manicured hands on her waist. "It's always good to see you and Jason at my palace. And you brought Cole with you? We love a good muscle boy in our midst."

"Yeah, he finally made it to the club. I can't believe it," I said.

"Me either, hunny. What's he doing here with us homosexuals? Is he going through a psychological change in his life?" Day said with a smirk.

"Chile cheese, he's straighter than Madam C. J. Walker's hair," I said. "He's gonna be on his best behavior. You performin' tonight, babe?"

"Don't downplay my position now, I am a *headliner*, thank you very much. I get more coins in my paycheck than the other girls. Lord knows I need 'em because I have to pay my cable bill and snatch me some groceries. My fridge is on E," Day Day said, waving to the group of cute guys coming through the door. "I want whatever man that's going to be at my house tonight to have something to snack on besides yours truly."

"Then what's going on?" I asked. "Where is your dress?"

"This one left it at the house," she said, pointing at her friend, Korey, who sauntered our way with a long garment bag. "He abandoned it like it was a broken-down Chevy on the side of the road."

Korey was a pecan pie-colored piece of work with cheekbones as high as the heavens. He was a senior studying hospitality management at Morrison during the day and getting his cosmetology license at night. His makeup skills were so on point that Day Day made him his personal beautician. If Korey wasn't a *lady,* he could get a taste of my stuff.

"You wouldn't have this dress if it wasn't for me." Korey stuffed the bag in Day Day's arms. "You should get ready 'cause the show's gonna begin soon."

"Hunny, boo. These kids can wait," Day Day batted her false eyelashes. "The show starts when I say it does."

"If you don't get ready now, the only coins you'll be snatching are the pennies in my ashtray," Korey sucked his teeth. "That means you'll have to find a sugar daddy. And we know you don't have the looks for that."

"Is the library open?" Day Day gasped. "Because you are *reading* me tonight. Don't pay him any mind, Tyree. He always wants all eyes to be on him."

"I don't need attention Dayneisha. I am *drowning* in attention. Get you some," Korey held his head high. After being around Day Day from sunup to sundown, Korey was not in the least bit moved by her shenanigans. They threw shade back and forth but at the end of the day they were the very best of friends.

"Korey, since you snatchin' wigs, when are we gonna see you get all dolled up?" I asked.

"Not anytime soon," he snickered. "I'm giving sex siren, not butch queen in drags. I don't need five layers of pancake foundation like these other girls. I am naturally flawless. Besides, Dayneisha is servin' enough fish for the whole club."

"Yes and I'm giving you *daytime* fish. Get into these 'look at me' legs! You can't take it," she laughed.

Just as I turned to find Jason and Cole, the DJ played one of my favorite songs by Trina, the baddest bitch in hip-hop. Nobody could resist her raunchy lyrics and unstoppable bass. Her voice was a seductive call telling me to join her on the dance floor. Day Day and Korey were gonna have to do without me for a while.

"Bye Tyree! Catch you after the show!" Dayneisha said. She understood my craving for body motion.

I stomped toward the dance floor like my name was Naomi Campbell. Whenever I walked in the club, I was a supermodel serving European runway. I wasn't looking left; I wasn't looking right. It was all about *me,* and I was focused on werkin' it. I had my Topshop shirt on and my devastating skinny jeans were snug as a bug in a rug. I worked my hips to the beat like the kids never saw before. On the dance floor, I could be whoever I wanted to be.

Trina's hardcore rap faded out and the music switched to deep house music with a hard-hitting groove. The room went wild. The floor vibrated from people banging their feet on the wood beneath us. The kids did their best to hold on to drinks and make that ass clap at the same time. They weren't doing a very good job 'cause liquor splashed every which way. See, this was exactly why I didn't drink. I didn't need to be messy to have a good time. I decided early in my college experience that I would stay away from that toxic garbage. I refused to blame alcohol for any portion of my behavior.

That didn't mean I couldn't step out for a night on the town. The Alibi was one of my favorite places in the city to enjoy myself. It wasn't much to look at, but it was way better than anything in Jackson where I was raised. My hometown was cool and whatnot. People just seemed to have more going on for themselves in Tampa. In Mississippi, not too many people ever left the towns where they grew up. Morrison took me away and I hadn't looked back since.

I did miss my daddy. Cecil Iversen was an older man in his 60s, with fuzzy black hair that thinned at the top. He was never without his bifocals or a funny joke for his son. His spirit was young and fresh. I was the one who had to keep up with him because my daddy was forever making sure I was happy. That meant going on mini adventures from time to time. He had me in art classes, summer camp and all kinds of after school activities. I could make a macaroni necklace before I knew what two plus two was.

My daddy was a lawyer with a successful practice. His office stayed busy because he got along with everybody who came through. He was highly regarded in the Jackson community for his service. Before I came to college, I would hang out at his front desk and do my homework. When his secretary called in sick, I answered the phones for him. No matter how much work my daddy had, he always made time for me.

I can't say me and my mother had the same relationship. That woman was so not into me being gay. Not that she called me out of my name or beat me; she was just a shady person. She'd call me something rude on the low like 'girl' or 'queen' and not in a 'yass queen!' way. More like 'I wish you would act like a man in my presence.' Family or not, nobody wants to be around that kind of attitude.

When I was twelve years old, my mother left us to be with a guy she met at a jazz festival. The same one we used to go to as a family for years. It broke my daddy's heart when he found out that my mother cheated on him. It hurt him more when she packed her bags and walked out. Without any warning, my father had a son to take care of by himself. I was different from the other boys. He knew that from that get-go. I wasn't the baseball playing Boy Scout he planned for, but he was there for me whenever I needed him.

Daddy sometimes drove me to the Northpark Mall because he knew it was one of my favorite places in Jackson. We'd spend hours going into the different stores, not buying a thing. It wasn't the clothes or the products I was interested in; it was how each store in the mall was its own universe.

Bath & Body Works had candles and light-colored wood on the walls that made me feel like I was at a spa in the country somewhere. When I went into H&M, it was like stepping into a disco. The store had sleek white walls and fierce mannequins slipped between the racks. They were the audience and I was the star of the show. Latest fashions modeled by yours truly.

For my 16th birthday, my daddy took me to the Mall of America in Minneapolis. I got my life! There were so many stores I couldn't take it. I must have hit all 400 of 'em! My eyes were the size of balloons pacing the corridors. Each nook had a unique design that enticed the passing shoppers. I browsed everything from kids' toys to high-end furniture. It was like I had died and went to mall heaven.

Growing up, I always wanted to have a career in something related to fashion. The industry was about beauty, fun and expressing yourself. That was me to a tee. The funny thing was that I loved clothes, but I couldn't sew a lick. It was the presentation I was into. That trip to God's gift of a mall was my indication that I much preferred the marketing side of fashion to anything else. I decided before I enrolled in college to pursue a fashion merchandising degree. After the clothes were made, it would be my job to figure out how to make 'em sell. It was still in that creative zone I wanted to be a part of.

I thought about going to school in New York or L.A. because that was where the companies and designers were. From what I saw on TV, it seemed like those places were too fast for me. I was a country boy through and through. Also, I didn't want to be so far from my daddy.

Morrison had one of the most prolific business schools in the South and the best out of all the other historically black colleges. Tampa was a half-day ride from Jackson. If these tired children ran me low, I could hop in my car and drive on the I-10 to the Mississippi state line.

Getting into college was the easy part. Figuring out how to pay for it was another thing. Daddy made decent money from his practice but didn't have a ton saved up. When I got accepted to Morrison, we had to think through our finances. Daddy agreed to pay for my housing and I did work study for spending money. The school gave me a student loan to cover my tuition. That was thousands of dollars that was eventually gonna come out of my pocket. I wouldn't worry about it until that first bill came. For now, my only problem was getting a good view of this drag show.

"*Hello,* everybody!" Day Day's high-pitched voice dominated the club. A good chunk of the boys who were dancing went straight to the bar to get a refill. The rest of 'em hustled to get to the open tables for a good view of the show.

Some of the gays acted like they weren't into drag queens. I didn't know if it was a masculine thing or what, but those of us in our right minds knew this was the real entertainment on tonight. What the down low types didn't understand was that these girls didn't wanna be women. They earned a living the same as everybody else. They just happened to wear fabulous gowns while they did it.

When Day Day took off that makeup and big hair, she was a boy. A femme boy, but no less of a man. Jason didn't care for her, but he needed to get a clue and buy a vowel. He was missing out on a beautiful individual.

Day Day was on the stage holding a microphone, poised like she was Aretha Franklin ready to give an encore. She had on a long, tan overcoat that covered everything from her neck to her feet. I couldn't wait to see what was hidden underneath it. The flashes of red peeking out the bottom meant there was something extra sickening in store for us.

"Good evening, lovelies! My name is Dayneisha Divine, and I am your diva-stating host tonight! The Alibi welcomes you and we certainly welcome your money. If you're in this place, we know you got paid! Be sure you get a drink from the bar and tip those sexy bartenders while you do it. Their gym memberships ain't cheap and neither am I, hunny. We accept ones, fives, tens and twenties. We do not discriminate. And if you see my boyfriend Ben Franklin you tell him he needs to come see me, alroight?"

Day Day walked regally across the stage, making sure everybody was good and ready for the show. The kids ate up every word that left her ruby lips.

"We've got some exceptional talent performing for you," Day Day announced. "Coming first to the stage is Miss Feroshima Foxwoods from At-LAN-tah Georgia, dahling. She drove down in her Buick and she's ready do it to it. A round of applause for Feroshima!"

Day Day exited stage left as Miss Foxwoods sashayed from the right. The girl had on black leather booty shorts and a matching jacket with a high gold collar. White topaz chandelier earrings dangled next to her shellacked face. Her song was an old school dance number, Crystal Waters' "100% Pure Love." The curly black wig and hooker heels she flaunted moved and grooved across the stage.

Feroshima exaggerated every word of her lip sync while she expertly collected the dollars people held out for her. She caressed each boy's hand as she took the bill to let him know she appreciated the gesture. In the second chorus of the song, Feroshima threw the fistful of money in the air to make it rain. The whirlwind of cash made the performance more exciting and freed her hands for more tips.

Korey handed Feroshima a five, then parked in a seat next to me. "What do you think about her?"

"She's turnin' the party!" I said as I did the snake in my seat.

"Dayneisha is next. Get ready for real talent."

As the lights went low, Feroshima scooped the decent stash she'd earned from off the floor. The smoky room was quiet except for the faint sound of record scratches. "Oooh-ooooooh..." The sweet, sultry voice of Beyoncé whispered over the speakers.

Two notes into the song and the boys lost their damn mind as if Destiny's Children descended from a white cloud into the room. If there was one way to get the gays peeing their panties it was Beyoncé. Her song "Yes" was the slow jam that got them together. Day Day was a smart girl for picking this one.

The spotlight brightened and there she was. Dayneisha Divine wore a floor-length, red latex evening gown and a jet black, bouffant wig so high it almost touched the ceiling. The light caught every curve of her body as she slunk from here to there. She gave Jessica Rabbit a run for her money. Yes *gawd*, mama! Go in!

When Dayneisha lip synced, she gave face *and* body. The way she angled her hips you would think she hopped off the pages of the September issue of Vogue magazine. Those toned arms of hers were the only giveaway she had something extra downstairs. Otherwise, she was all woman. The kids got their dollars out before Day Day could get into the first verse. She gently collected the bills, letting them float to the stage beneath her. Get into that glamour!

All of a sudden, the slow jam stopped and the pulsating beats of Beyoncé's female empowerment anthem "Run the World" boomed around us. The boys by the bar stuck out their necks to see what the fuss was about.

My girl tore the bottom half of her gown away to reveal a red, latex swimsuit underneath. She had on copper-colored nylons that made her legs look exceptional. And she used those stems! She gave kicks; she gave twirls. Day Day got *down* on the stage. Some of the other queens gave watered down, third lead vocalist performances. Dayneisha served one hundred percent Sasha Fierce.

Without pausing for breath, Day Day jumped straight up, kicked her leg to a ninety-degree angle and death dropped to the ground. The line of guys crowding the stage lost their minds! Dollars flew everywhere! Day Day threw her fist in the air as Beyoncé shouted one last "Girls!"

Day Day's lip sync was tighter than her tuck. My ears rang from the rabid cheering and clapping going on around me. Korey ran to the stage and handed my girl a mic. She wasn't gonna let a lack of oxygen stop her from keeping the show going.

"How was that, darlings? Did you enjoy it?" Day Day gleefully moved a loose strand of hair from her face. "You have your girl feeling like royalty! I love it! This is why we perform, to make sure you boys are entertained, so thank you so much for the support. That's going to be it for us for now. Grab somebody and have fun tonight! Turn up the musiiiiic!"

When the room went dark, everybody who kept their distance at the bar came running to the dance floor. It was almost pitch black with purple lights surrounding the dancers. I swayed to the music that moved me. My arms reached up to the sky. With the lights down low, I could move any way I pleased.

I felt hands on my waist. I spun around expecting it to be Jason or Cole, but it was a boy that I had never seen before. I could barely make out what he looked like, but he had dimples that gave him a friendly essence. I ran with it, as one tends to do in the club. I couldn't resist such a noble gesture. He matched my rhythm while our hips gave life to the music. It was a fast house song, but I moved slow, pressing myself close to him. I wanted the boy to feel all of me.

I rotated my ass so he could get into my cake. I wasn't

pussy popping aggressively like the boys around us. I let my body ripple from my lower back to my ass. I didn't need words to let him know I had a high interest in the merchandise he was selling. I spun one more time so I could get a better look at his face.

"You're a fantastic dancer," I said. My voice was breathier than I intended it to be.

"You are too," he replied. "Better than anyone else here. I had to come over to see if I could get a dance with you. What's your name?" he asked.

"It's Tyree. What's yours? You from around here?" I whirled my head away from him and wiped the sweat from my brow in one smooth motion. Had to keep it classy. First impressions were everything.

"My name's Chris and nope, I'm from Gainesville. I'm here with my cousin for his birthday."

"Oh really? Where's your cousin?"

He pointed to the tables behind me where I sat earlier. I scanned the room to see who he was talking about, but there were so many people around us it was a lost cause. Chris delicately turned my head to face him.

"Hey, you didn't come here to check out my family," he said.

"You're right about that, sugar," I cooed. The music pounded faster and so did my heartbeat. I liked this one. His beard tickled my neck as we danced, making me feel good inside. Every guy in the bar should've been jealous of me and Chris. This was the kinda action they dreamed about getting at the club.

"Where are you from?" he asked.

"From Jackson, but I live here," I said.

"A Mississippi boy! What are you doing in the big city?"

"School," I said, "and talking to you."

"Oh yeah?" he clasped my hands in his.

"Well, Mississippi, I'm glad I ran into you."

So was I. His soothing voice made my knees quiver. My pants woulda slipped off my waist if there wasn't an Alexander McQueen belt holding them up.

Over Chris' shoulder, I saw Cole leaning against the wall by himself, playing it cool like always. He danced as best as he knew how, but Cole had no rhythm. Was that a two-step? Fix it, Jesus.

A boy in a baseball cap scooted toward him, in the hopes of getting a hello. When subtle didn't work, the boy placed his hand on Cole's ass and said something in his ear. Cole shoved him so hard that the poor soul fell over and crashed into a small table. Cole slammed his fist on the ground inches from the boy's head. Thank God, it didn't connect. The beefy security man from the entrance appeared out of thin air to bring an end to the fisticuffs.

"Can you excuse me?" I said to Chris. I took off in Cole's direction. The gossipy queens sidled over to the fuss, signifying to each other who started what.

I tried to wrench Cole away, but he wouldn't budge. He was too busy cursing at that damn boy. The vein in his forehead was gonna explode from anger. He wouldn't leave until he got his silly point across, whatever it was. This was humiliating! Here he was embarrassing us in front of everybody in the club, which I specifically told him not to do. The only way to save face was to end it myself.

"It's time to go! Right now!" I yelled.

I couldn't manage to get between the two of 'em, but the bouncer could. He grabbed Cole by the arm and hauled his ass toward the door. I followed behind them, saying everything I could to get Cole to stop the madness. He was so caught up in his melodrama that he wasn't listening to me or anybody else for that matter.

In the commotion, we passed Jason who had no idea what was happening. He saw that me and Cole were at the center of the action and chased after us. We had an entourage of gay boys following us out the club so they could have a story to tell their friends later. The music from the dance floor kept playing like the scene was nothing out of the ordinary.

"What happened?!" Jason yelled over the hubbub.

"What do you think? We're leaving!" I said as security threw open the doors.

COLE

This gorilla motherfucka wanna drag me out of the club? I needed to get back in there so I could crush old boy! Security had a grip on my arm that I couldn't tear myself away from. A bunch of people watched me as I got thrown outside. I picked myself up from the ground. The boys waiting in the line to get in whispered to each other about me.

"He was touching on me like he knew me!" I yelled. "I will wear him out!"

Tyree yanked me away from the entrance. "Don't forget where you are, Cole! This is a gay bar, in case you didn't get the memo."

He wanted to say more, but he knew that I was angrier than he'd ever seen me. I wasn't taking shit from him, from security and not from Jason, who was smart enough to stay out of it. No man was gonna disrespect me like that. I raced back toward the door to finish what I started. Tyree stood in front of me, blocking my path. I spun like a defensive guard to get around him. He stayed on me.

"Look, Cole," he said. "I don't know what crazy pills you took before you came, but you can't go fightin' people! I don't care if he put his hands on you! You got more sense than that!"

Tyree looked at me, then at the club. He was searching for somebody. Nothing but a gang of dudes along the wall smoking cigarettes. Whoever he was looking for, I didn't give a fuck. I got into his car and shut the door with a loud bang.

"Don't be slammin' my property!" Tyree said as he jumped in the driver's seat.

We motored down the road, away from the bars and clubs of Ybor City. The farther we drove, the better I felt. I hoped that man learned his lesson about stepping to me without permission. I caught Tyree glaring at me in the rear view mirror.

"Are you drunk?!" Tyree said angrily.

"Why it gotta be all that?" I spat back.

"I dunno, because you out there actin' like a foolywang? I told you don't embarrass me and you out here sluggin' people on the dance floor. What kind of sane person does that?"

"I didn't mean to go at him like that, I promise. But he came at me wrong."

Tyree let out a long sigh. I was a lost cause. He didn't have to say it out loud. The wrinkles on his face told me everything.

"I'm not asking you to apologize for your emotions, Cole. You felt the way you felt. But what you need to do is control yourself. You coulda handled that a lot better."

Jason agreed. Fuck what either one of them thought. I wasn't a violent man. But what he tried to pull was outta line. We were almost home when Jason perked up.

"Tyree, I saw you dancing with that guy. Who was that?" he asked.

"I can't say for sure. I was enjoyin' myself until I got distracted by *somebody*."

I didn't give a damn who Tyree was talking to. It was the last thing I cared about.

"Was he cute?" Jason asked.

"Yeah, but it doesn't matter," Tyree said. "Even if I wanted to see him again I know nothing more about him than his first name and the feeling of his body against mine. This night was a whole lot of things."

Tyree put on his blinker and turned onto our street. The dark road that led to our house was a trap. I didn't wanna have to deal with their judgment about what I did. I went straight to my room to get my duffel bag and a sweatshirt.

"I'm goin' to the gym. I'll catch you later," I said.

"You need a ride?" Tyree asked earnestly.

"Nah, I'll take the bus."

L.A. Fitness was the only gym I went to besides the one on campus. It was a haul to get there, but they had good equipment. It was late at night. The long rows of treadmills had nobody on 'em. The weight benches were empty. It was fine with me. I wasn't in the mood to have conversations with people who didn't know me. I threw my shirt in a locker and put on a black tank and my J's. Time to get it in.

Whenever I was stressed, I went to the gym for a good workout. There was something calming about running on the treadmill with my headphones strapped to my ears. It put me in a better place. I forgot about everything else. I started the timer on the machine to get the belt moving.

I made a serious mistake going in that club. It wasn't that I had an issue with gay dudes. If I did, I wouldn't be living with two roommates that were gay. I was already jumpy being in there. That bold move was enough for me to set it off.

It was good that we got thrown out when we did. I didn't know how much longer I coulda stayed anyway. It was one thing to kick it with Jason and Tyree at the house. It was another to be surrounded by thirsty ass men who couldn't keep their hands to themselves.

I turned up the speed on the treadmill and counted my footsteps. 72. 73. 74. Running was what brought balance to my life. I ran all the time when I was a kid in South Philly just to have something to do outside of school. I liked it so much that when I got to high school I signed on to run cross-country.

I was sloppy back then, but I was fast. The coach convinced me to do sprints instead of distance running. He thought I'd be good at it. He was right. I got a heap of medals. We also won the title at the state championship twice in a row.

I'd been running for the Morrison track team since my freshman year in college. They had me doing the 100, 200 and 400-meter sprints and sometimes the relays. My teammates were taller and leaner than I was, but I had power. It took a real man to do what I did.

The 400 had the hardest training out of all the track events. Most of the fellas couldn't handle the endurance it took to make it to the end. The race put a runner through pain like they never felt before. I had the sprinting events down pat. That's why I kept winning. Not for the last couple of meets, but I was gonna bounce back soon.

Sometimes when I was feelin' in the mood, I got out of the apartment before the sun rose to run around the city. When I really wanted to get away, I rode the HART bus to Bayshore Boulevard. It was the best place in Tampa for a run. The path followed the edge of the bay for a couple miles. On most days, the sky was a calming shade of powder blue. The water wasn't that murky shit we had in Philly. It was like glass that hadn't been touched by a single person. The other side of the path had nothing but palm trees and Easter egg-colored houses.

There was more to see on Bayshore besides buildings and water. The females were out there all the time running in small ass sports bras, tiny shorts and neon shoes. They were an extra incentive for me to get out the house and run. Sometimes I'd give 'em a wink as they passed by to let 'em know wassup. Get at me, basically.

The area by Bayshore was a lot like the neighborhood me and my parents moved to when I was 16. You needed a magnifying glass to find the Black people. It was the opposite of South Philly where we lived for years. It all started because my father was a software engineer for SEPTA — the Southeastern Pennsylvania Transportation Authority. Him and his crew worked on the programs that kept the Philly trains in line.

My father worked his ass off. He put in overtime on nights and sometimes weekends to finish what he needed to do. He'd been working on the job for a long ass time when he got promoted to Senior Project Manager. The new role had him looking after two dozen engineers. He got a huge raise too. We weren't struggling before, but the promotion meant we had extra digits on our bank balance.

My mother was more jazzed than any of us. She was an accountant for the Franklin Smith Corporation. Instead of handling other people's money, she finally had her own to play with. I was surprised she didn't run out of her job with two middle fingers in the air.

We moved to a bigger house because we could afford it with the extra money. Our new place was still in Philly, but in the Chestnut Hill area. It was where people who had bank camped out. The living situation was an upgrade, but it also meant I had to transfer to a new high school too. I came from the hood where pretty much everybody around me was Black. Going to school in a white neighborhood was a total change.

Our lives went from backyard barbecues and spades tournaments to afternoon brunches and cotillions. Every other weekend, the moms from my school got together for a bake sale or a booster club event. I never went to any of that stuff. Not my style. Sometimes I couldn't avoid it.

Once in a while my mother would invite the neighbors to our house for lunch. They were the type of people with popped collars who pronounced "croissant" with a fake French accent. If they brought that noise to South Philly, me and my boys woulda laughed them off the block.

My mother loved every minute of it. In our old house, she shared a cramped closet with my father. After the move, she had one the size of some people's apartment. It was filled with brand name shoes and suit jackets, designer this and label that.

Moms bragged about my father's new money to anybody who'd listen. She'd be on the phone, her voice two octaves higher, talking about "Oh yes, we love the house! Four bedrooms can you believe it? Yes, it is truly wonderful." Fuckin' kill me.

Everything switched so fast. My parents never took the time to ask me what I thought about the changes. I didn't want to take away from their happiness. I wasn't the type to ruin a party when everybody else was having fun.

I loved my folks, but after the move it felt like they didn't care about me the same way they used to. Maybe it was because I was in high school. I wasn't their little boy anymore. I could take care of myself. But everybody wants their parents to check in on 'em once in a while. To say how good they're doing. I stopped hearing that. I got in the way of their lives, so my time went into track. That was the only option I saw for me.

I was stuck between two worlds. Too good for the hood and too Black for the white folks. My classmates at the new high school never gave me grief, but it wasn't like I fit in. There was a small number of Black students who went there. They all grew up on the same streets and went to the same private schools. When I came through, they knew from jump I wasn't from the area. They had their cliques already and weren't down to hang with anybody new.

I didn't sweat it. It wasn't like I needed a group of friends to hold me down. I had track for that. The team at the new school let me on before outdoor season because — let's be real — I was better than any of those bunk ass white boys. In class, I wasn't challenged academically. My teachers didn't think I could be an athlete and intelligent too. I did just enough to get the A. I knew I could put in more work, but why wear myself out for no reason?

My grades were good enough to get me in most of the universities I applied to. Out of all of 'em, I decided to go to a historically black college. My parents freaked out when I told them. They met when they were students at Carnegie Mellon in Pittsburgh. They wanted me to go there too. But Morrison offered me a scholarship. Carnegie gave me squat.

In the end, Moms was happy about the full ride. Paying college tuition woulda meant cutting into her beauty budget. But she never stopped telling me that I had the GPA to go to a "nicer" school. I knew what she meant. A white school. But after three years of being surrounded by 25-20s and Black people who woulda handed over a year's paycheck to be white, I needed to be around my people again.

I let the treadmill wind down. That was enough running for the night. Most times, I would run for a good hour or more. This go-round I decided to save it for another day. I had enough in me to hit the free weights. The 50-pound dumbbells on the rack were all mine. I checked myself out in the mirror as I lifted. Right, left, right, left. I admired the pop they gave my biceps. It was pure muscle. I only got a couple reps in when I got a text from my girl, April.

what r u doing?

workin out whatsup with u

Me and April first met at this same gym. She was over by the treadmills. I was on my way to do leg presses. I stopped what I was doing when I saw her. The mocha brown skin girl in a crop top and leggings owned the gym. The way that booty bounced every time her feet hit the belt had me hooked. Her curly 'fro flew everywhere. She had a vibe that was somewhere between hippie chick and nerd. April wore braces and glasses, which weren't my thing. I was cool with it because of everything else.

I had to get at her. There was an open machine next to her, so I went for the opportunity. Every couple of steps I threw glances her way. I caught a smile when she saw I wasn't wearing any draws. April's mouth watered watching the moisture run from my chest and drip down my abs.

Come to think of it, that was the same look Jason gave me when I met him at the Freshman Beach Party. He thought I didn't see him with his eyes on my package. It didn't get past me. I thought it was kinda funny. I'd never tell him because it would make him upset. His cover would be blown.

I stopped April on her way outta the gym. "What's a brotha gotta do to get your number?" I asked. She typed it in my cell and grinned. Since then, we've been together almost a year. April was different from the other girls I met at Morrison. She liked superheroes and comics. Storm from the X-Men was her favorite. Her personality was goofy, but I liked it.

We were cool at the beginning. Things went left when April got a job at the Forever 21 store by the airport. She stopped going to the gym. She wore sweatpants and T-shirts every day. She got lazy and let herself go. April was never as bangin' as the first time I saw her.

The sex was on point, so that was good. April had a pussy that would make Jason and Tyree reconsider being gay. The in-between moments when we weren't fuckin' were what made me not wanna be with her. She was on me at the wrong times, kissing me when I needed to study, texting me when she knew I was at practice. It was too much.

April rubbed other people the wrong way too. Some girls had what they called resting bitch face. April had sad puppy in the rain face. She constantly needed love. I made sure not to grumble in front of Tyree. He'd use it as ammunition to tell me I shouldn't be with her. April was a downgrade for me, he said. I deserved better.

No matter how aggravating April got, I liked her because she was there for me when I needed her. I didn't have to worry about her being out with other dudes. She always rolled with me. After a long day on the track, I could always count on my girl to wait for me 'til it was over. When we were away from each other, I would daydream about her opening herself up to me. My tongue tasting both sets of her lips. Her screaming my name. Then we'd meet in person and I'd be like here we go again. She was on me like a sexy leech.

I wondered if I should have just ended it with April, but I didn't do it. Breaking it off would mess her up bad. I was her first love. She wasn't mine. On the flip side, I was too dependent on April to let her go.

I wasn't going all out with the weights like I usually did. I'd make up for it when I was at the gym on campus tomorrow. I set them down on the rack and went to the locker room to get clean. It was a cool space with wood doors on the lockers and private shower stalls. There was pretty much no one around when it was this late.

Once I got my shirt off, I checked myself out in the mirror above the sink. My training had my cuts looking defined. Every muscle was taut. My tattoos were on point too. I rocked a sleeve on one arm with a Chinese dragon that one of my boys in Philly hooked me up with. The other one was a tribal tat on my chest. It made it look like I was ready to go to war. I flexed my arms and checked out the broad muscles in my back. Everything was fire. I had to snap a picture of myself.

I tugged my damp shorts down to right above my dick. Gotta show off the V cuts on my waist. Damn. The picture was hot. Now who would I send it to?

JASON

My head ached from the liquor that had become best friends with my circulatory system. The problem with venturing to a nightclub on a Thursday was showing up to class on Friday. Add Cole's tirade to the mix and my anxiety was at new heights. I pulled my cap lower over my eyes and kept walking toward the humanities building. It was the pleasant, sunny days like today that reminded me how beautiful the Morrison campus was.

Newer buildings were outnumbered by those constructed of brick and wood decades before I was born. The trickle of water from the school's stone fountains flowed peacefully like the Oconee River that wound its way through my hometown. There was lush, green grass everywhere, including the quad where most students could be found between classes.

In my restful moments before or after class, I, like other students, would lie on the quad and bask in the sun's glow. I nuzzled my head against the leafy grass while an orchestra of hurried footsteps shuffled past me. I bonded with the hallowed ground of Morrison State University.

Out of the a hundred or so historically black colleges and universities around the country, I chose to attend Morrison. Many HBCUs were founded between the 1850s and the turn of the 20th century. At the time, African Americans were denied enrollment at long-established institutions. If they were allowed to attend, the students faced non-stop discrimination from their White classmates and professors.

HBCUs created a safe space for Black students to pursue their academic goals. Morrison and other similar universities continued that legacy by enrolling hundreds of students every year. Even in more recent times, historically black colleges gave individuals who might not have otherwise received a higher education the opportunity to do so. That was why my fellow students and I cared so much about this school.

Everyone who went to an HBCU could recite the famous alumni that came before them. Thurgood Marshall and Taraji P. Henson attended Howard University. Martin Luther King and Spike Lee went to Morehouse and so on. For over a hundred years, Morrison helped students achieve their dreams. Influential politicians, scientists and civil rights leaders all roamed these halls. I aspired to add my name to the long list of scholars the school produced.

Morrison's enrollment wasn't as large as other HBCUs like Howard or Morehouse. However, we had hundreds of students from around the globe, which was wonderful to observe. Most who went to Morrison were from Florida or Georgia, but there were students from locales as far as Europe and Africa.

After more than a year at this school, I was a master of deducing a student's hometown based on their accent. A Tennessean or Carolinian drawl wasn't uncommon. The California students' crisp pronunciation of every word made them easily identifiable. Vaughn, on the other hand, had no discernible lilt to his voice. If he hadn't mentioned he was from Atlanta, I would've had no clue.

In my senior year of high school, I spent a great deal of time online searching for scholarships. I didn't want my mom to have to pay for my education by herself. She fretted knowing her relatively meager salary from the hospital wouldn't cover the cost of college tuition.

I received one scholarship from the Georgia NAACP for $3,000 and another from the local chapter of Zeta Phi Beta sorority for $1,000. But $4,000 wasn't enough to make a dent in a five-figure per year tuition bill. So I was surprised when I received a partial academic scholarship from Morrison. My 3.7 GPA was a lifesaver! My mother and I were over the moon because my collegiate future was secured.

The biggest worry that I didn't anticipate was living so far away from my mom. We spent 18 years of our lives in the same house. We no longer had each other's physical presence to fall back on. I soon came to acknowledge that I could be myself more in the unrestricted sanctuary that Morrison offered than I ever could back home.

One of the first things I noticed my freshman year was that there were a significant number of gay men on campus. Even some of the straight guys looked like they could be mistaken for being gay because they dressed so extravagantly. Students regularly donned bow ties, loafers and linen shirts. The only time I saw men my age dressed like that in Athens was during church service.

Despite the relaxed atmosphere, I wasn't ready to admit publicly that I was interested in guys. If I could have changed my sexual desire, I'd choose to be straight without question. I didn't want to sabotage my relationship with God and the foundation of everything I'd been taught.

I was late for my African-American history class. I didn't know why I was stressed about my arrival because Professor Rose was never there on time. Sometimes she didn't come at all. I wanted to say the marijuana she smoked in the confines of her office was the root of the issue. The incense she burned failed to overcome the lasting acrid smell.

Her impeccable record as an instructor outweighed any other deficiencies. Professor Rose made African-American history come alive for her students. The slaves transported against their will to the United States became more than just faceless drones. Our knowledge of the civil rights movement of the 1960s wasn't limited to Martin Luther King, Jr. and Rosa Parks.

She brought to life the stories of unsung heroes like Bayard Rustin, organizer of the 1963 March on Washington. She connected the boycotts in Montgomery and Greensboro to the Black Lives Matter protests. The professor was so adept at making every class intriguing that hers became my favorite.

I ran into the building as fast as I could. As I expected, Professor Rose wasn't there. The room buzzed with students doing last-minute reading or trading notes amongst each other. I said hello to my classmates and took a seat at a desk in the back. I thumbed through my notes hoping I had a few moments to go over the chapters I skimmed through. Recollections of our discussion on the leadership of W.E.B. Du Bois and Booker T.

Washington came back to me.

The ticking clock on the wall above the door said it was 9:13. If the professor didn't arrive fifteen minutes into a class, there was a mutual understanding that we would go ahead and leave. Just as the clock clicked to 9:14, the door opened. In came Professor Rose wearing the sly smile of a Cheshire cat, papers in hand.

"Class, open your books. Let's get into it," she said.

"We were almost out of here!" someone murmured.

Professor Rose wasted no time delving into the lesson. "So we've been studying W.E.B. Du Bois' theory of the 'Talented Tenth,'" she said. "Your texts were Du Bois' 'Up From Slavery' and 'The Souls of Black Folk'. Also, Booker T. Washington's Atlanta Compromise speech. You read through all of them?"

"Yeeessssss," we groaned.

The classroom door flew open a second time. My fellow students and I craned our necks to identify the last-minute attendee. Someone was later than the professor? Tasha Nichols, my friend and confidante, strutted in wearing a pink T-shirt with her books stuffed in an oversized Louis Vuitton bag. She was a curvy girl with an impressive bosom that she would be the first to detail how much she loved. "God gave the girls to me, why should I hide what I have?" she'd always say.

Tasha was *the* woman on campus. She was vice president of the student government association and was present at nearly every school function. If it had anything to do with Morrison, she was there. Like most of the other ladies in Alpha Kappa Alpha sorority, she was also on many of the school committees.

My first encounter with Tasha was in the line for freshman orientation in the school gym turned registration hub. We waited patiently as droves of incoming students enrolled. We had nothing but time on our hands and each other.

Upon realizing that the lines weren't moving very fast, both of our mothers left us to fend for ourselves while they explored the sights of Tampa. We spent the next two hours getting to know each other and discussing plans for our first year. Since then, Tasha and I shared many of the same classes and the tumult that came with them.

I loved Tasha… as a friend. She was a girly girl and incredibly smart. Besides Tyree and Cole, Tasha knew more about the private details of my life than anyone else. She was also the only other person who I told about my fondness for the male species.

"Sorry, Professor!" Tasha said as she swung around to the back of the class where I sat. "Running late. Sorority business. Skeeeeee-wee!"

It didn't surprise me when she did her high-pitched sorority call in class. It was the audible signature she and her sorors shared that announced their presence. Professor Rose, however, was not impressed. The corners of her mouth curled downward with contempt.

"Miss Nichols, please have a seat," she said with disinterest.

"Tasha, you're going to get in trouble if you come in late again," I said. She slid in the seat in front of me.

"Jason, you were supposed to hold up class for me!" she laughed. "I'm a grown woman with an agenda."

"As long as you make going to class one of the things on your schedule, you'll be just fine," I said. "Remember we're not giving the professors any reason to dock our grades this semester."

"And if they do, I'll blame you for being a bad influence on my attendance record," she smiled.

"If there are no more interruptions," Professor Rose admonished us. "Who would like to recap for the class what

the 'Talented Tenth' is? Tasha? Since you graced us with your
tardiness why don't you share with everyone?"

Tasha shot me the "oh no she didn't" eye roll before she
faced the professor. She stretched her arms out across the desk
dramatically as if she was gathering the strength for her next
statement. "Du Bois said the 'Talented Tenth' was the class of
educated Black people who had a responsibility to uplift the
whole race. They led the struggle for everyone else."

"Anyone want to add to that?" Professor Rose asked. She eyed
her students in hopes of obtaining an equally acceptable answer.

Matthew's hand shot up. He was a freshman who hadn't
gone a single class without saying *something*. The grumbling
from our classmates did nothing to dissuade him from offering
his contribution.

"Du Bois wanted us to get a better education and work on
issues between Blacks and Whites."

"Both correct," Professor Rose said. "Black people were
facing a host of problems in the late 1800s. There was poverty,
crime, poor education and health issues. He believed the
'Talented Tenth' would lead in resolving them.

A girl named Mackenzie, who prided herself in her
Afrocentricity, chimed in. "Professor, I think that's elitist crap.
To say only ten percent of Black people are gonna accomplish
something is not right. So the other 90 percent can't do anything
for themselves?"

"Perhaps Du Bois wasn't saying a tenth are *capable* of being
leaders," Professor Rose said thoughtfully. "But that a tenth
would *accept* the responsibility required to be a leader. Each
of us knows Black people in high positions who are mostly
worried about enriching themselves rather than the lives of
others. There are also people who donate to charitable causes,

but aren't necessarily leading anyone to action."

Many of the students nodded, including Tasha, who wasn't afraid to speak up if she had something to add. I didn't know if I completely agreed with what the professor said, but I couldn't develop a decent enough reason to argue against her statement.

"Let's refer to the text," Professor Rose said, opening a bookmarked page in her frayed book. 'The Talented Tenth of the Negro race must be made leaders of thought and missionaries of culture among their people. No others can do this work and Negro colleges must train men for it. The Negro race, like all other races, is going to be saved by its exceptional men.' Let's think about Mackenzie's statement. Do Black people need a select group to uplift us or can everyone do it collectively?"

Rahim, a guy who I had classes with since last semester, raised his hand. "It's like you said. Most Black people only care about themselves. They get theirs and they leave everybody else behind."

A girl sitting behind him agreed. "Movin' on up to a deluxe apartment in the white part of town," she quipped.

"Good points," the professor said. "Washington's Atlanta Compromise speech also touches on the subject. 'If anywhere there are efforts tending to curtail the fullest growth of the Negro, let these efforts be turned into stimulating, encouraging, and making him the most useful and intelligent citizen. Effort or means so invested will pay a thousand percent interest. These efforts will be twice blessed — blessing him that gives and him that takes.'"

Professor Rose looked up from the underlined pages in her hands. "It's important to remember that this speech was given in 1895 in a room of mostly white people. Washington fought against stereotypes and laid out a plan for the future that worked for both races. That's why it was later called the Atlanta Compromise. So how does Du Bois' position contrast with Booker T. Washington's plan for the success of the race? Mackenzie?"

"Booker T. wanted equal rights for Blacks, but he didn't want to piss off white people in the process. He wasn't thinking about Black people getting degrees. He wanted us to have good jobs. He thought white people would depend on us for our skills and because of that we would get equality down the line," Mackenzie offered.

Armani, a dimpled stunner who was a frequent contributor to the class, jumped in. "It's simple when you think about it. Du Bois wanted equality now and safety later. Washington wanted safety now and equality later."

Mackenzie was on the edge of her seat. "My thing is there'll always be a 'later.' It's not like white folks were gonna be like 'here you go' and give us equal rights. I can see making sure you got a job, but you gotta fight for something more than a paycheck."

Professor Rose listened with care to her response. "Class, you need to understand that most Black people weren't giving up one for the other," she said firmly. "They were literally dying for their right to get both better jobs and a better education. Our people faced a tidal wave of racism from a dominant society that preferred they had neither. None of you should take for granted that you are sitting in this classroom. Your ancestors paid a hefty price for you to walk out of here with a degree and a career."

Professor Rose scanned the room for a response, but everyone sat motionlessly. The clock ticked.

"Professor..." Tasha waved. "My fellow students and I

appreciate every moment we're at Morrison. We're extremely fortunate to be here."

Rahim threw a piece of paper across the classroom. "Boooooo! Don't be a suck up, Tasha."

"Rahim, please use your talents for something else besides bothering me," Tasha dismissed him. She tossed the crumpled paper into the waste bin.

"Class, let's get back to the lesson," Professor Rose said, halting the great paper war. "Here's a question: do you believe that you would be considered the Talented Tenth because you're attending a university?"

There was an audible mix of yeses and nos. I was so sleepy I was nearly falling out of my chair. I regretted choosing to spend last night in that den of iniquity. I uttered a muted "maybe." If the professor heard my oblique answer, she would insist that I explain myself.

"However you feel about the concept, I want to see each of you graduate and go on to do incredible things," she said. "Whether it's in four years or if it takes you five, six or seven, I want you to cross that stage. And most importantly, I want you to pass my class. Isn't that right, Jason Cooper?"

"Yes, professor," I said. Darn it, she saw that I was checking out.

"Now that we've digested both positions, tell me class: who do you think had the better plan for the Black community at the time? W.E.B. Du Bois or Booker T. Washington?"

Everyone yelled out Du Bois' name. I was silent this time, but I agreed. Professor Rose was surprised that our collective answer was so one-sided.

"Don't discount brother Booker T.," she persisted. "He was a successful fundraiser and educator. He also founded Tuskegee

University, part of our HBCU family. Have things improved since the Atlanta Compromise? How does this relate to Black people today?"

"A lot's changed," Armani said. "But there's a lot of racist people out there who don't want to see us be successful,"

"I absolutely agree," Tasha said. "People treat us differently just because we're Black. And some of them who owned slaves or set dogs on us in the 60s are still alive, or their children are."

"But we can agree that we've made progress," Professor Rose said. "Class, you have an assignment. I want you to identify someone who you think reflects the idea of the Talented Tenth and detail their impact on Black Americans. For my Booker T. Washington fans that don't ascribe to the theory of a modern-day Talented Tenth, I want you to pick an influencer that has pushed for education over civil rights. You understand?"

"Yes, professor," everyone said.

Great. More homework. I wondered when I'd have time to do it. The class was almost over, but the professor went on about the lesson. "Any questions about your assignment?"

"When's it due?" Rahim asked.

"It should be in my inbox by noon on Monday. No excuses. It must be five pages or more, double-spaced. If you read your syllabus, you know this counts for 15 percent of your grade. And I don't want to see any Wikipedia!"

Tasha and I stepped out of the humanities building and into the much needed fresh air. She directed us to a shady area near the quad where students rushed to and from class. Those for whom time was a luxury gabbed about school-related topics from astronomy homework to what was on the lunch menu. Students like Tyree who were blessed to have their own mode of transportation drove conspicuously down the adjacent boulevard.

"So Tasha, what did you think about the class? Are we the Talented Tenth?" I prodded her.

"It was an intriguing discussion. I thought the class was going to rush Professor Rose after that graduation comment," she chuckled.

"Me too," I said. "The professor wouldn't have stood a chance against a room of aggravated college students. Who are you going to write about for the assignment?"

"My friend, Jason Cooper."

I couldn't tell whether she was serious or not because she said everything with a gated smile.

"You're a talented guy. Why shouldn't I document your successes? You're a sexy bundle of academic deliciousness."

"Be serious, Tasha. You have to pick someone famous. I don't think writing about me is going to cut it."

"In that case, I'll do Jay Z or Michelle Obama or somebody like that. What about you?"

"I was thinking Cornel West. You know the prolific intellectual? Explaining his theories on racial justice might take more than five pages."

Speaking of complex Black men, I spied Tyree across the quad heading our way. He sauntered down the sidewalk with the air of a campus celebrity. His outfit no doubt took him most of the morning to assemble. A red Moschino belt accented tailored khakis and a blue gingham button down shirt. If I had to guess, I'd say the clothes totaled a minimum of $200, more than any college student who didn't have a trust fund could afford. I didn't know how he funded his enviable wardrobe.

"Hey kids, what's shakin'?" Tyree said as he approached. "Y'all got time to be standin' on the quad? I should be so lucky."

"Our class just ended," I said. "Tasha, do you know my roommate Tyree?"

"Of course!" she said. "We're both working on the Miss Morrison pageant."

"Tasha, you're a beauty queen?" I asked curiously. "Don't tell me you're running for Miss Morrison. I didn't think that was your style."

"Please," she dismissed the suggestion. "I'm coordinating the details for the pageant. But I am running for student government association president. We have an election coming up soon."

Before Tyree and I could add our thoughts, Tasha launched into an impromptu campaign speech.

"I believe I've been an exceptional SGA vice president. I've led this school and the ladies of Alpha Kappa Alpha Sorority, IN-corporated with fairness and grace," she said importantly. I could almost envision the American flag waving behind her, the red, white and blue billowing in the wind. "Can I count on you for your vote? Don't let your girl down."

"How could we not support Black excellence?" I said. "You're one of the treasures of Morrison State University."

"Awesome!" she squealed. "Thank you so much, love. And spread the word: there's only one person running for SGA Secretary. Also, we need someone to take over my old position. Can't have a president without a vice president. There's plenty of room for improvement in our relationship with the school. The student body is always saying 'we don't have a voice,' so we need to bring it to a new level next year. You guys ready for it?"

"Yes ma'am," Tyree said. "I'm all for hope and change."

Apparently we didn't have the necessary amount of enthusiasm to satisfy Tasha. "Come on boys, you have to be READY!" she goaded us. "Who's going to help me hand out fliers? I need capable Black men on my side."

"I have weak ankles, but for you Tasha, anything," Tyree said courteously.

"Great, thanks! And Jason can I count on you?" Tasha asked. She wouldn't accept anything other than yes. I wouldn't dream of turning her down because a "no" never entered her vocabulary if someone needed help.

"Tasha, you have my vote, but I don't have a lot of extra time," I said.

"Oh yes, I know! A little birdie told me you're pledging."

"Shhh! What are you talking about?"

Tyree looked at me with a raised eyebrow. "You kids have fun. I'm gonna mosey to my next class. See you 'round!"

After he left, Tasha lowered her voice to above a whisper. "So you're busy and you haven't been on Twitter lately. You have to tell me. Which frat are you pledging? Is it Alpha? I won't say anything, Jason. I'm your girl!"

"I have to go to class, Tasha. You're going to get me in trouble," I said, looking for my escape.

"And don't think I haven't noticed you haven't been walking on the grass either!" she yelled as I briskly walked away from the interrogation.

I didn't know how she found out, but Tasha uncovered the secret that I hid from everyone except my roommates. I'd been on line for weeks pledging Theta Pi Chi fraternity. When someone pledged a frat or sorority at Morrison, they literally disappeared. Almost every night, we were required to attend "set" where the Thetas grilled us for hours about the fraternity and its history.

When we weren't with our big brothers, we had to study everything they taught us so that we were prepared for the next time we met. A full night's sleep was a luxury I could no longer afford.

We'd been online for almost six weeks. Six. Long. Weeks. I worked hard to maintain my grades, but between pledging Theta, study sessions, and quality time with Vaughn, it was hard to stay on top of my classwork. I'd never consistently made Cs before this process. The first D I got on a test was like a two-by-four to the stomach. My reputation as an honors student was destroyed.

My teachers had to know what was going on. A precipitous decline in a student's grades was a ten-foot tall, neon billboard announcing they were pledging. I wasn't the first student at Morrison to go through the process, and I wouldn't be the last. Nonetheless, I could tell my professors were disappointed in me.

Pledging was a huge burden to carry, but it would be worth it when I was done. Joining a black fraternity meant automatically becoming a leader in one's community. When I first arrived at Morrison, I saw the Thetas on the yard conducting a canned food drive. I admired how the comrades in orange and blue worked together to perform community service that wasn't required of them. And they did it with smiles on their faces. Not only did they support the university and the surrounding area, but they were also there for each other.

As the year went on, I saw the Thetas everywhere, cleaning trash around the neighborhood, throwing school parties and going to church as a group. Last month, they organized a fundraiser that awarded scholarships to local high school students. I wanted to be a part of something bigger than myself. I had to pledge Theta.

Once someone joined a black fraternity or sorority, they were a member for life. I sometimes saw Thetas who pledged decades ago wearing their letters on campus. They chanted louder than many of the current students. Professor Rose described the Talented Tenth; Black Greek organizations were the epitome of that. They were the best and brightest the university had to offer.

It was common knowledge that fraternities only selected pledgees if they "knew" them. I hadn't met any of the Thetas face to face, but I wouldn't wait around for them to make the first move. I approached one of the guys at a school party and introduced myself. We had a surprisingly easygoing conversation. He instructed me to research the frat when I returned home.

I got the basics by reading the book "The Divine Nine" and gleaned what I could from the internet. The fraternity website said I needed a 2.8 GPA to pledge and 200 hours of community service. That was no problem. I volunteered more than 250 hours at a local elementary school as part of Morrison's requirement for all freshman students.

I had to ask my mom for assistance with the application fee. She was less than thrilled, not because of the $100 it required, but because I put her money and my time into a fraternity. She stressed that fraternities were similar to gangs: they ran in packs and new members were jumped in to be able to wear colors.

I explained to her that there were major differences between the two. Gangs weren't a positive force in their communities. They didn't hold leadership positions on campus or go on to become influential members of society. Also, Jesus and the twelve disciples were like a fraternity and they did okay. She wasn't pleased with my response.

What they didn't have on the application for Theta was that we were going to be hazed. It wasn't an "official" requirement to become a member, but I couldn't call myself a real Theta if I didn't go through it. I'm sure I could've been "paper" and simply signed on a dotted line with the national office. However, the paper guys didn't know much of anything about the fraternity. Pledging for them meant one week of written tests and a firm handshake at the end of it to send them on their way.

If I chose that path, I could've skipped the hazing with the big brothers and still received my letters. But for me, there was no point in coming into Theta through the back door. I wanted to endure everything the brothers before me went through. I wanted to walk the yard knowing that I was truly a part of the fraternity. By the end of the process, they'd be assured that I'd learned every detail about Theta that there was to know.

My brothers and everyone else on campus would respect me. I'd stick up for my fellow Thetas if we were ever in trouble and they'd have my back no matter what. I couldn't say a paper member would do the same. All that aside, I was going through hell.

The nights we met with the big brothers were called "set." It was supposed to be the time in which we were taught the history of Theta Pi Chi. Instead, it was more likely to be a succession of physical attacks by the Thetas while they commanded us to recite information we could barely remember. It was hard to detail the finer points of the fraternity when someone was beating you non-stop.

We also received random phone calls, sometimes in the middle of the night, with tasks we were challenged to complete. Show up here, go do this. A big brother needed us to clean his house or do his homework.

Before we began, I heard stories about what pledgees went

through and how brutal the process could be. There was no way I could've prepared for the mental and physical adversity I'd have to endure almost every day. Pledging was supposed to teach us how to bond like brothers. However, keeping that end goal in sight was difficult when we were blinded by continuous savagery.

Knowing that I wasn't going through the process alone made me more at ease… somewhat. There were four other guys — my "line brothers" — pledging with me. We did everything as a group. We studied, went to set and ate meals as one unit, though never in public. We were instructed from the start to never be seen in the same place at the same time. That way nobody outside of the fraternity would discover we were pledging. Mostly, it was because the Theta brothers didn't want the school administration to find out about the line.

The Morrison chapter of the fraternity was suspended years ago for hazing because one of the pledges launched into a rant on social media about what was done to him. He detailed everything in a frenzied attempt to liberate himself from the process.

Not only did the school shut the chapter down, but the Thetas weren't allowed to have another intake until all the existing members graduated from Morrison. The chapter was back and nothing about the ritual had changed.

When the Thetas first selected the guys who were going to be on line this semester, they lined us in a row by height. I wasn't that short, but I became the Number 2 on a line of five. At first I was worried I wasn't going to relate to my line brothers on any meaningful level. Just because we would pledge together didn't mean we were necessarily going to be instant friends.

But going through the fiery furnace expedited our

attachment to each other more than I assumed was possible. It was our love of Theta that brought us together. It had to be what kept us going.

Our "Ace," the guy at the head of the line, was Rodney Jensen, a sophomore. He was two inches shorter than I was and considerably thin for someone who was raised in the South. His dense afro sat atop his head like a halo. I hadn't met Rodney before Theta, but under different circumstances we still would have been friends. He was an agreeable guy and fun to be around.

His downfall in the context of set was his frailty. The Ace had the hardest time among us because he was often the first to be asked a question. He was also the first person punished if our answers came up short.

Our Number 4 was Jonathan Martin, Jr., a linebacker for the school football team. He was named after his dad, so everyone called him Junior long before he came to Morrison. He had the build of a pro athlete, steeped in roughened beauty.

I was anxious when I was notified we would be on the same pledge line. I'd never spent time around football players and didn't know what the convergence meant for the two of us. I was also unnerved that Junior talked about his girlfriend all the time. I'd gotten to know him better since the beginning of the process, but it was obvious we were very different people. If I ever told my line brothers that I liked guys, it would be Junior who would have the biggest issue with the revelation.

Our Number 5, the tallest and, therefore, the Tail of the line, was Chima Eze, a junior studying computer engineering. His mother was from Nigeria, but he was raised in Alabama where his father was a county sheriff. I knew who Chima was before we met because he was a tenor in the school's gospel choir. He didn't say much when he wasn't singing, but when he did it was profound.

Chima, he explained one night as we strapped on our boots, meant "God knows" in the Igbo language. It was fitting because Chima committed the fraternity history to memory faster than any of us. If we forgot a crucial piece of information at set, he was often the one to save the day.

Lastly, the Number 3 of our line was Vaughn. That's right, I was pledging with the guy I was seeing. For some, being initiated into a fraternity may have been the scenario sexual fantasies were made of. However, it was not as titillating as it sounded. Our time on line was no candlelit dinner. On the other hand, it was encouraging to go through the process with someone I knew so intimately. They called the strongest person on the line the "rock" and well, he was *my* rock.

Somehow word of Vaughn's sexual preferences hadn't spread to the Thetas, who incorrectly presumed he was as straight as anyone else. Neither he nor I corrected the big brothers. It was of no consequence to them whether we explored each other's bodies in our off hours.

I'd heard members say that there were no gay Thetas. I didn't believe that was true, but I kept my mouth shut. I also didn't want to cause any friction with my LBs. Maybe it wouldn't be a big deal if I said something, but this was a fraternity at a black college in conservative Florida. No way would I spill the beans without provocation.

A fraternity was the ultimate symbol of prestige and manhood. In Athens, I'd see Greek letters emblazoned on license plates, on shirts and tattooed on the hardiest of men. If becoming a Theta meant hiding a part of me, then I was willing to make the sacrifice. Vaughn and I wouldn't jeopardize the unrivaled springboard to success that Theta provided. I'd spent much of life hiding from my mother and the people around me. This would be more of the same.

I checked my phone to see if my LBs texted where set was happening tonight. Most times, it was at a big brother's house, but we weren't notified where or when we were supposed to arrive until a few hours before. Sure enough, we had a text from Chima saying that we were meeting at one of our more frequented destinations at 9 p.m. I hadn't quite figured out who lived at this particular apartment. The Thetas always waited for us at the door, and then we began the festivities shortly after. I did hear someone say that their girlfriend worked at night and they could use her living room. I was constantly on the edge of hallucination during set, so I didn't catch who said it.

I cut through campus to get to Carpenter Hall where I had English class in ten minutes. I'd been so sore recently that sometimes it was hard to walk. I motivated myself like I always did: by chanting "I *will* be a Theta man" with every step.

"What's it like to not be tired? I can't remember," Junior asked from the backseat of Vaughn's old Ford Explorer.

My line brothers and I were stuffed in the truck. Vaughn and I were in the front with Rodney, Junior and Chima behind us. Everyone wore the same black T-shirt, dark blue jeans and work boots. When we went to set, we had to dress exactly alike, down to our socks and underwear. We all wore the same plaid boxers that hit us at the knee. When we weren't pledging, Vaughn favored boxer briefs. To give his man parts the proper support, he explained. I should have been thinking about something else, but how could I not with my Adonis next to me.

"Another night with the big brothers," Rodney groaned. "I gotta be honest, I don't wanna go tonight."

Junior agreed as he laced his boots. "Me either, but it's not like we have a choice."

"Yeah, I guess you're right."

"Actually, we do have a choice," Chima said. "They're not dragging us to set every night. We can walk away from this anytime."

"True, but you won't get your letters," Vaughn said, keeping his eye on the road.

"And there's the problem," Chima mumbled.

"You guys think we're crossing tonight?" Junior asked sincerely.

"Who knows," I said. I didn't want to deflate his aspirations.

"It's possible," Vaughn said, counteracting my dour assessment. "If not, we only have a short time left anyway. Keep your heads high guys, we're in this together."

I much preferred the car rides Vaughn and I took around the city than the grim trips to set. He'd hum R&B songs as he steered us to his favorite hangouts on Bay Street or Channelside Drive. He particularly liked the Florida Aquarium. We'd been there several times to stare in wonder at the fish drifting by. I'd come to trust that he would always take me somewhere that I would enjoy, aside from set of course.

I'm sure each of us said a quiet prayer every time we drove to meet the big brothers that it would be our last night of pledging. When it wasn't, we convinced ourselves it would be the next night. So far this night had no more promise to be the end than any of the others.

We each responded differently to the stress of pledging. I resigned myself to our fate. Vaughn was out to prove himself to the Thetas. If they did discover he was gay, they couldn't say that he had ever backed down from a challenge. Junior, although he was straight, was on the same mission as Vaughn. He was one of Morrison's top football players. He had a reputation to uphold.

Chima and Rodney were at opposite ends of the emotional spectrum. Chima's strength was in outfoxing the big brothers. If they confronted us with what seemed like an impossible question, he ensured we were two steps ahead of them with a clever answer. Rodney wasn't as quick on his feet — both literally and figuratively. The big brothers often took pity on him. They acknowledged that because of his size he couldn't endure the same physical challenges as us.

I was the second worst after Rodney. I hadn't seen the inside of a gym since high school P.E. class and yet I held my own. I pushed through every round of sit-ups and stood firm when they yelled epithets in our faces. Inside I was dying, but I refused to show it.

We continued our funeral march to the apartment, winding the car through the darkened roads parallel to Bullard Parkway and its high traffic. The anticipation was always the hardest part of the journey. We never knew if it would be a hard set that lasted into the morning or if they'd go easy on us for just an hour. My four brothers and I thought silently about what was in store for the night when Rodney spoke up.

"I'm thinking about dropping the line," he said solemnly. "My manager is going to fire me from my job because I keep missing work for set."

"You're going to quit?" Vaughn said. "Rodney, don't. Not

after everything we've been through."

"Man, you can't be serious!" Junior added angrily. "You knew what it was before we got on line."

"Yeah, but I…" Rodney stammered.

"I feel you on the job problems," Junior said. "But you gotta figure something out. We've been bustin' our ass tryna get in this fraternity. You can't quit now."

"But I want to!" Rodney wailed. "Everything that's happened so far isn't what's wearing me down. It's thinking about how much more we have to go through."

Rodney's eyes darted back and forth looking for support from his fellow line brothers. Junior deflected his stares with silent anger.

"If you leave, you'll have nothing to show for your hard work," Chima said. "You'll be watching from a distance when we cross, too embarrassed to tell people that you pledged Theta too. Why make things harder than they have to be? Let's get in there, complete our tasks and go home."

Vaughn always made sure to park in the darkest corner of the apartment complex to make sure we weren't seen. Five guys dressed alike creeping around their home would make anyone suspicious. We got out of the Explorer, careful to make as little noise as possible. The only lights around us were from the swimming pool area across the way.

Rodney removed the snacks for the big brothers from the back of the truck. Each of us contributed whatever money we could so we could bring their favorites to set: chewy Chips Ahoy, pink Starbursts and an eight pack of cherry Cokes. Only one of us did the shopping on behalf of the rest of the line since we couldn't be seen together.

Each of us also took out one of the heavy cinder blocks that never left our side at set. God knows what we'd use them for tonight. Carrying it for long periods of time or raising them over our heads were previous uses. The burden was limited only by the big brothers' creativity. I'd be so relieved when I never had to see a cinder block again.

The dull scrape of our boots against the pavement marked our arrival at the apartment. It sounded like a party was going on inside. I tried not to let it upset me, but I was well aware that this doubled as a social activity for the big brothers. For us, it was absolute torture.

With his one free hand, Rodney knocked five times. The banter inside stopped instantly. Our dean of pledging Terrence Barnett, better known to us as Big Brother Genesis, answered the door and shooed us inside. We marched as one into the room with our heads down. We did our best to be on the same foot, but more often than not it was a clunky shuffle. It was hard to maintain order when we carried cement blocks the size of shoeboxes.

DP locked the door behind us and carried the snacks away from Rodney. We set the blocks down in a row on the carpet and formed the familiar line: Rodney at the front and Chima at the back. We huddled as close to each other possible with our arms wrapped securely around our LB in front of us.

Vaughn stood behind me holding my waist attentively. I kept my chin buried in between Rodney's shoulder blades, both out of duty and as a means of self-preservation. In the weeks we'd pledged, I memorized every contour of his neck. My eyes were focused forward, never to the side.

We'd been in the same room countless times, but I had no concept of what it looked like. A leisurely tour of the apartment was never on the agenda. We were not allowed to move unless we were expressly instructed to do so. I couldn't tell how many people were here with us, but I'd guess five or six, including DP.

The dean of pledging was the big brother that led the line and taught the pledges everything about the fraternity. He sometimes protected us when things went too far, but he had a high threshold for interference. His leadership role didn't stop him from doling out punishment where he saw fit. He was more likely to contribute to our "education" than any of the big brothers.

DP pledged Theta his sophomore year when the chapter was reinstated after its suspension for hazing. He was the only pledge on his line. I couldn't imagine what it would be like to have no one else to rely on under such duress. But he made it. It was his turn to lead the five of us through the process. There was also an assistant dean of pledging, Big Brother Major Payne. ADP's real name was Michael Sheldon. He was essentially the vice president of the line and led set when DP wasn't in attendance.

The big brothers all had quirky line names that they were given when they pledged. Some of them were easy to decipher; others were shrouded in mystery. Only the Thetas in the chapter knew exactly why they received them. DP was given the name Genesis because he was the first pledge in the fraternity's new era at Morrison. ADP was Major Payne because, well, it was obvious why.

"Hey, look who made it!" DP said mockingly. The big brothers heckled loudly, doing their best to unnerve us. They didn't have to try hard.

"They don't look too happy to be here!" one of them taunted. We were instructed not to smile during our time on line, but who would want to?

"Of course they are, brother," DP said as he circled the room.

"You're always happy to see us, aren't you fellas?"

"Yes sir, Big Brother Genesis!" we shouted.

"We'll see how you boys feel at the end of the night. Let me hear greetings!" DP barked at us.

The greetings were the preamble to set in which we honored the big brothers individually with humorous and flattering chants. If one of the Thetas wasn't thrilled with his greeting, there would be retribution at some point during the night.

"Greetings Big Brothers of Theta Pi Chi Fraternity Innnn-corporated!" we bellowed in unison.

"Greetings Big Brother Genesis! You are the originator! Never duplicated! Your leadership will guide us to the light!"

"Greetings Big Brother Major Payne! The leanest! Meanest! Roughest! Toughest! Soldier of all of Theta Pi Chi Fraternity!"

"Greetings Big Brother Dennis the Menace! The brother who can't be tamed! You are the prince of mischief who plays by your own rules!"

"Greetings Big Brother Blue Light Special! When you get turned on allllllll the ladies come running!"

"Greetings Big Brother Flatline! We were dead until you brought us back to life! We owe you from now until eternity!"

"Greetings Big Brother Motor Mouth! You are the fountain from which knowledge springs! Bless us with your words of wisdom!"

We exhausted ourselves running through the greetings. The quick delivery was challenging because we had to be in sync with our four other LBs. We couldn't omit a single word. The big brothers were on the hunt for any reason to feign indignation.

"Have you guys been studying?" DP asked. His question was both praise for our past work and a warning against any future mistakes.

"Naw, they ain't been studyin'!" one of the guys to our

left yelled.

"What's that? You haven't been doing your work? Why you say they haven't been studying, Brotha Flatline?"

"Cause I saw one of 'em talkin' to girls on the quad!"

"Oooooooh!" the brothers muttered to each other.

That was ridiculous! None of us was foolish enough to talk to a girl anywhere on campus. It was one of the many rules outlined at the start of the process. It was harder for Junior to abide by it more than any of us because his girlfriend also attended Morrison.

However, he had become so skilled at keeping his conversations with her private that I didn't believe for one second that he was the person in question. I couldn't call Big Brother Flatline out on his mistake. Flubbing a line or two of the greetings was a small infraction compared to talking back to the big brothers.

DP held a large wood paddle to Rodney's chin. "You been talking to girls, Ace?"

"No sir, Big Brother Genesis," Rodney pleaded.

"Okay."

DP shoved the hulking plank of wood in my face. I hated that thing more than I could ever say! Fraternity paddles were made of solid wood and had Greek letters burned into their polished surfaces. They came in all sizes: short ones the length of my arm and paddles so long the brothers could lean on them like a cane. And they hit us with them every chance they got.

Answer a question wrong, get smashed with the paddle. Don't know your information? Prepare for the worst. The brothers swung madly, sometimes delivering 20 or more crippling swats in a row.

At the outset of pledging, I estimated that the larger paddles would be the ones most likely to destroy us, but it turned out they were harder to swing. Most times, they landed in the same area on our butts, so the worst pain was at the beginning of the punishment. After the first few swats, I could anticipate what was coming and my body went numb.

The smaller paddles they wound like baseball bats, making sure to hit every part of our body that they could. The agony of being struck repeatedly consumed me until it was all I could think about. At the end of the night, my butt was colored with horrid shades of black and blue. It was so swollen that when I touched it, it was harder than my skull.

Some of the big brothers got a kick out of "giving wood." They were aware that the exercise in brutality sometimes went overboard. But who was I to argue? I had no recourse to say, "Excuse me Big Brother, could you please go lighter and to the left?" That would only provoke them to swing with all their might until they nearly beat the life out of us.

"You guys are talking to girls, but not one of you has something to say?" DP grilled us.

He tapped each of us on the shoulder with the four-foot plank of wood. My eyes were laser focused on the intricacies of Rodney's afro. Vaughn cradled me from behind to insulate me from retaliation.

"These rules are here for a reason," DP yelled. "If you can't follow them like you're supposed to, that means you gotta take the punishment! Get in the cut! All of you!"

The five of us got in the position that had become routine: squatting with our butts out, eyes facing the wall, our right arm extended forward with our hand making a tight fist. I tried to prepare myself mentally for the crack of the paddle against my body, but I couldn't. Even after weeks of playing this lethal game with the big brothers, I couldn't voluntarily prepare my body for injury. Someone turned the volume on the television to an unfathomable level. A drone of voices was the soundtrack to our misery.

I closed my eyes and envisioned myself anywhere else but in the room. Back in Athens at home with my books. SMACK! In Vaughn's dorm room watching cartoons. SMACK! Reading the Bible with my mother at the dinner table. SMACK!

The sting of the wood burned through my rear like a house set ablaze. Flashes of pain reverberated through every part of my body. Tears burned down my face as the swats blurred together. With every swing, I clenched my fist tighter and willed myself not to fall over. SMACK!

"Back in line, pledges!" DP commanded. "It's question time! If you haven't got the lesson about talking to girls, you better remember your information. If you don't, you're gonna be in the cut all night."

I rushed back into formation and collapsed on Rodney's back so forcefully I almost crushed him. The phantom swings of the paddle sent aftershocks coursing through every inch of me. I couldn't come up with a cohesive thought, but if I got any of the fraternity history wrong I had no doubts DP would make good on his promise. My splintered body begged me to concentrate.

"Where was Theta Pi Chi Fraternity founded?!" DP roared.

"Howard University, sir!" we shouted in the most assertive voices we could muster.

"What date was Theta Pi Chi founded?!"

"March 1st, 1916!"

"What are the fraternity's ideals, Number 4?"

"Brotherhood, fellowship, achievement and… and service,

sir!" Junior cried.

"Wrong!" DP paced the floor. His footsteps were deadened by the carpet beneath him.

"Ace, what are the fraternity's ideals?"

"Brotherhood! Fellowship! Service! And honor!" Rodney yelled assertively.

"Correct! But how is it that you have the right answer and your brother doesn't? Answer me that?"

"Aw hell naw!" the big brothers laughed mockingly.

Dang it, Rodney! We were supposed to be on the same page. If Junior made an error, Rodney should have done the same, even if he was sure his response was the better of the two.

"Big brother, I—" Rodney stuttered, fully aware of the misstep.

DP ignored him. "Who do you think has the correct answer, Number 5?"

"They both do, sir!" Chima said. His response didn't make sense. However, this was the alternate universe of pledging. If we didn't say the same thing, it would be our butts on the line again.

DP contemplated the conflicting positions. "How is it that they both have the correct answer? Number 2, who do you think is right?"

"They both are, Big Brother Genesis, sir!" I screamed.

"Number 3, which of your brothers has the correct answer?"

"They both do, sir!" Vaughn contributed desperately.

"Ace, you may have the right answer, but you are dead wrong!" DP's words sent a chill through my nearly broken spine. "You are a line! One unit! If one of you doesn't have the answer, then none of you do! That means all of you are getting in the cut! Why do you make me do this to you?"

The five of us slowly returned to our positions in front of the firing squad. My body hadn't stopped screaming for relief after the last round with the paddle. The hundreds of facts about Theta Pi Chi that filled my head turned to sludge.

"You are supposed to work together! No excuses!" DP swung the wood violently, piling onto the graveyard of bruises we already had.

The jeering from our big brothers magnified the aching. They went through this same infliction before and loved to see the tables turned. But that should have meant they knew more than anyone how much the strain damaged our souls.

"I don't want any goddamn individuals on this line!" DP increased the speed of the swats to our backs.

"No GDIs!" someone yelled from across the room.

"You boys are gonna get it right whether you like or not! Get back in line."

We wiped the perspiration and tears from our faces, flinging salty drops while we locked back up. I clutched my rear as if I could somehow control the searing pain. Rodney's sniffles echoed mine.

"Let's go again!" DP yelled to my defeated line brothers. "Who are the eight founders of Theta Pi Chi Fraternity, Incorporated?"

I whispered the names in Rodney's ear in rapid succession. I wouldn't leave the protection of the line if I could help it. Vaughn's grasp was far better than the paddle's sting. The line stumbled through the eight founders' names. We didn't have the same coordination that we had practiced, but it was enough to not set DP off again.

"Sounds like they need to study more," Big Brother Flatline complained sarcastically.

"I agree brother," DP said. "Your minds are weak pledges, so we're gonna make your bodies tough. On the ground!"

We lay flat on the fading carpet. The fibers were a rough pillow against my cheek. Suddenly, a crippling weight pushed into my back. The big brothers had placed the concrete blocks on top of us. To move them would require a Herculean effort.

"Ten push-ups!" DP commanded.

My body was so weak that the block felt ten times heavier than when we carried them in. I strained to lift the weight and myself at the same time. Somehow I managed to do the push-ups without it falling off. If it did, I'd have to start over. I moved slowly, keeping my eyes on the threadbare carpet below and blocking out the grunts of my LBs.

The big brothers were on the ground next to us. They yelled in our faces and did everything they could to discourage us. Big Brother Motor Mouth pushed his elbow into my back. It made it even harder to pull myself up. 180 pounds of rage were determined to crush me.

"Go all the way down! Up! Down!" DP towered over us. "There is no room for weakness in this frat!"

"Sir, yes sir," we responded with exhaustion.

Thirty minutes more of the exercise and the night was finally over. We dragged ourselves out of the apartment into the muggy air using whatever strength we had left to carry the blocks. There was an explosion of laughter from inside the apartment as the big brothers replayed the events of the night.

Anyone passing by would think it was nothing more than a run-of-the-mill house party. The only clue that something was awry was the five shuffling guys in drenched clothes trudging toward a Ford Explorer. Like us, it had seen better days. We rode in silence back to the dorms. There was nothing worth talking about.

We were two miles down the road when Chima broke the silence. "Junior, how could you forget the fraternity ideals?! We've been studying them all week!"

"I'm sorry! My mind blanked!" Junior said. "I meant to say honor, but I couldn't think of what it was. Rodney, you made it worse! Why didn't you tell 'em the same thing I said?"

"Somebody had to have the right answer," Rodney responded dryly.

"But they told us we have to be on the same page!"

"You should've had the right answer then!" Rodney shot back. "Don't put it on me!"

"And by the way, who was talkin' to girls?!" Junior was angry and so was I. "This is basic, day one shit! I can't even be around my girl on campus! You think I like ignoring her?"

Vaughn's mounting exasperation created more tension inside the truck. "You guys can't keep giving them reasons to jump on us!"

In the time since I met Vaughn, he never raised his voice to me. Pledging brought out the Mr. Hyde in every one of us. The pressure from the big brothers was more stressful than anything I'd ever encountered.

"None of us would do something on purpose to make them hit us," I said with restraint. "They don't need a reason to beat us down. They're going to do it anyway."

"I think my back is bleeding," Junior said, reaching under his shirt to make sure. "Rodney, I'm gonna fuck you up after we cross."

"Junior, you're not going to do anything of the sort," Chima intervened. "We're brothers. If you touch him, it is an attack against all of us. Just keep your cool so you don't do anything you'll regret."

One by one, Vaughn dropped our LBs off at their dorms. They fought sleep deprivation and the undercurrent of contempt toward the Theta brothers.

Rodney was the last one out of the truck. "I'm sorry, guys. I promise it won't happen again," he said.

Vaughn smiled tenderly at our broken line brother. "We know. Have a good night. Make sure you study for next time."

I recognized the same warmth that brought me peace whenever I was shaken. We rolled away from the dormitory leaving Rodney to think over his actions. Finally, Vaughn and I were alone. He lived in the dorms too and my apartment was the furthest from campus, but I was always the last person he took home. He stroked my left leg softly as a reminder of his affection for me.

"You okay?" he asked.

I was more worried about him. Vaughn didn't get angry often, but I could tell that tonight's ordeal with the brothers triggered something new in him.

"As good as I can be," I said. "We survived another night."

"Yeah, they didn't show us any mercy. We've had worse nights, though," he said, lightly stroking my shoulder.

"Probably, but every night is the worst night," I complained. "I'm going to need serious therapy after this. I don't want you to find me balled up in a corner somewhere shaking and mumbling to myself."

"Hopefully this is over before it gets to that point," he said. "Your LBs have your back. I have your back *and* your front."

Vaughn had never set foot inside my apartment for more than a minute or two because I hadn't yet told my roommates about our intimacy. Sitting in the car was the closest we came to spending time alone at my place. I caressed his back, careful not to touch any part that may have been hit with the paddle. He moved in for a kiss, resting my head between his charitable hands.

"Not tonight," I said, pulling away from him. "I have class tomorrow."

"You don't wanna crash in my room? I can cuddle you to sleep," he smiled in a way he knew made me melt.

"Vaughn, don't even try it," I couldn't contain my flattered grin. "One minute we'll be cuddling, the next you'll be inside me. I know how you are."

"Don't you mean how *we* are," he said innocently.

I exited the truck and walked around to his side where we met face to face. I placed my lips against his one more time. His tongue sought mine with urgency. Kissing Vaughn was a brief escape from the daily challenges that haunted me.

"I'll see you soon," I said.

"Yes, you will," Vaughn replied. "Hey, next time you go to the store can you buy more Icy Hot?"

"Why? Is your behind burning?" I joked.

"No, but yours will be when I get ahold of it."

The lights were off in the apartment. It was 1:30 in the morning, way past any of our normal bedtimes. My roommates were used to me coming in late. They understood that it was because I was pledging. How could I not tell them? I came home every night looking like I had a threesome with a bulldozer and a wrecking ball.

Tyree and Cole didn't know where I was pledging or with whom. My LBs and I only met outside my apartment if I was sure they wouldn't be home. Cole was always at track practice, and I made sure to text Tyree before I invited them over.

I quietly set my house keys down on the kitchen counter

and flicked on the light switch. There was a stack of dirty dishes in the sink. A half-eaten sandwich collected dust on the table. If Cole and Tyree thought I would clean that up, they'd better think again. My duties as a roommate did not extend to maid service.

My backpack that contained a collection of unread textbooks hadn't moved from its resting place in the living room. I had yet to finish my assignment for African-American history class or the homework for Calculus. I couldn't anticipate when I would finish it all.

The best I could do was step into the shower and scrub the stink away. The bathroom was messier than the kitchen. I stepped over the old towels and dirty laundry that were likely Cole's castoffs. As steam filled the room, I carefully removed my rancid clothes. I carelessly threw them on the back of the toilet. The spray from the showerhead stung my back, mostly in the places where I was hit repeatedly. I didn't need to turn around to know it was covered in black welts.

Instead of falling over like my body wanted to do, I steadied myself on the tiles of the bathroom wall. The water flowing over me always brought me back to life after a long night at set. In one of her books, Octavia Butler wrote that in order to rise from its own ashes, a phoenix first must burn. I considered those words frequently. Pain was temporary. Theta was forever. I ran the soapy washcloth gently over my wounds.

Someone knocked on the bathroom door. It had to be Tyree. Cole never bothered to interrupt if it was closed. It could have been April, but if she was at the apartment this late, she and Cole stayed secluded in his room.

"Hey Jason, that you?" Tyree said from the other side.

"Yeah, it's me. I'll be done in a second. Did you need

something from out of here?"

"Nope, just checkin' on you. How did tonight go?"

"Another evening of fun and adventure," I said as I soaped up.

Tyree was probably sitting outside the door waiting for me. I appreciated how much he cared about my well-being. With my mother 500 miles away, I had a friend nearby who I could rely on. I shut off the shower and wrapped a towel around my waist. One would think with all those cinder block push-ups I would've dropped weight but no, I still looked like a distant relative of the Pillsbury Doughboy.

Tyree and I sat on the living room couch. Him with a swift flourish, me very, very slowly.

"Where's Cole?" I asked, wiping off the rest of the water from my shoulders.

"Out with April, I think." He couldn't be sure and I didn't want to rouse him at the late hour.

Tyree switched on the TV. The laughter from a Tyler Perry movie did its best to lift my spirits. I caught my roommate inspecting the bruises on my back where the cinder block pressed into it. I put on a shirt that lay on the arm of the couch.

"I don't know how you keep goin' through it," he said. "Jason, this is some slave on the plantation mess! So what'd they do to you this time?"

I told him about set without going into the details. Someone on the line messed up. We got beat beyond belief. Nothing out of the ordinary. Then Vaughn dropped us off.

"Speakin' of Vaughn, what's going on with you and him? Y'all been mighty close."

Tyree's prying tone was a dead giveaway that he wanted to know if we were dating or something more. He wasn't getting a thing out of me tonight. I simply said no.

"Girl, please. You been eyein' that boy since you first saw him on the yard. Your tongue was waggin' this way and that. You tellin' me nothin's poppin' off with you two?"

I wish Tyree wouldn't call me girl, but what he suspected was true. I couldn't stop thinking about Vaughn. A week after we began chatting, I was caught off guard when I saw him coming out of the cafeteria. I almost tripped on a crack in the pavement to get over to him.

Vaughn strode with the easy finesse that was his hallmark. My initial reaction to Cole was merely physical. Vaughn and I shared a connection that transcended carnal desires. Tyree saw my blunder and would not stop laughing. He had no idea Vaughn and I already shared our private moments online and off.

A familiar beep snapped me out of my reminiscing. Tyree received a message on Grindr, the app he was fond of. It had been a while since I logged in to check out the index of single men in the area. With Vaughn around, I had no reason to stray.

Tyree looked at me as he thumbed through the profiles. Knowing my roommate, the app was open the entire time we talked. I smiled at him knowingly.

"You not the only one who wants to find a boo," he said mischievously.

"For your information, I'm not looking for anyone," I said. "So who's the lucky guy? Is he cute?"

Tyree read out the profile as if it were a poem by Langston Hughes written at the height of the Harlem Renaissance: "24 years old. Total top with Southern charm. Lookin' to chill and meet new people. Got a good job. Workout three times a week. Go hard or go home."

"Oh wow he sounds hot!" I exclaimed. "Have you guys

talked already?"

"He's been messagin' me for a day or two," Tyree said. "That's more time than I give most of these Negroes on the app. I cuts 'em off real quick if I suspect a trace of foolishness. But me and this guy are supposed to go out soon. This weekend maybe."

"Let me see his picture," I said, reaching for the phone.

On the screen was a chiseled Black guy enticing potential suitors with an overtly sexual display of his upper body muscles. Tyree went for the masculine type, so this one was a match for him. I tapped the screen to view his profile.

The first picture had the high quality I came to expect from my roommate. The selfie was captured with his phone held over his head to show off his best attributes: his boyish face and enviable torso. Tyree's pout was playful, but not too sexy.

"That's a nice pic, you look like a catch," I winked as I handed the phone back.

"Oh, I don't play around when it comes to the selfies. It's all about the angles!" he posed. "Got that good lightin' and er'thang. They gonna have to give me the Oscar for this one. Best art direction in a featured photo."

I interrupted his acceptance speech of the invisible award. "But your face is showing? You're not scared someone might recognize you?"

"Chile, these boys be five feet away when they hit me up on the app, so that ain't nothin'. The only thing I'm worried about is if somebody feels compelled to post my pics online. There's enough dicks and asses on the internet. I don't need my good stuff out there along with everybody else's."

"First you have to have photos that people want to steal," I said.

"I feel very attacked!" he gasped in false horror. "Don't be jealous, Jason Cooper. My selfies are *extraordinary*. The real thing is equally luscious. Come Spring Break the boys are gonna be runnin' across the yard to get at my milkshake. Trust and believe."

"You're going to use Grindr when we go to Miami?" I asked.

"Yes gawd! Why wouldn't I?" He thumbed through more profiles on his phone.

"I don't mind, of course, but please don't cause a scene when we're down there."

"*Excuse* me?" He stared at me with a significant delay to see if I was joking. Oh boy. What did I say this time?

"I'm not gonna be spillin' my tea, but if somebody wants to holla I'm not changin' who I am 'cause I'm in Miami."

Tyree's eyes bored into me the same way my mother's did when I didn't complete one of my assigned household chores. If I misplaced a pair of shoes or left books lying around, she would launch into a lesson on cleanliness backed by a line of scripture. There was an awkward pause before Tyree returned to his phone.

"I'm sorry, I didn't mean to be rude," I said. "I'm extremely tired."

"You're okay, but I don't like people tellin' me how I'm supposed to live my life," he said. "I worked hard to become a person I like. Nobody's gonna take that away from me. Including you."

"I understand. Tyree, you've always been so confident. How do you do that?" I asked. If there was one thing I admired about my roommate, it was that he was always himself, no matter the circumstances.

"I'm confident because I have to be. Hidin' who you are is

too much of a commitment. The people who have a problem with who I am are not the people I want around me anyway."

"I wish I could be that honest," I sighed. "I wouldn't have to lie every day, but I'd also open myself up to a new set of problems. I don't want to do anything that would destroy the relationship my mom and I have. She's my world. I can't picture a life without her in it."

"Listen, Jason, once you tell your parents, that's half the battle there. Your mother loves you," he affirmed.

"But I also know she wants me to be straight. She's made that very clear."

Tyree sucked his teeth. "You think I don't know what that pressure's like? I told you how my mother was before she decided to leave us. I hate to say this about the woman who birthed me, but thank God she's gone. Livin' with her was dreadful. Not only did I have somebody in the same house who gave me drama about the person that God made me, it was the woman who pushed me outta her uterus!"

"That's why she drove you out. She was trying to get rid of you," I laughed.

"Yep, she gave me an eviction notice and kicked me to the curb! But seriously Jason, you can't stay in the closet forever. It's not cute. You have to show folks that not all the gays are loud and rowdy like some people." Tyree cleared his throat and pointed at himself.

"It comes down to this," he said. "Who you are shouldn't have to be a secret. And if people don't like it, fuck 'em. Life's too short to pretend you don't like dick."

Tyree was too much! I doubled over in laughter because of his audacity. He roared because he had imparted his unique brand of self-help advice.

"Don't get me wrong, Jason. I'm insecure sometimes," he said. "But if I can make it, you can too."

"I'll work on it, Tyree. In the meantime, let's stay out of trouble, okay? We'll be away from home which means we need to have our guard up."

"Gotcha boo. We're still cool. No homo."

In the time we talked I completely forgot I'd just come from set. The pervasive aches served as a reminder. If I didn't get to bed, I'd never be able to get up in the morning.

"Tyree, I'm on my way to dreamland. I'll meditate on what you said."

"See you in the mornin', Jason. And don't be stompin' 'round the house like an elephant when you wake up. You may have an early class, but some of us need to get our beauty sleep."

TYREE

I checked Grindr again to see if my Southern charmer hit me back. The conversation with him was on point so far, especially considering texting somebody from Grindr for the first time was always stressful. Did they like you? Were they funny or just funny-looking? The good thing was that if it didn't work out, I could hit the block button and never have to hear from the man again. Speaking of, that guy in the club was super sweet. If Cole hadn't been carrying on like he was, I woulda got a nice date out of it. And he was pretty? What a wasted opportunity.

I wish I could meet somebody like Cole, minus the heterosexual part. When we moved in to our apartment, I didn't realize how hard having a straight roommate would be. Seeing a fine ass man in your home, knowing you can't have him was a struggle. I'd never tell Cole because that would mean no more of him walking around the house with no shirt on.

The funny thing was I wasn't always crushing on him. My friends were like "ooh your roommate is so sexy." I'd be like, "who him? That's Cole, ain't nobody payin' him no mind."

But with all these people coming at me, talking about how cute my roommate was, one day something clicked. I saw the beauty in him too.

Cole bringing April around was a constant reminder that he was off-limits. I couldn't stand that girl, but then again she probably didn't like me either. No woman wanted a sissy — let alone two of 'em — around her man. Me and her tolerated each other for Cole's sake.

He stuck up for me when April oh so casually called me a "punk" during one of our conversations. I swear to God he almost decked her in the face. She thought she was being cute calling me out my name, but that was the last thing I was gonna take from my roommate's side hoe. It was the moment I knew Cole would be by my side, girlfriend or no girlfriend.

Times like that made me wonder if there was ever a slight possibility of Cole and I getting together. Under that thug visage was a smart guy. He tried to hide it, but I saw his transcripts. All As and one B.

The only time he showed any sign of academic success was when I was almost gonna fail my freshman English class. Cole stayed up all night making me a cheat sheet for the final. And I passed! Nothing like a man with brains *and* body. I told Jason a while back how I felt about Cole, but he would never understand how complex our relationship was.

Somebody's keys jingled in the door. Speak of the devil. Cole drifted into the apartment with his book bag slung over his shoulder. He wore Nike sweats and a graphic tee from Walmart I took scissors to and made it sleeveless for him. He looked like he had a helluva night.

"Whattup," Cole said lazily.

"Wassup, where you been?" I pried.

"Had a kick-back at one of my boy's houses," he slurred. "Man, I'm hungry. What's in the fridge?"

"Just some collard greens and corn bread, some candied yams, a little potato salad, fried chicken, peach cobbler and a few slices of ham."

"Really?"

"Hell no. There's frozen dinners in the freezer."

Why did it smell like weed in here? The scent of fresh Mary Jane attacked my nostrils. "You been smokin' too?" I asked.

"I might've sparked one up."

He went about his business in the kitchen, not paying me any mind. After his introduction to my stash of fine colognes, you'd think he'd take advantage.

"How you gon' run track and smoke weed? How does that work?"

"Ain't a big thing. Smoke ain't gonna bring me down. I'm unstoppable," he said as he popped a Lean Cuisine in the microwave. Cole plopped down next to me while the microwave stirred and laid his head in my lap. Ooh! What was I supposed to do here? This was a first. That weed must've been mighty powerful.

"No April tonight?" I asked. I lightly massaged his forehead to relieve his stress and my panic.

"Nah, she had to study. Why you up? You're usually out for the count by midnight."

"Because I'm not tired yet. Jason just left outta here to go to bed not too long ago."

"He sleep?" Cole asked indifferently.

"I think so. It's time for me to hit the sack too."

"Alright then. Peace."

Cole disappeared into his room, the smell of weed and microwaved ravioli trailing behind him. The combination would have been an instant turnoff from anybody else. Cole's hard-body physique and good-natured spirit made him hard to resist.

I threw myself on my bed, landing on the jumble of soft pillows. I had Intro to Marketing tomorrow. It was the one class I took that was related to my major. Because of that, it was the class I loved the most. I couldn't wait to get into my real coursework and do internships so I could get one step closer to my success.

The long and short of it was I wanted to make my daddy proud. He would love to see me be a businessman and a pillar of the community just like he was. Also, I'd have a family of my own one day. I was a long ways off from birthing babies, but a good first step would be getting my career off the ground.

Before I got to Morrison, I was worried that my daddy was alone in the house by himself. Turned out my first year in he got married again — this time to a woman named Valerie. He had been seeing her off and on for a while. They met when he represented her in what he told me was a messy divorce case. She came to the office about six months after it was over and asked him out for coffee. I was surprised when he said yes.

My daddy worked so hard he didn't have time to date, or at least that's what he used to say. But when Valerie came around, he was happier than a kid on Christmas. She was cute too: a petite thang with long, wavy hair and cinnamon brown skin. She was borderline mousey and wouldn't speak much unless she was spoken to, except when she was around my father. He brought out the best in her.

Me and Valerie didn't quite connect with each other when we first met. She was suspicious of this nelly boy gallivanting around the house. I figured we could break bread the best way I knew how — over shopping.

She was the kind of girl who looked okay from the knees up, but those Target leggings and buckle shoes weren't doing her any favors. I got her out of her Sunday school teacher clothes and put her in pumps and pencil skirts. You would've thought I was a saint! She would not stop thanking me.

By the time I was done with her, Valerie had a few pieces to jazz up her wardrobe and a more open outlook on me. She insisted that she didn't want to replace my mother. I didn't want her to feel like she should. That wasn't her responsibility.

After we cozied up, Valerie would invite me to church, but I always turned her down. My daddy and I used to go to the Baptist church not too far from Jackson State and that was nothing but trouble. The saints in the pews were two-faced. Sister so-and-so and the other Black folks in there sucked their teeth at the *homosexual* in God's house. They'd wave their church fans and preach about love your neighbor, and then talk about me like a dog a minute after the closing prayer!

Whatever happened to "Let him who is without sin cast the first stone"? Not that I thought being gay was a sin, but the way the church folks told it I was on the same level as murderers and thieves. They only tolerated me because they liked my father. He was a welcome member of the house of worship.

The irony of it all was that church was filled to the rafters with gays. The way the minister of music banged on his keyboard, it didn't take Olivia Benson from "Law & Order" to figure out he crept around with Jackson's finest bachelors. And there were more fish in the choir than you could shake a ten-foot pole at. And yet the preacher was hellfire and brimstone this and Sodom and Gomorrah that.

One day, he was deep in another one of his sermons on how homosexuality was an unforgivable sin. I wanted to stand up in the middle of that church and call him out. "All have sinned and fallen short of the glory of God" was written there in Romans, chapter 3. Why was being gay the worst possible thing a man could do? My father felt me tensing up. He held my hand to calm me down.

I let the reverend finish his hour-long condemnation, but that was the last time I set foot in there. I was like the 7UP cake at the end of a church picnic — gone. I'd get my religion by myself without cackling hens judging me from behind those Holy Ghost satellites they called hats.

Being gay in the South was *work*. It wasn't like people didn't know you were gay, they just didn't want you to talk about it. And they didn't take kindly to a man doing anything they saw as womanly. I wanted to pledge Theta, but the fraternity boys gave me static for the same reason.

"There are no gays in Theta. Period," one of them told me to my face when I asked. Yeah right. With all that Carmex popping on his lips, if it wasn't him, for sure some of his brothers were bumping booties on the low. I thanked God every day that I had a father who loved me for who I was, but men like him were one in a million. A lot of gay folks didn't have that kind of unconditional love.

My phone beeped. It was another message from the guy from Grindr. I wished he had hit me up earlier because I was about to crash, but getting a chat from this cutie was everything I needed.

hey babe
i mean homie. whatsup?

                                                        was that a slip or....

oops yeah
we still meeting soon?

                                                                      yes
                                          we'll lock down details ltr
                                                  catching zzzs ☺

Professor Akende scribbled on the whiteboard faster than he could talk. I jotted down the bullet points in my workbook, doing my best to keep up. He was from Africa like a lot of the professors at Morrison. Sometimes it was hard to understand what he was saying through his thick accent. He hailed from Nigeria as he pointed out the first day, along with instructions that we better not fail his class. Handing in work late was a surefire way to flunk out.

The professor had on the same blue dress shirt and khakis he wore almost every time I saw him. His back was always turned to us during the lectures, so I had just a partial understanding of what the front of him looked like.

There were about 25 students in the room with me. That was a lot for Morrison. Most times, there were only 10 or 15 in a class. The day's lesson included phrases I hadn't heard before, like "behavioral segmentation" and "category need." It might as well have been in Scandinavian. I didn't know before this class how technical marketing could be. Nothing I couldn't handle if I continued to stay in my textbooks. I did not slack when it came to my studies.

"Market size is important when you are establishing your new business because you have to determine the potential growth rate," Professor Akende said. "You cannot target 100 percent of the population. So let's say you are opening a new restaurant. You would first have to analyze the market."

The professor wrote "targeting" in wide letters on the board. That meant we could count on it being on a test. I followed suit and added the new phrase to my notes.

"You have to ask yourself these things when you start. What are the demographics of your intended neighborhood? Are there other restaurants in the area? What is their customer base? How can you market your business so it is different from your competitors?"

Looks like I wouldn't be starting a restaurant for a while. Not without a ton of research first. Selling clothes had to be easier than hawking burgers.

"If you open a restaurant and sell every kind of food," the professor continued, "you would have to keep a very large inventory and market to wide a range of customers. Because of this, your menu will be very long and confusing. So we analyze the market. In this particular case, we will need to select what food we are going to sell. So let us pick one. What kind of restaurant should we open?"

"Soul food!"

"Asian food!"

Everybody yelled, mostly because it was almost lunchtime and they were hungry. I wondered what they were serving in the caf. Something fried or rice and gravy. They *always* had rice and gravy.

"Okay, I heard the soul food. If you were to open a restaurant in Tampa, who would be your direct and indirect competitors?"

"Bob Evans."

"Denny's!"

"Denny's is the soul food? Okay. If you say so." The class snickered at the suggestion.

"The next step is 'positioning.' This is the space we occupy in the customer's mind relative to the competition. Think about your luxury brands. Louis Vuitton. Porsche. Are they the best? Possibly. Perhaps not. But they have positioned themselves as superior through marketing."

"Yes, but they also cost more," a girl in front of me named Monica said. "If something is expensive won't people automatically think it's a luxury item?"

"That is right," the professor answered. "But the price is also a part of the marketing. They are not looking to attract customers with limited financial resources because that is not their consumer base. If you were to see a person who looked very poor driving a Porsche, you would consider the product to be less valuable. So it is not only how you market to the customers, but also how the customers market your product for you."

I think I got what he was saying. Back in the day, Louis Vuitton created a new line of bags to market to younger customers. They brought in the designer Marc Jacobs to give the brand some spice. He collaborated with cool artists like Takashi Murakami on the rainbow bags and the Stephen Sprouse ones had Louis written in neon graffiti. Everybody bought those suckers up. But after they came out you could get that Ooh-Wee Vuitton knockoff from anybody on the street. The rich folks who were buying the real thing stopped because they didn't want nobody thinking they had fakes. Goes to show, when you were good, somebody out there would always try to copy you.

"Okay class, what is perceptual mapping and how does it relate to positioning? This was part of your assigned reading." Professor Akende waited for an answer.

"You, Mr. Butler. What is a perceptual map?" the professor said, calling out this scrub boy Keyshawn who was three seats away from me.

Keyshawn stuttered and stalled, but he couldn't come up with the answer. Typical.

"I see you have not been studying your lesson," the professor said. "Who can tell me what a perceptual map is? Tyree, please share."

I had no problem with him calling me out. Unlike other people, I actually did the reading.

"Perceptual mapping is a way to visually represent the position of a product or brand relative to the competition." Bam. Couldn't tell me that wasn't the answer.

"Gay ass nigga," Keyshawn said. "He be positionin' on dicks."

Everybody in the room cracked up at his "joke." I heard him and the professor did too, but our teacher didn't say a word. Professor Akende's back was turned to the class. That didn't make him deaf. Looked like I was on my own.

"Yo daddy be positioned on my dick," I yelled back.

"That is enough!" Professor Akende finally said. "No language like that in my class! Back to our lesson, please."

I was so heated I couldn't listen to the rest of the lecture. Keyshawn could yell "faggot" with a megaphone and none of the professors would bat an eyelash. It wasn't my fault he didn't know the answer. He wasn't gonna make me feel some kinda way for being on top of my education.

I didn't have time for this. I dug into my textbook until it was time to go.

My next class was down the hall from Professor Akende's. Normally I loved walking through the Business building because it was one of the newest on campus. It had gleaming windows that filled the place with sunshine. But there Keyshawn was, at the end of the walkway yammering away with one of his boys.

The death stare he shot my way meant he was still mad about what happened earlier. I couldn't avoid him because my Statistics class was on the other side of where he stood. All the sunshine was sucked outta the building.

This did not have to be awkward. I found myself looking anywhere except in Keyshawn's direction, walking as normal as I possibly could. I didn't want him thinking I was backing down. He kept his eye on me as I got closer. That scowl of his coulda burned a hole into the side of a building.

"That's the faggot," he said loudly to his friend.

I got in his nasty face. "What did you say to me?"

He didn't respond, but I could tell from the way his lip quivered he wanted to. Keyshawn would not stop me from living my life. I had a class to get to and knowledge to obtain. I kept moving until I passed him up.

"Yeah, keep suckin' dick faggot," he shouted. The other students on their way to class stopped in their tracks.

"Oh hell no! Who you think you callin' a faggot?" I said. "I ain't yo damn faggot."

I rushed toward Keyshawn like a linebacker, shoulders down, so I could ram him in his gut. He blocked me without much effort. When I spun around to land a solid punch, he pushed me dead in the chest. No matter how much the blow hurt, I would not let myself be dominated by this fool. My adrenaline kicked in and so did my desire to let him have it.

"You like to touch on other boys, huh?!" I said, attempting to sneak a jab into his fat stomach. "You wanna cop a feel? Is that what it is?"

His friend grabbed me by the waist and lifted me off the ground, tearing me away from my target. The force of his grip took the wind out of me. He didn't know I refused to be defeated. Not no way, not no how.

"Get off me! I SAID GET OFF ME!" I screamed.

Keyshawn laughed his ass off while I wrestled myself away from his friend's hold on me. "Yeah whatsup now, bitch nigga?" he taunted.

I threw my arm back to elbow the man in his gut but whacked him in the nose instead. He howled like a banshee as I made my escape. Blood oozed from his face down to the sides of his twisted mouth. More students bunched in to see us fighting. The commotion was loud enough for my stats professor Miss Ramirez to poke her head out of the classroom. She forced herself between me and Keyshawn so we didn't rip each other apart.

"What is wrong with you two? This is a place of learning!" she shrieked.

We were surrounded by students who wanted to see the prizefight keep going. Phones and cameras were out like they were paparazzi on a red carpet. I didn't want my face all over social media, so I scooped up my bag to leave.

"Keyshawn, I wish you would call me a faggot again," I challenged. "I will wear you out!"

"Fuck you!" he screamed. "Don't let me catch yo punk ass off campus!"

"I wish you would come at me! I will whoop your ass from here to next week!"

I stormed away without another word. This was the type of

mess that made me not wanna go to this school. I couldn't take on the world every time somebody looked at me sideways. This was supposed to be the era of gay marriages and equal rights and here I was getting right hooks instead.

Sometimes I wished I was like the white gays on the covers of glossy magazines. They didn't have to put up with this mess. Their friends and loved ones threw them parties when they came out of the closet. They gushed about how brave the person was and pledged to support them for life.

That would never be my reality. People came at me left and right just for existing. I wasn't a fighter, but I felt like I was constantly forced to be one. My tongue was way sharper than my uppercut. This shitstorm was enough to drive a man crazy.

I fired off a couple texts to Jason to tell him about the battle with Keyshawn. He responded right away.

> have you talked 2 someone on campus?
> a counselor?

I loved Jason, but he could be dense as hell sometimes. A counselor? After that boy tried to whoop my ass on school property?

I was madder than a demon in a vat of boiling oil. What got me even angrier was that I looked like the hottest of hot messes. My brand new tangerine polo from Zara hung off me like a rag and a button was missing. Fantastic. This much was obvious: I wouldn't be going to class for the rest of the day. I was supposed to do work study at the Academic Office later, but I would go ahead and get my hours now.

Somebody from an 813 area code was calling my phone. It looked like a school number. No way was I gonna answer that.

I was in no mood for anymore headaches.

I took a few deep breaths to compose myself before going into the office. The only reason I was here was because I loved this job. It was the one place on campus that was never hostile. No one ever fought me over a transcript request.

The other thing I liked about it was that I led tours for students who wanted to come to Morrison. We got a lot of questions on everything from how they could get into the university to where they could park their cars once they were here. Us campus ambassadors were supposed to know every fact possible about the school.

As always, a row of prospective students sat on the Academic Office's plush gray sofa. They were waiting their turn to talk to one of the staff. Natalie was behind the counter and Andrea typed away at the computer we shared.

Natalie did work-study with me, so we had the same amount of hours, but she did the earlier shift. She was one of those "long hair, don't care" girls with skin the color of dark chocolate and a sew-in weave you couldn't clock with a microscope.

Andrea was more low maintenance in her blue jeans and baby doll shirts. Her light brown, shoulder-length hair complimented her luscious frame. Andrea was an alumna of the school and got a full-time job in the office when she graduated. She was more senior than me and Natalie, so she kept us in check. If we slacked, she pointed out documents that needed processing or emails that needed to be read before the day was out.

"I'm glad you showed up so you can help me with these applications," Natalie said. One quick look at me and she knew something wasn't right. "Did you fall down the stairs or something?"

"It's no big deal," I sighed. Everybody in the office didn't need to know about the minor valleys of my life.

"Yes it is!" she protested.

"Tyree, come in here, please." A no-nonsense voice called for me from the nearby office.

My boss Miss Bert heard us. Her real name was Bertha Wallace, but she insisted that everyone call her something less formal. She was a big girl with gray hair, buttery brown skin, and a thing for pantsuits and floral blouses. Sure enough, she wore a navy blue number and a shirt with a vivid pink flower pattern.

Miss Bert's title was Director of Admissions for Morrison. She coordinated the freshman and recruitment events. She was also on the selection committee for the school, so she reviewed a lot of the applications to decide who got in. I always wondered if she ever saw mine. Miss Bert looked at so many she probably wouldn't remember and I never asked.

"Good afternoon, ma'am," I said, fixing myself in the doorway of her office. I always marveled at the gifts people had given her that she kept around her desk — small masks from Zimbabwe, seashells from Antigua, a stuffed poodle wearing a Sigma Gamma Rho sweater and postcards from around the globe. Miss Bert gave me the same suspicious once-over that Natalie did. Nothing got past her.

"The dean's office called here looking for you, Tyree. They don't ring my phone unless it's important. Are you in trouble?"

"No, Miss Bert. Havin' a bad day, that's all."

"What happened to your shirt?" she asked. I twisted myself away from her to hide it. "Sweetheart, you look like you went one on one with a hurricane. The Tyree I know who comes into this office looking stylish is not the person in front of me."

I stood there silent as a stone. I had work to do and it wasn't gonna get finished with me in here yapping about unimportant matters.

"You're not going to tell me what's wrong?" Miss Bert asked patiently. "You can always come to me for anything."

I shook my head no. She seemed disappointed that I wouldn't confide in her, but I didn't want to give Keyshawn any more of my energy. Miss Bert and I had many conversations about my personal life up to this point. Yes, she was my boss but she was also a listening ear. Miss Bert had two decades more of living than I had. She never held back on advising me on how to best go about life.

"You better go see Dean Simmons because they did not sound very happy," she said with concern. "If you need me, I'm a phone call away."

The dean's office was in the old-as-dirt administration building. The floorboards creaked as I walked inside. Paintings of school presidents and benefactors who donated serious cash lined the walls. I hadn't been inside since my first week of school. It wasn't like I had a reason to. The only students who met with Dean Simmons were the ones getting suspended. They were probably gonna bounce Keyshawn's ass out of Morrison.

The secretary waved me through to the office. Dean Simmons sat waiting for me behind a wide mahogany desk. Aside from working for Morrison, he was also a deacon at a church nearby. His office was a shrine of fraternity plaques and old pictures of him with famous alumni. He motioned for me to sit in a brown leather chair on the other side of his desk. I was prepared to give a detailed account of my encounter with those sons of bitches.

"Mr. Iversen, you're aware of why I called you in here. Tell me what happened in the Business building earlier," he said firmly.

I told him about how I was on my way to my next class when Keyshawn called me out in the hallway. Him and his friend double-teamed me, I explained. I waited for the dean to respond to my account.

He carelessly tapped a stapler on his desk. "You should've reported it to campus police instead of losing control and fighting another student. We have rules in place to handle these sorts of things. If someone is bothering you that much, you should ignore them and move on."

"So you're tellin' me if somebody physically assaults me that *you*, the dean of Morrison State University, think I should ignore it? Please tell me how that makes a lick of sense."

"If you carried yourself with the dignity of a Morrison man and not walk around campus like a..."

"Like what?" I cocked my head.

"Like someone who isn't behaving like a Morrison man. Do you think fighting in school hallways is acceptable?"

"No, and I wasn't tryin' to pick a fight. I was confronted, plain and simple. If he thinks he can call me a faggot in the middle of the damn hallway, I'm well within my right to defend myself."

"Watch your mouth young man," the dean said. He hunched forward and rested his hands on the desk that separated us.

"Mr. Iversen, we do everything we can to stop these incidents, but you share some of the responsibility. Have you tried acting less... flamboyant? You know, less gay? We wouldn't want you to attract the wrong kind of attention."

"Wait, 'less gay'? How exactly do you propose I do that, Dean Simmons?"

"We don't tolerate harassment on this campus. The gentlemen were wrong to put their hands on you. But the Bible speaks very clearly about homosexuality. Leviticus 20:13 says 'If a man lies with a male as with a woman, both of them have committed an abomination.' There's a place for everyone at this school if you respect the values we were founded on."

This man who was supposed to be representing the students at Morrison was lecturing me on my sexuality! I thought I was heated earlier, but he was two words away from me flipping his desk over.

"Let me stop you there," I said. "You were married, right? To Mrs. Simmons?"

"My personal life is not the topic of discussion, Mr. Iversen," he said defensively. "We're talking about you and your issues. As I was saying, the Bible—"

"I'm just asking a simple question."

"My wife and I are separated," he responded.

Everybody on campus knew him and his wife were not separated, unless that's what they called divorce nowadays. She walked outta his office with a box of his stuff and hadn't been seen around since. Nobody said anything to his face, but the whole school was chitchatting about him behind his back. It was no secret that the former Mrs. Simmons left him because he was pushing up on one of the ladies in the athletics office. I wasn't gonna let that one slide past me.

"I think you mean divorced, Dean. Since you wanna bring out the Bible and lecture me on *my* life, I'm sure you read First Corinthians. The part that says 'Whoever divorces his wife, except for immorality, and marries another woman commits adultery.' And that tacky Theta tattoo I saw on your arm last homecoming? No tattoos either. Leviticus 19:28, since you're so fond of that chapter. If you gonna try to read somebody, you best take a closer look at your Bible. You ain't the only one who knows scripture."

I leapt to my feet. "I don't know what's worse, being attacked by my classmate or by you. Can you explain that to me?"

"Mr. Iversen, sit down. This doesn't have to be a confrontation," the dean said. He was quickly getting agitated but not as much as I was.

"I'm not spendin' one more minute in this office," I said. "I've had quite enough, thank you. Dean Simmons, gay people on this campus are catchin' hell every day and this school ain't doin' shit about it. If you looked around, maybe you would see it for yourself. Instead of worryin' about me and my sins, why don't you do your damn job."

I threw the door open and stormed past the secretary. Her eyes were wider than dinner plates as I slammed the door behind me. I thought the dean was gonna hand down justice and at the very least suspend those guys. And yet I was the one getting told off. I probably wasn't the only one he had that conversation with either. I wasn't expecting a lot from the administration at Morrison, but support in any form or fashion would've been appreciated. Why was I the one who was in the wrong just because of who I was?

So let's see: I couldn't go to class. I couldn't go back to work-study. What the hell was I supposed to do? I texted Cole to get direction.

in chapel come thru

ok b right there

After the conversation with the dean, the *last* place I wanted to be was chapel. It was the same as church but held at the school for an hour on weekday mornings. Attendance was mandatory or else good luck with graduating. I didn't know before I came to Morrison that the school was Baptist or affiliated with any religion. I thought I got away from that holy business. Come to find out most HBCUs were connected to one of the church denominations.

I strolled into the chapel like a bad bitch. They wouldn't see me shook. No, ma'am. This relic had seen better days. The white paint on the walls was chipped and the carpet that used to be burgundy faded to a bland pinkish gray. Years of people trampling through for services and lectures was enough to wear it out. This place went all the way back to 1901 when they used to have classes in here. There were only 50 students back then. The school renovated it several times since, but it could use a few more overhauls.

As always, there was a local preacher at the front talking about how we students needed to motivate ourselves. His suit had shoulder pads the size of Volvos. His tie was broader than the Mississippi River. The dark hanky in his hand got a good shake every other word. The students in the room were unmoved by his theatrics.

"So you fightin' now?" Cole asked as I eased next to him in a pew near the back of the room. "You were on me for gettin' into it at the club. You over here throwin' bows on your classmates."

I did a double take. "How'd you know that? I only texted you asking for your location."

"Everybody knows about it, Ty. There's a picture going around on Twitter of you and the dude goin' at it. Why do you think he was messin' witchu?"

"I don't know. Sexual frustration? Your guess is as good as mine."

Cole considered the many reasons I would come outta pocket like that. "Let me ask you somethin', Ty. Have you ever thought about startin' a group on campus for gay students? You would have somebody to talk to that knows wassup."

"Hell naw. Are you forreal? That would cause me more problems," I said exasperated. "I'd be putting a target on my back if I joined a group. It's enough that I'm a confirmed homosexual. I don't need to add being the official face of sodomy at Morrison to my list of extracurricular activities."

The chapel monitor keeping watch from the back row shushed me, but I paid her no mind. She should've been worried about having a resuscitation machine for the preacher. The way he hollered at the students he was bound to go into cardiac arrest. If he didn't bring it down a notch, they were gonna have to take him outta the chapel on a stretcher.

"Me and the dean talked about what happened, by the way," I said to Cole. "He wasn't any help. Blamed it all on me. The conversation was a fucking mess."

"Watch your language, man. You're in God's house," Cole shrugged apologetically at the students in the next pew.

"Sorry. I was cussin' at the dean too," I smiled.

His face went south like he'd sucked on a bitter lemon. "What?! You wanna get suspended?"

"If that woulda got the message through to him, then yeah. I'm not into these so-called Christians who use the Bible as an excuse to persecute other people and that's precisely what he did. All my life, the church has been tellin' me I'm goin' to hell for being gay. If that's true, I better get my sunscreen and shades because that ship has sailed."

"I'll get you holy water you can splash on those people when they come at you," Cole said. "But good job standin' up for yourself. That took balls."

"I'm a pro at takin' balls," I kidded. "But you were aware of that already."

"Scratch that. I'm gonna need a gallon of holy water for you," Cole said playfully. "Hey, you comin' to the track meet tomorrow?"

"I'll be there with bells on. Me and Jason'll be in our same spot in the bleachers."

"Cool. Heads up, April's comin' over to the house tonight to cook."

Lawdy Jesus. Every time April was at our apartment Cole turned into a mushy, Romeo wannabe. And she was nobody's Juliet.

"In that case let me find somewhere else to be," I said. "I'll see if Jason wants to go to the movies. I need to be as far away from you two as possible."

Our preacher friend closed out his sermon with one last shake of the hanky.

COLE

It smelled good in the apartment. Like spaghetti and garlic bread. April cooked in the kitchen while I kicked back on the couch. Waiting on her gave me time to check out that ass. I was a sucker for the way it jiggled when she stirred. She did that shit on purpose. It was one of her ways of keeping me around. Cooking was another. Couldn't be mad at somebody who was feeding you. When the pasta was done, she set a big plate of it on the table for me.

"Thanks, babe." I kissed her. She tasted like oregano. I dipped into the spaghetti, swirling it on my fork to get at the sauce. April wasn't the best cook, but a man could only eat so much McDonald's. I could make magic on boxed mac and cheese, but it was nothing like the meals April made for me.

"How is it?" she asked.

"It's great. Tastes like somebody's mother made it."

"Hey now!" she smiled. "Nothing but the best for you."

It wasn't *that* good, but I didn't want her to stop cooking for me. Every man should come home to a good woman and a good meal.

"See, what would you do without me?" she said.

"Eat Ramen noodles out of the package. Add hot sauce and crushed Cheetos and I got a five-star meal."

"Boy, you better be glad I cooked because that sounds nasty! And don't even think about making that for me. You can save that for your friends," April said, slurping on a noodle. "Do you miss living in the dorms at all?"

"Not really," I said. "Bein' in a building with all guys around me is not my style. If I live in an apartment, that's more time for me to spend with you on this couch."

"What about the bonding? The new experiences?" she asked. "Cole, you can't tell me you don't miss that."

"I have to live on campus to bond with people? I thought I was doin' that with you here."

"You know what I'm talking about," she bit into the pasta. "It's like a slumber party every night with the girls in the dorm. And it's the only place I can get my hair done for 20 dollars."

I scooped the last of the tomato sauce on my plate with a piece of garlic bread. April was still working on hers. "Cole, what do you really like about me?" she asked thoughtfully. "Besides the food?"

She better not have cooked this meal for me to give her compliments all night. If I said something physical like the titties, she would stab me with her fork. The first reasons that popped in my mind were reasons I didn't like her. She asked too many questions. Her laugh was annoying. The only thing she kept up was her hair.

"I like your enthusiasm," I said.

"My what?" she snapped.

That came out wrong. Shoulda gave my answer more thought.

"You love life," I bounced back. "You're spontaneous. It's always a good time when I'm with you."

"That's all?" she crossed her arms.

"What do you mean, that's all? Whatchu want me to say? You sound like you already had an answer in my mind."

She rolled her eyes. "You're supposed to tell me I'm the most beautiful girl you've ever seen. That when we first met at the gym you wanted me to run into your arms."

April thought she was a "10", but she was more like a "7." I wouldn't tell her that to her face. "Ay, how's the job goin' by the way?"

"They have me working the worst hours," she said, scraping the last bit of spaghetti off the plate. "I have to close out, so it's on me to clean the store and lock everything up. Oh, and check the cash register to make sure it has the correct amount of money."

"Why? Somebody pocketin' cash?"

"No, nothing like that," April added the plates to the sink.

"I don't want anything to stop you from comin' out and supportin' your boy."

"I have two jobs," she declared as she settled back onto the couch. "Being your cheerleader is the best part-time job a girl could ask for. Are you worried about tomorrow?"

"Honestly? Yeah. There's gonna be a lot of runners with fast times out there," I grumbled.

"But none of them are you."

April swiped her curls outta the way to land a soft kiss on my neck. Her tongue rolled like a pro to my ear. She pushed her breasts against my arm. She kept teasing me. Her firm nipples hinted at what she wanted. I let her do her thing, but I knew where it was gonna head. I wanted to get in that, but I had to be on point tomorrow. Coach told us all the time, no sex before a meet. I could be like fuck it and spend time with my girl, but I needed to bring home a win.

"Not tonight, baby. After the meet, I promise," I said, pulling away.

"Are you serious?" She slumped back on the couch. "Aren't you my boyfriend? I wish you put as much energy into me as you did that damn track."

"You drawlin', April," I shot back. "What happened to you being my cheerleader? You knew when you met me what my schedule was. It's not like I'm out here doin' nothin'. I'm runnin' my ass off!"

April was pissed, but it was the truth. I couldn't let her dictate what I should or shouldn't be doing. I was done talking. I cracked open the Constitutional Law book I had to read for class. This jawn was thick as my arm with every law known to man in it. The chapters were almost 200 pages each. I turned to the section on religious liberty.

"Oh, it's like that? You gonna ignore me?" April said.

"I got work to do."

"Yeah okay," she said, snatching her purse off the counter.

"You can stay over if you want," I said.

"For what, Cole? No, I'm gonna go. Have fun with your book. Make sure I hear from you tonight. Smoke signals, telegram, I don't care how you do it."

She left outta the apartment so fast, the breeze behind her

flipped the pages in my book. Thinking about the night kept me from concentrating on the words. The long paragraphs of text read like chicken scratch.

I'd been so out of it lately. April wanted me to be a good boyfriend. My teachers were pushing me to be a better student. Coach wouldn't stay off me until I was the best runner in the state of Florida.

I couldn't satisfy everybody. Sure, I could do better than what I put out on the track or in school, but I didn't want to. For what? I could graduate without getting straight As. It wasn't like it made a difference for my parents either. I was in school and getting my degree. They weren't worried about what their son was doing. I bet if I lost my scholarship it would make them care.

Tomorrow was another early day on the field. On nights like this when I couldn't sleep, I popped a Unisom. It would have me snoring in minutes. But I didn't feel like getting up to snag the pill from the bathroom. I figured I'd get a game of Bejeweled in instead. I had to think about something else besides April. Yeah. Five diamonds in a row.

The track meet today wasn't like the ones we usually ran in. It was an invitational on our home field. That meant we hosted the other teams from the Mid-Eastern Athletic Conference or MEAC for short. I didn't know why Coach Jackson thought having the other schools compete on our track was a good idea, but here they came.

Morgan State, Maryland-Eastern Shore, Bethune-Cookman, FAMU — They stepped off their buses and onto the field. The bleachers were about a quarter full. It was mostly our team's friends and family. It was never crowded for a track event, even on a big day like this where we were representing Morrison.

Coach Jackson stood watch over the team while we warmed up in the grassy infield. He used to run back in the day when he was a student. He even had a few championships under his belt. Now our mentor was pushing sixty. With age came wisdom, I guessed.

Every time Coach was on the field, he wore a white polo with the Morrison eagle on it and mirrored aviator shades so we couldn't see his eyes. I think it was so he could scope us out without any of us knowing who he was looking at. He was a good coach. During the meets, he monitored our performance from the sidelines. He kept us going whether we wanted to or not. That motivation was the difference between a winning and losing team.

There were 14 of us that ran on the men's team at Morrison, including five other sprinters and me. We were one team, but when we got to a meet, everybody broke off into groups. Mostly it was because we had separate training regimens. The long distance runners practiced by themselves. Us sprinters rolled in our own pack.

There were also the jumpers (long jump, high jump, pole vault) and the throwers (shot put and weight throw). Each event called for a different state of mind. That's why we stuck with people who thought and competed the same way.

I'd known most of the other sprinters on the team since my freshman year. There was Cedric from Tampa, Sergey Petrov, who joined this year, Maxwell Abernathy, Vanilla Nick, and Marshall Moore.

Everybody was cool for the most part except for Marshall. If you went by his times, he was the best runner on the team. Like me, the man had an athletic scholarship that paid for his tuition and housing. Off top, a track scholarship at Morrison was hard to get. Mostly it was the white runners from Eastern Europe who got 'em.

Marshall was fast, but he was also an asshole. One of those conceited light-skinned dudes that the females checked for when he was on the track. Some runners talked a good game, but couldn't back it up. Problem was Marshall was as good as he constantly told us he was.

Marshall was the only man who made me feel like I wasn't worth shit. He didn't even try and his personal bests killed mine. If that wasn't messed up enough, he ran anchor in the relay too. We needed to work together if we wanted to take first.

Marshall wasn't the only man who could run on the team. All of us had good credentials. We never won a MEAC championship, but we'd placed at most of the meets we competed in. If we were gonna come through against these other teams we needed better facilities soon.

Morrison wasn't the best place to hold a meet. The gym was trash and they hadn't updated the weight room in a decade. Coach Jackson was frustrated because he wanted something better for us. It wasn't gonna happen. Most of the money went to the school's football team.

Those boys hadn't won a championship in a long time and the stands were *still* packed. There were 50,000 people at the Tampa Football Classic every year. Morrison alumni showed up to the game cutting the school checks, no problem. And because HBCUs weren't making bank like they used to, the funds went right back to the football team.

Track, volleyball, golf, tennis, and the other sports got the scraps. Most of the students here didn't know we had a track team. If they did, they weren't showing up for meets. It was cool, though. We did it for the love of running. We'd perform whether the school supported us or not.

It was almost the end of outdoor track season. I needed to get my times up badly. I was far from where I used to be my first year. Coach helped me out by putting me in the 100 and 400-meter race today. They were events he knew I could place in. He also put me down for the 4x100 and 4x400 relays with Marshall and the crew.

If I was gonna do any good I needed to focus on my drills. Coach had us doing high knees. We jumped from one foot to the other with our legs at a 90-degree angle, keeping a fast pace. No slacking. The intense exercise gave us a good stretch before we went out on the track.

"Let's get those legs up!" Coach yelled. "If you're not sweating, you're not ready to compete! I don't want to see you going through the motions!"

We finished out with accelerations and stretches before Coach stopped us. I coulda gone on longer, but I was fine with ending it there.

"You guys come around, listen up! I want to see that Eagle spirit when you run today. This is our home! We need to show these other teams what Morrison is capable of. Marshall, you've been doing really well in these last meets. I want all of you to do the same," Coach drilled us. "You might be running your individual races, but remember track is a team sport. Every point counts!"

"We gon' run circles around these fools!" Max shouted.

"That's the spirit I'm talking about. Go out there and do it!" Coach said. We went off in different directions toward our events. We were amped for the day ahead of us.

The way a track meet worked, we scored points for the team

by placing in individual events. First place got us five points, second was three points, and third was one point. For relays, it was five points for first or nothing. If one of the fellas on the team was down a few points but smashed it in his other events, we could come through with a win.

From where I stood in the infield, I spotted April, Jason and Tyree in the stands waving at me. Sup folks. I was surprised that April came after our showdown last night. She looked more chill than when she left. Our time apart gave her more time to consider her man's priorities. I shot them a thumbs up. As soon as I did, Marshall slithered next to me.

"So you gonna man up on the track?" he taunted.

"Don't worry about me," I grumbled. "Worry about your events. I'm runnin' my own race. You should do the same."

"You heard Coach, track is a team sport," Marshall narrowed his eyes. "And you run like a bitch. That means when you mess up like you always do it makes me look bad."

"I'll show you who's the bitch when I'm the first one to cross the line. I'm 'bout to put it down. Just wait and see."

"Cole, you sound gay as hell," he said with a dry laugh. "Bro, the only thing you've put down is low times and weak performances. The nerds in the math club could do a better job on the track than you can."

Marshall turned his back to me before I could say something. He swaggered away toward the starting line of the 200-meter race. "Good luck out there," his voice faded under the noise from the bleachers.

I would've taken that as words of encouragement from anybody else. The way Marshall came at me, he was saying I didn't have a chance.

I warmed up more in the infield before my event: skips,

squats, leg swings and lifts. I needed to be ready to put my best out there, even if Marshall didn't think I could. I was inspired by my other teammates. I watched while they gave it everything they had against the competition from the other schools. Andrew Greene dove into the pit to land his mark in the long jump. Kevin Davis conquered the pole vault with a filthy swing over the bar.

The voice of the announcer came through the crackling speakers. It was time for the 400-meter race. I pulled off my warm-ups and stepped onto the track. My red singlet with "MSU" in block letters was tight on me. Anybody looking could see my bird when I ran. My left nut was bigger than everything in Marshall's tiny jock, so I had that on him. The most important thing about my uniform was that it moved when I did.

My competition lined up next to me. Savannah State, Howard, Bethune-Cookman, FAMU, Coppin State, South Carolina State and Delaware. It was our first step toward bragging rights. These fellas had better uniforms, slimmer frames and probably got in more drills than I did. I would have to push hard to catch up with them. I rotated my arms while the announcer said our names and lane assignments.

"In lane two, Colin Hill. Morrison State University!"

I clapped it up for myself, forcing my palms together to jolt me outta my funk. I could hear my troop in the stands chanting my name.

"Runners, on your marks," the announcer said between the static.

I pushed my feet into the metal blocks. Our track was smaller, so we had two laps to run. Two hundred meters each. I focused on the white lane markers that would guide my path.

Everybody in the stands was quiet as we readied ourselves.

"Set."

I lifted both knees off the ground. It was time to go.

The sound of the starting gun cracked in the air. I shot out of the blocks and accelerated into the curve to pick up all the speed I could. The crowd woke up out of their coma. I was off to a good start.

My legs churned as I raced into the first straightaway. I had to find my rhythm. If I went too fast, I'd be hurting before I made it to the finish. Too slow and I'd be left behind. After the second turn, I made up the stagger until I was alongside the other runners.

As I raced into the second lap, I heard April's loud ass in the stands. That girl was gonna leave me soon if I didn't dedicate more of my time to her. I didn't mean to make her mad, but I had a race ahead of me. I couldn't change that, as much as she wanted me to.

Oh man, I lost focus! My rhythm was off. I fell behind the other runners. I saw their backs ahead of me, which should have never happened. I needed to pull through! I fought the screaming in my legs to pick up speed in the last 100 meters. It wouldn't matter. Even if I gave it my all, I couldn't come back to make first.

My head went down as I raced across the line. I slowed to a stop and let my breathing come back to normal. The scoreboard showed my name in third with a time of 48.98 seconds. I placed, but that wasn't close to my best. I couldn't say I lost for a good reason either.

"What was that?" Coach pulled me to the side. He was so angry about the finish he almost spat on the track.

"I dunno, Coach," I scrambled for an answer that would

satisfy him. "Comin' outta the last turn I lost it. My head wasn't in the game."

"Cole, what is going on with you?" he flailed his arms. "You're better than this! We can't win this meet unless everybody's on the same page and you're in another library, my brotha. This team needs every point it can get, so don't muck it up in the 4x400."

There was more pressure on me in the upcoming event than there was in the solo. The 400-meter relay was sorta like my last race. Instead of one runner — just me — there were four on each team. We had to do two laps each and pass the baton to the next man. The last runner crossed the finish line and brought us to victory. One bad link on the team could throw everything off. That was why I liked running individual events. It was one man against the others. The only person I wanted to rely on was me.

I jumped in place to get my heart rate up. The first leg for each team moved into their lane. Marshall was at the line stretching with the baton in his hand. He was gonna lead off for us in the relay. Sergey would go after him, I was in third and Nick was fourth to close it out.

"Gentlemen to your marks," the announcer prepped. The speaker system had enough stress on it today. If it gave out to mechanical failure, I wouldn't complain. It would give me more time to get ready.

When the gun went off, the first legs in the race blasted out of the blocks without hesitation. Two laps in and it was time to switch to the next runner in the relay. Marshall connected with Sergey for a crisp handoff of the baton. Good job. I moved to the line with the other third legs. The lower half of my body was set to run. The upper half twisted around to keep tabs on my teammate's distance from me.

Once Sergey came out of the curve, I launched myself

forward to match his pace. He held the long, silver baton out for me to take control of it.

"Stick!" he yelled to me. Sergey slapped the metal rod into my waiting hand. I took my charge and ran with it like a champ. Me and three other men ran neck and neck for the lead. I picked up speed around the last turn so I could get the baton to Nick. I shoved my arm forward to pass it to him. Instead of connecting, it slipped out of his hand and stayed in mine. Dammit! He looked back at me with a clenched jaw that warned me not to screw it up again.

I made the pass one more time with my eyes locked on his cycling arms. This time it was good. The baton was his to carry forward. That terrible handoff put us behind. We were in seventh place with only one man bringing up the rear and he looked like he was injured. The boos from the stands made me feel worse.

I moved off the track, bending over to catch my breath. Ahead of me, Nick flew to rejoin the other runners. We were done before he crossed the line. I didn't have to look at the scoreboard to know we lost the relay at our own invitational. Me, Marshall and Sergey waited for Nick to finish the race out.

"Why didn't you two make the exchange?!" Marshall yelled at us.

"Cole didn't get it to me!" Nick shouted back. He refused to take the blame. He didn't have to. The team knew it was my fault.

"We had this, Cole!" Marshall fumed. "I'm not blowing my season because you can't get it together! If you weren't spending so much time getting your booty licked by those faggots you'd run like you were supposed to."

"Why you always up in my face, Marshall?" I stepped back.

He shook his head irritably. "Because your game is weak, that's why. If you're going to keep running like a sissy, just tell us you're gay. It's cool. At least we'll know what's up." Both Nick and Sergey turned their backs to me. It seemed like I was always putting myself in situations where folks were either coming down on me or leaving me to fend for myself.

"I ain't no sissy," I said.

"Here's the thing," Marshall looked me up and down. "I think you are. I heard your boyfriend in the stands calling your name."

"That ain't my boyfriend; that's my roommate. My girl is sittin' there next to him."

"Oh, so you're bi?" he laughed mockingly. "This man goes both ways! Every way except the finish line apparently."

I wanted to punch Marshall in the face so hard his eyeballs would meet the back of his skull. Nobody came at me like that!

The people watching us from the bleachers could see something was wrong with our team. I fought the anger and contained myself. I wouldn't make this a repeat of that night in the club. It wasn't until Coach made his way over that Nick and Sergey called Marshall off.

"Why are you arguing in front of our competition?!" Coach Jackson roared. "Where is your self-respect?"

Marshall rushed to defend himself. "Coach, I don't think you should let someone run who isn't at the same level as the rest of the team. Cole's the reason we lost the relay."

Coach wasn't moved by Marshall's complaining. "Everybody lost. He isn't the only one running out there. But Cole, if you bring that piss poor stunt to my field again, you'll be on the curb faster than last week's garbage. *Both* of you," he said pointing at Marshall. "I don't wanna hear another word."

Marshall shot me a dirty look and mumbled something to

himself. "I said I don't wanna hear it, Moore!" Coach grunted. "Cole, walk with me."

We headed to a part of the field away from the nosy bystanders who were waiting for me to get my punishment. That was a messed up relay. Worse than any race we ran as a team. Coach already sensed I was beating myself up. I didn't need him to rub it in. He looked more concerned than anything.

"Cole, you frustrate me," he said gloomily. "You have so much potential and you're not living up to it."

I couldn't come up with a decent explanation to give him. No matter what I said, it wouldn't take back the win I handed the competition. "I'm havin' an off week," I stammered.

"Your whole season has been off and your work ethic is shit," Coach roasted me. "Marshall and most of the guys on the team are running five miles every morning in addition to what I have you doing for practice. I can always count on you to do the bare minimum."

Did he think I was gonna apologize for doing what he told us to do? If he wanted more, he should've said something. I wasn't a mind reader.

"Coach, my girl's been on my back, I got classes I hafta study for—"

"And you think you're the only one?" he stopped me. "It's always someone else's fault that you weren't at your best. I don't want you thinking about your damn girlfriend when you're out there on the field. Pussy doesn't win you races! You have to go out there and compete! You're a politics major, right Cole?"

"Political science, yeah."

"What do you want to do after you graduate?"

"I dunno yet," I sighed. It was the truth. My future was TBD. "I'm thinkin' about it."

"There's your problem," Coach said. "Remember this: good students make good athletes. At the rate you're going, you'll leave Morrison with nothing but a piece of paper with your name on it and nowhere to go."

The frantic cheering from the stands drowned out our conversation. Somebody must've run a good race. I couldn't tell who won, but it would be cool if it was one of the boys from our team. Coach needed something else to concentrate on besides me. What I did after I graduated wasn't his problem anyway. I would never see him again after I crossed the stage.

Coach shook his open palm in my face to bring me back from my daze. "I'm taking you out of the 100 and 200 at the MEAC championship. But I'm gonna have you run the 400 and a leg on the relay. You better not disappoint me, or you're off this team."

"Aight Coach, I got this," I said with courage I didn't fully feel.

"And any issue you have with Marshall, drop it," he said. "I want you to step up your practice too. I better see you on the field an hour before everyone else building up your endurance. We gave you that scholarship because we want you to excel."

"Yes, sir."

"Now grab your stuff and get out of here. I'll see you Monday at practice."

I walked back to where I left my bag and threw on my warm-ups. Why did I have to be the one he called out? I was already decent. Extra practice wasn't nothin' but his way of punishing me. If it wasn't for the scholarship money, he coulda kept that extra hour.

Him taking me out of the other two races was a good thing. It just meant that I could concentrate on going hard on the other two. I may have been slipping, but I was still one of the best runners out there. Coach was the one wearing me out with four races in a single meet. If I didn't run at all, he would be the one looking stupid.

April sat by herself in the bleachers fiddling with her hair. I waved for her to meet me outside by the car. As I walked out, I ran into Nick by the gate toweling himself off. Nick was one of a few white students who went to Morrison. He overcompensated for it by always being extra friendly. He didn't need to. Everybody liked his cheery personality.

"Ay, I'm sorry it didn't go down the way we practiced," I said sincerely.

"It's only one meet, Cole," Nick said. "We'll have another chance at the next one. In the meantime, Spring Break will give the team an opportunity to recuperate. We'll be ready to win."

"Yeah, you're right. I'm gonna take advantage of it. Me and my boys are planning on driving to Miami for the week. 'Bout to get into dirty deeds that don't have anything to do with relays or sprints or Coach Jackson."

"You said Miami? I'm going too! We should plan to hang out if you have free time."

"No doubt. Coach told me to head home, so I'm gonna take off. Let me know how the rest of the meet goes."

"You got it, brother."

My roommates and April were on the hood of Tyree's car waiting for me to get there. I was surprised that they perked up when they saw me. I didn't represent like I should have. I was ready for them to come down on me. Instead, April ran over to give me a hug. "You did great, baby."

"Yeah right, I flopped on that track," I said.

"It was cute," Tyree said. "What took you so long?"

April eyed me suspiciously. She saw Coach Jackson pull me to the side for our long conversation. Either she hadn't told

Tyree yet, or she wanted to hear it directly from the source. I could never admit to Ty that the back and forth with Marshall was partly about him. He wouldn't take it well at all.

"Just track stuff. You wouldn't be interested," I blew it off. "In case you're wondering, Coach is still gonna have me run at the MEAC."

"I don't see why he shouldn't," Jason said. "Your performance in the race wasn't the best, but it wasn't awful. You didn't fall on the track or cause a pile up or anything."

"I think you looked sexy out there, babe," April spared me from another one of Jason's uninspiring inspirational talks. "You shouldn't let your teammates get to you. You're Cole Hill! You're my track star."

She kissed my cheek as I slid my hands over her hips. The way she curled her tongue against mine reminded me what she wanted. April was practically begging me to fuck her. I was stupid for not getting at my girl last night. I slapped that ass. I wanted her too.

"Let's wrap it up!" Tyree said to us. "Y'all two lovebirds are holdin' up progress. Some of us have places to be."

The only place I wanted to be was in my room, swimming in April's pussy. I needed to release some tension and I was about to do it inside her.

After the meet yesterday it was nice to get a chill moment on the quad. Me and the boys were sitting on one of the only benches on concrete. Jason would get his ass kicked by those Theta boys for walking on the grass. We also made sure not to sit by any of the plots for the Greeks either. It didn't give us a lot of options. Almost every tree or rock at Morrison was painted with Greek letters.

I texted April while the boys gossiped about the latest news on campus. It wasn't the kind of talk I cared about. Something about a girl who got caught fucking her boyfriend in the dorm room while their roommate was supposedly asleep. That was nothing new for Morrison. Jason did his best to get Tyree to keep his loud talking down.

"If I'm makin' too much noise for you, why don't you go over there and sit by the Theta plot?" Tyree joked.

He pointed to a tree near us painted blue and orange with a gold plaque at the bottom. The founding date of the fraternity chapter was carved into it. I passed that plaque damn near every day going to class. Even when the Thetas weren't there, no other students were allowed to hang by their tree. I'd never seen anybody get slugged, but no one wanted to deal with the consequences.

Jason could drown in the drool coming outta his mouth whenever he looked at it. "One day that tree is going to be mine too," he said puffing his chest. Until then, I'll make sure to stay 100 feet away from it. Tyree, you can pay it a visit on my behalf if you want."

"Oh no, that's your business," Tyree said. "My name is Bennett and I ain't in it."

Jason hung his head. "What sucks is the part of the quad next to it used to be my favorite cool-down area. I would settle into the lawn under that maple tree and watch the leaves rustle above me. I'm looking forward to the day after I cross when I can sit anywhere I want. I'll be Greek then and there will be no limit to where I can go."

I changed the subject. I didn't need this man getting emotional on me. "Jason, you gonna get a line jacket after you cross?"

"Yes!" he returned to his normal upbeat self. "It'll have my line name and the fraternity letters and every Theta insignia I can fit on it. It's going to be awesome! Just wait."

"Why don't you buy it now so you'll have it ready when you finish pledging?" I asked. I knew the answer, but I wanted to rile him up.

"Are you kidding me, Cole? I'd be kicked off the line if they *thought* I owned anything with Theta on it."

"Let's be real. You just wanna stroll and wear your fraternity letters," I teased.

"The same way you wear your track outfit on the yard so the girls will look at your penis?" Jason was serious about the accusation. Instead of taking it further, he backed down. "By the way it's not the jacket that makes you a Theta. It's the hard work that you put into it. It's more than another article of clothing hanging in a closet. It represents a commitment to the fraternity."

Tyree butted in. "Speaking of hard work, how you feelin' after the meet Mr. Track Star?"

"You saw me. I wasn't doin' too hot out there," I said. "I was in a better place after I came home. Me and April talked things over."

"Couldn't have been much of a conversation," Tyree cackled. "You were bangin' down those walls last night! That poor girl!"

I lightly slapped him upside the back of his head. Jason giggled along with Tyree, who hadn't stopped laughing like a maniac. "You can't be hittin' me, you beast. I will not allow my delicate skin to be disturbed by your unnecessary roughness."

While we poked fun at each other, one of the dudes Jason was pledging with came rolling up the quad. He had a cool stride for somebody who was pledging every night. If it was me, I'd be dragging myself across the pavement. His energy level seemed to get higher the closer he got to our bench. "Whatsup everybody," he nodded to us.

Jason spent a lot of time with his fraternity boys. This one I'd seen around more than the others. Vaughn was his name. I wondered if they were getting it in. Jason was my boy. If he was going out with somebody, he'd tell me. We didn't keep secrets between us roommates. We made space for Vaughn on the bench.

"You boys got set tonight?" I asked.

Me and Tyree basically became invisible to them. Jason was deep in conversation with his line brother. His bashful smile gave away that something was going on. Our Theta-to-be looked up long enough to answer my question. "The Miss Morrison pageant is tomorrow and a few of the Thetas are in it, so no set. Tyree and I will be backstage helping out and Vaughn's an escort for the contestants."

"Making sure Morrison's finest women don't go unprotected," Vaughn added. "We have a run-through later today. Cole, you going to the pageant?"

"I'm plannin' on it. I'll hit you boys up when I'm there."

"Cool. Don't forget to come backstage and say hey when you get there," Vaughn said, standing up to leave. "Well, I just stopped by to say hi. I have to go to my next class. Jason, hit me up on Skype tonight?"

Yeah, they were definitely fucking. Two grown ass men didn't be on Skype like that.

"Sure, Vaughn," Jason said with pleasure. There went that corny ass smile again.

JASON

The amber streetlight filtering through my window highlighted a pile of unworn clothes on my bedroom floor. I needed to find something suitable to wear to the pageant tomorrow. Tyree was the fashionisto, of course, but I didn't plan to show up in jeans, or worse, the gym shorts I was wearing. I had to look presentable, even if we would be backstage for the duration of the show. I laid a pair of slacks and a crisp shirt on the bed.

On my desk was one of my most invaluable possessions: a Swatch watch with a black band Vaughn gave me two months after we met online. It wasn't the most expensive timepiece, but the significance it held was priceless. I'd never been given a present on a day other than my birthday or the holidays.

Vaughn presented the token of his affection outside of my last class that day. The gravity of the moment was slightly marred because of my discomfort with being in full view of passersby. I cupped it in my hands, admiring the gift where no one else could see. I'd wear it to the pageant tomorrow as a symbol of my attachment to him.

The Skype tone from my laptop rang through my bedroom. I darted toward it to answer the call I'd waited for all day. I hurriedly pressed the green button to accept the video chat. My heart fluttered when the image of Vaughn's darling face appeared on the screen.

Vaughn stretched out in an old office chair watching me arrange myself. The only light in his room came from the bluish computer screen. "Hey there handsome," he said flirtatiously.

"You're the handsome one," I replied. "Can you see me okay?"

"Yeah babe, you look great," he said. "Was your day as good as you look?"

His compliment made my heart flutter. "It wasn't hectic like I thought it would be," I said. "Finals and the chaos that come with them aren't for a while. How was yours?"

"I got an A on the English Lit paper that I'd spent a week struggling with. It was a relief to know it turned out okay."

"That's great news, Vaughn! I knew you'd ace it. You're a smart cookie."

"Aw, thanks. But don't let it get out that I'm a geek in disguise," he said bashfully.

Vaughn was no geek. There were guys on campus that delighted in making sure their outward appearance mirrored their perceived intellect. They would never call themselves geeks or nerds — those labels were taboo. And yet they wore slacks with creased cuffs and argyle socks in every color. They proudly toted leather briefcases and peered through thick-rimmed, non-prescription eyeglasses.

Vaughn didn't need to put himself on display like that. The man on my computer screen looked more like he should be on the cover of Men's Fitness than Wired Magazine.

"You may not think I'm a geek Jason, but I am," he said. "I just happen to be smooth with it. You should see me when I'm dressed up for the pageant."

"A large portion of the school will be watching you. Does that make you nervous?" I asked.

"No, but even if it did, you'll be backstage looking out for me."

"For sure," I said. "Do you have your tux?"

"Yeah, they took the escorts to Men's Wearhouse and got us fitted. It's a good look for me. I wish I could keep it after we're done, but it's an Oscar de la Rental. The main thing is they wanna make sure we don't look like bums when we're next to the girls."

"You'll be the most well-dressed homeless person they've ever seen," I said appreciatively.

"Thanks for believing in me, Jason. Let's say you were competing in the pageant, what would your talent be?"

"I'm not much of a vocalist, but probably singing," I said shyly. "I'd want to perform a song that would win the audience over. Something uplifting."

"I didn't know you could sing!" Vaughn exclaimed. "I wanna hear something… please?"

I should have known I couldn't make a declaration like that without showcasing my so-called skills to him. I rarely sang in public or to anyone other than my toys when I was younger. I could hold a decent note, but I couldn't come close to the singers on the radio or the soloists that fronted Morrison's concert chorale. For Vaughn, I'd make an exception, just this once.

I launched into one of my favorite songs, Phyllis Hyman's "Be One." It had a soft, bluesy tone that carried so much emotion. "Be One" was about hesitation and love and giving in to what you truly felt.

I closed my eyes and let the words move through me. I pictured Vaughn as I crooned, my voice gently tickling the harmonies. Like the man Phyllis sang of, Vaughn broke through so many of the barriers I'd surrounded myself with. Before we met, I never imagined another guy would have the impact on me that he did.

I drew out the last line: "Go ahead and fall in love." I opened my eyes to Vaughn's glowing approval. My face reddened as he applauded my efforts.

"That was really good, babe!" he said with a smile. "We should give you the crown and sash now. You're a winner in my book."

"You liked it?" I bowed my head. "I was just playing around."

"I'm serious. You can sing, Jason. You should get a record deal. Be the next Rihanna."

"Are you calling me a girl?" I kidded. "Am I the female in this relationship?"

"No, nothing like that. And it's weird hearing you say 'relationship.' I think it's the first time I've heard you say that word since we've been together."

I sidestepped his questioning stare with a matter-of-fact explanation. "All human beings have relationships. Ours happens to be closer than most. But to be fair, most of the time we spend with each other is at set."

"Having paddles swung at us and lifting cinder blocks until we pass out. Yeah, it's real romantic."

For the first time, I saw the exhaustion in Vaughn's eyes that he was always so good at hiding. "Jason, every night I go to bed wishing that you were lying next to me. I wish I could be your big spoon again. Do you miss me too?"

He slowly removed his shirt to show off his solid as steel pectoral muscles. The blue light from the computer screen gave his anatomy an otherworldly glow. If this was his attempt to distract me from thinking about pledging he was doing an *incredible* job.

I was hypnotized by the spectacular display in front of me. I gingerly pulled my shirt over my head as a thank you for his gracious favor. There was a dark bruise on my shoulder from the other night at set, but we ignored it. Vaughn ran his fingers across his lips and along the peaks of his hairless chest. The gaze of his seductive brown eyes was my permission to let my hands travel below my waist.

My fingers tugged at the drawstring of my shorts. They fell quietly to the floor. I moaned as I played with myself just out of the view of the computer's camera. I could have backed up in my seat or moved the camera farther away, but I wanted to make a show of my self-exploration. His desk chair squeaked as he sat up from his chair to see more.

"Yeah, that's what I'm talking about," he said with bedroom eyes. "You got me hard as hell in these draws."

"Then take them off."

He removed his patterned boxer briefs and held them up to the camera with a mischievous smile. Seeing Vaughn's exposed manhood reminded me how much I'd missed spending nights with him curved behind me. He'd reach around to play with my nipples while sensually nibbling on my ear. My toes curled when he teased the nape of my neck. More than anything, I missed him being inside me.

I loved when his body blended with mine as he made his home between my legs. He knew when to go slowly and when to make me scream in ecstasy. When I was with him, I always made sure there was a pillow nearby to bury my face in. Without it, every floor of his dormitory would hear his name trumpeted repeatedly.

From the way Vaughn stroked himself intently, it was obvious he missed me too. I stood up from my chair and balanced my knees on its seat so my rear faced the camera. Neither of us cared about any unimportant scars the paddles may have left on my round buttocks. I slid my body up and down as if I was riding on top of him. The mock sensation of straddling his pole left me breathless. I was so lost in exploring the contours of my body that I almost forgot he wasn't in the room.

"Damn, I wish I was in that ass, baby," he moaned. His right hand pumped at lightning speed.

"Me too, Vaughn. Make me yours," I panted.

My hands brushed against my nipples before traveling to my waiting hole. I opened myself up more, pretending my fingers were Vaughn's. I wanted his flesh against mine. I writhed at the image of Vaughn entering my vulnerability.

The room whirled at a dizzying speed as I lost myself in his love. I couldn't bear the tension any longer. Hearing him on the verge of erupting was enough to bring me to orgasm. His screams enveloped me as hot liquid splashed across my stomach, creating a pearly trail down my thigh.

When I opened my eyes to survey the damage, Vaughn was wiping his screen with the abandoned underwear.

"Whoa, what happened?" I asked.

"I came on my computer!" he laughed. "Do you know how to get cum out of a keyboard?"

"No idea!" I giggled. "But after you're done, can you help me clean up?"

"Anything for you, babe," he teased. "Since I can't cuddle you through a computer, you owe me a kiss next time I see you."

"I'll give you more than that."

Jason. The nagging voice of my mother broke through my post-coital intoxication. I refused to acknowledge the invisible presence that frowned on my and Vaughn's exchange. It was him I wanted, not the shame she insisted came from such an act.

I didn't choose to fall for Vaughn. Nature made the decision for me. Each moment with him made me more empowered and yet more conflicted. I sought my resolution in the man in front of me.

"Have a good night, handsome," Vaughn smiled. "I can't wait see you tomorrow."

Neither could I.

The pageant was supposed to begin soon and yet the auditorium was in near chaos. Nothing was ready. A flurry of people ran around the stage putting together last-minute touches. The lights needed an adjustment to illuminate the decorations that hadn't been set in place. Empty boxes and bric-à-brac were scattered where the presentation would occur. The frenetic energy was a testament to how important the Miss Morrison pageant was to the school and every one of its students.

The winner of the annual contest was the face of the university. She made an appearance at almost every school event, outfitted in her tiara and sash. Sometimes she arrived as a solo act, other times she was backed by the royal court. Her four cohorts each represented their year at Morrison. The incoming senior class voted for Miss Senior, the next crop of juniors elected their queen, and so on. The royal court was the glamorous entourage that trailed dutifully behind her.

Tyree told me that, besides impressing notable guests, the real reason we had a Miss Morrison was to inspire the school's benefactors to donate more money. That's why past winners were so devastatingly gorgeous. Beauty could weaken the defenses of any man. Before tonight's contestants had a chance at mingling with the wealthy elite, they needed to impress the 400 students in the arena watching them vie for the title.

Tyree was perched on a ladder at the rear of the stage hanging a crimson banner. Gold letters that spelled "Miss Morrison State University" were stitched into its velvet surface. I positioned myself at the last rung to ensure Tyree didn't fall off.

I was also in charge of the music for the night. It was my responsibility to make sure the contestants' tracks were lined up on my laptop. The extent of my DJing experience was a playlist or two on my Spotify account "jasonatmsu." Other than that, I knew as much about the craft as any other amateur. I was thankful to not have the same problems with my computer that Vaughn did last night or I'd be in serious trouble.

Derrick assumed the role of pageant coordinator, double-checking that the girls and escorts hit their marks on the stage. It was a daunting amount of work for an hour-long show. Ms. Marshall, the director of student activities, was more than glad to let him take the lead. The Dayneisha Divine I knew that wore women's clothes and ruled the club from her sequined throne was gone. Derrick temporarily traded in his dresses for somewhat normal attire for a man. However, the diva attitude remained.

I stayed far away from him. Saying hello to Derrick at the Alibi was tolerable. Being seen with him as he swished down the school's pathways was not. I agreed to help because even though Derrick was in the position of power, I wouldn't miss a chance to help Tyree.

Darnell Cook, the emcee for the night, reviewed the notes on his white index cards. He was the most qualified among us to be the face of the show. Darnell had ambitions of being the next Black president one day, following in the footsteps of his hero Barack Obama. His look was presidential, down to his collection of cufflinks and tie clips. Darnell was one of a few students who made the honor roll in both fall and spring semesters his first year. Three years later, his personal streak remained unbroken.

The stage lights shone on Tasha, who checked items off her to-do list. She was armed with gaffer tape and an extra microphone. If the pageant wasn't such a monumental production, she and I would sit back laughing at the commotion. Instead, we both worked hard to make sure the show went smoothly.

"So who do you think is gonna win?" Tyree asked as he tied the banner to a beam.

"If I was a betting man, I'd pick Alexandra," I said. "Everything about her says pageant winner. Who do you think will take it?"

"These things are so unpredictable it's hard to say," Tyree mused. "I'm not pickin' anybody just yet so you won't hold me to it after this is over. Check with me after the talent section. That's the make or break moment. By the way, have you seen Cole?"

My answer was overwhelmed by Derrick's screaming. "You girls need to rehearse like you are competing! How do you not have on heels? Tammy, please go change your shoes so we can finish this part."

The other contestants waited patiently for her return. It gave Tyree a moment to scrutinize them from his view on the ladder. Despite his caginess, I could tell he approved of one or more of them.

"You know they used to have a swimwear competition, but they cut it out," he said to me. "The administration said Miss Morrison is a 'lady'. She would never have a reason to wear a swimsuit. Personally, I think they should bring it back. Can you imagine Miss Morrison and the royal court hoofin' it on the football field wearin' matching bikinis? That's the beauty queen I wanna see!"

"Would they wear high heels too?" I asked.

"Of course! Attendance at the games would be double... triple! Those horny old alumni men wouldn't know what to do with themselves," he giggled as he climbed down.

Hanging the banner was our last task before the show was scheduled to begin. We stashed the ladder behind the curtain and watched the four contestants practice the opening dance number. Derrick paced the wooden floor watching them like a hawk. They weren't going for Miss America, but he made them perform as if they were.

"Remember what we rehearsed, girls. You walk to the front of the stage, strike a pose, then walk back and twirl. Got it? Walk, pose, walk, twirl," Derrick said, spinning in a perfect circle.

"Give me ladylike steps, please! And big smiles! I want you to show off those pearly whites. Yes!" he exclaimed as the contestants widened their grins.

"Let's go over the introductions," he said, motioning to them. "You're going to take turns introducing yourself. You'll say 'My name is,' then your name, your major and give us a sentence about why you want to win Miss Morrison. And keep it brief. Don't give me no 'I Have a Dream' speech because I will shut you down darlings."

One of the girls laughed into her hands. Derrick shot her a dirty look that assured her he was not to be taken lightly. I didn't blame the contestant for cracking up. It was hard to be serious in the presence of a man who wore a white mesh tank top and pink Converse.

"You can read what you're going to say from a piece of paper," Derrick instructed, "but I highly recommend you memorize your lines or speak from the heart. I'll give you girls a ten-minute break. Get a cup of water and come back so we can continue in a timely fashion."

The four ladies strolled backstage, except for Alexandra who stayed behind to practice her dance number. Derrick dabbed himself with a soft hand towel.

"Tyree, you're on curtain duty tonight," he said. "Keep an eye on this area for me so these womenfolk can get to and from the stage without denting their 'dos."

"I got you, honey bun," Tyree said.

Derrick turned to me smacking his lips. If he planned to share one of his cutting remarks I would gladly head home.

"Do me a favor, baby? Get the music ready for the opening number. After that, we can arrange the mic stands and make sure all that's working."

"Yes, sir," I said with distaste.

"Sir?" he paused. I didn't believe anyone had called Derrick "sir" in a long time. He drummed his French manicured fingers on my shoulder. I recoiled from his touch. "Alroight, I see, Jason. You wanna act brand new because we're swimming with these fish. Tyree, you better get your friend."

Derrick rushed away to find the contestants, leaving Tyree to scold me about my lack of couth. No matter how I "straight" I decided to be in public, I should always be respectful, he warned. I wouldn't want someone to react to me in the same way. I considered what he said, but stuck to my plan to distance myself from our fearless leader.

From where I stood, I could hear Derrick scolding the contestants. "Okay, you've had enough of a break. Let's go ladies!"

Students and faculty members filed into the auditorium chatting excitedly. They wanted the best seats to watch the future queen, whoever it would be, up close. Tyree and I took our places behind the burgundy folds of the curtain.

From our vantage point, we could see the stage and the first few rows but were out of the girls' way. My laptop sat next to a desk lamp on a small table that would serve as my station. On a far wall was a large mirror with light bulbs dotting its frame where the girls could apply their makeup. The dressing rooms for the contestants were just outside the stage door.

Someone shut off the majority of the lights backstage. Tyree sealed the curtain. I shared the same eagerness for the show to begin that the girls did. Last year, I observed the pageant from my seat in the audience. Experiencing it from backstage would be much cooler.

My anticipation evaporated when I discovered DP was one of the escorts. I spied him helping one of the other Thetas move the glitzy set pieces into place. If Vaughn alerted me earlier that I would spend my night off from set under DP's watch, I wouldn't have volunteered to help Tyree. Vaughn was likely caught up in the hoopla and I hadn't thought to ask. There were many reasons to back out of my duties, but I refused to disappoint Tyree.

The contestants were clad in their business wear. They stood next to the escorts who were suited in impeccable black tuxes. The crew wore regular street clothes. I was the only person who wouldn't appear onstage that was dressed for the occasion. Even Tyree wore a polo shirt and faded skinny jeans. It was another stylish outfit, but more casual than what I chose.

Derrick herded everyone into place, using his pen and clipboard as a cattle prod. "Let's have everybody over here. We're gonna do our best to begin on time. Faster, please! Let me see those feet move!"

Lighting captains, prop masters, queens and escorts rushed to heed Day Day's command. Vaughn and I were separated by the commotion. We both smiled upon seeing each other. He threw in a wink to up the ante.

With everyone all ears, Derrick ran through the show. "We're going to kick it off with introductions and then we're going into the talent portion," he said. "My ladies, make sure you change quickly for the question and answer. We're going to have an easy show."

He paused for a moment of sincerity. "Remember girls, you don't have to worry about the judges. If you get the students behind you, you're a sure thing. Wear the crown. Be the crown. You are the crown. Are there any questions, concerns or commentary before we raise the curtain?"

No one piped up. "Okay then, five minutes 'til show time!"

The contestants raced to the mirror to make final adjustments before the show got underway. Double stick tape was applied to their décolletage. Body glitter was passed around like cigarettes. Lipsticks were flung without regard.

Tyree tossed an escaped mascara wand toward the mirror. "Thanks for comin' by the way, boo. I know you coulda been elsewhere tonight."

"No problem. Are we still going to be friends if I screw up the music?"

"If anything goes wrong, that's your ass! Don't make me go ham on you!"

Tyree and I laughed heartily until we heard a crash that stunned everyone around us. One of the guys hauling the props struggled with an artificial palm tree higher than his head.

"I'll be back," Tyree said. He ran over to help wrangle the renegade tree.

I checked my laptop to make sure the playlist was set. DP's shiver-inducing voice crept behind me. "You having fun?"

I spun around and straightened up. "No sir," I mumbled. I stifled the internal screaming that came with his presence. My eyes grazed the dark wood floor beneath me.

"We may not have set tonight, but don't get too comfortable," he warned. "You and your LBs are gonna get your asses handed to you if you don't get it right when I see you again."

"Yes, Big Brother Genesis."

"Don't call me that name when we're not at set. There are too many people around," he said, gesturing to the ambling crew. "What did I say about discretion?"

DP had said plenty. He drilled the word into us when we got wood or as he slammed his hands into my back. If he saw me on the yard, he'd grip my shoulder forcefully and say it in my ear. At this point, any indiscretion was beaten out of me.

I had one rare moment away from the big brothers and I couldn't enjoy it. I just wanted to go one day without thinking about pledging! Whatever dignity I had was replaced by discretion.

"Don't go far after this," he said before joining the other escorts. "I'm watching you, number 2."

What made DP more terrifying is he didn't look like the type to inflict pain. When I met him at the Theta interest meeting, he struck me as a well-educated student with a welcoming disposition. He carried himself with the regal authority most Morrison men embodied. Behind closed doors, he was an accomplished sadist. His mind constantly churned out new ways to haze us.

Tyree waited until DP was out of the way before he scurried toward me. His warmth was the blowtorch that cut through my disappointment.

"What did he say?" my roommate asked.

I was so shaken I couldn't think clearly enough to process the warning. I shook my head at Tyree and eyed the stage. My brief encounter with DP would not ruin my night.

"Good evening, students and faculty! Welcome to the Miss Morrison State University pageant!" Darnell spoke into the mic. The audience greeted him with energetic applause. "We're thrilled you came out to help us choose the next representative of our esteemed university. We have a great program planned for you, so please show the contestants your love. Let's meet the four ladies who are going for the crown!"

That was my cue. I pressed the play button on the first track on the list: Whitney Houston's version of "I'm Every Woman." The ladies instantly flashed their prettiest smiles and floated to the stage in a single line. The quartet was decked out in dark-colored business suits with starched white collars and heels, except for Alexandra.

If anyone wasn't aware that she was a member of Delta Sigma Theta they knew now. Alexandra opted to ditch the sober hues for a crimson pantsuit that represented the colors of her sorority. Melinda, the contestant whom I wanted to win, was subtler. She wore a small pink and green Alpha Kappa Alpha brooch on the lapel of her blazer.

The girls strutted the length of the stage, then performed the dance number they'd rehearsed. I was impressed. They executed each of Derrick's patented spins. Some of them added their own personal flair. With one last twirl, they each walked to the mic to introduce themselves.

First up was Lauren. Her height and muscular frame were similar to that of the other girls on the volleyball team. Serving and spiking molded her into excellent shape. Someone pressed out her natural hair so it fell past her shoulders.

There was a rumor circulating on campus that Lauren was a lesbian. Then again, every girl who was athletic and not sleeping with fifteen or more guys on campus was allegedly gay. Lesbian or not, she and the voluptuous girls on the volleyball team were the reason male students packed the stands of the gym to watch them play. The women's volleyball games had higher attendance than most of the university's other sports.

"Good evening! My name is Lauren Daley! I'm a junior mass communications major from Delray Beach, Florida. I believe a queen is a wise and intelligent leader. Because these are skills I possess, you should select me to be the next Miss Morrison State University."

Lauren received a round of applause as she took her place next to the other girls. Next up was Melinda, who drifted like a fairy tale princess toward the microphone. She had fair skin with light brown, almost blond hair that fell in waves around her radiant face. Melinda's plum lipstick made her toothpaste ad smile look even more dazzling. I was startled by the daring pink shoes on her feet.

"Oh boy, those heels are high," I said.

"Yes, but they look gooooood!" Tyree said in awe. "Life's too short for a pedestrian heel. Nobody's gonna be like 'ooh isn't our queen modest?' They want a girl who can serve it in a pair of six-inch slingback stilettos."

There was an impassioned rumble in the auditorium as Melinda assumed her place on the stage. The audience simmered down long enough for her to introduce herself.

"My name is Melinda Rousseau, and I hail from Tampa, Florida!" she announced.

A chorus of high-pitched "skeeee-weeees" erupted across the auditorium. Not only did her sorors cheer her on, but Melinda also received the endorsement of her fellow residents from Tampa too.

"I am a nursing major with a minor in communications. I have learned that you are a product of the people you know, the experiences you've had and the God you serve. I thank you for your support!"

"Yaaaaaasssss mama, she did that!" Tyree said above the prolonged applause from the crowd. "I'm *living* for her. She better get 'em goin' from jump!"

The audience was equally inspired because they hadn't stopped cheering even though Melinda had already finished. Tammy, the next contestant, waited patiently at the microphone. She was a butterscotch blonde with hazel contacts and a wide rear end. She was short and stacked like most Southern women. She wasn't fat, but she was dangerously close to it.

"Hello, my name is..." She paused until the room settled down. "Hello, my name is Tammy Barnes, and I'm from Tallahassee. I'm a second year psychology major. I'm ready to take my place in the universe thanks to Morrison."

The audience clapped politely. The chance of Tammy winning the title was slim. She was only a sophomore and didn't have a wide circle of friends like the other contestants. You didn't need to be in a sorority or the prettiest girl to win Miss Morrison, but it sure helped.

"Mmm, I don't see it for her," Tyree confirmed.

Alexandra's sorors shouted her name with glee before she reached the microphone. The red suit combined with the intense lights made her bronzed skin gleam. She smiled through the lively response until she found the right time to begin.

"My name is Alexandra Webb, and I'm a criminal justice major from Mobile, Alabama!"

"OO-OOOOP!" her sorors chanted the Delta call in response.

"I believe in positive motivation for the student body of Morrison State as well our alumni. Together, we can make our school the pinnacle of success, recognized far and wide!"

Alexandra spun on her heels and returned to the line of contestants. Her posture was reminiscent of the Egyptian goddesses that once ruled ancient Africa.

"Thank you, ladies!" Darnell waved his trusty index cards at the group. "Give them another round of applause! Tonight's winner will not only take home the title of Miss Morrison State University, but will also receive free tuition for the year of her reign, a $1,500 book scholarship, a clothing and travel stipend, and will go on to compete in the Miss HBCU pageant this summer!"

"And remember our class queens that will make up the royal court — Miss Senior, Miss Junior and Miss Sophomore — will be voted on during the student government elections in a few weeks. Let's give our ladies a hand as they prepare for the talent portion of our evening."

The contestants glided in our direction, leaving the audience to buzz about the jaw-dropping prizes Darnell outlined. Most students at Morrison would give their right arm for that kind of financial package. Once the girls were safely behind the curtain, they scrambled to the dressing rooms to change into their next outfit.

"It's my pleasure to introduce our wonderful judges for the night," Darnell gestured to the front row. "We have Quinton Briggs, the current president of the Student Government Association! Next to Quinton is Johnson & Johnson executive and Miss Morrison 1972 Angel Allison Dawson! And finally we have Ms. Marshall, our director of student activities!"

The audience responded with earnest praise. The jazz quartet struck up a number as Darnell left the stage assuring everyone that the show would resume soon. Tammy stood apprehensively at the edge of the curtain. She searched the faces of the attendees that would analyze her every move.

"I think I could've done better. Did I do okay?" she asked Derrick. His primary concern was whether her loitering would delay his pageant.

"You did great, sweetheart. Now get yourself together for the talent," he said, ushering her to the dressing room. "We don't wanna run behind and make our guests upset."

Lauren, who had changed into a maid's uniform, read over the lines for her monologue. While she waited, the prop master set an armchair and a woven rug on the stage. Once everything was in place, Tyree reopened the curtains for her solo act.

"How's the show goin' fellas?" Cole appeared behind us.

Thank God I wasn't the only one who dressed up for the pageant. Cole wore a dark gray, long-sleeve shirt and dress slacks. He had also shortened his beard to a more distinguished 5 o'clock shadow.

I opened my mouth to say the show was going well so far.

However, Cole was under the spell of the alluring contestants. He couldn't seem to keep his eyes off the ladies, despite having a doting girlfriend.

"Nuh uh, Cole," Tyree snapped his fingers in front of our roommate's infatuated face. "You not about to get me in trouble messin' around back here. Stay away from the talent."

"Don't worry, I'm not into the beauty queen type," he woke up. "Too much work."

"So you sayin' you don't wanna carry a good lookin' woman on your arm?" Tyree giggled. "It's not too late. We can get you a tux."

"Nah, I'm good. I'll leave it to the experts." Cole moved closer to check out my laptop. "Jason, how'd you get this gig? I didn't know you were a DJ."

"You're right, I'm not," I said. "But I do have a laptop, and I'm very good at pushing buttons."

Tyree edged Cole away from my station. "Jason, you're doin' great, so don't let this man mess you up. Here Cole, come stand by me."

Lauren curtsied as she wrapped up her monologue. Melinda had transformed from a chic business executive to a leading lady. She was stunning in a short, black sequined gown. Her hair was pulled back into a neat bun. I hit play on the instrumental version of "Lift Ev'ry Voice and Sing" that she requested. Melinda belted out the anthem in a resounding, but shaky alto. Her wild gestures dramatized every overblown lyric.

"Facing the rising SUUUUN! Of our new day beguuuuun! Let us march on! 'Til victory is wooooooonnnn!"

Melinda piled into the next verse with more unrestrained passion than the first. If she sang the third verse too, she might run out of breath before the song was over. Thankfully, she finished out with the chorus. Her last hurrah was a run that hit every note on the scale. The audience loved it. They cheered with more fervor than they had all night.

Tyree was in a daze. "Well okay! That chile was tryna raze the buildin' with that singin'. You hear her?"

"I did," Cole said as Melinda exited the stage toward us. "Nobody's gonna tell her that was bad?"

"Shhh, keep your voice down," Tyree elbowed him. "These girls is already fragile. Yes she was givin' Ma-hell no Jackson but I don't want her or anybody else soakin' their tears into one of our shoulders."

"You won't hear nothin' from me, Ty," Cole said. "But somebody should say something to her."

Tammy was next at the mic. After Melinda's vocal cartwheels, I was relieved our next performer didn't need music too. After a brief introduction from Darnell, Tammy recited an original poem written about her favorite aunt. She didn't give Maya Angelou a run for her money, but it was solid.

After Tammy finished, Alexandra strode onto the stage wearing a lengthy, white liturgical dress that caught the air as she moved. She picked a slow gospel number to accompany her dance. It was the kind of song in which you could hear the churchgoers in the background worshipping spiritedly along with the singer.

Alexandra began with her arms outstretched to the ceiling, then pirouetted quickly to make her dress float around her. The expressive worship was similar to what the dance ministry at my church in Athens performed every third Sunday. Alexandra's steps were triumphant as if the Holy Spirit guided her movement.

"Praise Him!" someone in the crowd yelled with zeal.

Alexandra ended with a dramatic collapse to the floor, her left hand stretched high above her. The audience leapt to their feet with a deafening roar. I wouldn't have been surprised if someone circulated an offering plate through the aisles. Alexandra infused church into the secular auditorium.

"Give it up one more time for contestant number four, Alexandra Webb!" Darnell said with gusto. "If you thought that was good, next is the question and answer part of the pageant. As we all know, Miss Morrison must be able to speak with anyone at a moment's notice. The next section will test that ability. Let's clap for the contestants as the jazz quartet gives us another number."

When Tyree closed the curtain, the backstage chaos returned to its noisy din. The girls jostled for the makeup scattered on the table in front of the mirror.

"Has anyone seen my shoes?"

"Can I borrow someone's eyeliner?"

"Hurry ladies!" Derrick said emphatically. "We need you to be onstage soon!"

Darnell swooped in from the dressing room with fresh cards. He now wore a silver sharkskin suit complemented by a Kente cloth bow tie and a gold pin with the Alpha Phi Alpha fraternity seal on it. Tyree gave him a thumbs up and raised the curtain.

"Ladies and gentlemen of MSU, let's welcome back our contestants!"

The audience fell silent while I dialed up the volume on a soulful ballad by the R&B singer Maxwell. He crooned about the love of his life as the contestants glided by in their finest evening wear. One by one they emerged from behind the curtain, cradled by Vaughn and the other escorts. The refinement of the guys' matching tuxes matched the ladies' style exquisitely. The four pairs posed as I faded out the music.

Darnell seized the moment, deepening his voice. "In my hand are the questions selected by our judges. Our first contestant is Miss Lauren Daley."

Lauren's escort walked her into the spotlight. Her athletic figure was completely transformed by the womanly lace sheath dress she wore. It had a long train that trailed behind her daintily.

"Lauren, you look like a million bucks," Darnell said. "The question for you is: If you could be on the cover of any magazine what would it be?"

"My own," she said without hesitation. "I'm starting a magazine from scratch and every issue is going to have me on the cover. Like my hero Oprah."

There was a brief pause while her fellow students digested her response. It was a great answer, but a touch of humility would have worked to her advantage.

"Give her a round of applause," Darnell said. The crowd obeyed with a few short claps.

"Up next is contestant number two, Miss Melinda Rousseau."

Vaughn nobly carried her on his left arm across the stage. Everything about him was breathtaking, down to the polish of his shoes. I wanted to rip the tuxedo off and expose his rock hard body and huge... smile. As I recalled the night before, my erection pressed against the zipper of my slacks. I wished I was the one he was holding on to.

Tyree nodded approvingly at the pair. "So good. She's servin' Ebony Fashion Fair, haute couture for your nerves."

"What?"

My focus was on Vaughn and nothing else. So much of our

experience together was through the partition of the computer or in the extreme closeness of set. Vaughn stood on the stage soundlessly communicating his longing for my companionship. The beauty queen was a poor replacement for the connection we shared.

Melinda was an outstanding vision in her ivory strapless dress. A strand of pearls draped elegantly around her neck. I'd let her have him until the end of the show.

"Contestant number two," Darnell spoke. "What do you think is the best thing about attending Morrison?"

My answer would be Vaughn.

Melinda smiled sweetly. "Morrison encourages me to be a better person who can accomplish anything I put my mind to. The Bible says I can do all things through Christ who strengthens me. Our university reinforces those words for me every day. If I were crowned Miss Morrison, I would carry on the tradition of the inspirational women who came before us."

Melinda's response was exceptional and, unlike my enamored consideration, appropriate for the occasion. Tyree and I clapped for her along with the audience.

"I see you, soror!" an AKA yelled from the back of the room. "Skeee-weeeeeee!"

I snapped a picture of Vaughn with my phone as he guided Melinda to her place next to Lauren. It was Tammy's turn to speak. The third contestant's dress was covered in sequins the color of flat champagne. It was also several sizes too large, except in the back. Her rear looked as if it was begging for emancipation from her control-top underwear.

"Jesus, take the wheel!" Tyree exclaimed. "That gown needs prayer. She's too cute to be wearin' somethin' like that."

Darnell was unfazed. "Contestant number three, the

question for you is: Would you ever send a nude picture to your significant other?"

A collective gasp rose from the auditorium. Tyree was gobsmacked. "Ooh, there is no good way to answer that!" he said incredulously.

"That was random," Cole added. "Who came up with these questions?"

"That sounds like a Day Day move," Tyree speculated.

"Figures," I said.

"Was that shade?" Tyree eyed me.

"It was no more shady than that cheap question," I replied.

Tammy did her best to not let Darnell's query and the collective reaction to it upset her. "No, I don't be sendin' no nasty pics," she fidgeted. "My goodies are between me and my husband — when I get one. My body is a temple. And my doors ain't open for everybody."

"Okayyyyyy. What was that?" I threw my hands in the air.

"It was a mess is what that was," Tyree said. "I got elementary school kids I tutor who coulda given a better answer than that."

"Maybe she'll get… what's that thing? Miss Congeniality?" Cole said.

Tyree laughed him off. "Boy, they don't have nothin' like that here. Her reward is that they don't boot her off the stage."

I couldn't decide whether Tammy's self-satisfaction was a result of tenacity or ignorance. She was, in all likelihood, going to lose the contest. If she was aware that the circumstances were not in her favor, I had to give her credit for pressing on.

DP strutted by us wearing a freshly-pressed tuxedo, Alexandra in tow. There was no paddle in sight and yet I cowered in his presence. His unnatural grin only made me more uneasy. Had he ever smiled before? I couldn't remember.

While I hid behind my laptop, Tyree fawned over Alexandra. "They are not ready for miss girl's floor length gown in that burgundy! She is selling it!"

Alexandra did look sublime. The only students in the building more animated than Tyree were her sorors. They yelled her name at an unequaled decibel. Once the supporters quieted down, Darnell raised his card to read her the question.

"Contestant number four, Alexandra Webb. What do you think is the biggest issue facing the African-American community today?"

She gracefully lifted the microphone to her lips. "The most important issue facing us is… um. I would say…" Alexandra laughed nervously as she searched for an answer. It wasn't a good sign. Darnell said it best earlier — you couldn't be Miss Morrison without the ability to handle a softball question. There were many responses that she could give that would suffice. She took her time to cycle through each one.

"The biggest issue is that we don't connect the way we used to," Alexandra finally spoke. "Like, um, with social media and the internet we need to find ways to get together like my family does every Sunday. Or we used to before I left for college. I can work with people from various walks of life and as Miss Morrison I will be a great ambassador for the school."

"Oh my goodness gracious," Tyree said. "I didn't see that comin'. What did she say her major was?"

"Criminal justice," Cole offered.

"Makes sense 'cause that was a crime against humanity. They gonna lock her up for that one?" Tyree said in amusement.

Alexandra's answer and Melinda's overwrought song during the talent portion were equally questionable. It was up to the judges to decide which contestant excelled beyond her peers. The competition remained a toss-up. Alexandra waved with her fingertips to her sorors. She then spun on her heel back to her place between the other girls.

"Thank you, ladies. Let's give a handclap to our contestants!" Darnell said as the girls disappeared backstage. "While the judges are tallying their scores we'll have another selection by our phenomenal jazz quartet."

There was a stifled scream behind me. Alexandra tripped on her dress just as the curtain closed. She was sprawled out on the floor, nursing the gown that now sported a long rip on its left side.

"Motherf—!" Our alarmed faces steered her away from more colorful words. "Fudge cake! Someone help me, please!"

One of the lighting guys rushed to lift Alexandra back on her feet. Derrick was visibly annoyed. His pageant was again being delayed.

"Look, it's too many of you all backstage, so if you don't need to be in this area, please scoot!" he shooed us away. "We are trying to put on a show! And I'd like to do it without sending anybody to Tampa General."

Alexandra sobbed as people drifted away from the damsel in distress. Globs of black mascara dripped down her face, pooling at her quivering chin.

Derrick did everything he could to console her. "Baby girl, it's nothing needle and thread can't fix."

Like a street magician, Derrick whipped a sewing kit out of thin air. His fingers worked quickly to thread the dress closed.

Cole backed far away from the one-man knitting circle. "Fellas, I'm gonna go watch the show from my seat. Come find me after."

"Okay, catch up with you soon, tiger," Tyree called after him.

A few more stitches and the giant tear in Alexandra's gown was mended. She smiled briefly, then started to wail again. "I broke a nail too!"

Derrick's patience ran thin. "Girl, the judges can't see your nails! They're in the audience! Wave with the other hand if you have to."

As Alexandra did her best to reverse her tears, Tasha peeked around the curtain. She handed Derrick the scorecards from the judges.

"Who won? Is it Melinda?" I asked Tasha.

"Boy, I can't tell you!" she scolded. "I have to get back out there, but let's talk after."

It wasn't like Tasha to spoil a surprise, but I figured I'd ask anyway. Derrick stashed the sewing kit in his pocket and pulled a fat red marker out of the other. He shuffled through the scores, oohing and aahing over the results. Once he was satisfied, he jotted something on a blank index card and handed it to Darnell.

"Make sure Charmaine has the crown please," Derrick instructed. Tyree passed the sparkling rhinestone tiara to last year's Miss Morrison. She held it delicately, inspecting it for any flaws. Each turn in her hands revealed a kaleidoscope of glinting light. I wondered how she felt about relinquishing her title to the next queen. Charmaine was pensive as she readied for her final walk.

"This is the moment we've been waiting for," Darnell said to the hushed crowd. "Let's bring out our reigning Miss Morrison Charmaine Keyes, who will help me crown this year's winner."

Charmaine moved regally across the stage in her slick gold gown. She blew grateful kisses to the students in the audience. The four contestants filed out behind her clapping anxiously.

"Good luck, girls!" Derrick yelled after them.

Alexandra and her broken nail were last onto the stage. She recovered from her fall, thanks in part to Derrick's handiwork. Her blinding smile masked any insecurity the upset caused. No one could tell the dress ever ripped. The four girls positioned themselves in a single line to receive the news. A rustle of anticipation swept through the audience.

"We've counted the judges scores," Darnell drew out the suspense. "The name of our new queen is in my hand. Congratulations to each of you. And the winner of the Miss Morrison State University pageant is..."

The auditorium exploded with students shouting the names of their favorite contestant. The jazz quartet furthered the tension with a slow drumroll. The girls held hands and smiled to ease the butterflies in their stomach. Tammy grinned as if she was sure her name was next to be called.

"The winner is... Alexandra Webb!" Darnell exclaimed.

The room erupted in applause so thunderous the auditorium floors rattled. The jazz quartet launched into a triumphant version of the school song. It paired well with the clicks of a hundred camera phones documenting the climax of the evening.

Alexandra cupped her mouth with both hands in genuine surprise. Her cheeks flushed red as she digested the news. Our new queen bent slightly to allow Charmaine to place the tiara on her head. Darnell draped a silk sash with "Miss Morrison State University" inscribed on it over her trembling shoulders. Alexandra wore them both proudly. It was as if she'd been practicing for this moment since she was a young girl.

"Oh my gosh!" she mouthed repeatedly.

The students, faculty and judges gave her an energetic standing ovation. Alexandra floated back and forth on the stage saluting her well-wishers. DP offered her a large bouquet of white roses. The tears that nearly did her in earlier were replaced with cries of joy. I clapped too, but I couldn't believe the judges scored her higher than Melinda.

"How did she win after she gave that awful answer?" I asked perplexed.

"Both of her sisters were Miss Morrison before her," Tyree said, continuing his handclap for the winner. "This school loves its legacies. There's no way on God's green Earth they weren't gonna give it to her."

Tyree wasn't thrilled about the choice either. From his blank expression, I could tell he'd already come to terms with her win.

"I still think Melinda was better," I said sullenly.

Darnell discreetly interrupted Alexandra's victory walk. "Congratulations! What do you have to say to everyone?"

"I am feeling so blessed," she announced. Her eyes twinkled brighter than the stones in the crown. "I want to thank the judges for selecting me to be the face of Morrison State University. Most of all, I want to thank my fellow students, especially my sorors of Delta Sigma Theta Sorority, Incorporated! OO-OOOOP!"

"OOOOO-OOOOOOOP!" the Deltas in the auditorium enthusiastically returned the call.

"Congratulations again to our reigning Miss MSU, Alexandra Webb!" Darnell said.

People were already filing out of the room noisily as he said his parting words. Darnell moved closer to the microphone to drown out the stragglers talking up a storm.

"Remember, voting for student government officers will take place in a few weeks. We look forward to seeing you then! Have a good night!"

When the house lights went up, the students who worked backstage rushed to congratulate Alexandra. She gushed as she accepted the praise.

"That's it everybody, good show!" Derrick said to the remaining crew. "Thank you so much! You all are wonderful. Before you leave for the gym party, let me have you get your stuff first. Don't leave nothing behind or I'm taking it home with me."

I set my laptop into my backpack. The ladies were surrounded by a throng of supporters. Melinda looked delighted as if she'd won herself. A friend of Tammy's attempted to uplift the contestant's broken spirit, but to no avail. She was upset about the results and no words could change that. I admired her for entering the pageant to begin with. Putting oneself on display for the school to judge had to be a taxing experience.

When Tyree, Cole and I entered the school gym, a fog of body heat engulfed us. Yesterday, it was where the men's basketball team dunked their way to a victory. For tonight's party, the hardwood was transformed into a dance floor populated by hundreds of lively students. Many, like us, came directly from the pageant to continue the celebration.

My roommates and I waited on the perimeter of the court while the fraternities and sororities strolled through the mass of people. For the Greeks, "strolling" wasn't the same as a leisurely walk in the park. For them, the term described a form of dance. It consisted of the brothers or sisters snaking their way through the room in a single line, dancing and marching with coordinated arm movements. The sight of it was both intriguing and intimidating for someone who wasn't Greek.

Each of the frats and sororities had their own version of strolling. The AKAs stepped from side to side with one pinky in the air. The Zetas positioned their hands to form a "Z" as they worked to the music. The Deltas always flashed their pyramids, palms out with their index fingers and thumbs touching. All the Greek letter organizations, including the Alphas, Sigmas, Iotas and SG Rhos, performed signature moves that were passed down for generations.

I couldn't wait to show off the Theta sign after I crossed. I could have done it anytime in the privacy of my room, but even alone it felt like a violation of a sacred rite reserved only for the Thetas.

The men of Omega Psi Phi kicked, jumped and barked their way through the gym. They were also referred to as "Ques" — pronounced like cue ball. Each of the distinctly muscular guys wore boots spray-painted gold, and purple shirts with their fraternity letters on them. The squadron threw up their "hooks," angling their arms to represent the Greek letter Omega. The students near them backed away to avoid a lethal kick to the face. No one wanted a trip to the infirmary because they inadvertently interrupted the fraternity's strolling.

"I said one! Two, three, four, five!" the Ques chanted. "Party hard, we Que Psi Phi! Six! Seven, eight, nine, ten! Back it up and let's do it again!"

Some of the fraternity members had an Omega branded into their legs and arms. The raised skin from the mark was a permanent symbol of their commitment to the fraternity. I could *never* get a brand. There was no way I would let someone plunge a red-hot poker or wire hanger into my skin. For me, that was worse than anything we'd done during the pledging process. However, I understood why the Ques did it. The brand would be visible for life, as would their dedication to Omega Psi Phi.

If I crossed I might get a tattoo, but nothing too showy. Also, it had to be somewhere I could hide it. My mom wouldn't approve of me marking my body in any way. If my tattoo were hidden, she wouldn't know about it unless I showed it to her.

The men of Kappa Alpha Psi shimmied their shoulders through the gym while rhythmically pantomiming the act of brushing their hair. The Kappas had a reputation for being the pretty boys on campus. They stroked their chins to the music and winked at the girls in the room who watched them with pleasure.

Unlike the Ques, the Kappas' attire varied. Some sported red "Kappa Alpha Psi" T-shirts. Others were dressed to the nines in cream linen suits with crimson neckwear. Reese, Lauren's escort in the pageant, was in step with his brothers. He wore a red rose tucked into the front pocket of his tux. Reese skillfully twirled one of the infamous striped Kappa canes. He had the tricks down, spinning the waist-high cane in his hand, then behind his back in one fluid move.

Watching a Kappa twirl a cane had the same thrill of watching a singer on a television competition show. You hoped they were good at their trade. If they hit a wrong note, it made you cringe. Whether it was a success or a disaster, it was exciting to watch. If a Kappa accidentally dropped his cane, nearby students would discreetly boo the offender. They rarely had a chance to do so, given the fraternity brothers' mastery of their art.

Tyree was equally mesmerized by the line of Kappas. "Look at him do his thang!" he exclaimed.

I'm pretty sure Tyree wanted to pledge Alpha Phi Alpha, though he never admitted his choice to me. He hadn't attended any interest meetings or parties for any of the fraternities, so I couldn't say for sure.

There was a commotion at the entrance of the gym. A line of Deltas strutted through the door with Alexandra leading the way. Our new queen had changed into a red blouse and slim white pants. The crown remained on her head; the sash draped thoughtfully over her shoulders.

"We got the Deltas in the building!" someone shouted. The music switched to Cheryl Lynn's "To Be Real," the sorority's go-to song for strolling. Everyone respectfully cleared out of the way. The ladies bounced to the song, sliding one leg out at a time and accentuating each move with two claps. Their line was a mass of spinning hair, except for Alexandra's mane. It remained in place thanks to the hairspray she used earlier.

"OOO-OOOP!" the Deltas cheered as they formed the pyramids with their hands. "Who are we? My sisters and me? We are the soul-stepping sorors of DST!"

Watching the sororities stroll was always captivating. It was obvious that days of practice went into perfecting their moves. The unity of their performance was a reflection of their sisterhood.

The students who previously were cutting loose on the dance floor stood by in awe watching the action. Their gaping mouths and star-struck eyes revealed their desire to be Greek too.

No student wanted to be a "GDI" — a goddamn individual. Everyone in the gym who wasn't Greek would pledge if given a chance. Most of those who said they wouldn't were lying. There was a mysterious aura around the fraternities and sororities on campus. It was as if they knew something about life that no one else did.

After the Deltas' song faded out, the party music returned to the gym. Some of the Greeks continued to stroll. They were crowded out by students who were intent on dancing. Someone shut off the jarring overhead lights. It was officially a Morrison gym party.

The girls in short shorts rotated their hips on guys steadying themselves behind them. The cumulative grinding in the gym could have powered a locomotive. I had nothing to offer in the way of dance, so I stood by like a passenger on a train platform.

My phone buzzed insistently. I already knew who the sequence of texts were from and what they said. God help me. I searched the court for DP's grimace but saw nothing. His head start gave him more time to devise the unpleasant tasks our line would endure when we arrived to set.

"Y'all wanna get out there and dance?" Tyree said to Cole and I.

"I can't!" I yelled over the music. I showed him the alerts on my phone. I could sense Tyree's indignation, even in the dark. No matter who I chose — my roommates or my line brothers — I would leave someone disappointed tonight.

Vaughn pushed his way through the party to get to me. "It's time to go!" he said. "My car is parked outside Mosley Hall. I'll meet you there!"

Tyree pulled me close as Vaughn dashed away. "Y'all gonna leave right now? It's just getting started."

"You know what I'm going to say, Tyree. I have to."

Cole put his arms around our shoulders. It eased my apprehension and agitated Tyree.

"Let the man go, Ty. He's gotta do what he's gotta do."

"I'll be so glad when this is done," Tyree said. He gave me a lengthy hug. "No more interruptions!"

"It'll be over soon!" I promised him.

"It better be, or me and the Thetas is gonna have words," he sulked.

Cole pushed me in the direction of the exit. "Go 'head. We

don't want you to get in trouble."

It was another night of suspension between dedication and despair. The two went hand in hand at set. I concentrated on the routine that preceded every encounter with the Thetas. Get the snacks, carry the blocks. A knock on the door. Discretion. The five of us entered the room as a line.

"Greetings!" Rodney called out.

"Greetings Big Brothers of Theta Pi Chi Fraternity Innnn-corporated!" we bellowed in unison.

We ran through the greetings for each big brother, complimenting them on attributes they may or may not have possessed. They smiled with satisfaction whenever their name was highlighted. We knew the greetings so well we didn't have to think about them, only move our lips in mimicry.

"Where my greeting at?" someone said derisively.

It was a voice I didn't recognize. I pressed my balled fists against Rodney's chest. It was my hint to him that we needed help with information.

"Big Brother Alcatraz," he whispered back.

I shared the name with Vaughn, who passed it down the line. Timothy Vendrick, or Alcatraz as we knew him, went to the University of South Florida in Tampa. I didn't know who it was when he spoke because Alcatraz had only been to set once before.

I hated when Thetas from other chapters visited. Set became an all-night affair consisting of them quizzing us on the tiniest details about the fraternity. They were much harder on us than the big brothers from the Morrison chapter. They mostly wanted to show off their supremacy over us.

"I can't get no greeting?" Alcatraz asked again impatiently.

No, because you're lame and you're never here. The words I wished I could say would never leave my mouth.

"We're gonna skip that greeting for now," DP ignored Big Brother Alcatraz. "We got a long night ahead of us. You got your blocks fellas? Get on up."

Rodney, Vaughn, Junior, Chima and I lay our burdens lengthwise in front of us. We stood precariously on them with one foot. We had to relay any information that was asked of us while maintaining our balance. We could switch from one leg to the other if the strain became too much to bear. If we fell, the reward was ten swats with the wood. The brothers gathered around us, ready to pounce the moment we toppled.

"Don't you disappoint us, pledges!" Big Brother Major Payne screamed.

Big Brother Alcatraz chose me as his victim for the night. He stood so close to me that the hot air from his nostrils drilled into my neck. I located a small crack in the wall to concentrate on. It curled through the plaster of the wall, a river of uncharted territory waiting to be navigated. I was the captain of my ship. I was Noah in the ark avoiding the rain. I was surrounded by vicious animals. I had to keep the peace.

"Pledges! List the chapters of Theta Pi Chi fraternity! Starting with Alpha chapter!" DP barked.

I lost sight of my ship. What would become of me?

My line brothers and I rattled off the names of the chapters and the campuses where they were founded. "Alpha chapter! Howard University! Beta! Harvard University! Gamma! Dartmouth College! Delta! New York University!"

Big Brother Alcatraz screamed the chapters along with us. He was an inconsistent parallel to our near flawless recitation. Venomous spit flew from his mouth with every syllable.

"Lambda Chapter! Morgan State!" we continued.

"Morehouse College!" he yelled back at me.

DP whipped his head around to where I stood. "Who messed that up?!"

The five of us on the line looked around at each other in a panic. We knew the founding dates forward and backward. No one knew what to say, but we would not take the punishment for something this dolt messed up.

The Lambda Chapter was founded on the Morgan State University campus in 1932 by seven students: two seniors, four juniors and one freshman. The Thetas from New York University traveled to Baltimore in 1931 to help found the new chapter. These were facts I'd bet my life on.

"None of us did, sir!" I pleaded to DP.

"You saying I don't know my information?" Alcatraz shot back. He avoided the criticizing stares of the other big brothers. "You calling me a liar, pledge??"

"No sir, Big Brother Alcatraz!" I winced.

With one relentless punch, the visiting Theta sent me flying backward off the cinder block. My head nearly missed a glass coffee table that inexplicably took up space next to us. For Christ's sake! What was wrong with this man?

"Yo, chill!" DP yelled. "Ay back off, Tim! The only person messing with my line is me!" DP had never cursed at any of the big brothers in front of us before.

Lying in repose on the carpet wouldn't do me any good. I stood to my feet and rejoined my LBs who were stunned by the turn of events. The moment that I was out cold was the most I'd seen of the room since we'd been online. My ribs ached from where Alcatraz's fist connected with them. I was grateful DP called him off. However, it didn't mean we would be spared from the rest of set. My health was the least of the brothers' concerns.

"Don't disrespect me and my line!" DP shoved Alcatraz into the next room.

We and the remaining big brothers listened closely to the muffled argument. How did a member of a fraternity go about punishing someone he took an oath to protect? Would it be an argument or escalate to something more? We weren't privy to such exchanges between the Thetas.

After a lengthy discussion, Alcatraz stormed back into the living room and plopped on the couch behind us. DP followed clutching Master of Disaster, a splintering old paddle that was used on Theta pledges for decades. The ear-shattering crack it made when it connected with our body drowned out any cries of pain. In the hands of a skilled man, it was a destructive force.

"Yo line up!" DP commanded. He slapped the enormous paddle against his leg. DP examined us like a drill sergeant who demanded perfection from his recruits.

My four LBs and I pressed close to each other. Heads down, eyes forward. I kept my imagination in check because it would only heighten my panic. Without warning, a pack of the big brothers rushed at us like football players.

They did everything they could to make us let go of each other. We were helpless punching bags with no hope of retaliation. The only way we would make it through the brutality was to keep ourselves upright. We could not allow them to defeat us.

"Don't let them break the line!" DP said adamantly. "A

fraternity is a bond! It must not be broken!"

I fastened my arms around Rodney to shield him from the big brothers' assault. Vaughn clutched me with all his might. If they managed to separate us, the punishment would be ten times worse. The shoving got more brutal by the minute. Their body-checks were unrelenting as they pounded into our weakening torsos.

"Stay strong, stay strong," Vaughn repeatedly murmured in my ear.

It was more a prompt for himself than it was for me. This couldn't last forever, we told ourselves. The attacks kept coming. A rush by three of the big brothers to our unsteady legs finally sent us crashing to the ground. There was only so much I could take! So help me God I wanted to march out of the door and never look back!

"Alright, step off," DP said to the other Thetas. He poked us with the paddle while we picked ourselves up from the carpet. "Step forward and touch your ankles!"

DP doled out ten backbreaking swats to each of us. A shroud of blurry tears clouded my vision as the swinging paddle slammed into my backside. The big brothers took their turn wailing at us with the vicious plank of wood. Being ripped apart with shards of glass would have been bliss compared to our persecution.

"Line up! We're going on a field trip," DP announced.

I didn't have the mental capacity to process what he meant by "field trip." I could barely move, much less leave this torture chamber. My LBs were equally confused. Set always began and ended in the same location.

"Aw shit," Junior cringed in fear.

The policeman's flashlight shone in our wearied faces. He demanded to know why five men in similar clothing were crouched on their knees in an empty field. The big brothers surrounding us couldn't offer a coherent explanation. Rodney whimpered inconsolably next to me.

I was scared out of my mind not knowing what our fate would be. I couldn't go to jail! I was a straight-A student before I met the Thetas! DP was supposed to take care of us! I'd heard stories of how encounters with police ended with Black men and women in the hospital or worse. I expected we would also meet a tragic end. I was wrong.

DP negotiated with the officer, who kept one of his beady eyes on us as they talked. We were on the track team and practicing for an upcoming meet, DP told him. It was a terrible excuse, one that he reluctantly accepted.

I suspected the lawman was a member of a fraternity — possibly Theta — and that he had been in a similar position before. He examined the row of sweaty college students shifting in the wet dirt and the guardians standing over us. The officer lumbered back to his waiting patrol car. He assured the dispatcher that everything was fine. Nothing here but kids playing a game.

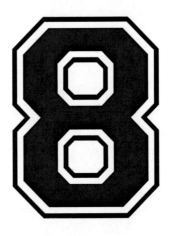

TYREE

Oh yes ma'am, it was about to be on tonight!

That shower had me fresher than a rosebush in a French garden! I had a date with that sexy boo daddy from Grindr. His name was Will; he was 23 and lived in Tampa. He didn't go to Morrison, which was great because I didn't date guys in college anyway. It was too messy.

His profile also said he was "discreet." That meant he was either a closet case, married or ugly as hell. And since I already saw the pics on the app it must've been number one. If it was number two, I'd be ghost like my name was Casper. I refused to be anybody's homewrecker.

It had been a minute since I was out on the town with any man, so my excitement was sky-high. He hit me back talking about he wanted to chill. It gave me pause. On the app, "chill" meant ending up naked at somebody's house with your clothes scattered on their floor.

I did my best to control my thirst. Will's shirt was off in every pic he posted. In the last one, his dick was hanging out. I gagged when that picture popped up! It definitely had girth, but if he thought he was getting these cookies without a proper date, he had another thing coming. A dick pic was not the way to my heart.

Will wanted me to send one back, but I honestly didn't keep naked pics on my phone. Besides, what would I look like working as a marketing executive and there were booty pictures of me on the internet? I would rather he waited and see my goodies in person.

Will said he was a top, which was good because I was a vers bottom, emphasis on the bottom. Regardless, I had no plans to be a ho on the first date. If he said he wanted to chill, that was exactly what we were gonna do. No bottoms' diet for me either. I didn't want any kind of temptation. But I would take a condom to be safe.

I smoothed hair butter through my curls to keep them nice and silky. My American Eagle boxer briefs with the bananas on 'em waited for me at the sink. They were my favorite because they made me look like a gay Josephine Baker. I was ready to shake my shimmy.

I'd be lying if I said I didn't have any hesitation going into this. You never knew what somebody was gonna be like when you met face to face. They could be a weirdo for all I knew.

I wasn't on the app looking for love, but it'd be nice to find somebody to spend time with. When the man of my dreams came around, he'd better be open to every bit of love I had to give because when I loved, I loved hard. That's why I couldn't be a ho.

Hoes didn't fall in love with the first man who came their way.

When I opened the bathroom door, Jason and Cole were standing in the hall. "Y'all need the bathroom?" I asked.

"Nope," Jason shook his head with a grin. "Just making sure our roomie is set for his date."

"You should put on that Tom Ford cologne," Cole said. "You gotta seduce with him your fragrance."

"Puh-lease," I ignored him. "I don't wear Tom Ford on a first date. It's Issey Miyake time. Jason, how was set last night?"

"They kicked our butts. No surprise there," he sighed. "Just when we thought it was over, they took us to an empty field and made us exercise in the rain. I did more sit-ups and push-ups than I could count. The only reason we stopped is because the police drove by."

"Oh my god!" The situations those Theta boys put him through were getting more awful every week.

"So what'd you do?" Cole asked.

"We didn't say anything, but DP told them we were practicing for a track meet."

"Track practice? In a field at night? They believed that?" Cole said angrily. "If I can't wear your fraternity letters, how you gonna go around claiming the track team?"

"Relax Cole, it's not a big deal," Jason said. "There was a flashlight in our faces and we were almost put in handcuffs. At that point, we would've said anything not to get arrested. I promise I'm not gunning for your place on the team."

"Whatever bruh," Cole dismissed him. "Ay Tyree, what time you headin' out?"

"I'm supposed to pick him up at 8. He lives in Temple Terrace," I said.

"That's a drive from here," Cole said. "Shouldn't you be

gone by now? You don't wanna keep the man waitin'."

"Psssh! Don't rush me!" I swatted them away. "I gotta look my best. Even when I'm late, I'm worth the wait, don't you think?"

Jason laughed his ass off. "Okay, but you need to get out of here soon. We don't want your carriage to turn into a pumpkin."

"Don't be bitter. It's not a good look on you," I said, smiling. I reached to close the door, but Jason held it open.

"Boy, if you don't get out of this bathroom!" I said.

Once my outfit was on point and I had a splash of smell good on me, Jason and Cole walked me out the door. They acted like two parents sending their kid off to prom. All I needed was a corsage and a limousine to set it off.

"Bye! Make good choices!" Jason yelled as I opened the car.

"And don't come back with spots on your dick," Cole chimed in.

Ooh, they were gonna let me have it before I got five feet from the apartment! "See y'all later! Wish me luck!" I honked the horn and drove off.

It was a ten-minute ride to Will's apartment. When I pulled up, the first thing I noticed was how crusty looking the outside of it was. The building wasn't like the newer places you'd see in most of Tampa. To make matters worse, the dingy white apartment had an iron fence around it to keep away any ne'er-do-wells.

The man who walked out was the opposite of the broke down shack he lived in. Will was even hotter than his pics! His bulging arm muscles were bursting out of his striped shirt with the rolled up sleeves. His face was a work of art thanks to lovely bone structure. Will's hot chocolate skin and short afro topped everything off nicely. What I saw on my phone before was what was in front of me. Yes, gawd! I breathed easier.

"Wassup, why you late?" he said without so much as a hello.

"That's on me," I said. "I wanted to look good for you. Hi to you too."

"Sorry man. Thanks for pickin' me up," he settled into my passenger seat. "Been lookin' forward to this, that's all. Come here." He kissed me on the lips, then slipped his tongue in my mouth. He tasted like mint leaves and infatuation. The kiss went on for longer than it should have, but damn that felt good.

"Hmmm, that's wassup," he popped a stick of fresh gum in his mouth. "Are you as sweet as your kiss?"

"I might be," I said in my best seductive voice. "You keep it up and you'll see for sure. We still headed to IHOP?"

"Yep, 'bout to go at the pancakes. That okay with you?"

"Works for me," I said. I hit the gas and headed left down Bullard Parkway. There were IHOPs everywhere in Tampa, including one between our apartments. Out of the corner of my eye, I inspected the man who looked so damn good on the app. "It's nice to meet you in person."

"Yeah, you too. You were scared I was gonna look like a monster or somethin', huh?"

"No," I said. "But I'm glad you look halfway decent or else I might've sped off from your apartment with the quickness."

"I'm glad you didn't. You're lookin' sexy yaself," Will said, stretching the gum with his tongue. Ooh, this sweet talker was smooth!

"You always flirt with everybody like this?"

"Only you, baby."

This one was turning up the charm to its highest level. Will was forward for my taste, but cute enough for another date. We'd see how this all shook out. If anybody other than Jason or

Cole asked how we met, I would never tell them about Grindr or that our first date was at an IHOP. I wasn't gonna shade him for wanting to save money, but a restaurant with senior specials on the menu was so not classy. I'd say we strolled by the harbor under the moonlight. Something more romantic.

I'll admit that with some of the guys I talked to before, I fell head over heels within a few days of meeting them. It never ended well because they could only hide their flaws for so long. My hopes of finding my soulmate kept slipping through my hands.

Cole told me I should start a guy at 50 percent and work my way up rather than starting at 100 percent into 'em from jump. That was easier said than done. I was a visual person and if that body was saying something I liked, I would communicate right back.

I hunted for a parking space, but the lot for the IHOP was taken over by other people's cars. Pancakes must've been real popular tonight. I swooped past where everybody who came before us settled in and pulled into a strip mall next door. Not too bad. Most of the stores were closed, so there were lots of spaces close enough to the restaurant. All we needed to do was cross over a strip of grass that was taken over by high palm trees.

We both got out of the car and cruised across the lot to the entrance. Will opened the door and motioned for me to go in first. He was a gentleman too? Ooh yes!

The hostess showed us to a booth in the rear by the bathroom. "Sorry kids, all the other tables are full," she handed us menus. "Your server Diane will be right with you." She left for the entrance where other customers waited.

I'd never much favored sitting with my back to anybody's door. I never knew what was behind me and I didn't like surprises. Just in case some mess went down and I needed to run, I didn't want to break a heel in the process. I had to be on my toes living in Mississippi 'cause my neighbors were known to carry shotguns. Most folks thought Tampa was just a sleepy city in Florida, but anything could happen here too.

"So whatsup?" Will bit his lower lip.

"Nothin'. Sup with you?"

"Not a whole lot." Will scanned the menu. It looked like he was more interested in the food than me. I was tastier than anything written on there.

"Where you from?" he asked from behind the list of pancakes.

"Jackson, Mississippi, but I go to school in Tampa. What do you do?"

He unrolled the napkin from the paper wrapper. "I work at the nutrition store in the mall. The one on the second level by the food court." That explained the nice body. "I see y'all college boys comin' by the store. I be watchin' you."

"Why? You think we gonna steal somethin'?"

"Nah, I'm lookin' for who gets down. I'm tryin' to come home with somethin'." The waitress returned before I had a chance to ask him how his booty safari was going.

Diane set waters and straws on the table. Will was ready with his order: a steak omelet, a stack of blueberry pancakes and a lemonade. I ordered the Simple & Fit omelet with sauce on the side and a fruit salad. Gotta stay slim and trim. Diane wrote it out on her pad, scooped up our menus with a smile and headed off to get our drinks.

Will waited until she walked away to give me that sly smile again. "So what you get into?"

Every gay man on planet Earth, Mars and Jupiter too knew what that question meant: what sex position did I favor? Was I a bottom, top or vers? I wasn't giving him the info that easily.

"You mean like what do I do after school?" I said coyly.

"Naw, like whatchu get into? You a bottom?"

Angels in heaven! If I had pearls, I'd be clutching them! There was no being modest with this one!

"So you like big dicks?" he blurted out. My goodness, who didn't? But what kind of man asked that in public? The people in the booth behind him thankfully didn't hear what he said. An older man in a Jacksonville Jaguars sweatshirt and a woman I assumed was his wife went about their meal.

"I like pancakes," I maintained my composure.

"Hold on. Somebody is textin' me." Will held his phone under the table where I couldn't see it. Wait a minute. I owned an iPhone too and I'd know that chime anywhere. Was this boy on Grindr? Oh, hell no!

The waitress set two steaming plates of food in front of us. If she hadn't, I woulda snatched that phone away from him. "Anything else, guys?"

"No, that's it. Thank you, ma'am," I said.

Will stuffed the omelet in his mouth like it was his last meal on Earth. I watched in disgust as he chewed his food. Tiny pieces of egg fell in his beard. He finally came up for air long enough to ask me to pass him the hot sauce.

"I don't usually meet guys off Grindr," he said chomping away. Lies. "And I'm not lookin' for anything serious," he added.

"Yeah, me either," I said. More lies. Neither one of us told the truth and we knew it. That was the line the gays were supposed to say to each other so they came off as virgins pure as fresh snow instead of high-traffic slut pieces. With Will carrying on the way he was, I was almost ready to call it a night. I didn't because it was still possible that this was going somewhere.

"You have any favorite places to hang out in Tampa?" I asked, popping a grape in my mouth. Please say something good or me and this omelet were packing up and heading for the hills.

"I don't be around gay people like that. You won't see me at the clubs or nothin'."

And yet he was on Grindr. Spare me the down low act, sir. Also, that wasn't what I asked him.

"Soooooo what do you do then?" I persisted.

"Work. Go home. Not much else."

This boy was testing me. My patience and attraction for Will were running low. I started noticing other things about him: his yellowing teeth, the chest hair that looked like taco meat. And these one-syllable responses grated my nerves!

Despite my frustration, I wouldn't take leave from my proper manners. I couldn't walk out and leave him miles from his apartment. I set my sights on the last bit of omelet on my plate. I couldn't wait to text my roommates once this was over.

We were done with our meal, but Diane was missing in action. The hostess at the register was too far away for me to catch her eye.

"Damn, where she at?" Will said, losing his patience. I'd been lost mine. "If she doesn't come back soon I'm callin' the restaurant."

I dropped my fork to the table. "Please don't do that. It's so not necessary." This had better be a joke. Oh no. It wasn't. Will was looking up the number on his phone!

"Found it!" Just as the hostess answered the call, our waitress came back. Thank. God. He hung up and cheesed at Diane.

"Will that be it for you?" she asked. This woman had no idea what kind of fuckery this man was about to put her through.

"That's it," I said. "Can we get the check?"

Will thrust his empty cup in her face. "And more lemonade."
"Yes, sir."

Diane came back with our receipt on a black plastic tray. She set it down on the table next to Will's juice. "Take your time."

I waited for him to show courtesy and pick up the bill, but this fool looked the other way! He thought I was paying for this by myself? It was his idea to go out in the first place!

"Are we gonna split this?" I asked.

"You got it. I'ma go to the bathroom." Sure enough, Will jumped outta the booth, leaving me with the bill and two empty plates. I couldn't believe it! I had half a mind to leave him money for a taxi and dip out. But I wasn't the type to dine and dash. I handed Diane my debit card and smiled like I didn't wanna throw the container of butter pecan syrup at the bathroom door.

Will returned with a smirk like nothing happened. If this was his idea of a joke, I wasn't laughing. I signed the receipt. Almost forty dollars for everything. I waited until Diane cleared the table before I said a word.

"Can you at least pick up the tip?" I couldn't believe I needed to ask him that. He fished in his pocket and set three crumpled dollar bills on the table. "We good?"

This nigga here. That was it for me. I hustled out of the booth toward the parking lot. Where was my damn car? I didn't care if he was following behind me or not. If he wanted a ride home, he'd better catch up.

"That was delicious," he picked his teeth with his pinky. "I gotta come here more. How was your food?"

"It was great, thank you very much."

Will plucked a Black & Mild cigar from his pocket and prepared to light it in front of my face. He had to be kidding me! I sighed loudly. "Please don't smoke in my car!"

"You got it, baby." He tucked the cigar behind his dirty ass ear as we rounded the bend to where Candy was parked. We were the only car left on this side of the lot. I inspected my windshield for a ticket. Thankfully, there was nothing there. We got in and I slid the key in the ignition. I would drop Will off at home and be done with him forever.

He stopped me before I turned on the car. "Hold up for a minute. Let's talk."

I moved my hand off the key and gave him a thorough once-over. I had no words for this hooligan. He leaned over to slip his foul tongue down my throat.

"Excuse me!" I snatched myself back before he could get close enough to touch me. He could forget about getting any of this after that show he put on at dinner.

Will yanked me toward him so fast I bumped my bottom lip on his teeth. I tasted bitter blood oozing into my mouth. What was wrong with him?! While I contemplated what to do next, he slid his pants toward the floorboard and whipped his dick out of his gray Hanes underwear. The sound of him slapping it against his thigh made me cringe in horror. "Yo, come and get it."

"Get what? I don't know what you think this is—"

Will forced my head into his lap before I finished my sentence. He thrust his dick down my throat so hard that I couldn't breathe. The muscles that I admired when he first got in the car were used as weapons against me. The gearshift stabbed me in my chest as I tried to wrestle away. The sweet playboy act was gone. It was replaced by a growling savage with every intent of having his way with me.

"You little bitch. Ain't this what you wanted? Get this dick!" he hollered.

I did everything in my power to pull away from the pig, but his hands were clamped around me like a vise. My lungs cried out for relief. I gagged so hard that he loosened up his grip for a split second. It was enough for me to wiggle away from him and tumble out of the car.

"What is wrong with you?!" I yelled. My keys! I grabbed them and slammed the door in Will's face. The parking lot around us was dead quiet except for the hum of the traffic nearby. Was anybody seeing this? I hustled back toward the IHOP. Will barreled out of the passenger seat.

"Oh, you gonna run away, huh?" Will dove on top of me, causing me to lose my balance and hit the pavement. He rolled me over to face him. "Yeah wassup! You the one actin' like you don't want this!" he growled.

His fist connected with my jaw as he took his anger out on me. Fire engine red blood dripped from his lips. I swung wildly to avoid another blow to the head. I couldn't get off the ground because he was stronger than I was.

Will clawed at my upper body to keep me from getting away. My elbows dug into the gravel. Before he could drag me to the car, I jerked my legs back with all the strength I could gather and kicked him square in the gut.

"Aughhh, you piece of shit!" He clutched his stomach from the pain I sent his way.

"How you think that feels!" I screamed. I bolted away from the monster. He had lost his everlovin' mind! I raced out of the parking lot, around the median and past the lights of the IHOP. He screamed after me, but I was already sprinting down the block. I cut a quick left onto a dark side street and kept running until I couldn't move another step. I looked around to make sure he wasn't close. Will was nowhere in sight.

Every part of my body was in horrible pain. I could run away from Will, but not the bruises he so lovingly bestowed on me.

I slowed down to a brisk walk. I was in a residential neighborhood and I didn't want none of these white folks calling the police on me. I made it far enough away from Will that he couldn't catch up. I looked around in a panic to make doubly sure. There was no telling where he was. Thank God there were no streetlights out here 'cause I looked like a raggedy nightmare. I collapsed on the curb beneath a street sign.

I was frightened out of my wits. No matter how worn out or beat down I was I couldn't stay here. I somehow managed to keep my phone with me. My fingers fumbled as I dialed Cole's cell number. Please answer! Please!

"Hello?" he said distractedly.

I described the brawl with Will, the words rushing out of my mouth. I rattled off everything that I could remember, from the moment we stepped into the car to the fresh wounds I got from being dragged across the parking lot.

"He attacked you?" Cole said astounded. "What the hell is goin' on? Where are you?"

"I'll text you the intersection," I said between sobs. "*Please* come quick, Cole! I don't know where he is. I'm by myself and the car is at the IHOP. It's nobody out here but me."

"Okay, sit tight, Ty. We're on our way."

"Thank you! Please hurry."

I sat petrified on the curb. My phone shook in my hands. A mix of blood and salty tears dripped down my face and splattered on the cement below me.

I wanted to scream until I ran out of words, but I couldn't. My body shut down from the shock of Will's behavior. I got blindsided by a man that I thought had so much potential.

That act he pulled in the restaurant was disturbing, but I never could've known he would come at me in such a vicious way. I still felt his rough hands holding me down. All because I refused to have sex with him in my car in a parking lot.

I didn't deserve to be thrown around like a useless rag doll by him or anyone. For the better part of my life, I absorbed everybody else's cruelty toward me. Then I was the one who was expected to keep a level head. I had to exist for some other reason than to constantly suffer at the hands of other men. Sorrow and grief were heaped on me like dirt on a grave. Being buried six feet under would be far easier than having my happiness ripped away from me day after day.

Will should've just done me a favor and killed me. My time here on Earth was nothing less than damnation. If I was in actual hell, I'd at least know where I stood. Instead, I was surrounded by demons in disguise, hiding behind masks of sincerity.

What sounded like gunshots came blasting from a single-story house across the street. They were firing at me! No, that wasn't it. For once, I had nothing to worry about. It was the sound of dominos being slammed on a table. For a second I thought it was the shot to the head that I was craving.

The wild voices inside were having a good time playing their hands. That was supposed to be me tonight! I was supposed to be the one enjoying myself! Instead, I ended up laid out in a parking lot with a maniac on top of me. I coulda been at home in my bed reading a book or watching TV. Something other than watching the blood thicken in my trembling hands.

If I stayed in one place, it wasn't no telling who was gonna come around the corner. I got on my feet and circled the block, stumbling every couple of steps from having the wind knocked out of me. The fourth time I passed the intersection where I first laid out, a pair of headlights came shining down the street. For a second, I thought that Will somehow drove off in my car and was coming top speed in my direction. I readied myself to run the opposite way when I saw that it wasn't my Camry. It was a Ford Explorer.

Cole poked his head out the passenger window. "Tyree? Let's get outta here. Hop in the back."

I stumbled his way to inspect what was supposed to be my ride away from this nightmare. Jason sat patiently in the driver's seat.

"Who's car is this?" I said suspiciously. I didn't need not one more surprise.

"Worry about that later," Cole said. He got out, opened the back door and waved me in. "Here let me help you."

"Aah! Watch the elbow!" I screeched as he lifted me inside.

Cole closed the door carefully and directed Jason to drive off. He didn't budge. Jason was horrified when he saw that the upper half of me was splattered with blood.

"What did he do to you?" he exclaimed.

His reaction was enough to make me break down in tears again. "He grabbed me and tried to rape me in my car!" I cried.

"Rape? What a shithead!" Cole said angrily. "You wanna call the police?"

"And tell them that a bum I met on an app made me suck his dick in the parkin' lot of a IHOP? I'll pass, thank you. And who's car is this?!"

"It's a friend from school's," Jason said. "They let me borrow it to come get you. Where's your car?"

My stomach was in knots from the exhaustion. I rested my

head against the window. "It's back at the restaurant. I didn't have a chance to lock it, I ran outta there so fast. For all I know, he ripped out my car seats and is draggin' my carburetor down Dale Mabry Boulevard."

"We'll swing by to make sure it's safe," Jason said. "You didn't notice anything wrong with him when you met? Did he do anything suspicious?"

"Look, I don't know okay!" I snapped. "He didn't exactly have 'rapist' written on his forehead. What do you want me to say? That I sat there and let him slam my head into the pavement? I'm done talkin' about this, Jason! No more questions! Take me to my car so we can go home!"

I slumped in my seat and conjured up my own world where assholes like Will didn't exist. If I hadn't got away from him would he have decked me out there in the parking lot? I sniffed a few times to hold back my dripping nose and the anger I didn't get to take out on him. I held one hand in the other to keep them from shaking.

"I know you said no more questions," Jason opened his yap again. "But do you want to go to the hospital?"

"I'll be fine," I insisted. "Let's go get my car, please. Make a right here."

Jason pulled into the driveway of the restaurant and around the trees to where my car was parked. The doors were closed and Will was gone.

Before I budged, Cole inspected the shadowy strip mall to make sure Will wasn't hiding out. "Jason, you take the truck back to the apartment. I'll drive Tyree's car. Ty, who do you wanna ride with?" Without a word, I hopped out of the back seat and into the front next to Jason. The last place I wanted to be was the scene of the crime. There might as well have been a chalk outline around my car because I was dead inside.

Jason seemed to be in a rush when we filed into the apartment. "Guys, I have to go to set," he announced. "Tyree, are you sure you don't need anything?"

"Go 'head. I'll see you when you get back," I said. So much for friends standing by your side.

If all was right in the universe, it would've been me pledging instead of Jason. If I was a big fraternity man, people wouldn't mess with me. They'd think I was high and mightier than I truly was. I'd have a support system to back me up. Here Jason was going through the process that I wanted to do since the very first day I came to Morrison.

I dragged myself to the bathroom and shut the door behind me with the weight of my body. What a night. What a terrible, awful, completely messed up night. My elbows were bruised beyond recognition and my bottom lip was slit open. My back was dark red from the blood and dirt stains where I got dragged down. The more I took account of the damage, the more I cried.

I ran the hot water until the tub was filled halfway. I dumped whatever was left of my clothes in the trashcan. I let the water rise to my neck. My wounds burned like hellfire.

Time after time, I found myself chasing after men that were either deeply troubled or emotionally unavailable. They broke my heart but never tried to break my bones like Will. I wish I could say he was the first man to terrorize me.

My second year of high school, I went on a date with an older man named Charles. He worked as an assistant in the computer lab of my school. I was 16 then, but I told him I was 18. We would sneak away after my classes were over and ride down State Street in his Jeep. Afterward, he'd drop me off and wish me a good night. In the morning, I'd find he left a bottle or two of mocha Frappuccinos or a 100 Grand candy bar on my porch. He remembered that they were my favorites. It was the closest thing to romance I ever experienced.

He started out nice, but things went south after weeks of dating on the low. One time after a trip to see a movie, Charles parked the car outside my house. We gabbed on and on about which scenes were our favorites. He suggested we continue the conversation in my room. My father might be home, I told him.

I liked Charles, but I didn't wanna risk my daddy finding me fooling around with a male stranger. I don't care, he said. We won't make any noise. I felt like I couldn't say no so invited him inside. We'll just talk, I thought.

When I wouldn't give Charles the ass he so obviously came for, he stood up and cursed me out with the vilest words I'd ever heard. He went to strike me, but he saw me flinching in terror. He looked for something to throw instead. The man hurled one of my lamps across the room. It broke into pieces and so did my heart. Thankfully, he didn't lay a hand on me.

"Cock tease," he fumed as he stomped away. "And I know you're not 18."

I was incredibly depressed for months after that. When my daddy inquired as to why I was so down I told him I had a crush on a boy at school who didn't like me back. He gave me a whole lot of love and support but didn't press the issue.

My father checked in every so often to see if my crush came to his senses. The answer to that was, of course, no. It took time, but I forgot about Charles. I convinced myself it was just a one-time unfortunate ordeal.

I shuffled through our medicine cabinet until I found a Band-Aid and the Neosporin. I bandaged myself as best I could before returning to the living room. Cole was half-watching SportsCenter.

"Hey, bruh. You look better," Cole said soothingly. I threw a blanket over my shoulders and eased in next to him. The announcers on the TV were going on about a game-changing slam dunk. I wasn't interested in anything they had to say. My best bet was to occupy myself with the Black Enterprise magazine on the side table. Three successful Black faces smiled at me from the cover.

Cole sorted through our junk drawer. It was where we kept the knickknacks that didn't have a home elsewhere — paper clips, hand tools, take out menus, ketchup packets and the like. He pulled out a warm ice pack.

Cole tossed the lukewarm pouch into my lap. "I used this when I hurt myself at an indoor event last semester. It's no good to you right now 'cause it's not cold."

Then why did he bother to give it to me?

"Wait, don't count me out yet. Let me get you the next best thing." Cole came back from the kitchen with a Ziploc bag filled with ice cubes.

"Thanks," I said groggily. I gently pressed the bag against the tender skin on my elbow. "So you *do* know your way around the kitchen. That's new."

"If you thought that was impressive, you oughta see me sort the silverware. I got skills, bruh."

"That's a talent you can make money off of," I chuckled through my soreness.

Leave it to Cole to make me smile when I had no intention of doing so any time soon. No man except my daddy ever cared for me the way Cole did. He was my Superman tonight. I fought my instinct to cuddle up to him. Would he mind if I lay in his lap? I didn't doubt that he would. I pulled the blanket tighter instead.

"You feel like talkin' about what happened yet?" he asked. "I only got the overview on the phone."

"Mmm no. How 'bout we talk about our favorite sports teams," I said sarcastically.

Cole gently nudged me. "Hey, you could use some fresh air. You wanna ride with me to Walmart? I'm gonna get a few things for Spring Break."

I considered his invitation. It was better to be with a hardy Black man like Cole than alone with Will's destruction haunting me. I said yes with slight hesitation.

We had almost pulled up to the Walmart when I had second thoughts about going inside a grocery store. I was so preoccupied with my rumble with Will I forgot every time I went in that Walmart, I saw somebody from school. It wasn't too late for us to go home. I took a gulp and shook my head to clear out the anxiety. What did I have to lose at this point?

Any another night I woulda felt some kinda way about the guy skateboarding between parked cars with a 12-pack of Charmin under his arm. Same for the redneck in the camo trucker hat and Confederate flag shirt by the sliding doors. Clearly I was out of fucks to give tonight.

The automatic doors swished open. The blinding fluorescent lights hit me like a sledgehammer. I shoulda got sunglasses before we left the house. Every shopper in the market could see the cut on my lip. I reminded myself it wasn't the worst thing anybody ever saw in a Walmart.

"We need to come up with a signal in case we run into people we know," I instructed Cole. "If you see somebody who looks like they go to Morrison, I want you to holler 'hoo-dee-hoo!' I'll dive behind the collard greens in the produce section."

"Man, you crazy," he said, pushing an empty shopping cart. "I got you covered. Let's see, what aisle are people from Morrison least likely to be in? The book section?"

"Boy, don't play. I'll bet they're in the frozen food aisle 'cause at this hour weedheads like you be raidin' this place for the late night snacks."

"Wait, isn't that the dude from—"

"Who?" I ducked my head and swerved the cart into another aisle.

"Just keepin' you on your toes, bruh!" Cole howled. "You moved so fast it looked like a fire drill."

I playfully slapped him on his thick skull. "You shoulda seen how I hit it outta that IHOP parking lot. When I tell you I was leapin' over cars and small children to get away from there…"

"I bet," he grinned. "You can coach me for my next meet. Look, it's the frozen foods, your favorite section."

"You know me too well," I smiled.

I added a handful of Marie Callender's meals to the basket. At the next aisle over, Cole tossed in Chili Cheese Fritos, tortilla chips and ranch dip. I snagged bigger Band-Aids to patch me up. The cart filled up fast with groceries and other personal items I needed.

"I can give you a ride to the school infirmary tomorrow if you wanna get tested," Cole said. "I want you to be safe."

"It didn't go that far, but sure why not."

"It'll be good for you, Ty. Don't let that man bring you down."

"Oh, I won't."

"You gotta report him too. Puttin' aside how you feel, when you get down to what he did was criminal. You can't let him get away with it."

"I hear you," I sighed. "But it won't undo anything. I just wanna move on, Cole."

"I'm not gonna make you do anything you don't wanna do. But you don't want him trying that with anybody else."

"Yeah, but why does it have to be my cross to bear?" I said.

"It's your call. I'll support you no matter what." Cole scooped an oversized bouncy ball from the rack near the toy aisle. "Was the food good, though?" He bounced the bright pink ball to me.

"It was delicious. Thanks for asking." I tossed it back and smiled. Superman.

Cole may try to act hard, but he was just as playful as any of us. His personality was bright like the bouncy ball, even if he didn't always show it. That's what I loved about him. Unlike other people, the part of himself that he kept hidden was positive instead of terrifying.

Cole put the ball back in its cage. "Brace yourself, Tyree. I got another big question for you. Why you messin' with these roughneck dudes anyway?"

I grabbed the cart by the handle to stop us from walking any farther. "Who should I be shacked up with? A hotshot track star?" I teased. Cole chuckled. I dropped sunscreen in the cart.

"I don't think April would appreciate that," he laughed. "What you need is a bookworm. Somebody who can do your homework for you. Hold your books while you go to class."

"Who says I can't do all that by myself?" I retorted.

"I know you can. What I'm sayin' is you need somebody in your life that'll make you happy. Everybody has a soulmate out there somewhere."

"That may be true, but after tonight's freak show, I'm skippin' men altogether."

After we filled up on food and vacation necessities, we pushed the grocery cart over to the registers. As always, there was a long line and only one cashier. Walmart didn't ever change.

"Look, it's a lane open over there," Cole pointed. Sure enough, a girl turned on the light at the next aisle. I placed my groceries on the belt, swiped my card and put in my pin number. "Card Declined" flashed on the tiny screen.

"Yo card ain't workin'," the cashier said. I checked her name tag. Jamisha.

"Thank you, Jamisha," I said coldly. "Let me try again."

I gave it another swipe. Card declined. She sucked her teeth and exhaled her stank breath on my groceries.

"Damn it all to hell!" I screamed. I was so frustrated I almost heaved the grocery cart across the store. A line of impatient customers behind us watched me about to break down and cry in the Walmart. I had more embarrassment in the last 24 hours than I could handle. This was absolutely the worst night of my life.

"Whoa whoa I got you, Ty," Cole held my hand. "Put my groceries with yours and I'll take care of it."

Jamisha was unbothered by Cole's generosity or my hysteria. She scanned his groceries while Cole swiped his card through the machine. It was approved. "Thanks, Cole. I don't know what I'd do without you." I said.

"You'd do the same for me, bruh," he winked.

"Not anytime soon, I can't. I'm gonna go to the financial aid office tomorrow and see if I have money there."

"You don't hafta pay me back, Tyree. Just worry 'bout gettin' sleep."

I couldn't believe my card was declined last night. I checked my bank balance and sure enough my funds were *low*. I wasn't dead broke, but I had no business buying a cart full of groceries. At least I got my money right. The financial aid office gave me a fat refund check they'd been holding on to. It was almost a grand, enough for me to stash some away and get a bite to eat.

I sat in a black and red booth at Steak 'n Shake waiting for Jason and Cole to make their appearance. Dinner was gonna be on me tonight. It was my thank you to my roomies for rescuing me after that catastrophe with Will.

I never heard back from him. Not that I thought Will was gonna call seeing as I blocked his number and his profile on the app. Still, I couldn't get him off my mind. He was somewhere in this city. I was scared to death that I would run into him. I escaped him once and he wouldn't let it happen again if we came to face to face.

Keyshawn was an even closer threat since we had classes together. He was free to terrorize me after his pardon from Dean Simmons. The so-called administrator would say my punishment from Will was my fault too, same as Keyshawn. I wanted to vanish into thin air. Then, neither Will, Keyshawn nor the dean would be able to hurt me.

I let myself settle into the squishiness of the red vinyl booth.

Nothing like a strawberry milkshake to ease the mind. While I waited, I sipped from the glass and watched two elderly men and a family next to them chomping on burgers. If my roommates didn't come soon, I was gonna sneak in between those people and help myself to an onion ring.

As I considered how to go about feeding myself, April came bouncing through the entrance followed by Cole. The sweatpants she wore had a stain on the thigh and she was chewing gum like a baby cow. Cole looked fine as always in track pants and a silver Nike tank that hugged his upper body.

"Hayyyy Tyree!" April reached in for a hug like we were the best of friends. She squeezed me, but I barely touched her. Whatever food group that was dripping off of her better not have rubbed on me. If it did, I was gonna lay hands on the girl. Did Cole think I was paying for April too?

"So you got your money squared away?" Cole asked.

"Yep, dinner's on me. I'll pay you back for the groceries when we get to the house."

"I told you don't worry 'bout it, Ty. But I won't turn down a meal. Thanks, man," he said.

"Thank you, Tyree!" April hollered.

Looks like her meal was going on my tab too. If it was up to me, she wouldn't get nothing but ice water.

"We passed Jason when we were comin' off the bus stop," Cole said. "He told us he'd be here in a minute."

Cole pointed toward the Ford Explorer loitering outside. It was the same one they picked me up in yesterday. Jason angled his way into the window and was talking to somebody in the driver's seat. It was too dark to tell who it was. Look at him hoin' at the Steak 'n Shake.

After he wrapped up the conversation, Jason floated through

the door with a smile. My roommate was always a positive person but never this easy, breezy, beautiful.

Jason was keeping a secret. He was in the closet, so it wouldn't be the first. I thought we were cool! Whatever it was, he'd tell me when he was ready.

"Hey, guys! How are you?" he said.

"Not as good as you," I replied. "Who was that?"

"It was one of my line brothers. We have assignments we have to complete for set."

I shook a straw at him. "Were y'all talkin' about pledgin'… or somethin' else? You was givin' a good ole seduction lean into the car. Some people ain't got no shame!"

"Wooooooo!" April exclaimed.

Girl. Shut up. I could tease my roommate, but she couldn't. I wish April would keep her comments to herself.

"Can't I talk with someone without it being considered flirting?" Jason brushed me off.

"Yes, you can," Cole confirmed. "Don't let Tyree stop you from handlin' your business, Jason. You're a man who's got responsibilities to take care of. But you gotta tell us, what was goin' on out there?"

"Some things I'd like to keep to myself," Jason replied.

The waiter picked a grand time to come by our table. We rattled off our orders: a guacamole Steakburger and Diet Coke for me, a Frisco melt with onion rings for Jason and a 7x7 burger, vanilla milkshake and a plate of fries for Cole. April copied my style and asked for a strawberry milkshake too. Normally I'd have a salad, but I was in desperate need of comfort food. This wasn't the time to eat like a rabbit.

"Don't think you're gettin' off that easy, Jason," I said. "Spill the tea, gurl. Do the Thetas know you're on Team Rainbow?"

"No and I'm not going to tell them, even if they ask," Jason said resentfully. "Please don't feel obligated to inform them either."

"Don't you think they're eventually gonna find out?" Cole pressed. "Let's say you're at a frat party. They ask you why you not tryna get at any females. Whaddyu say?"

"The truth. I don't see any women I'm interested in."

I coughed loudly at his vague answer. "Here's what you do," I said. "Tell 'em you're on a diet and you're allergic to fish. Tacos make you queasy."

"You guys give him a break," April said. "Are you out of the closet, Jason? Personally, I thought you were straight until Cole told me what the real story was. I haven't seen you with any guys on campus."

"You won't see him around girls either," Cole noted. "Except for Tasha."

"And we're just friends," Jason said. "Some people think we're together. I don't say anything that would make them think otherwise."

Our waiter set down the milkshakes and a tray of piping hot food. April snatched Cole's cherry from his shake and popped it in her mouth.

"This is what the doctor ordered," I said as I dug into my meal. The burger spoke to my soul. The grease dripping down my chin was like holy oil anointing my spirit.

While Cole ate, April lavished him with sloppy kisses on his cheek. It was enough to make my stomach turn. Steak 'n Shake was not their personal bedroom! I couldn't stand how she flaunted Cole in front of me. Whether she did it on purpose or not, April was about to get checked. She better get her grubby paws off my roommate.

I put a stop to their public display of digestion. "Cole, how you got a track meet next week and you eatin' this greasy food?"

He washed down a fry with a sip of his shake. "I don't put on weight 'cause I wear it out in the gym," he said confidently. "It's not a problem if I go off my diet once in a while. What matters is that I hit it when I'm on the track. Anyway, my body's rock solid. Ain't that right, baby?"

"Yes Coley-cue," April kissed him. She stuffed one of his fries in her mouth.

"Besides, it's my cheat day," Cole grinned.

"Mine too," Jason said.

"Every day's your cheat day, Jason."

Oh no, he didn't. "Cole, you put the 'hater' in heterosexual," I said.

"And you put the 'ho' in homo," he laughed.

As long as I'd known Jason, he was always self-conscious about his body. I didn't understand it. He wasn't anywhere close to being fat. Had he seen those big Southern boys bulldozing their way through the campus?

Jason spent a lot of time staring at himself in the mirror or comparing himself to other men. I felt where he was coming from. With Cole and his super-sized muscles in the house, who wouldn't have a mental complex? If I didn't have a slim European waistline myself, I would've lost my mind too.

"I might be eatin' this burger but I'm bringin' body to Spring Break," I announced. "Now er'body got gas money for the trip, right? If not it'll be me and my lovely vehicle Candy ridin' by ourselves to the city."

"You rich now pahtna," Cole laughed. "Don't worry. We got our money. The tank'll stay full."

"How can you guys afford a hotel?" April bogarted her way into the conversation. "Tyree, I get you're paying for dinner, but none of you have Miami Beach money! Did you rob a bank or something?"

She laughed like a wild hyena. Bitch, what? I folded my arms and stared at her until she stopped her incessant cackling. Why did I put up with her troll ass? My financial matters were none of her concern.

I didn't bother to look in her direction. "For your information April, my daddy travels a lot," I said. "He has reward points at the Sheraton. We're gonna use 'em to stay there."

"Oh okay, that's cute. How many beds?" she asked.

None of your damn business, ho!

"Jason and I will share a bed and Cole can have his own," I growled.

"Interesting. Well, I can't go because I have to work, so you guys have fun."

Nobody invited your sloppy ass!

"I'm gonna miss you, Cole," April fawned over him. "Don't forget to text me while you're down there."

Not if I could help it. I'd toss Cole's phone in the Atlantic Ocean before I let him spend our vacation talking to this trick.

"Have you guys been to Miami before?" April asked us. She was unaware of the ass whooping she was fixin' to catch.

Everybody shook their head no except for Cole. "I did once back in high school. Me and the track team went there for a meet. We didn't get to see much of the city."

"And you have a meet when we get back," Jason added.

"Right. It's the finals for the MEAC. The last meet of the season. Coach is puttin' the pressure on me. I gotta step it for the team."

"Speaking of," I paused for effect, "Tell us. What's it like bein' in a locker room with all those *men*?"

"Bul, why you gotta play with me like that?" Cole smirked. "We in there washin' up after practice, not suckin' each others' dicks. That's my lady's job." April puckered her lips and tickled him playfully. Get a damn room!

"But yeah fam, I gotta set personal records at this meet," Cole said. "Marshall's givin' me shit because I've been fallin' behind my times in the 400-meter relay. The fellas are talkin' about me when they think I'm not listenin'. They're saying how I'm gonna bring the team down. Marshall is the only one besides Coach who says it to my face. He thinks he's the leader of the team."

"So you guys really don't get along then?" Jason asked.

Cole stared at the table. "Nope. I wish he would transfer to Florida State. Then I wouldn't have to deal with him. Marshall likes to hear himself talk. If he wasn't ragging on me, it'd be another man on the team. Enough about him. Jason, how'd you get a break from pledging? I'm surprised they let you go for a week."

"The campus will be vacant and DP wanted to leave town just like every other student," Jason said. "You won't hear any of us on the line complaining about it. But when Spring Break's over, everything will be back to normal."

"How long you been on line now?" Cole asked.

"Too long."

Jason looked so defeated it made my heart cry. I understood that it was his choice to continue pledging, but it didn't make his suffering any less tragic.

I planted a kiss on his head. "Don't you worry about it, boo. When we're down in South Beach you can work on your tan so it's as dark as your ass."

"Thanks Tyree," he smiled weakly.

COLE

I almost fell over carrying Tyree's big ass suitcase out to the car. This jawn was almost taller than I was and heavy as shit. "What the hell's in this thing?" I asked him.

Tyree set grocery bags with Little Debbie snack cakes in 'em into the trunk. "Don't you worry 'bout that, Cole. I gotta be prepared!"

That was his way of saying he had 15 different swimsuits, a tank top in every color, 12 pairs of sandals and enough sunscreen to cover the city. It took me 20 minutes to pack. It took him two hours. He liked his options. I dropped the suitcase in the trunk on top of mine.

"Careful, watch out for the food," Tyree cautioned. "We got the snacks and the suitcases. The hotel reservations are on my phone. What else? Jason, you got everything?"

"Hold on, let me check." Jason peered through the car windows and patted his pockets. "I probably forgot something, but I likely won't remember what it is until we're on our way. Oh, I stopped by SunTrust bank to get traveling money. Do you guys need to go to an ATM before we leave?"

"I'm good," I said as I opened the passenger door to Tyree's ride, Candy. I never got over him picking that name for his car. "Does anybody need to use the bathroom before we go? I got empty bottles back there if you need 'em."

"That's nasty," Tyree cringed, "but good to know in case we get stranded in the wilderness. Thank you for your thoughtful preparation, Cole."

"You're welcome, bruh," I laughed.

"I locked the door unless one of you needs to get back in the apartment," Jason said.

Tyree did one final inspection. Everything was good. He ceremoniously closed the trunk. "I think we're good to go! Let's hit the road, boys. It's 3 p.m. If we get outta here now, we can get to Miami by 7."

Tyree jumped behind the wheel. I rode shotgun. Jason lounged in the backseat, playing a game of Scrabble on his phone. I'd counted down the days until Spring Break. Also, it was my first road trip with the boys in the two years since we met. You had to trust a person if you were gonna ride in the car for four hours together. We were that tight.

"Somebody turn on the white lady so we can figure out where we're goin'," Tyree said. A few taps on my phone and we had directions to Miami Beach.

"Follow the signs for 75 South," the GPS instructed.

"And we're off!" Tyree squealed. "Cole, can you put on music for us? And none of that white boy mess Jason be listenin' to."

"What's wrong with my music?" Jason asked.

"I can't deal with no Maroon 5 or Coldplay mess while we're drivin' down there. This is a party!"

"Tyree, how can you be sure that you don't like Maroon 5 if you don't listen to them?" Jason said. "You should give them a try."

"Oh, don't think I'm not a man of the world," Tyree replied. "I heard enough of their music to know I don't wanna be served a loaf of Wonder Bread on this trip. When I drive, we listen to what I want. When you're in this seat, you can play Maroon 5 to your heart's content and I promise I won't say anything."

"Sounds good to me," Jason said with satisfaction.

"And by the way, you're never drivin' my car."

We heard that rule enough times before to know he wasn't kidding. We could borrow Tyree's car whenever we wanted. If he was in it, he would always be behind the wheel. No need to ask. We joined the other cars speeding down the freeway. I looked for music to put on that both of the boys would like. Raekwon? Nah too hard. The Roots? Too laid back. I had to put on something they could ride to. Their version of "hard."

Jason finished out his Scrabble game. "Tyree, you say you don't like that music, but I'll bet you're going to end up marrying a white guy one day. You'll both live in a house by a river where you'll sip vodka tonics and listen to the dulcet tunes of Celine Dion."

"I don't mind," Tyree huffed. "If he puts the house in my name, sure. I'll take a splash of cream in my morning coffee."

Jokes aside, I couldn't imagine Tyree getting with a white boy. My roommate loved Black men. The darker, the better. "Nubian kings" he called 'em. Unless something changed, I didn't think the swirl was going down anytime soon. Not unless the man had Bill Gates' money or looked like Channing Tatum.

I pushed play on the songs I kept just for Tyree: Trina, Lady Gaga, Diana Ross, Karen Clark Sheard, Patti LaBelle. His "divas." I'd been on enough car rides with these boys to know what would get them going.

The first song was a Big Freedia joint Tyree loved. It was the New Orleans bounce music that turned the energy to 100. They got into it right away. Both of them were poppin' in their seats as we drove a cool 60 miles per hour down the highway. "It's Big Freedia! The queen diva!" the supersonic voice repeated. The rhythm had me throwing 'bows too.

The next song was a chill R&B cut. It was probably for the best 'cause these boys were gonna twerk their way outta the car.

"It's our first road trip together! You guys excited?" Tyree asked.

"I am," I said. "You gotta tell your pops thanks for us."

"Oh, I told him. He said to have fun and be safe."

"It's good to leave school behind for a while," Jason poked his head between our seats. "I want to see a new place and meet different people."

Tyree agreed. "Jason, do you like goin' to Morrison? I never asked you straight out."

"Totally! The professors know our names and sometimes the personal challenges we're facing. It's like everyone who works on campus wants me to succeed. Even the cafeteria ladies say hello to me every day. I have you guys to count on, but if I didn't, I'd never believe for a second that I was going through college alone."

"Besides the issue with the dean, I'm with you," Tyree said as he switched lanes. "I love that the school is so small, half the campus knows your life story. But it's what you said, people care."

"You need to be worried if they're not talkin' about you," I said.

"You ain't never lied," Tyree snickered. "So what about you, Cole? Is Morrison what you thought it was gonna be?"

"For the most part. I'm with Jason. I didn't think the professors would be so friendly. They give us more assignments than we can handle sometimes, but I also feel like we could kick back and play Xbox with 'em. The other cool thing is my classmates are smart. They got school spirit too. A few months into my first semester I realized I was the only person at Morrison who didn't own a MSU T-shirt."

"And now you have like eight of them," Jason counted on his fingers.

"Probably more than that," I said. "I do wonder how it woulda been if I went to a white school. I'm not sayin' I have regrets about comin' to Morrison, but it's always been at the back of my mind."

Jason propped himself between us. "I applied to a few places that weren't HBCUs, though going to a black college was never one of my top priorities. It came down to money. Every school I applied to offered me a scholarship to come. Morrison presented the biggest financial aid package. I couldn't turn down something so generous."

"Did you ever get a chance to visit the campus before you said yes?" Tyree asked.

"No, I visited other campuses but my first time seeing Morrison was the first day of school. Nevertheless, I'm glad I came," Jason said. "The food in the cafeteria could use work. I've gained ten pounds from the grease they serve us and this is coming from someone who grew up in Georgia."

"Speakin' of food, I'm hungry," Tyree stretched out his

hand. "Jason, pass me a honey bun from back there. When we get to Miami I gotta do better. I want a Cuban sandwich. Ooh, Jamaican food too. I wonder if they have curry goat?"

"Yeah, you are hungry bruh," I said. I was daydreaming about my next meal too.

At Morrison, I discovered food I never heard of before. The thing about living in Florida was there were more people from the islands than I'd ever met in Philly. Jamaicans, Trinidadians, Haitians, Virgin Islanders, Bahamians, every part of the Caribbean was represented.

My roommate freshman year before I met Jason and Tyree was from the Bahamas. His boys would come through our room to hang. They said they were speaking English, but I couldn't understand a word of it. Keeping up with their accents was a struggle. The more I hung around them, the more I picked it up.

My roommate and his crew used to take me to the island parties where they had good ass food. Callaloo, conch, jerk chicken, whitefish, goat stew and spicy dishes I never tasted before. I was a long ways away from cheesesteaks. Sometimes the Jamaican Club would get up with the other Caribbean students to bring foil pans of food out to the yard. You could get a nice meal for five bucks a plate.

I could never forget the first time I ordered a curry chicken sandwich. They put a whole chicken breast, bone and everything, on a piece of white bread. Then they drowned it in sauce from a squeeze bottle. I didn't know how to eat it. Everybody behind the table busted out laughing at how confused I was.

"Try it nah man," my roommate said. "You go like it." He was dead on. It took work to get it down, but it was one of the best things I ever ate.

The opening piano and horns of Jennifer Hudson's "Love You I Do" came through the radio. I forgot the "Dreamgirls" soundtrack was on my phone. It wasn't my type of music. It was another one of those tracks I kept for Tyree. He didn't waste any time turning it up. My roommates' over-the-top singing made me laugh my ass off. "Y'all are so gay!"

"You better believe it, boo!" Tyree said.

Jason and Ty watched that movie about 30 damn times. First thing in the morning, after dinner, whenever the feeling struck them. Even with my door closed and headphones on I could hear them ripping those songs apart. Jason would never do that outside the house. Tyree wouldn't hesitate to sing the soundtrack and dare somebody to say something to him.

"Ay Tyree, you ever done the drag queen thing?" I asked. I turned the music down.

"I thought about it, but I'd rather leave it to the professionals. I'm too masculine to be wearin' makeup and heels. I'm trade boots, hunny."

"What does that mean?" I asked. I couldn't keep up with his lingo.

"Know this: I got high levels of testosterone and an Adam's apple that won't quit. Also, I'm not tuckin' my penis away for nobody. No ma'am Pam, not with a honey-baked ham."

I didn't know if I believed him. With some encouragement, we could probably convince him to get dressed up for one night. Everything Tyree did was a show. It wouldn't be that much of a stretch for him. I wanted him to put his same energy into driving. We were moving too slow. There was a giant red F-150 truck creeping on our tail. A line of cars was behind it. We'd never get to Miami in good time if he kept it up.

"Bruh, put some weight on that gas pedal. You see we

holdin' up traffic, yeah?" I said.

"I'm doin' 75!" Tyree eyed the speedometer. "If they wanna break the law they can go around me."

"Yes, try to keep it under 80," Jason said. "The city will still be there when we arrive."

It was Tyree's car. Let him do what he wanted. I wasn't much of a driver anyway. Before I went to high school, my mother did all the driving for the family. She would pick me up from school. We would talk about our days. How work was going for her. If the family needed a break from South Philly, we cruised up to Atlantic City. I missed that. Once I got a bus pass our time together in the car didn't happen as often.

The sky was clear, but up ahead smoky clouds were coming at us fast. Sprinkles hit the windshield like pellets out of a BB gun. Streaks of rain came out of nowhere and pounded the car. The rumbling of thunder had us shook. Another mile in and it rained so hard it was like Armageddon outside.

I rolled up my window to keep the spray from other cars from getting on me. The traffic slowed down to a crawl. Blinking hazard lights switched on. For a while, they were the only thing we could see through the bands of rain. The wind was so powerful it almost pushed our car off the road.

"Can you drive in a storm?" I elbowed Tyree.

"I can handle anything Mother Nature throws my way," he replied.

The rain disappeared as quickly as it came. The sky was back to being its normal baby blue. A few of the leftover clouds didn't get the message that the storm was over. Other than that, we were good. That was typical Florida weather there. Always unpredictable.

Jason rolled down his window to enjoy the sunshine. "I hope

it doesn't rain in Miami too," he said.

The weather app on my phone said it was 84 degrees. "We'll be aight."

The thunder and lightning brought excitement to the trip. Without the weather coming at us hard, the car ride started to get boring. I fiddled with my iPod to keep myself interested.

"Hey, we should play a game," Jason sat up. "Like 'I Spy' or find license plates from each of the 50 states."

That was too lame for me. "Y'all go 'head. I'm gonna rest my eyes," I said. I wanted to catch a nap before the fun got started.

Who was honking the damn horn? I woke up to Tyree beating on the steering wheel at the other cars in traffic. I wiped the spit from the corner of my mouth. My man was going through trouble.

"You want me to drive?" I asked groggily.

"Ha! What's up, sleepyhead? Thanks, but we're almost in Miami. Get into it," he pointed at the road signs ahead. Sure enough, we were less than five miles away from the city. I could hardly sit still waiting for us to get there.

I stretched my arms and admired the sunset drifting over the water. The sky went from sunny blue to warm shades of orange, pink and navy. Up ahead, the neon lights of the Miami skyline called to us. We made it!

Touching down in South Beach was like driving into the livest street party ever. Wall-to-wall people cruised the avenue. They were having the best time of their lives. Latin music and warm air blew through the palm trees lining the street. On either side of us were hotels the color of rainbow Skittles. In front of them were sidewalk cafés crowded with people eating and laughing. A good number of 'em were sipping on drinks the size of skyscrapers. That's what I wanted to get on!

We drove five miles per hour along with the other cars creeping down the street. There were Mercedes, Lambos, Corvettes and more! They were *ballin'* out here. Everybody was doing the same thing we were — watching the beautiful people go by. I poked my head out of the car to get a better view of the Miami females.

Instead of beach bunnies, a group of gray-haired old ladies in way too small bikinis walked past us. I popped back in the car with more speed than I ever put on the track.

"See, that's unnecessary!" I said in horror. "Why do they hafta be out here like that?"

"I thought you loved good-looking women." Jason chuckled.

"Not senior citizens! I'm lookin' for dimes, not these Social Security broads. We need to find mamis who are gonna turn the party out."

"Like these girls here?" Tyree asked.

Man oh man! A group of curvy Latinas made their way past the intersection. They basically had dental floss on. Their swimwear was so tiny it barely covered their golden, glistening titties. The girls were more enticing than anything I saw in Tampa *or* Philly. This was the sexiness we came to Miami for.

I went to thank Tyree for pointing them out, but he was focused on something else. I should've known me and the boys were looking at two different things. They were out here eyeballing this musclehead in a small yellow tank on the left side of the street. He had diesel arms and tree trunk legs coming out of green camo shorts. He had the gay G.I. Joe swagger on lock.

Tyree's body was almost completely out of the window. "Hey, you shol' is sexy! Look at him all oiled up and stuff. Hey boo!"

The cars behind us beeped their horns to tell us to keep going. Tyree wasn't paying 'em any mind. The only reason he sat in his seat was for the five more dudes on the next block up. There were gym rats on every part of the street. I lost count of the juiced up brothas floating down the street like Macy's Thanksgiving Day Parade balloons.

"Tell me we're goin' to a straight club at some point," I sulked. "I don't wanna be in gay bars the whole time we're here."

"There are ladies in the gay club," Tyree said. He knew more than anyone there wasn't a woman within a mile of a gay club. If that was the situation, they were either interested in other females or I had to pat 'em down first to make sure they weren't packing more than I was. I loved my roommates, but I needed to see pussy on this trip.

Jason laid out a solution. "How about this: tonight the three of us go to a gay club. Tomorrow we can go to whatever club you want, Cole."

"I'm down for that," I said. That was a relief.

"Cole, do you need to meditate before we go out?" Tyree asked. "I don't wanna see you goin' buckwild if one of these boys wants to get your number again. It's not they fault you cute."

I rolled my eyes so he could see my disgust. "Tyree, I came to relax. Nobody's 'bout to make me come outta pocket tonight."

We pulled into the hotel driveway. A doorman in a white uniform was there ready to usher us in. "Welcome to the Four Points Sheraton," he greeted us. The temperature outside the car was tropical. Vacation weather. The Sheraton was low-key compared to the other hotels we drove by. It was like somebody's mansion.

"This is nice!" Jason said. He was already out of the car and heading to the lobby. He jumped for joy as he looked around.

"You guys get the suitcases. I'll go check in," Tyree said. He dashed to the entrance, leaving me and the doorman behind. I gave Jason a moment to soak it in before I yelled for him to come back. We got as many bags as we could carry. The rest we left in the trunk while Tyree wrapped up at the front desk.

"Let's hit it to the room boys," Tyree said, handing us both a key card. We towed the suitcases into the elevator and down the long carpeted hall. We were ready to kick off our Spring Break! "This is us. Room 506."

Jason was first inside. He dropped everything at the door and flopped on the bed closest to us. "It was fun riding with you guys, but I am so glad to be out of that car!" He wasn't the only one.

The hotel room was on point. The blue walls and white bedspreads gave it an ocean feel. It was dark outside, but I could see the lights from the beach shining on the other side of a tall hedge.

"Cole, you can have the bed by the window," Tyree said. "Jason, we'll bunk together in this one. If you come with me to get the rest of the bags, we can pick up somethin' to eat while we're out."

"I'ma stay here," I said. "Can you get me some food too? Nothin' too heavy. I don't wanna be full when we go out." Tyree and Jason agreed. They left me alone in the room.

I stepped on the narrow balcony to look at the stars. The sky was mostly pitch-black. I wanted to light up a J to celebrate the end of our trip. I decided to sip on something instead. I filled a Solo cup with the Smirnoff and pineapple juice stashed in my bag.

Finally, time to myself. This was the most peace I had in a while. I was constantly in the apartment with my roommates. When they were out, April was over. The volume at our place was always high because of the rowdy conversations.

Still, it didn't come close to how hype the dorms were. Every other night there was a party going on in somebody's room. The fellas were always yelling when they came down the hall — sometimes at 3 a.m.

One time freshman year, I was studying for my English class when one of the guys pulled the fire alarm. Water flooded everywhere. They turned the hallway into a Slip 'N Slide. It was fun, but those interruptions killed my concentration. I swirled the ice cubes in my vodka and pineapple. Never mind. It was too quiet. I reached for the remote to cut on the TV.

"Adult movies! Right at your fingertips," a sexy voice announced.

Folks were still buying hotel room porn? They hadn't heard of the internet? I could have 15 different Ebony videos lined up on my phone in five minutes if I wanted to. I flipped through the channels until I got to a rerun of Real Diva Housewives of something or the other on BET.

If Coach saw me lounging around watching reality shows, he'd kick my ass, then make me run ten laps. I wondered what Marshall was up to? Putting in time at the gym, no doubt. I should see if the hotel had an exercise room or something. Nah, fuck that. I was gonna take it easy this week.

"Knock knock! We're back!" Tyree and Jason came in carrying white plastic bags and the rest of our suitcases.

I got excited when I saw our dinner. "Wassup? What y'all get me?"

"Chicken wings from the restaurant up the street!" Jason said. He set a Styrofoam container on the desk. "There's a liquor store next to it so if we need to refresh our supply we're covered. There's also a lot of places to eat around here."

Tyree did a dance while he chewed on a saucy wing. "We were gonna go to this pizza place that was smellin' delicious, but it was crawling with people. No complaints though 'cause this is gooder than a mug."

Jason inspected the open bottle of Smirnoff on the desk. "Looks like someone got started without us."

"Yeah, I couldn't wait on you boys too long," I said. "Go ahead and have some."

Jason poured a swallow of vodka in his soda cup from the restaurant. We sat together on the bed watching Tyree shake his ass like he was in a music video.

"Cole, when you get a chance you should go down to the lobby," Jason said. "There's a bar where girls are hanging out and a basketball game was playing on the TVs. That's totally up your alley."

"I'm good. Plus, the liquor in here is paid for. I'm saving my money for food and entertainment."

"Same here," Jason sipped from his cup. "I'm doing by best to leave Miami with more than lint in my pockets. What do people do in this city do besides drink and lie by the water?"

"Party. Find somebody to go home with," I said.

"Is that your plan for tonight?"

"I don't have a plan. Wherever the streets of Miami take me is where I'm goin'."

"Cheers to that," Jason said. We raised our cups.

It took Tyree a good 45 minutes to get ready. He put on a brand new Miami Heat basketball jersey. That jawn was so small and tight it looked like it came from Kids Foot Locker.

"You don't even like sports," I laughed. "Do you know who plays for the Heat?"

"No, but that don't mean I can't *look* like I watch sports," he said. "I might snatch me a Miami ball player, so I need you to holla if we run into one of 'em. Hook a brotha up. So do I look like trade?" He spun around to show off the outfit.

"If you're trade, then I'm the president of the United States," Jason said.

"Hello, Mr. President! Happy Birthday!" Tyree cooed in an affected sultry voice.

I dug through my suitcase to find a pair of sneakers to wear. "Aight you two. Let's get it together so we can make it to the club before the party's over."

"And don't forget we need to get gas," Jason said.

Tyree smothered lotion on his arms. "Jason, we not in danger, girl. The tank is not that low. Let's get the gas *after* the club. I don't want to go in there smellin' like pump number one."

We took our places in the car and drove toward Downtown Miami. Coke-white yachts in the canals pointed the way. Glass skyscrapers whizzed past us we got closer. The vibe of the area was different from South Beach. It was more of a real city than the Disney World we were staying in.

By the time we got to our destination it was almost midnight. There was no sign on the building we were headed to, just a door with one floodlight over it. Two bouncers in black suits were posted against a brick wall. There was a velvet rope next to them for people to line up. No one stood in it. What was going on? It looked sketchy as fuck.

"This is it?" I frowned.

"Yep, this is the place," Tyree said. "Club Cakes on

Northwest 26th Street. Don't worry! All the best gay clubs look like abandoned fallout shelters from the outside. This is gonna be fun!"

Here we go again. I felt bad about how I acted last time I went out with Tyree and Jason to the club. I thought I'd be able to keep it together. I was wrong. Having dude pushing up on me brought me out of my element. I shoulda taken it as a compliment and walked away. I would be on my best behavior this time. I wasn't planning on getting carried out by security again.

April's name popped up on my phone. It was a long text. I didn't bother to see what it said. If I was doing this club thing, I didn't want a picture of April in my head.

The security at the door checked our IDs, then pointed us down a dark hallway. At the end of it was a chocolate girl with braids sitting in a booth with a cash register. A muffled Jay Z joint played on the other side of a dark curtain.

The big posters on the wall advertising the coming events caught my eye. Every one of 'em was dominated by a ripped Black man with a greasy body. The gay dudes that passed this way probably studied every detail of the poster boys.

Tyree tapped me on the shoulder. "It's never guys that look like that in the club. You show somebody sexy on the ad and they got you like a worm on a hook. Hurry up, where your money at?"

I handed the cashier a $20 bill. She gave me my change and a neon green wristband. I did a double take when I walked through the curtain. There were only ten or so people in the place. Music and laser lights were going, but the club was a ghost town.

"See, you was rushin' us and there's nobody here," Tyree said.

"That means we have the club to ourselves!" Jason cheered. "We can drink until the party starts."

The DJ warmed up the room with uptempo R&B tracks from the 90s. The hot party starters would come later. Behind the counter of the bar was this sexy female bartender. She reminded me of the Latina chicks we saw on the beach earlier.

Her hair was dyed blond; she had a diamond nose ring and the biggest titties I'd ever seen on a girl with a small waist. I could see through her thin wifebeater shirt. She didn't have on a bra and both of her nipples were pierced. Damn, it was like that in Miami? My new wifey was busy cleaning glasses and setting bottles of liquor on the shelves.

Tyree strained his voice above the music to get her attention. "Excuse me, miss. What time do people usually arrive at your lovely establishment?"

She finished wiping down a glass. "Hey boys, we're open 'til 6 a.m., so most people don't show up 'til 1 or 2."

"Oh girl!" Tyree gasped. "That late? This is definitely not Tampa!"

"You're from out of town? Welcome! We're glad to have you," she and her nipple rings exclaimed.

Focus, Cole. Concentrate on her light green eyes, the curve of her mouth when she talked, the hair that caressed her shoulders. Anything but her tits. She's gonna think you're a perv. "What's your name?" I asked, moving closer to her.

"Whatchu need to know that for?" she said playfully. "It's Bianca. What's yours since you're asking questions?"

"My name's Colin, but everybody calls me Cole. You got a man, Bianca?"

"I do not. But the way you're talking you sound like you're straight."

"That's because he is," Jason volunteered.

"If you like girls what are you doing here?" she asked.

"Yeah, Cole," Tyree said accusingly. "Why are you in this club flirtin' with this lovely young lady when you have a *girlfriend* at home?"

Bianca wasn't bothered by Tyree's interference. She moved closer to me, resting her tits on the counter of the bar. "I'm here to serve you drinks, papi. Not fall in love. Unless you give me a nice tip then I'm yours."

I had a tip for that ass.

"How about shots, guys? On the house." Bianca poured Patrón Silver into four small glasses. She slid them to us.

"Oh, no thank you, I don't drink," Tyree said, backing away from the bar. "The only alcohol that's comin' anywhere near me is communion wine and that's just grape juice and prayer. I'll have a Shirley Temple, please."

"How about you take this shot and I'll have a Shirley Temple for you after you're done." Bianca handed him the tequila.

"Mmm-mmmm, gurl! You wanna get me liquored up so somebody can snatch my booginity! You ain't right!"

"Just this once, Tyree?" Jason pleaded. "It's a special occasion. We can toast to my freedom from set."

"All this peer pressure! I can't stand it," Tyree said, shaking his head. "Bianca, you see what they do to me?"

"It's okay! See, I'm having a shot with you." She raised a glass.

The four of us pounded them down in one swallow. Tyree looked like he just went a couple rounds in a boxing ring. Not bad though for a man who didn't drink. I put two singles in the tip jar on the counter.

"Gah! You lucky I like you, Bianca," Tyree said.

"I like you too, papi," she winked. "Here's your Shirley

Temple. You guys want a real drink?"

"Two whiskey sours, please," Jason said.

She mixed up the drinks for us. Jason got one cherry. She dropped three in mine. "Enjoy! Come back when you're ready for a refill. I'm sure I'll see *you* later," she said, raising a perfectly arched eyebrow at me. My dick twitched in response.

"You see the cushions on that girl?" I elbowed Jason as we walked away.

"Bianca liked you, Cole. She almost gave you the entire jar of cherries."

Tyree stopped suddenly. "But she forgot to put one in my Shirley Temple! I'll be back." He ran to the bar while me and Jason scoped out the club.

Some fellas on the dance floor were getting it in to a Biggie remix. The rest sat on carpeted benches along the walls soaking in the atmosphere. Tyree came back, satisfied with the fresh cherry in his soda. We hung near the center of the club and watched people coming through the curtain ready to party.

The guys were mostly Black and Latino, but there was a different kind of diversity. There were both masculine and feminine dudes. A good number wore the minimum amount of clothes they possibly could. A few of them had on oversized T-shirts and toothpicks tipping out of their mouths. Old heads in mesh tank tops mixed in with young bulls who snuck in on their friend's ID. All that and not one girl.

The DJ was perched in a booth on a platform high above the dance floor. He spun the latest hip-hop tracks to get people moving. He was a big dude with cornrows past his shoulders. Oversized headphones were wrapped around his neck.

"Let's go! This ya boy!" he yelled into the mic. "We bringin' it to you live every Friday and Saturday night at Club Cakes!

How many of y'all came to party?!"

"Over here!" the three of us raised our glasses in salute.

"You show me love, I'ma keep mixin' hot music for y'all. Before the go-go boys come out, we gonna give away a free bottle of Grey Goose vodka to somebody out there. We call it 'body shots.' We'll give you the liquor, but you gotta show off that body! We wanna see six packs in this bish. Who wanna show us what they got? Let me see you represent, fellas!"

Everybody on the dance floor was wild and ready a second ago. The dare had grown men looking around at each other all shy. Somebody needed to step up to the challenge. No one made a move. I almost dropped my drink from Jason and Tyree pushing me toward the DJ booth. "What are y'all doin'?" I said.

"Go 'head and give 'em that ebony thunder," Tyree said with a wide grin.

"Tyree, you ain't about to drink none of the liquor if I do, so why do you care?" I said.

"You right. I took one shot and that's enough to last me a lifetime. But your ass better go up there and get that free bottle! Think of it as payback for your shenanigans last time we were in a club."

"Do it, Cole! It'll be fun!" Jason urged me. My phone rang again. April. What was with this girl? She couldn't leave me alone for one night?

Jason took my phone outta my hand and replaced it with the whiskey sour he was babysitting. "Drink this." For someone who was into Jesus and being a good Christian, Jason was a lush. And an enabler. Something must have happened since he got to Morrison 'cause he was less of a stiff these days.

"Y'all really want me to do this? Fine. Whatever." I finished off the cocktail until the only thing left was ice cubes. Done. The liquid courage was in my system. I had better not regret this.

As soon as I raised my hand to volunteer, the place turned into a zoo. In that moment, I understood how females felt when me or another man got at 'em when they walked down the street. The fellas around me were acting like wild monkeys in cages. They whistled at me as I rolled to the platform.

"Yeah, baby!"

"Work that thang!"

Cheers from other men to take my clothes off? Why did I listen to my roommates? There were plenty of other guys who'd be better at this than me. I was the last man who needed to be on some Magic Mike shit. Yeah, I'd get drinks out of it, but I had my own money. There was no turning back. I was gonna show these dudes what a real man's body should look like.

"Wassup homeboy. What's ya name?" the DJ asked as I hopped on the platform.

"My name's Cee." The whistling boys down front climbed over themselves to get a view of the action. Their tongues wagged like they'd missed a few meals.

"Aight, Cee. You ready to score this bottle? I'ma get you the music and let you do ya thing. Let's go!"

The DJ started off with a crazy air horn, then fired up a dancehall track. I thought he was gonna put on Rick Ross or something! I wasn't no Jamaican! What would the West Indian fellas do? I pictured the island parties. What did they call it? Dutty wine? Whatever. I went with it.

I gyrated my hips to keep up with the tropical rhythm. That wasn't gonna work. I couldn't do what they did. I stuck to what I knew best. I lifted my shirt in slow motion. Not all the way, just enough so my fans could see what's up. Yeah. I had it.

The DJ shut the music off. "Ay, you think 'cause you a pretty boy we just gonna give it to you? You gotta show us more than that, dawg."

More? What did I look like? A stripper? Before the DJ could play the song, Bianca climbed up to the platform and kissed me. I let down my guard as she slipped me her tongue. That was a helluva motivator!

"Get off the stage, woman!" the DJ laughed from his gut. "You supposed to be behind the bar! You're depriving these people of their drinks! But forreal give it up for my girl, Bianca. I don't mean to tell ya secrets, but she goes both ways, fellas. So if you like pussy and got good credit, I'ma hook you up. Mr. Cee what's your FICO score?"

"Uh...."

"Don't worry, these boys don't care if you paid. They just wanna see you dance. Come on wit' it!"

Bianca and that kiss got my bravery up. I took off my shirt to show the body I spent nearly every day in the gym to get right. Arms? Shoulders? I had that and more. Bianca's eyes sized up every part of me. Just like I wanted her to. I pulled my shorts down past my underwear so she could see the weight in my draws. The boys below me screamed so hard my ears rang.

I avoided looking at any of 'em. I let my body talk for me. I matched my torso to the West Indian drums. The club was in a trance watching me work. The only time I felt this type of control over people was when I was on the track. Heads everywhere were tilted up at me. Every roll of my hips, crunch of my abs, pop of my pecs and flex of my biceps drew them in.

The music winded down. My spectators gave me the love I deserved. Yeah, buddy.

"Let's give it up for Cee! You earned that bottle homeboy," the DJ pounded my fist. "That's gonna be it on the body shots, but y'all keep it live! If you like what my man Cee did, you gonna enjoy the strippers that'll be out here soon."

I came off the platform feeling like a champ. The appreciation was cool, even if it was from a room of gay dudes. I wasn't thinking about them. Bianca and her nipple rings had drawn me in. I met her at the bottom of the platform as the music got louder. "You did a great job up there!" she said with a high-five. "Are you sure you're straight?"

"Yeah, no doubt!" I said at the top of my lungs. "Thanks for that kiss! I couldn'ta done it without your help."

"I'm glad I could be your inspiration," she giggled. She pointed to Tyree at the bar. He gleefully held an unopened bottle of Grey Goose. "Looks like your friends already got your trophy for you."

"So can we meet up later tonight or…?"

"I have to go back to work, but you should call me some time." She slid a piece of paper into my hand. Her name and number was on it. "786 471-5385. XO, Bianca."

"Don't forget," she said as she walked away.

"You bet I won't."

Jason and Tyree came rolling over with the Goose. For a second I thought they were gonna pour it over my head like a Gatorade shower. It woulda been appropriate since that was an all-star performance.

"Look who became an entertainer!" Tyree grinned. "You better werk, you showstopper!"

"And April likes you!" Jason said. "Oops, I meant to say Bianca."

"I see what you did there," I smirked.

Tyree handed me the vodka and a glass of ice. "Looks like we're square. Just don't go buckwild on us tonight. If you do,

I'ma put you up on that stage again."

"I'm so chill, Ty," I said. "Y'all the ones I wanna see enjoyin' yourselves. Get out there and have fun."

Bianca was right about people coming in later. It was 2 a.m. and the building couldn't fit another person in here. I found a place where I could watch the action without being in the way. I didn't wanna ruin another party. Besides, the fellas in this club were no joke. Some of these big body niggas looked like they just busted out of prison. I'd be stupid to get into with a man who thought taking it up the ass was a form of entertainment. Ain't nothin' tougher than that.

Some of the wallflowers camped out on the benches gave me the *look*. That lick the lips, lusty eye contact thing females did when they were feeling a man. They were probably dreaming about what I looked like naked. As long as they didn't touch me we were good.

I wondered how Jason and Tyree felt about being surrounded by straight people every day. It made sense they would wanna go to at a gay club when we went out. It was awkward for me to come in here. They probably felt the same way when they were at a function with girls and guys dancing on each other.

"All my party people in Club Cakes tonight!" the DJ competed with the booming music. "We servin' it up hot and fresh out the oven! Fellas in the building let me see you shake that shit!"

I let myself get lost in the stream of dancers. The ice-cold vodka loosened me up more with each sip. The guys were squeezed in so tightly they couldn't help but dance with the stranger next to them. Nobody cared. I started not to either. They didn't give a damn what the music was or who was around them. I was solo but far from alone.

The strippers the DJ promised took their places on the black boxes scattered around the room. All they had on were jockstraps stuffed with dicks the size of paper towel rolls. The boys in the club fell out of their rhythm getting a glance in.

Over on one of the boxes in the center of everything was a stripper with a slim but muscled out body. He wore Timb boots and a purple fitted cap. His dick struggled to stay inside his light blue briefs. "Andrew Christian" was written on the waistband of his underwear.

He called to Jason with his oversized package. As Jason moved closer, the stripper flopped his dick in my roommate's hungry face. Jason stuffed a handful of bills in the man's draws as a thank you. Stripper dude jumped down off the box and lifted Jason on top of it. He laid my boy out on his back and held his legs in the air. The slow grind the man put on him had Jason about to lose his mind. I hoped he wasn't too drunk to enjoy getting air fucked.

From what I could see, Jason loved every minute of it. That wasn't a surprise to me. My boy wilded out when he got liquor in him. Jason needed to get a boyfriend. Somebody who could work him out the way the stripper did, but on the regular.

Jason took a break from the ecstasy long enough to dig into his pocket. Out came another bill. He slid it between the stripper's draws and his clean-shaven crotch. Besides me, only one or two other people were looking their way. Other than that the club belonged to Jason and "Andrew C."

Damn, my phone kept buzzing from April texting me. It would have to wait until tomorrow. She could go a day without hearing from me. Being together didn't mean we needed to talk everyday. I put the phone in airplane mode.

Jason hustled through the crowd toward me, sweating like a

beast. He inspected the almost empty bottle in my hand. "You okay, Cole?"

"I am and it's about to get a lot better," I eyed him. I finished off the bottle and set it on the bench. "Let's dance."

I was so twisted I couldn't walk straight. I had to keep it cool so I didn't bust my ass before I got to the car. Was that rain? Ha. It felt like I was at a water park or something. Like I was Shamu. I was ready to do tricks and flips. The water on my skin was what I needed after coming out of that hot club.

Tyree twirled around in the street. "Ooh, that party was everything! Did y'all live?"

"I loooooove Miami! Wooo-hooo!" Jason slurred. Tyree stood behind him to keep the man from falling.

"Ew, Jason you're greasy!" He sniffed. "Oh my God, you smell like a stripper!"

"That's the scent of love! And baby oil."

"You lost your religion in that club," Tyree said devilishly. "But how 'bout a round of applause for Mr. Colin Hill! He gave those dancers a run for their money! You think you was cute on that stage showin' off your goods?"

"You know you liked it," I said. "When you wear it out in the gym like me what else you gonna do? Show it off."

"Boy please, you ain't the only one with body!" Tyree lifted his shirt to reveal the ridges of his abs. Was he hiding a Bowflex or NordicTrack in his room? I knew he had a nice shape on him. I forgot he was cut too.

"That's aight. You still not on my level." I fell out in the back seat of the car. Loose off the Goose. I hadn't been on one like this in a while.

"Don't forget we need to get gas," Jason said shakily.

Tyree offered Jason his hand to guide him inside. "Okay, let's do it 'cause I do not wanna be stranded on the streets of Miami. Cole, find out where the nearest gas station is."

The screen on my phone was blurry. Cold air from the AC helped get my mind right. "It's a BP four blocks away."

"That's where we're headed then. Jason, get your drunk ass in this car."

I wasn't sober enough to pump the gas. No way. I didn't trust myself. I had enough energy to get snacks outta the store. I needed something to soak up the liquor. I left Jason and Tyree at pump number one to fill the tank. It was colder than a mothafucka in the store. The chill hit me like a December snowstorm. The fridge where they kept the sodas was even cooler. I picked out a handful of mango Arizonas and an Arnold Palmer.

"Cole, what are you doing here?" Marshall and Nick were standing behind the fridge door. I almost dropped the damn juices.

"Oh wassup! I forgot y'all was in Miami," I said, gripping the cold cans. They were the only thing keeping me in my right mind. The two caught me off guard. I wasn't ready to entertain anybody at a gas station in the middle of the night.

First April was on me, now my teammates. If I saw Coach Jackson or one of my professors, that was it. I was blasting on niggas.

"You look like you came from a party," Marshall said accusingly.

"Yep, a club near here," I said. "I'm winding things down."

"Which one are you coming from?" Nick asked. "Cameo? King of Diamonds?"

If I told 'em I went to a gay club with my roommates it would be a wrap. "It was somewhere on South Beach," I said. "I can't remember which one."

"Don't party too hard," Marshall said. He stuck his finger in my chest. "You had a rough time at the invitational, didn't you? We don't want a repeat of that disaster next time we're on the track."

"It's nothin' I can't handle," I said, pulling away.

Nick stepped between us. He was always the one to keep the peace. "Have fun, Cole. Check out the parties on Collins Avenue when you can. We'll see you when we're back on campus. Let's go, Marshall."

I couldn't tell if Marshall held back because of Nick or because it was Spring Break. I'm glad he didn't waste his words on me. I didn't want a lecture in the juice aisle at a convenience store.

I let them leave before I paid for my drinks. There were a hundred gas stations in Miami. Why'd they have to be at this one? And the same aisle too? They'd probably followed us around like they were the CIA. I wouldn't put it past Marshall. When I got outside, I didn't see either of their cars anywhere. That was a relief.

Jason's smile drooped into a suspicious frown. He saw that something was wrong with me. "Cole what's going on? Was there something scary in there?"

"I ran into two of my teammates," I coughed.

"You can go with 'em if you want," Tyree offered. "You don't hafta stick around us third wheels."

"Why would I wanna do that?" I said. "I'm havin' a good time with my roommates. Let's get back to the hotel, though. That bed is waitin' for me."

I opened my eyes slowly. My head was groggy from a night of hard partying. I'd slept in my clothes and my shoes dangled off my feet. It was almost noon, way later than I was used to waking up. Jason and Tyree were already eating breakfast at the desk by the bed.

"Hey, sunshine. How did you sleep?" Jason asked between bites of hash brown.

"Better than I thought I would. How 'bout you boys?"

"Right as rain," Tyree said. "We're headed to the pool if you wanna come." Tyree tossed something in a yellow wrapper in my lap.

"An Egg McMuffin? Y'all had time to go to Mickey D's?" This sandwich was about to disappear.

I'm glad they went. If it was up to me, I wouldn't have left the bed until it was time for dinner. But I didn't come to Miami to lounge in the hotel room all day. I finished off the sandwich, scraped the cheese out of my teeth and dug through my suitcase to find something to wear to the pool. Jason held up his green shorts with the Hawaiian print for us to see. Very nice. Tyree pulled out what looked like a cross between a Speedo and tighty-whities. Was that black rubber?

"You gonna give the old ladies out there a heart attack," I said.

"I am not myself unless I'm borderline indecent," Tyree said with satisfaction. "What you thought I was gonna wear? Somethin' demure? That is *not* how I do thangs. Even my pajamas are fierce."

"Don't you slept naked?" Jason said.

"They're so fierce they don't exist!" Tyree winked.

Why was I surprised by anything this man did anymore? Over the top for me was an ordinary day for Tyree. I didn't want them to kick us out of the pool because of him. I put on something more appropriate for going outside: yellow shorts and my flip-flops from the Dollar Store.

"Hey, those are the same trunks you wore at the freshman beach party," Jason said.

"Oh yeah. I can't believe you remember that," I said. "It's where we met for the first time."

"It was unforgettable," he said under his breath. "I'd never been to the beach before I arrived at Morrison. Can you believe that?"

"You're kidding me," Tyree said. "You lived in Georgia and never drove to a beach? That's a shame."

"My mother never took us," Jason said. "I don't know if it's because she didn't have the time or didn't want to, but yeah, we never went."

"Before you get weepy on me, come put sunscreen on my back." Tyree handed him the slippery container. "After the pool we can spend as much time on the beach as you want."

"Let me get that after you," I said. The backpacks with the liquor were on the carpet by my feet. "I need a re-up. Jason, you want me fix you somethin'?"

"Yes, but I'll get it." He took two small bottles of orange juice and poured out half of what was inside. Then he filled the empty space with vodka. Anybody who wasn't looking close would think it was 100 percent OJ. It was straight liquor in there.

"Y'all didn't have enough last night?" Tyree said. He was covered from head to toe in a thick layer of sunscreen.

"If you don't wanna get a hangover, keep drinkin'," I said. "That's what I heard. From somewhere…"

We stashed the drinks in a bag with our towels. The three of us rode the elevator down to the pool area. It was hotter than an oven outside. The water looked like it would be a relief. Tyree was the first over to the blue lounge chairs under the palm trees. He rushed to throw a towel over his head.

"Ooh, it is hot as Hades!" he yelped. "Jesus, be an umbrella! Cover me, Lord."

"You should prolly jump in the pool instead of bakin' out here in the sun," I said.

"Y'all go 'head. I need to work on my tan. I wanna be golden brown and luxurious by the end of this trip."

That was fine with me. Most of the people in the pool were here for Spring Break too. A few Black girls with neon bikinis and big jewelry dipped their feet in the water. Everybody else splashed around having a good time. We didn't see anybody who worked at the hotel. Jason and I downed the bottles of the OJ/vodka concoctions.

"Anymore left?" I asked him.

"Yes, here you go."

He handed me another round. I finished most of it before I dived into the pool. It felt so good. My head was buzzed, but the rest of me loved being suspended in the water.

Jason cannonballed into the pool, sending water everywhere. "Hello, Cole! What's up with you stranger?"

"Go away you weirdo," I joked. "I see you strugglin' a bit there. Can you swim?"

"No, I can't float without a tube and I don't see any around," he said. "The good news is this pool is only four feet deep."

"Your mother did you wrong when it came to the water. Here, lemme teach you. Lie flat and kick your feet," I said.

I held my palms under his back and guided him across

the pool. My left hand cupped his head to keep it from going under. He shut his eyes as he bathed in the water. His skin became liquid in my hands. I kept the touching to a minimum in case somebody was watching us. Jason relaxed as I carried him from one end to the other. He got the hang of the floating after a few minutes.

"Think you can do it by yourself?" I asked.

"Not without your help, but I'll practice more later."

"I'ma hold you to that. Your moms will be impressed when you finally go to a beach together. Did you tell her you were comin' to Miami?"

"No freaking way," he said, making small waves with his hands. "Spring Break is a foreign concept to her. She'd tell me I should use the time to study."

"Your grades could use the help," I said.

"Look who's talking. If I'm not mistaken, you're in this pool with me, Cole. I don't see any textbooks in your hand."

"I thought we were in biology class right now," I laughed. "You tellin' me I ain't gettin' extra credit for helpin' you swim?"

"I'm going to say no."

An hour in the sun and more alcohol than I shoulda had meant we were tore up. Jason's eyes were bloodshot red and not from the chlorine in the water. My boy was blitzed.

"Cole can you answer something for me?" Jason did his best to wade my way. "It's not a big deal. Simple question, really. Do you think it's bad to drink during the day?

"No sir. Why? Are you drunk?" I asked.

"Possibly," he slurred.

"Me too, bruh."

Tyree laid out on his lounge chair like an African queen. All he needed was pool boys to fan him with palm leaves. His eyes were fixed on Jason and me. Was he ever gonna get in the pool?

"Tyree, can you hand me that bottle next to you?" I asked.

He pretended like he didn't hear me. I held on to my shorts as I climbed out of the pool. The orange juice bottle was warm. We shoulda got ice before we came down. "Ay, I'm 'bout to go upstairs to get another drink," I said to Tyree. "Jason, you want anything?"

"I'll come with you," he tiptoed to the edge of the pool.

Tyree suddenly got his hearing back. "Can one of you bring my cell phone? It should be on the counter in the bathroom."

"Sure thing," I said.

I didn't realize how drunk I was until I walked around the pool. I grabbed a towel to cover me up. Get out on that side, I gestured to Jason. The part of the pool away from the girls. If I slipped on the wet ground, I didn't want 'em see me get a concussion.

"Last night was incredible, Cole," Jason said. "You went from fighting guys in the club to taking off your clothes in front of everyone. That's impressive. I'm very proud of you."

I pushed the button for the elevator. "I wasn't trippin'. It was all in fun. That's what we came to do. By the way, I saw that stripper who was on you."

"But do you know why? Oh, I didn't tell you what happened! He was rubbing against me and I wanted him to go away so I could dance. I pulled out what I thought was a dollar from my pocket and put it in his underwear. When I went back to the bar, I realized I gave him a fifty-dollar bill! That was supposed to be my drink money!"

"You shoulda gone up to him and be like 'Ay stripper, I'm sorry but I'ma need my $50 back.'"

"How would it look if I asked a dancer for a refund? That's

not okay."

"It's your money tho!" I laughed.

"I agree, but at that point it was a lost cause. After you and I danced, he followed me around the rest of the night."

"You sure it wasn't 'cause you were sexy and he wanted to get on that?" I grabbed Jason's ass as he put the key card in the door.

"Cole, that's ridiculous. I'm a respectable gentleman—"

"Who likes fuckin' other respectable gentlemen."

"That's not what we were discussing!"

Jason opened the door to the room. He tossed the key casually on the desk. I let the towel drop from my waist as I fell back on the bed. That liquor had me messed up. I could handle one more cup of something, though. I was a champ.

Jason pulled more bottles of orange juice and vodka out of the bag. He was dripping wet from the pool. Water rolled from his shoulders, down his spine and collected at the top of his ass. I walked up behind him quietly while he finished pouring. Before he turned around, I pulled him down to the bed.

"Get away from me. You're drunk," he said, swatting me playfully.

I moved a pillow out of my way and tugged at his waistband until his body pressed against mine. His wet shorts made my dick ready to stroke. "Wassup?" I said.

"What's up with you?" Jason fondled me through the fabric of my trunks.

My piece was on brick from his touch. Jason pulled my shorts off and threw them to the side. He licked me from my neck down to my stomach, making circles as he went. His tongue stopped just before he got past my waist. "You sure about this?" he asked.

"You talk too much. Bring that ass over here."

I only had to say the word. Before I knew it, Jason's face was buried in my lap. He fought to take my ten inches into his greedy mouth. He went up and down, slurping and sucking, his tongue playing with the head. I closed my eyes and concentrated on the mouth doing its magic on my long shaft. He bobbed up and down, the tip hitting his tonsils on repeat. I didn't want to let him know how good it felt, but I couldn't hold back my moaning. I was betrayed by my own dick. I wanted this.

I flipped him over so his face was deep in one of the pillows. I climbed on top of him and guided my dick into his pleasure spot. He arched his back to invite me in. I slipped my piece into the warmth between his firm cheeks. He reached around and kissed me hard as I got my rhythm going inside of him.

I braced myself against the bed while I ferociously slammed my weight into his ass. The pool water mixed with my liquids to open him up to me. With every thrust, my grunts got louder. I prepared myself for the fountain that was ready to erupt. He turned over to face me as I pulled out. He furiously jacked me off like his life depended on me getting my nut.

"Ahhhhh! AAAAAAHHH!" I exploded on his chest, sending cum flying everywhere. He kept stroking me off until the last drop leaked out. Jason closed his eyes and lay out on the bed. His hands and body were drenched with my kids.

"Fuck!" I finally stopped shaking. I threw my head back into the feather pillow next to him. I waited for the swirling in my brain to stop. Wait, was the door to the room open? I squinted through my haze to see Tyree standing in the doorway. He was horrified watching us recover from our session. Jason saw him too. He sat up fast.

"Y'all are in here having sex?!" Tyree yelled hysterically.

"What is wrong with you two! I can't believe you would do this behind my back! You assholes!" He took off from the room, his tears flying behind him.

"Wait, Tyree!" I shouted. I threw on my shorts and chased after my roommate. By the time I got to him, he was out the door. "Tyree!" I caught up to him and reached for his arm. He yanked it back, but I wouldn't let him go.

"What Cole? What could you *possibly* have to say to me? 'Cause whatever it is I don't wanna hear it!"

"Come back! Look, it's not—"

He snatched his arm away and doubled back to the room with an impressive sprint. I got to the doorway a few seconds after him. Jason was still on the bed, butt-ass naked. He had cleaned himself up with a towel. "Tyree, please listen!" Jason pleaded.

Tyree ditched us for the bathroom. He slammed the door behind him. Jason picked up his clothes from the floor. I tried my best to comfort him. "At least he's back in the room," I said.

The bathroom door swung open violently. Tyree charged past us with an armful of his stuff. He dumped it on the bed and threw his suitcase next to the pile. Shorts, shoes, wet towels, toiletries, belts, hats — it all got tossed inside. Me and Jason were stone-faced watching Tyree go apeshit in front of us. He finally got everything he brought with him in the bag. He zipped it so fast he almost split it in two.

"Y'all wanna get left in Miami? You best get your asses packed."

Between me and Jason, we couldn't figure out what to do next. Jason's watery eyes begged me to say something.

"It ain't worth all that," I said. "For real. We got a couple days on the hotel left. You ain't tryna leave now are you?"

"I wanna go home! Right now!" Tyree dragged the suitcase toward the door. He threw his car keys directly at me. They almost hit me in the head. "And you're driving," he commanded.

"But I'm not sober." So much for not letting anybody drive his car.

"You have 30 minutes," he growled. "Get yourself a black coffee or whatever it is you need to do. I'll be in the lobby. *Thirty minutes.*"

There wasn't much traffic as we drove up the I-75 freeway toward Tampa. The sky was clear. The radio was off. There was nothing to distract us from the tension in the car. Tyree rode in the front wearing the biggest, darkest shades he owned. He hadn't said a word since we left the hotel. Jason was in the back sleeping off the liquor. I couldn't drive us away from Miami fast enough.

I had one eye on Tyree and the other on the road. "Are we gonna talk about it or are you just gonna not say nothin' for the rest of the trip?" I asked him.

Tyree didn't bother to look my way. "The next thing that comes outta your mouth is gonna be a load of crap but go 'head. Talk."

"Why you givin' me grief? You act like I went in there and said, okay I'ma have sex with my roommate. You think I'm goin' around every day gettin' sucked off by dudes? It's nothing like that!"

My statement made him even madder. "Cole, please don't act like your dick accidentally popped outta your pants and landed in Jason's mouth! You think I'ma be okay after I saw that? You done lost your damn mind! You're a liar and a messed up human being!"

"What's this got to do with you, Tyree? We live together. You ain't my girl! I don't owe you an explanation! This ain't about you. This is between me and Jason."

"So you have no idea why I'm upset?" he shouted at me. "You are so damn ignorant sometimes! You don't care how any of the things you do affect the people around you. Get your head outta your ass, Cole!"

"Tyree, I still don't see what this has to do with you!" I yelled back.

"Are you *that* dumb, Cole? I've always liked you and not just as a roommate. You had my love until I walked into that room."

"What are you talkin' about?!" I shook my head in confusion. "This is news to me! When were you gonna say somethin'?"

"Don't act brand new, Cole!" Tyree snapped. "What about that 'I'll always be there for you' speech back at the Walmart? Stop playin' this role like you a good person who cares about somebody. If you did, you woulda thought twice before you had sex with Jason on our hotel bed. If that's what you wanted and you decided you like men now, you coulda at least came to somebody who cares about your sorry ass."

"Fuck you! I got a girl."

"Not anymore you don't."

"The hell is that s'posed to mean?" I was so heated I wanted to throw him out the passenger door.

I couldn't believe it was going down like this! I messed with one of my roommates and the other was in love with me. I knew being around these dudes would get me caught up one day. None of this was my fault! Jason was the one who pushed on top of me. I was drunk!

My foot jammed on the gas, giving the car speed. The needle

on the dashboard spun past the 70 miles per hour mark. I held on to the steering wheel. I forced myself to concentrate. If I didn't, I was gonna run us off the road and into a ditch.

"You ain't shit, Cole," Tyree looked away from me. "You can't run a lap, little dick havin', punk bitch. I knew you got down from the moment you walked in the club."

Tyree wanted to get me upset. I wouldn't let him. He didn't know anything about what was going on in my head.

Bianca got me juiced up. Me and April were away from each other too long. Can't say this was the only time I ever fucked with a dude. This was what happened when I was away from a girl too long.

At that preppy high school I went to, the Black girls didn't waste their time with me. Success for them meant a white boy in a pink polo shirt and seersucker shorts that cost more than some people's rent. The ones whose daddies handed them keys to a Mercedes for their birthday.

That was far from who I was so they counted me out. I wasn't a prospect for them. The Black girls might not have been feeling me, but a few of the gay white boys were. They hadn't been around somebody so "urban" before. They wanted to make their fantasy of getting worked over by a big Mandingo Black man come true.

Some of 'em found excuses to get close to me. They'd watch from behind the fence at meets or invite me to get tutored. This one time, a classmate of mine named Blake invited me to his place for a study group. When I showed up, I was the only one there. I didn't sweat it. He told me to follow him to his room. Blake wore cargo shorts and nothing else. When he turned around, I saw he had a fat ass booty for a white boy.

We hit the books for a while. Blake told me I could lie out

on his bed if I wanted to. While I was into my AP Calc book, he pulled at the zipper on my pants. I flinched for a second, but I let him do what he wanted to do. It was just head. Nothing more than that. After I nutted, he wiped me down and we went back to studying.

I rolled to his house a couple more times after that. We had classwork to take care of. Eventually, he let me smash.

As long as I didn't touch him and kept my eyes closed it felt like I was going at some pussy. If he started to shout, I gripped his mouth to shut him the fuck up. Blake never told his family about our studying. He didn't want a reputation for sleeping with Black men. That was cool with me. What we were doing didn't need to get around.

I only let Blake throw it back because not having a girlfriend then gave me blue balls like a mothafucka. Every man has a dry spell. They need that special kind of attention. If I wanted to fuck and somebody wanted to give it up, I was gonna go for it. Ass was ass to me.

After I graduated high school, I had girlfriends back to back. That was part of why I didn't want gay dudes touching me. Shit was in the past. I didn't wanna put ideas in anybody's head. Didn't matter who I might've fucked around with once or twice or who it was in that hotel room, my roommate or whoever. I would always be straight. It was gonna stay that way.

"What is that noise!" Tyree temporarily snapped out of his rage.

Dammit, it was sirens. There was a cop car with its lights on coming behind us. I flicked on the turn signal and slowed down to pull over to the shoulder. Jason was laid out snoring. "Tyree, put your seat belt on and don't talk," I scowled.

The cop was a white guy. Right away, I was scared for my

life. In Philly, police would pull me and my boys over for no reason. Even if we weren't doing anything, they found an excuse to stop us.

One time I was coming out of the Foot Locker when two officers surrounded me. A store down the street was robbed by somebody with a gun. I matched the description. Black guy, they said. Sixteen to 30 years old. That described most of the people in the damn neighborhood. They let me go, but not before they slammed me on the car, handcuffed me and forced me to stand on South Street for an hour. I had the right to remain silent, but not to speak up for myself.

Ever since then, I never let my guard down around the police. The people who were supposed to be protecting me. As my window rolled down for the officer, my fake smile got bigger. I needed to come off as unthreatening as possible so he wouldn't haul our asses off to jail. I couldn't run track if I was behind bars.

"Hi, how's it going officer?" I said. I was careful not to say too much.

"Afternoon, boys. I pulled you over because you were going mighty fast. 76 in a 50-mile-per-hour zone."

"My bad, officer. I didn't realize it was that fast. I'm a good driver. I promise."

"Everything alright back here?" The policeman tapped on the back window. Jason shot up in his seat. He almost bumped his head on the roof of the car.

"Oh crap!" he exclaimed. "Did we do something wrong?"

"Are you okay, sir?" the cop asked sternly.

"Yes, I fell asleep," Jason said, keeping his panic under control. "Are we under arrest?"

"Is there a reason that you should be?" the cop squinted his eyes at us.

No sir, we said. Tyree was surprisingly cool with it. Before we got pulled over, he was ready to tear my head off. No one was dumb enough to cause a scene in front of a cop. Not even Tyree at his worst.

"Let me see your license and registration," the officer said as he came back to my window.

"It's my car, sir," Tyree said. He slowly reached in the glove box. Out came his insurance card. I passed it through the window along with my ID. I waited for the bad news. Was that it for us?

"We go to college in Tampa," I added desperately. "We were in Miami for Spring Break. We're on our way home."

I played my education like a trump card, hoping it excused us in some way. Maybe he'd think we were different from "other" Blacks. We weren't troublemakers or thugs or… niggers. I didn't want him to get restless 'cause he saw a carful of Black men riding together.

"I'm writing you boys up for speeding," he handed me a ticket through the window. "You have 30 days to take care of this. Slow down and have a good afternoon."

"We will. Thank you, officer," I said. I couldn't remember the last time I was so relieved. We dodged a bullet. Literally.

It wasn't until I saw his taillights down the road that I said anything. Jason shivered like he'd been floated out on a glacier. Tyree hadn't moved. He should have been grateful I got us out of that. He could've been wearing an orange jumpsuit for Spring Break instead of swimwear.

"You're an idiot, Cole," Tyree grumbled.

"And you're acting like a bitch. Man up."

"Can you guys just stop?" Jason pleaded. "It's not that

serious! This isn't worth losing our friendship over."

"It might be!" Tyree snorted. "See, that's your problem, Jason. You don't understand how serious this is. Please don't be a dumbfuck."

"I'm not… that word."

"That's debatable," Tyree huffed. "Why are we sitting here? I don't wanna waste anymore of my time with you two."

He wasn't the only one. I drove us the 300 or so miles to Tampa. Back to reality. It was the longest car ride of my life. The only break from the silence was Tyree's heavy breathing. He made a beeline for the apartment as soon as I stopped out front.

"You at least wanna get your bags?" I yelled after him.

He shut the front door so hard it almost came off the hinges. I took that as a no. Jason was at the trunk pulling out his suitcase. He walked away with his head hung low.

I smashed my fists into the hood of the car with a brutal thunk. It left a mark that Tyree would always remember. I ignored the pain shooting through my arms. I messed this up. And I never texted April back. I didn't want to talk to her or anybody else, but she always sensed when something was wrong. I had a long list of things she didn't need to know about and we'd only been in Miami for a day.

JASON

Cole didn't come home last night. I texted him almost every hour since we returned, but he hadn't responded to a single one of my messages. I wished that he would reach out so he could share what was on his mind. I needed to know if he was agonizing over our rendezvous as well. I turned my phone's ringer to its highest setting. He had to call eventually. We couldn't escape a resolution.

I scrolled through my phone one more time, then tucked it away. Spring Break was yet another issue that I had to contend with. I juggled my sorrows like roaring chainsaws, hoping to keep them in the air before they butchered me.

Vaughn and I were in Lettuce Lake Park, a forested area just outside the city limits of Tampa. If the quad was my safe space, then this was a sanctuary. The miles of trees that surrounded me on all sides were magnificent in stature. Millions of leaves dangled from the branches like facets of a precious gem. Above the tree line was a sky undisturbed by the rows of glass buildings that paralyzed the natural beauty of Tampa.

My feet hadn't touched a blade of grass since we began pledging. I wouldn't dare defy our big brothers' instructions. Luckily, I was protected from the forbidden surface by the wooden boardwalk that looped through the park.

I waited near the restrooms where Vaughn excused himself before we began our afternoon excursion. I was alone with my thoughts and the crisp air that swept through the cypress trees above me. As much as I wanted to speak to Cole, I welcomed the retreat Lettuce Lake presented. Our apartment was a landmine. It would be wise of me to avoid it. Being anywhere near Tyree and Cole would only further disturb our broken triangle.

In the chaos of our sudden departure, I hadn't taken stock of how traumatic Tyree's discovery must have been for him. He disclosed to me early last semester that he was smitten with Cole. However, I'd assumed that over time the puppy love lost its bite. Tyree waited so long for mutual affection that he knew would never actualize. In downplaying his emotional ties to Cole, I may have squandered the closest friendship I was ever blessed to have.

If given the opportunity, I would tell Tyree how much I regretted the misdeed with our roommate, but I doubted he would believe me. He witnessed firsthand the abandonment of his trust. In the time since we arrived in Tampa, I replayed the scenario in my head to determine what I could have changed. Making sure the door was locked should have been our primary task. Not sleeping with Cole was also an option, albeit one that I was too intoxicated to favor.

With the recent changes in my life, my moral compass had spun in so many directions. Tyree was the unfortunate victim of its disrepair. In spite of everything, I would always be his friend. If Tyree voided our friendship, it wouldn't undo the past. Maybe he recognized that and needed time alone. Things would return to normal once this blew over. One day soon, we would look back on Spring Break and have a good laugh, I was sure of it.

Vaughn ran up next to me and draped a loving arm around my shoulder. "Did you wash your hands?" I asked playfully.

"You're saying you don't want my germs?" he joked.

"There's a lot of things I want from you, but your germs are not one of them," I smirked.

The planks of the boardwalk creaked beneath our feet as we navigated the park. The rich, golden sunlight that filtered through the trees lit our path like the Yellow Brick Road leading to Emerald City. The call of birds drowned out the dull roar of the nearby 75 freeway. A group of turtles swam playfully below us in the marsh, their tiny feet kicking beneath them. There were signs warning us that alligators also made their home in the lake. We didn't see any of the scaly creatures, but I narrowed my walk to the center of the path to be sure. I had enough danger in Miami.

"Thanks for coming," Vaughn said. "I'm glad you could spend the extra time with me before we go back to set. How are you feeling about starting our 'lessons' again?"

"We've been pursuing this so long I kind of wish we didn't have the break," I sighed. "It's a reminder of what life was like before pledging. It's tough transitioning back to a captive state of mind."

"We're getting close to the end, though," he empathized.

"That would be great," I said. "I'm tired of the smelly clothes and my hair is wilder than the animals in this park. The hardest part is only the big brothers know for sure when we're crossing. We have to keep going until they say the word."

"True," Vaughn said wistfully. "Also, I hate that we're not together as much as we used to be."

"What do you mean? We see each other all the time."

"I'm not talking about set, Jason. When the five of us go our separate ways and I'm back in my dorm alone without you, I feel like a piece of me is missing. Yeah, we talk on the phone, but it's not the same as seeing you in real life. You and me occupying the same space together is the best feeling a guy could ask for."

Vaughn held my hand tenderly. He rested my body against the wooden rail of the boardwalk. The splintery pine dug into my back as he greeted me with his lips. His words were delectable, but not enough to convince me to kiss him so explicitly in a park. I didn't care how much I had fallen for him.

"What are you doing?" I thwarted his advance. "There have to be at least twenty people on this boardwalk. I want to kiss you too Vaughn, but this isn't the place for it."

Vaughn was bewildered by my reaction. "No one's paying any attention to us. Jason, what are you scared of? Are you my boyfriend or what?"

I wish I could have said yes. The word flowed so easily for him. For me, it remained a struggle to vocalize. I never had a boyfriend before. Despite caring deeply for Vaughn, I wasn't ready to attach the label to our union. Was there a manual that outlined the rules of a relationship? I hadn't seen it. One thing was for sure, I wasn't ready to kiss in a public space surrounded by strangers with prying eyes.

Vaughn's forehead wrinkled with disappointment. "Jason, I care a lot about you. You're an incredible guy and one of the most amazing people I've ever met. When you pull away, it's like you're saying you don't wanna be with me. It's not like I want you to carry a rainbow flag through the streets of Tampa. It's just a kiss."

"But do we have to be so open about it?"

"So you show me love in front of strangers. Is the world gonna end?"

My mom would answer yes to that.

"Here's the issue, Vaughn," I said. "I don't want to be the 'gay guy.' It's easier for me to have people believe that I'm straight than give me a hard time about feelings I haven't worked out for myself."

"Babe," he gently touched my arm. "You care too much about what other people think of you."

"I also don't know what God wants for me," I said. "Am I defying His will by lying with another man? What we're doing goes against everything I was taught growing up."

"Jason, we're not breaking any laws here. We're two guys who have gotten close to each other. Look, I'm not gonna push you to do something that makes you uncomfortable. I do hope that one day you might be more laid back around me. I want you to sit by my side when we're in the caf, not across from each other like we usually do. You're good for giving me that half handshake, half hug thing. I want a real embrace from you and not just when we're alone."

I always thought Vaughn had my best interests at heart, but he wanted me to flip a switch and become someone else! That wasn't fair! "Let me ask you something then, Vaughn. If you're so out and proud, why don't you tell the big brothers you're gay?"

"For the same reason you haven't," he said. "Because I want to cross Theta."

"And you don't think that's dishonest? If we're going to be their brothers, shouldn't they accept us for who we are?"

"They should, but the reality is they're not letting anybody in the frat they think might be gay," he said defensively. "We'd be dropped without a second thought."

"So why all this talk about being out and proud then, Vaughn? Are you planning on telling them after we receive our letters? Why does the entire campus have to know we're having sex?!"

A few heads turned when I said the "S" word. A park was not the best place for this conversation.

"We both know that I'm not talking about sex," Vaughn said unshaken.

I lowered my voice. "It feels like we're creating more trouble for ourselves than we need to."

He considered my words as we proceeded to cruise the length of the boardwalk, past the leafy canopy overhead. From our new vantage point, the glassy surface of the lake reflected the acres of verdant foliage around it. I needed the same strength God gave the firmly rooted trees.

Up ahead, a wooden observation tower rose three stories into the sky. Children, families and couples climbed the stairs to snap photos of the magnificent view. Robinson Crusoe would be jealous. We settled next to one of the benches near the base of the observation tower. A white heron descended on the railing adjacent to us.

"So how was your Spring Break?" Vaughn asked hesitantly. "You guys came back early. Everything okay?"

Oh no. I hoped we could enjoy our time in the park before we discussed the subject. I wanted us to have the most pleasurable experience possible. I surveyed the birds nestled in the trees praying they'd warble to me what I should tell Vaughn.

"It was fine," I dropped my head. "We went to a club and danced all night. Oh, and I accidentally gave $50 to a stripper."

"What? You could've given me the money. I would've danced for you." Vaughn playfully rotated his crotch at me. I appreciated the gesture, but I could barely crack a smile.

"That's not it," I said with a heavy breath. "There's something else I have to share with you. Cole and I, we, um… we messed around," I blurted out.

Vaughn stopped abruptly. The birds halted their song. "What do you mean 'messed around'? You had sex? With your roommate? How did that happen??"

"We had a lot to drink and found ourselves in the bed together. Do you seriously want me to go into the details?"

"How far did it go, Jason? Was it full-on sex?"

"It was. We went all the way," I admitted grievously.

Vaughn pulled away from me in disgust. The wheels turned in his head as he considered whether my infidelity was a roadblock or a hurdle we could overcome. No matter how intoxicated Cole and I were, it didn't excuse me from having sex with my roommate. What made matters worse was Vaughn and I hadn't been intimate in a while. I gave Cole the love that I owed my guy. I prayed Vaughn would forgive me. I would understand if he didn't.

I shuffled my feet waiting for his response. Vaughn's next statement would determine if we remained side by side on the boardwalk or with one push over the railing I would become alligator food.

"So let me get this straight, you fuck your roommate and

you don't want to kiss me?" he said incensed.

"I swear it meant nothing. I had to say something to you because I don't want us to keep secrets from each other. It only happened once. I wouldn't betray you!"

"But you did, Jason!" he yelled. "That shit is unforgivable! How do I know it won't happen again? You two live in the same apartment together… the same one you won't ever let me into. The only time you don't treat me like a friend is when we're having sex and that's only happening once in a while. Were you feeling that neglected this week?"

"I missed you every minute I was there!"

"No, you didn't, Jason! Stop lying to yourself about who you are and what you want! Why would I want to be with you when you keep dragging me along? Why don't you just break it off with me? Then at least one of us will be happy."

"That's the last thing I want."

"This is what I'm going to do," Vaughn said contemptuously. "I'll drive you to set tonight because you're my line brother, but don't say a word to me. If we're not at set, I don't want to see your face or hear you speak.

Vaughn fumed with scorn. I didn't realize how much he meant to me until I stood to lose him. I wish I considered at the time what I'd be giving up by cavorting with Cole.

One by one people were disappearing from my life; now I lost Vaughn too. It was a taste of the betrayal Tyree must have endured. I was wrong, but no manner of apology would dull Vaughn's anger and disappointment. I surrendered to temptation and tossed his love to the side. The heron that served as a witness to our falling out flew away.

Something was different. It was 8 p.m., the time at which we were instructed to arrive to set. My line brothers and I were in our dreary uniforms preparing ourselves by the truck like always. The smell of weeks of body odor radiated from our clothes.

Instead of waiting for us in the apartment, the big brothers stood outside by a row of running cars. The headlights were switched off. Before I could process what was happening, they pinned us against the truck and wrapped long pieces of fabric around our heads. "Don't say a word," DP snarled.

Someone pushed me into what felt like the back of an SUV. The collision tore through my existing wounds. I had no sight, but from what I could tell, two of my LBs were tossed in after me. We were a tangle of limbs attempting to organize ourselves.

I heard the driver's door open and someone hop in. "Let's go," it said. The voice was muffled, but it sounded like Big Brother Flatline. I came to expect surprises while we pledged, but I couldn't bear it anymore. I was absolutely done with not knowing what was going on in my life.

"Vaughn, are you there?" I said in my lowest whisper, careful not to alert our chauffeurs of the exchange.

"Shut up, Jason. This is it," he responded curtly. He was very much still furious after my admission.

Suddenly I was aware of the importance of the moment. Were we going to cross? God, I hoped we were! In an instant, my desperation withered away. I was more optimistic than I ever was in our long saga of pledging. That would explain why everything was so different tonight!

Besides Vaughn, I couldn't tell who else was in the truck with us. I wasn't curious enough to find out, so I maintained my silence. The last time one of us talked when we weren't supposed to it didn't end well. The drive lasted for what felt like an eternity before it came to a swift halt.

"Get out!" a blistering voice demanded.

Someone dragged me by the legs down to the cold ground. I could hear the same aggression happening to my line brothers. I blindly reached out my hands to search for them. Rodney shifted his dejected figure so he stood in front of me. Vaughn stationed himself behind my back and locked his arms around my chest. Our line was reunited again. Where exactly, we didn't know.

Between our panting, I heard the cyclical crash of waves somewhere nearby. Each roar sent a jolt through my unsteady feet up to my fingertips. As long as I was standing, I would take on anything the big brothers threw at us if it meant that I could cross.

"How long you been on line?! Ace?" DP's voice brutalized our eardrums.

"Nine weeks, four days, and about ten hours Big Brother Genesis, sir!" Rodney shouted into the darkness.

"You pledges still wanna be Theta men?"

"Yes sir!" we said.

"Tonight you're gonna prove it. Brothas…"

Rough hands ushered us through the mushy ground toward the sound of the waves. What felt like thick ropes were tied securely around our wrists. First our sight was taken away from us with the blindfolds; now we were bound together with no chance of separation. This night couldn't get worse, although I suspected it would.

Our motley crew stumbled over each other as the Thetas pushed us closer to the waves. The rising water quickly soaked through my boots, then the bottom of my pants. Were they going to push us into the ocean? The answer was a terrifying yes.

My nose and mouth burned from the sting of seawater that monopolized every orifice of my body. I gasped for air as I attempted to break free of the ropes that anchored us. My LBs scrambled frantically to escape the water too, but the struggling only weighed us down more.

The Thetas intended to kill us! I wanted to be a member of the fraternity more than anything else, but I didn't come here to die! Stop tugging!

I fought my way through the panic long enough to realize that we weren't actually underwater. In a moment of clarity, I formulated a plan for how we could make our escape.

"Wait until the tide moves out!" I screamed.

When the water swept away, I jerked myself to my feet. There was a weight pulling at the rope against my wrists. The hurried gasps that trailed below were unmistakably Vaughn's. The breaths that were once sexual in nature evolved into plaintive cries of a man confronting his death. I wouldn't allow either of us to be undone by this cesspool. I was determined to equal the valor that he showed me.

I flung my body back as hard as I could until my line brother crashed into me. The frenzy stopped. The five of us on the line were one again. Waves splashed at our feet as if it were just another peaceful evening.

Someone untied the ropes that restrained us and removed the wet blindfolds. I could've sworn we were completely submerged, but the water only rose to our ankles. I didn't care. We almost died! If they tried to drown us, who knew what else these jerks would do!

Our line was so stunned from the ordeal that we didn't notice the big brothers on the shore carrying flickering torches. The flames illuminated the night and our stewards' pride in the five men standing in front of them. This was the light we'd been chasing since the beginning! We dragged ourselves out of the water toward their exuberant ovation. The Thetas' congratulations traveled along the moonlit shore.

DP stood in front of the pack, the proudest of them all. "Brothas!" he yelled. "You are now members of Theta Pi Chi Fraternity, Incorporated! Men of service, honor and distinction! We welcome you to the brotherhood!"

Oh my God! It was over! Finally! Junior kicked up sand and punched the air in jubilation. Rodney was dumbfounded. He walked in circles as the news settled in. His smile could not be restrained. Chima fell to his knees, shaking his interlocked fingers to the heavens in prayer.

A startled thrill blossomed from deep within Vaughn. His justified resentment toward me was overshadowed by the culmination of our trying times together. He buried his head in my shoulder to hide the tears of joy streaming down his face. We absorbed the moment as one. To everyone else on the beach, we looked like new frat brothers congratulating each other. But we knew better.

"Shirts off!" DP commanded. We did as we were told and stripped ourselves of our ragged tops. DP placed a silver dog tag around each of our necks. I ran my fingers over the metal. The Greek letter Theta was etched into its smooth surface. I finally had my letters! It was everything we worked for. The memory of the trials we endured together was already beginning to fade away. It seemed insignificant compared to the honor we were bestowed.

"Everybody look at me," DP called to us. "The word fraternity means brotherhood. We support each other, no matter the circumstances. Through suffering comes wisdom. Pledging is about learning to deal with hard problems and walking away with your head high. You have a spirit that can't be defeated. I don't want any of you holding grudges because of this process, you hear me?"

"Yes sir, Big Brother Genesis!" the five of us shouted.

"No more 'Big Brother' either. We're all brothers. I want you to wear the Theta tag under your clothes when you're on campus until after the probate show. That's when you'll become official. After that, we'll represent the blue and orange together!"

They were the words I'd always aspired to hear.

"For the new brothas, I want you to go home and get cleaned up," DP said. "Tomorrow night at 8 we're gonna start practicing for the probate show. Wear black. Whatever you have in your closet. Let's give 'em love!"

The brothers walked side by side with us through the sand. Instead of a single line of five, we proceeded as a unit. They were our "prophytes," formerly known as our big brothers. We were their "neos."

Brother Motor Mouth jogged to my side. "Congrats, Jason. You didn't think you were going to make it, did you?"

"For a while there, yes," I admitted. "I knew I wasn't the strongest one on the line, but I refused to be the weakest. I wanted to prove to you guys that I could see it through."

"You did that and more," he said. "Hey, Vaughn!"

Motor Mouth tossed my fraternity brother the keys to his Explorer. The truck was parked at the edge of the beach adjacent to the cars that brought us here. After exchanging congratulatory handshakes with our new brothers, the line — Rodney, Vaughn, Junior, Chima, and I — climbed into our chariot, the five newly christened members of Theta Pi Chi.

We were tired, wet and covered with sand, but we were beyond excited! I couldn't wait to tell everyone I'd ever met that we crossed! I hadn't anticipated that reaching the lowest, most stressful point in my life would make me more devoted to being a Theta man forever.

My LBs and I overcame every difficulty we faced, despite the odds against us. The individuals who came into the process unsure of themselves and each other evolved into a five-man army. It was up to our line to carry the Theta banner, not only for the men in the chapter but on behalf of the thousands of brothers we had yet to meet.

"Whattup y'all we Thetas now! Yeahhhhh man!" Junior shouted. Chima did his best to play it cool. With light roughhousing and a hardy shake from Junior, his grin broadened to irrepressible laughter.

Rodney held up his dog tag for us to admire. "Guys, I can't believe we made it. Look at it!"

He and Chima clinked their metal necklaces against each other in a toast. Vaughn soundlessly reached his hand over the cup holders and placed it on my lap. Our line brothers were too entrenched in their revelry to notice our affection.

"Let's go to my girl's apartment to celebrate!" Junior said. "Y'all down?" Vaughn quickly put his hand back on the steering wheel.

"I'm in, but is she going to be there?" I asked. "Like DP said, we have to keep the news to ourselves until the probate show."

"She's out at her cousin's place. It'll just be us," Junior said. "Can't wait for that show! It's gonna be the best they've ever seen!"

He was right about that! The probate show was the culmination of the pledging process. It was when we declared to the student body of Morrison State that we were members of the illustrious Theta Pi Chi fraternity. A probate was a concert, family reunion and a red carpet premiere all rolled into one sensational night. People gathered on the quad by the hundreds to see them, whether it was a fraternity or sorority or if the line was 50 people or three.

I never went to a Theta probate show because I was intent on going to my own one day. I did turn out for the Alphas' and the Sigmas' debuts last year to get a sneak peek. There were several components to prepare. We needed to rehearse the fraternity songs, a stepping routine and anything else the brothers planned for the evening.

"By the way, do any of you guys know how to step?" I asked. The coordinated stomping and hand-clapping to produce a drum-like beat was far from anything I'd ever done before. Like strolling, it was an essential part of the Black Greek experience. From what I'd seen at step shows it required a tremendous amount of practice to pull off. I would need my brothers' assistance to ensure we blew our observers away.

"I can step!" Vaughn, Chima and Junior volunteered merrily.

"I tried back in high school," Rodney shrugged. "It took me longer to get the moves down than everybody else."

"We're your brothers," Chima said to him. "We'll practice as long as we have to for us to nail it."

"So how 'bout this?" Junior said. "We'll meet at my dorm in an hour. Vaughn, can you pick us up?"

"Not a problem," he nodded. "It'll give us time to get cleaned up."

"Yeah do that, 'cause y'all are funkier than a squirrel's nuts," Junior joked.

Chima sniffed himself for confirmation. "I have many containers of soap that I plan to use as soon as I am in my room. Feel free to stop by if you need some."

One by one, Vaughn dropped off our frat brothers at their dorms. They each raced inside with a joyful spirit I hadn't seen in them for weeks. When Vaughn parked the truck outside my apartment, I gulped and made my plea. I hoped to benefit from the goodwill of the evening.

"Please understand how much I regret betraying you, Vaughn," I said. "We're meant to be together. I don't want one stupid decision to come between us."

"Jason, you're my boy. I care about you more than anything," he said. "I'm hurt, but I appreciate you 'fessing up. I have to ask…is this gonna be a regular thing with you and Cole?"

"Absolutely not. I'm all yours unless you say otherwise," I said resolutely.

Vaughn drank in my vow with a broad grin. I kissed him passionately and relentlessly to articulate my commitment to him. I couldn't contain the lust that was pent up inside me during his absence.

My time in bed with Cole was eye-opening, but it was the way Vaughn loved me dearly that reinforced what we had was much more than a drunken fling in a hotel room. My heart belonged to the man sitting next to me.

Our oral gymnastics came to a sharp end. Vaughn shifted hesitantly in his seat. Every cell in my body screamed for a second more of his caress.

"You want to come inside with me or—" I began to ask.

"I want to," he said, kissing me again. "But I don't wanna

hold the other guys up or rush the time we spend together. Trust me, you and I will need more than an hour. I'm gonna give you brotherly love you'll never forget."

I bit my lower lip in anticipation. Just thinking about what Vaughn had in store for us warmed me inside and out. Reluctantly, I adjusted my throbbing girth and opened the truck door. "Wait…" he said.

Vaughn pulled me toward him, kissing me more intensely than before. With one hand, I lifted the lever under his seat to slide it as far back as it could go. I needed every inch of room possible to seat myself onto his cruise control.

I arched my back against the steering wheel, inviting him to do what he pleased. His hands slid under my shirt until they reached my waiting nipples. I moaned with delight as he tugged at them delicately. My fingers teased the growing manhood buried under his damp pants. I had to have it. He stopped me before I released my prize from his zipper.

"Later," Vaughn whispered. I agreed, but not without disappointment.

I stood on the road until his truck drove off into the distance. I knew Vaughn intended to make good on his promise to give me the affection I longed for. However, I was through with waiting. I longed for him to hold me. I wanted Vaughn's appetizing kiss.

The only sound in the apartment was the jingle of my dog tag. I rushed to undress until it was the only article of clothing against my skin. I was so pleased to never have to wear the horrid rags from set another night. I would torch them, but I wouldn't want our neighbors to suffocate from the fumes.

I had to call my mom! I dug out my phone from my castoffs, searched through my "Favorites" and dialed her number. She picked up on the first ring. "Hello?"

"Hey, mom. Guess what?"

"Is something wrong?" she said with alarm. "Are you okay?"

"Yes, I crossed tonight! I'm a Theta!"

There was a long pause. I didn't expect my mom to be overjoyed by the announcement. She didn't think I should have pledged in the first place. But I wanted her to understand how much it meant to me.

"Congratulations, baby. I can tell you're on cloud nine."

"I am, very much so," I said. "I can't talk long because we're going to celebrate, but I wanted to tell you the good news."

"I'm your mother, Jason. No matter what it is, I should be the first person you call," she said. "I love you. I always will. Don't stay out too late because you have school this week. And stay away from those fast girls."

"Of course. I love you too, Mom. Talk to you tomorrow?"

"Yes, baby. Go have fun. Remember to keep God first in everything you do."

I ran to the bathroom to rinse off the sand that found its way into every uncharted crevice I had. My hands shook with elation as I slid on fresh clothes. In my hurry to meet Vaughn outside, I almost didn't notice Tyree sitting on the living room floor. His expression was distant. "You crossed?" he said, shifting his gaze to me.

"You heard me on the phone? We did! Just about an hour ago," I exclaimed. I danced a jig around the living room. My dog tag swung noisily around my neck. Tyree was not impressed.

"Good for you," he deadpanned. Tyree marched past me with his arms folded. He sullenly removed a glass from the kitchen cabinet and slowly dropped in three ice cubes. Clink. Clink. Clink. He poured cold sweet tea into the cup until it almost overflowed. He sipped.

It wasn't the reaction I was hoping for from him.

"Okaayyyyyy." I struggled for what to say next. "You're not still mad about the hotel, are you?"

"Chile, please," he said. "I have other things to think about."

"Is Cole home?" I asked.

"Am I his babysitter? No, he's not."

"When he gets back, please don't say anything about me crossing. I want to tell him myself."

"Whatever." Tyree assumed his previous position by the couch, the glass of tea in hand. He sipped.

A ring on my cell phone notified me that Vaughn was outside. I was in too fine a mood to let Tyree and his theatrics bring me down. "I'm heading out. Catch you later!"

I heard a faint "yeah sure" as I closed the door behind me.

TYREE

Fuck. This. Shit. Jason came in here talking about he crossed. As if Miami wasn't enough of a gag! First he slept with the man I loved; then he snatched my dreams away! I wanted to pledge! I was supposed to be with Cole! And Jason got everything!

I left them alone for two seconds and they were off having sex like whores! Did I miss something? Wasn't Cole supposed to be straight? All this time I held myself back for nothing. Jason didn't care about Cole the way I did! His closeted ass was just looking for the next man to hop on.

Hot tears streamed down my face as I stormed around the living room. I didn't bother to wipe them away. I was tired of pretending that the things people said and did to me didn't cut me to my core. I got beat in parking lots, I was called a sissy the moment I set foot on campus…I had no more dignity left. These so-called men acted tough when they were with their boys, but would fuck me the first chance they got. There was no end to the bullshit I went through! I was stupid to think I was important to anybody, let alone Cole.

I stared down my reflection in the bathroom mirror. I bet no one would notice if I wasn't around anymore. We finally got rid of that fag, they'd say. I was a joke. I could save them the trouble and end it myself. But how would I do it? Jump from a high building so that my bones broke into thousands of pieces? Let somebody beat my head in until I bled out on the yard?

People were always telling me who I should be or how to live my life. They were not about to tell me how to die. I was already dying inside. Might as well take myself out before anybody else could. I would not shed blood for another damn person besides myself.

I didn't need convincing to kill myself. Life did that for me. I just needed the means to do it. A gun would end everything. One shot to the head. But I didn't have one. I had to find something that could help me carry it through. I pulled everything from the medicine cabinet down into the sink. Nothing but grooming products, aspirin and Cole's stupid sleeping pills. None of that was gonna help me! I needed something more.

The kitchen. I tore through the drawers to find something to give me peace. Our old kitchen knives were too dull to make the kind of mark I needed them to. Off to the side was the junk drawer. Under the leftover ketchup packets was an X-acto knife. My unheard prayers were finally answered.

I flipped the razor in my hand. I slid it out of its black case to bring out as much of the blade as possible. I needed every part of it if I was gonna do this right.

My soul was tired. The voices circulating in my mind insisted that I go on. They commanded me to die. Don't be a coward, Tyree! I glided the razor vertically from my wrists to the veins in my restless arm. With the first cut, the red liquid began to seep out like a leaky faucet that could never be fixed. I pushed the razor in deeper until it disappeared under my skin.

The blood poured from my arms but not quickly enough to satisfy me. I turned the razor to my legs. I stabbed myself again and again and again until my leg was drenched in blood. A small piece of the blade broke off in one of the jagged cuts on my thigh. The bitterness dripped from my wounds and landed on the kitchen floor in red splatters. The art they made was the last creative thing I would ever do.

I slowly slipped to the floor, my hands clutching the metal blade — my savior.

The beep of machines flooded my head as I woke from what was supposed to be my eternal sleep. Small electronic meters next to me blinked non-stop. They were persuading me to wake up. A clear tube shoved in my arm led to the blood-soaked gauze and bandages that taped me together. I sat up to get a better understanding of the ghost-white room I was laid out in. "Where am I?" I asked weakly.

It wasn't my apartment and it wasn't heaven. Not unless the good Lord installed heart monitors by the pearly gates.

"You're at Florida Hospital," a woman said. "Mr. Iversen, you passed out after severe blood loss from your self-inflicted wounds."

The answer came from a brunette doctor in a white coat

and scrubs. She stood at the foot of my bed watching me over her glasses. Cole was next to her in a blood-stained shirt. His eyes were glassy from crying. I reached for the bandages that covered my aching scars. The doctor took my hand and put it back on the hospital bed.

My head was throbbing. Every extremity I had felt like it was run over by a freight train. The fluorescent lights overhead and the sun coming through the window attacked my eyes. The extra strain was more than I could bear.

"Can you close that, please?" I asked. It was harder to speak than I thought it would be. The doctor pulled the curtain closed, but it hardly dimmed the room.

"Mr. Iversen, I'm Dr. Edwards," she introduced herself. "Your roommate found you and called 911 before any critical damage occurred. We would normally ask anyone who isn't of direct relation to you to remain in the waiting room, but I understand your father is in Mississippi. Do you mind if your friend stays in the room?"

He was *not* any friend of mine. Cole waited until I was in a hospital to be by my side? I was so angry I couldn't manage to give the doctor the absolute "no" I wanted to.

"Is he gonna be okay?" Cole asked. He shoved his burgundy-stained hands into his pockets.

"He's stable," Dr. Edwards said. "We've given him stitches for the wounds. Fortunately, you got him to the hospital just in time and the injuries weren't fatal. Mr. Iversen, we also gave you something to relax you. We'll need to keep you here another day to monitor your health. Also, we want to make sure you don't attempt to harm yourself again. I'm going to ask you a few questions, if that's okay. How are you feeling?"

"Great," I muttered. I wasn't giving this lady any more words than were absolutely necessary. I was laid out in a hospital bed wrapped like a dead and gone mummy. Playing 21 questions about my life wasn't at the top of my agenda.

"Any drug use? Alcohol?"

"He doesn't drink," Cole said.

"Mr. Iversen, any alcohol or drugs?"

I couldn't answer her because Jason loudly ambushed his way into the room. His widow in mourning act was completely excessive. Cole guided him to one of the folding chairs against the wall. "Calm down, Jason. He's awake. The doctor is checking on him."

"Who is this?" the doctor said impatiently. The interruptions stopped her from doing her work and me from coming to terms with the fact that I wasn't dead. This place was turning into a three-ring circus. I was not here to put on a show!

"I'm his roommate," Jason said between crocodile tears.

"Both of you can stay, but you're going to have to be quiet," the doctor instructed. "Mr. Iversen, any existing medical conditions? Do you have a history of mental illness in your family?"

"No."

"Mental illness?" Jason gasped.

"Sir, please. Keep the outbursts to a minimum or I'll have to ask you to leave," the doctor flared. "Mr. Iversen. Tyree. Have you ever thought about hurting yourself before this incident?"

I kept telling this woman "no"! Couldn't she leave me alone in peace? No, she kept going with her line of questioning.

"So what led to your decision to hurt yourself?" she asked. "This was a particularly severe form of self-harm. Was there any recent trauma in your life?"

This so-called "doctor" had a medical degree and she still

needed to ask me that stupid question? "Yes," I said.

I wanted to tell her everything, but I couldn't. The people most responsible for my troubles were in the room. She sensed that might be the case. "Would you prefer to talk in private?" she asked.

"No, it won't make a difference," I said.

She sighed but continued like I told her to. "As I mentioned, aside from the blood loss there wasn't extensive damage. Somehow, you didn't hit a nerve," she said. "One of the nurses will be in shortly to dress your wounds. After we release you, I'm recommending you follow up with one of our staff psychiatrists to evaluate whether we need to prescribe medication. You're over 18, so we're not required to call a parent or guardian. However, I've asked your roommate to make sure you follow through with my instructions."

Cole nodded to the doctor. Please, anybody but him.

"Can you two come over here?" the doctor gestured to Cole and Jason. "We'll be back, Mr. Iversen. Push the button on the bed if you need anything."

My irritation was at its boiling point watching them talk about how unbalanced I was. If this was an attempt to keep their powwow on the hush, they needed to try harder. It was a small room and the doctor wasn't talking nearly low enough. I could hear them saying things about how I was a danger to myself. Treating me like I was a child.

"He's likely to be on edge once we release him," the doctor said. "Keep him away from any sharp objects like knives or scissors you may have in the house. You should check on him regularly. Keep the door to his bedroom open at all times. Also, make sure he schedules his follow-up appointment."

"We will," Cole said.

"Take care of yourself, Mr. Iversen," the doctor announced

to me.

After she walked out, Jason rushed to my side. I rolled over quickly to turn away from him and Cole. I wasn't supposed to see these traitors ever again. I couldn't succeed at life, so I didn't know how I thought I'd be any better at ending it.

They kept me in the hospital for two days. I'd been inside the apartment for just as long. Jason and Cole had searched high and low for anything dangerous that I could use to hurt myself. Some things in my room were moved or completely missing. My chest of drawers that was once organized by color was a wreck. The tag team mostly left me alone except for the occasional peek through the crack of my door. They didn't dare disturb me.

Ever since Jason and Cole brought me back to my room, I had no desire to go anywhere else. In my mind, the bandages around my arms and legs kept me tied down to the bed. My punishment was to live in the purgatory I created for myself.

The soreness from my injuries went away somewhat. That wasn't the issue, though. I did the most drastic thing I possibly could to escape life. Yet here I was in my same bed with the same thoughts. Every single time I'd been attacked or disrespected replayed over and over. I rubbed my head hoping it would bring sense back to my troubled mind. That didn't work any more than killing myself did.

Now that I was alive I needed to consider what my future would look like. To an outsider, I didn't have the worst life ever. I was in college and in good health. There were starving children in Africa, my mother would say when I was younger.

Just because I didn't have the biggest problems in the world didn't mean they weren't worth losing my mind over.

I told myself my struggles were insignificant. Just ignore them and don't tell anyone else, I thought. But eventually the smaller issues collected like raindrops into a wide puddle that swallowed me whole. I couldn't admit to myself I was depressed. That's where I went wrong.

I hadn't decided whether to call my daddy or not. Hurting him was the worst part of what I did. There was no way to properly tell my father that I slashed myself open with a razor because I was desperate to end my life. I didn't want to leave him with a tragedy on his hands but what was worse? Me living a miserable life or hiding my struggles to make him and everybody else around me feel better about themselves. I would not lose my sanity helping other people hold on to theirs.

For sure my daddy would be scared after our conversation, but he'd do his best to get me feeling better. "Time heals all wounds," he'd say. Even if that was true, the physical scars may heal, but the mark on my life they left behind would never go away completely. I went way too far for things to ever be the same.

Somebody knocked on my door. It wasn't closed all the way and Jason and Cole knew I hadn't gone anywhere. I appreciated their phony courtesy, but I didn't feel like talking to either one of 'em. They knocked another time. Those two were gonna keep pounding on that door until I let them in. I would do it only so they could leave me be.

"Door's open," my voice cracked. It was the first time I'd said anything out loud in days.

Idiot and Dumbass shuffled to my bed with hangdog expressions. Jason opened his mouth to ask me something, but all I got from him was air. "It's been a week, Tyree," he finally said.

"Did you come in here to give me a calendar update?" I asked.

"No," he said without looking me in the eye. "We wanted to see if you're doing better. Are you?"

"I'm not lookin' for a pity party," I said between clenched teeth.

"We know," Cole sighed. "Just seein' where your head is at."

"What you really wanna know is why I did it," I said defiantly. "That's what it is, right? Things were sooooo great and I'm always soooooo happy. I had no reason to wanna kill myself. But I can only take so much. Y'all pushed me over the edge. As much as I've dealt with in my life, I never thought it would be the people closest to me other than my family who would hurt me the most. I trusted you two and you shat all over our friendship."

They were stunned like what I said was news to them. Jason and Cole could never put themselves in my broken shoes. They had no clue what I went through. I gave up on them understanding me the moment I made that first cut.

"You are not in high school anymore," I continued. "You need to grow up! I don't care how drunk you were when you were laid in that hotel! The fact that you would do somethin' that cruel behind my back is complete nonsense. What makes it worse is that you refuse to see things from my perspective."

"We're doing our best," Jason said. "We might not understand everything exactly, but we want to. Cole and I feel terrible about Miami. We weren't thinking clearly."

"That's right, you weren't. You guys are just like everybody else. Every hateful word people say, every time they do me wrong, it chips away at my well-being. I had enough of it!"

"I'm sorry, Tyree," Jason stammered.

"I *don't* accept your apology. Don't think 'cause I'm talkin' to you right now that I've in any way forgiven you."

"I'll pray for you," he said.

"Go pray for yourself."

I sprang out of my bed toward Jason. I had every intention of clawing his lying eyes out. Jason leapt back just in time to avoid being slashed in the face with my fingernails.

"Tyree, stop it!" Cole hollered. If he didn't come between us when he did, I would've ripped Jason's throat out.

"Give us some time to talk, Jason," Cole panted. The nitwit left the room mouthing another weak "I'm sorry." Cole wasn't sure what to say to me, so he sat there looking like boo boo the fool. Unless his plan was to give me the sincere apology I deserved from him, he could follow Jason out the door.

"Cole, I expected so much more from you," I said defeatedly. "I never told you I liked you as more than a friend 'cause I didn't wanna make things uncomfortable between us. But you hurt me more than that boy at IHOP ever could."

"I'm straight, though!" he protested. "I don't want you stressin' over somethin' that was never gonna happen. That situation with Jason and me is something I never shoulda done, but I love females. I ain't gay. If you can't get that through your brain, then I don't know what to tell you."

Cole handed me a napkin from the nightstand for me to clean myself up. "I'ma let you have ya alone time. You should see the psychiatrist like the doctor said. You need to talk it out."

He scooped up the pile of leftover cereal bowls and left me sitting there dumbfounded. I wished he never came in the room! Nothing changed! Cole could not give a single damn about me. I would not trap myself in the apartment with these two Judases. I would not let them bring me down to their level. I crawled out of bed and hobbled toward the mirror on my dresser.

I looked like a mess. My hair hadn't seen any product since Miami. A week's worth of stubble took over my face. Somebody needed to hose me down with a fire hydrant because the awful smell in the room was disturbing my nostrils. Before I did anything, I would call my daddy. I wanted to hide the death that never happened from him, but I couldn't go on without hearing his voice. I cradled my cell phone in my hands gathering the strength to dial his number.

When I got to the admissions office, Miss Bert was at the counter with a stack of manila folders in her hands. Natalie and Andrea were at their workstations typing away. The office was exactly the same as it was before I left. No one knew about the trauma I went through the past week. I hid my scars under a black, long-sleeve shirt and pants so they wouldn't find out.

Miss Bert glanced my way. "Welcome back, Tyree. Your roommate stopped by and told me you weren't feeling well. You've been away for a while. Is everything okay?"

"I'm not sick, Miss Bert. I just haven't been feeling like myself lately."

She saw right through my non-answer. "Here, come talk with me in my office."

She closed the door and we sat across from each other. Her face softened. "Listen, Tyree, I care about you not only as my employee but also as a student and an individual. If something is wrong, you need to tell me. I can see you want to keep your emotions private and that's okay. But I can't help you if you don't open up."

Attempting to hash things out with Cole was a disaster but it was much easier to confide in Miss Bert. Without my mother around she filled a void for me that was left open for years. Miss Bert was real and present and she cared.

My boss and adviser listened kindly to my every word as I described what could've been the end for me. She was sympathetic and never interrupted. There was no judgment coming from her. When I was done, she exhaled a heavy "God bless."

"I'm going to share with you what someone told me when I was younger," she said with care. "In college, you're going to struggle either academically, financially or spiritually and sometimes all three at the same time. That doesn't mean you give up, Tyree."

"I keep telling myself that, Miss Bert, but I don't always believe it. This school is breakin' me down no matter which way I turn. When I got my acceptance letter from Morrison, I felt like I would finally belong somewhere. So far, that hasn't been the case."

"Why are you looking for validation from other people? Tyree, you are meant to be here. You think I didn't go through your application before you started working in my office? You've got the goods to be successful, dear. I need you to know that. You're at this school for a reason."

"I know why I'm here, Miss Bert. It's the people around me that are draggin' me down. They don't even bother talkin' about me behind my back. Just when I think I'm over a run-in with one jagwagon, somebody else'll laugh or point or call me a name and I'm back at square one. It's this never-ending cycle of hate comin' my way."

Miss Bert nodded with understanding. "Tyree, people will

point out your flaws so they can feel better about themselves. They'll talk about you regardless of what you do. If you let them know you're hurt by their words, then they've won. Live your life the way you want to, Tyree. The haters don't wanna see you be successful."

"What you know about haters, Miss Bert?" She cracked my face with that one!

"Oh, I got haters! You think because I'm up in age they don't have it in for me too? I just brush them off with a big broomstick!"

That was enough for me to lose it. I laughed until I was almost exhausted. I had two choices: joy or tears. Laughter felt so much better than the other option. It was a weight off my shoulders for me to let it out. Miss Bert howled along with me.

"All jokes aside Tyree, do you. Be yourself and don't stress over what anyone else has to say. Whenever you're feeling down, remember there are people in your life who love you, including me. Now give me a hug."

She embraced me like my daddy used to do when I was going through it in high school. There were hills to climb and it would be a long road before I made it over.

Miss Bert flipped through one of her folders and handed me a sheet of paper with a list of names. "We have a group of students coming in from Hillsborough High to do a campus tour. You should show them around. It'll take your mind off everything. Get yourself together like I know you can. I'll have them wait outside."

I took a fistful of tissues from her desk so I wouldn't look like I was crying my eyes out. It was time to put on my game face. Sure enough, when I stepped out of the building, there was a crew of high school students kiki-ing outside. I gave the rehearsed intro I'd said many times before.

"Hello everybody my name is Tyree Iversen. Welcome to Morrison State University." The round of applause from my group made me a little prouder.

"I'm gonna take you around to see our historic buildings and landmarks. You can ask me questions at any time, just stay close so we don't lose anyone. Let's head this way."

The 20 or so students shuffled behind me chatting with each other until we reached the main entrance to the school. "Morrison State University" was etched into the wrought iron gate. The school seal topped the arc. The students' eyes were as big as mine were when I first visited the campus.

As we passed under the gate I talked through details about the school's history. "Morrison State University was founded in 1901 by the Reverend Alfred Morrison. He was a great man who had a vision for a place of higher learning that welcomed students of color. The university was a destination for African-American students to receive a college education when they were being turned away from predominantly White schools."

I walked backward and faced the students at the same time. It was a skill I mastered early on because it was easier to point out what they should be looking at. I peeked over my shoulder every so often to make sure I didn't trip over anything. Also, I didn't raise my hands above my head so I wouldn't show off the bandages wrapped around my arms. The students didn't notice a thing.

"On your right is the humanities building. It was constructed in the 1920s and is one of the oldest buildings at the university. Classes were first held in the chapel, then in here once more students enrolled. On your left is the Academic office where students can register for classes and find out more about the programs offered here."

A girl with her hair in natural twists and a "Black Girls Rock" shirt threw her hand up. "When do you have to pick a major?" she asked.

"The way it goes is you declare your major on your application, but you can change it anytime," I said. "Your first year is mostly general education courses. You start takin' classes for your major sophomore year. Another question?"

I nodded to a boy with a box fade who had his hand up too. "What made you want to come to this school?"

I kept a prepared answer for whenever a prospective student would ask me that. I had to be myself in spite of everybody else.

"I came because I wanted to be a better version of myself," I said. "You can't accomplish your goals without an education. If I'm gonna get a degree that'll change my life I better do it at a school that's settin' Black students up for success. Let's keep walkin'."

The katta-kat-kat of snare drums echoed through campus, which meant band practice had kicked off. Sure enough, as we rounded the bleachers, the school band was on the football field with their instruments tucked under their arms. Instead of the full uniforms they wore at football games, they had on white Morrison T-shirts and maroon jogging pants.

The music director Mr. Washington stood on a high ladder yelling orders into a megaphone. I couldn't make out what he was saying, but I sure wouldn't want to be under his watchful eye.

"Hey y'all, this is our football field, home of the MEAC champion Morrison Eagles!" I said to the students. "The first game on this field was held in 1956 against Savannah State. When it's not football season, the band uses it for practice. Altogether, there are about 150 students in the band. Some of them are music majors, but a lot of 'em are studyin' one of the 100 or so other majors the school offers. You can sit in the stands and watch them practice if you want."

The students scrambled to grab seats that would give them a good view of the action. The chances of catching the band practicing were always high since they marched on the field almost every afternoon. That's what made them so damn good. They put in work.

When the band members weren't in class, they were going over their routines. An HBCU band wasn't like the corny ones at the white schools. Our band would get you on your feet. They'd play the latest hit song like it was a Mozart symphony with choreography from start to finish.

At the last game against Norfolk State, everybody was bored because neither team had scored a point. Then halftime came around. The Morrison band lit up that field like it was the Fourth of July. People came running back from the concession stands, dragging their poor children behind them because they knew better than to miss the party.

The band came through the football field dancing and marching in formation. Those cymbals spun like they were Neo in the Matrix. The percussion section took it back to Africa with their beats. It was fantastic.

Today, the ten Eaglette dancers were on the field in their usual place in front of the band. Their full name was the Morrison State *Electrifying* Eaglettes. "Electrifying" didn't begin to describe these girls. The way they moved was feminine allure personified. Their footwork and synchronized arm movements made it look like they were signaling the fiercest plane on an airport runway. Straight guys fell over themselves to get a look at the Eaglettes.

The outfits they wore were a huge part of their appeal. Those things were so skin-tight every ass shake and body roll came through loud and clear. On performance days, they wore long, silky weaves that dripped from the top of their heads to their juicy hips.

The band on the field wasn't giving us more than the occasional toot on their horns. Mr. Washington looked over at me and the tour group in the stands waiting patiently for them to play a song. That man loved an audience. With one wave, the band lined up and stood at attention. He lightly moved his wand from side to side as they launched into a melodic performance of Stevie Wonder's "If It's Magic."

The slow songs like this one were my favorites. The sweet sound pulled me in and didn't let me go until the song was over. There was no denying Morrison ran me low, but moments like this were worth sticking around for.

Most of the students were fixated on the band or buried in their phones. Two boys next to me were as into the music as I was. They were skinny little things, both with dark hair. One of 'em had olive skin and what appeared to be Latino features. He looked older than his friend who had straight teeth and greenish hazel eyes. On the younger one's backpack was a button with a rainbow on it. Boom. Gay. They caught me looking in their direction.

"Those girls are fierce!" My Latino friend exclaimed. His wonder warmed my ice-cold heart.

"They sure are. Y'all wanna try out?" I kidded quietly. I hadn't completely recovered after my heart to heart with Miss Bert.

"Dancing's not my thing," he said. "But I do wanna join a fraternity if I come here."

"A fraternity?" I coughed. No, ma'am. "Okay, what's your name?"

"Javier," he said politely.

"And I'm Russell," his friend smiled.

"Thank you for the tour! This place is so cool," Javier said. "Are you in a fraternity?"

"No sir, I'm more of a solo person," I said, shaking my head.

"Mr. Tyree, can I ask you a question? I don't wanna blow up your spot but are there any other gay people at Morrison?" Damn, he done clocked me too. Gay recognized gay, so I couldn't be totally mad.

"There's a few here and there," I said. "Some of them are outta the closet. There's also the ones who don't advertise."

"So people aren't out at this school?" Javier asked. "I heard most HBCUs don't support guys like us. Is that true?"

Javier's statement brought Russell's mood down. "Yeah, we looked at places like Florida State 'cause they have gay groups for the students," he sighed.

"We don't have school-sponsored groups or events on campus," I said with regret. "There are cliques, but they don't have meetings or anything like that."

Javier wasn't swayed. "Let's say me and him kiss on the field somewhere..."

"Eww, you my play brother! We don't do that," Russell protested.

"I'm saying what if I get a boo? Someone very sexy, of course. If I wanna give him a kiss before I go to class is everybody gonna come for me?"

These kids were *fast*. Tonguing somebody down on the football field? "It don't matter if you're gay or straight," I said. "If two students are kissin' on campus, people will talk about you. You'll be alright, though."

I knew that was far from the truth, but I didn't want them coming to this school thinking they weren't going to be safe. I gave them a smile that I hoped they couldn't see through.

"Ooh, you think I could get a letterman jacket if I come here?" Javier asked.

"For what sport?" Russell teased.

"I don't know. Good grades? I got those. Instead of an M for Morrison they can put straight As on the back."

The boys shared a laugh between them. The final drawn out note from the band got a big round of applause from the group of students. Mr. Washington and the Eaglettes waved appreciatively in our direction. We shouted our thank-yous toward the field.

"Okay everybody we have to get goin'," I announced. "Follow me this way."

We climbed down from the stands toward the student center so they could get a bathroom break. The kids rushed inside. They were going on and on about the band. Russell and Javier followed the crowd, talking about our conversation.

I wanted them to be okay if they came to Morrison. They shouldn't have to go through the same crap I did. It wasn't right for any of the students to have to walk around in fear. Our administration couldn't hide behind school traditions when it wanted something to go away that they saw as troublesome. Progress would not stop because our school officials chose to ignore it.

Nobody cared about the gay students, but I did. I couldn't sit helplessly on the sidelines anymore. I was gonna be the Harriet Tubman of this school and lead the way. Somebody needed to help the students and incoming classes understand they had a safe place at Morrison. The only way this school would change its outdated sensibilities was if I did something about it.

Where was my phone? I needed to text Tasha. She was always somewhere in the student center. A minute later, Tasha came bouncing out of the doors as bubbly as ever. "Heyyyyy! What's up, babe?"

"Tasha, I wanna run for a position in student government. Is it too late for me to put my name in?"

"Not at all! We would love to have you! You did such a good job at the pageant. That's the kind of work ethic we need for SGA. We don't have anybody running for vice president if you're interested in that."

"Vice president?"

"Yeah, can you believe it? Nobody's signed up yet and we're days away from the election. There's one student running against me for president and three going for Secretary. The other slots have one person running uncontested. Vice president is a great fit for you, Tyree. If I win, we'll get to work together! What do you think?"

"I'm in, girl. Where do I sign up?"

"So amazing!" Tasha squealed. "I'll get your name on the ballot. You need to come to the student activities office before the end of the day to be certified. You're running alone, but you should get a campaign together for the elections next week. You want the student body to know who you are and why you want to be vice president."

"I can do that, no problem," I said. I was already creating a checklist in my mind of the things I could do.

"Also, there'll be tables on the quad on election day for you to pass out flyers. You can arrange it however you want. Sound good, boo?"

"Yes, thank you, Tasha!"

"I'm so thrilled for you, Tyree! I have to head inside but don't forget to stop by the office! Byeeeee!"

That was the motivation I needed. Both me and this school were gonna change. From here on out I'd set my own path. The first stop on the road was vice president of the Morrison State University SGA.

Should I tell Jason and Cole? No, they could go fuck themselves. Or each other. And yes, I was still mad about it. Let me text my girl Day Day.

guess whos running for SGA vp ☺

Before I could put my phone back in my pocket, it was already ringing.

"Oh my godddddddd!" Day Day shouted in my ear. "You better get your politics on, Tyree! Werk!" He was more ecstatic than I was, "If you're going to slay the scene you'll need a fierce campaign manager. I can offer you my services. I'll give you the friends and family discount."

"Ain't nobody runnin' against me, Day," I said into the phone. "What I need a campaign manager for? And you work in the student activities office. Wouldn't that be suspect?"

"You right, but we gotta get *someone* to vote for your ass or else you got no votes and no vice president. I'll handle everything on the low, I promise."

"Day, I trust you as long as you don't blow it out the water. Let's go 'head and meet tomorrow so we can talk it over."

"Yes, we'll get posters, a banner…ooh and buttons with your face on 'em," he laid out the plans. "I'll talk to you soon, girl!"

I called the students back from their break to keep the tour going. I was in a better place than I was this morning. I was gonna tear the roof off this school.

"Vote for Tyree for SGA vice president! Let's make Morrison outstanding!"

A group of ladies in tennis skirts paused at my table to pick out a piece of candy. I smiled and handed them a flyer. I was on the quad with the other candidates who'd set out their spaces on the grass.

My table didn't have as many students dropping by, but it was the best looking one. I had a stack of handwritten flyers and glass bowls of purple Jolly Ranchers. Under that was a cerulean tablecloth and placemats I borrowed from the house. I wouldn't be a marketing major if I didn't know how to turn a space out.

Day Day made a sign for me — "Tyree for V.P." in fancy, handwritten letters on neon poster board. He watched from far enough behind me that it didn't look like he was campaigning on my behalf. Tasha's table across the walkway from mine had bright pink and green balloons everywhere. A group of her sorors handed out flyers for her. I blushed when she blew me a kiss. Having her support meant everything.

"This table is looking mighty clever!" Day Day sauntered toward me. I knew he couldn't stay away for too long.

"You helped, Day," I said. "You're like a fairy godmother makin' my wishes come true."

"Without the wings and the magic wand. Those are on layaway," he said. "So, I never asked you, Ty, why are you doing this? You woke up one day wanting to be SGA vice president?"

I didn't tell him about the... incident. Mostly because he'd freak out more than my daddy did and I hadn't even told him the whole story. He insisted on driving to Tampa to come get me. It took an hour and a half to convince him there was no need for that. I told Day Day about my heated conversation with Dean Simmons instead.

"That kinda attitude is so old school," he groaned. "We need someone like you to get in there and change things up."

"I agree. What was Morrison like when you were in school?"

"Tyree, I was so focused on my future matriculation I wasn't thinking about this school and its issues. Don't get me wrong, I was Morrison's most welcome guest at school functions and football games, but my mind was on getting what? My diploma. After you graduate, none of this will matter, boo. You'll be long gone and hopefully not look back."

"But the dean will still be at this school when I leave. A new group of students are gonna come in and have to deal with Dean Simmons or whoever comes after him."

"You're right. So be that leader! Fight for what you believe in. I've come to understand that sometimes just being yourself is a political statement. Put me on a stage with a heap of makeup and a sickening wig and that's my form of protest. You have to find yours, baby."

"Has there ever been a gay person on the SGA before?" I asked. "Or am I the first one?"

"I'm sure there's been a closet queen in there somewhere. I'd bet my life on it. If you want an answer with deep research, I'll find out for you later. In the meantime did you vote yet?"

"I'm going to soon. I hear I'm the best candidate on the ballot," I winked.

"I know that's right, girl! I can't vote, but if I could it'd be tens across the board for you. Let me watch the table and you go 'head on. I'll make sure nobody runs off with this delicious candy in these pretty little bowls."

There were a bunch of students in the caf ready for politics too. Miss Marshall and Quinton Briggs, the outgoing SGA president, were at a small square table passing out ballots. "Hey boss man, good luck," Quinton said as he handed me a slip of paper.

I was the only one on the ballot for VP. The students could leave the box blank if they wanted to. God willing they wouldn't do that. The first line was for Student Body President. I put a tick by Tasha's name. I filled out the rest of the ballot for Secretary, Treasurer, Parliamentarian and Member at Large. I saved Vice President for last. There was my name on a line by itself.

Tyree Iversen.

It was weird to vote for myself, but it would be silly if I didn't. This position was bigger than me. I filled in the box and handed over the finished ballot. I was certified and official. When I got back to the table, Jason and Cole were there picking through the candy. I didn't have the patience nor the will to put up with these two. Where did Day Day go?

"Hi, Tyree!" Jason reached out to me. I blocked his hug like I had on Wonder Woman's bracelets. He looked disappointed, but he could save those tears for somebody else. "How's it going out here?"

"So far so good. Meetin' new people," I said curtly.

"Cool," Cole went in for a Jolly Rancher. The candy was sweet, but his mood was sour.

"Whatsup with you?" I asked.

"Did you tell him?" Jason nudged Cole.

"Tell me what?"

"April broke up with me," he confessed. My expression didn't change. If this was his attempt to get sympathy points from me, he came to the wrong place. I stopped caring the moment I held that razor in my hand.

"That's too bad," I said as blatantly insincere as I could manage.

"Yeah, it is what it is," he mumbled without acknowledging my sarcasm. "Can't say I didn't see it comin'. I'm so used to having April around I almost texted her about the meet tomorrow. Are you guys gonna come?"

"I don't think so," I said sternly.

"Try to make it if you can," he hung his head. "I should take off. We're ridin' to Orlando early tomorrow. I gotta rest up. Good luck with the campaign, Tyree."

"Yeah, thanks."

COLE

The University of Central Florida's track stadium stood there waiting for me and my teammates as we got off the bus. This was where it was gonna go down. I wasn't ready for how majestic the place was.

The facilities at UCF were better than anything at Morrison. It held more than 2,000 people. The infield grass was an acre of green carpet. The lines on the all-weather track were freshly painted and the metal bleachers look liked like they were shined up for hours. If I ran in a stadium like this, I'd be the Michael Jordan of track.

It was the third day of the MEAC championships and my first day running. I had two events today. One solo run in the 400-meter and the 4x400 relay with the team. The relays were the last events of the day. The other ones went by quickly except for the long distance events. Those lasted forever.

So far, the Morrison men's team was in fourth place at the meet. Maryland-Eastern Shore and Hampton were in second and third. Bethune-Cookman University was in the lead with 55 points. B-CU was a black college in Daytona Beach, a couple of hours drive away from Tampa. They were a powerhouse in the MEAC. Last season, they swept through the events. Their team left the other runners in the dust.

The heat sheets outlined who was running from the other schools. Some of them had great times, but one misstep was the difference between winning and losing. If we wanted to win this thing we needed to get our asses in gear.

I texted my parents this morning to let 'em know I was competing in the championship. They didn't hit me back. I wasn't surprised though. They hadn't come to see me race since I was in high school.

Any other day, I would've been looking for my roommates in the stands. Not having them here was actually a good change for me. It meant no distractions. I channeled my disappointment, anger, frustration and the negativity from last week into my will to do better. I wouldn't let myself bring the team down.

Before we went our separate ways to get warmed up, Coach Jackson gathered us around. We needed motivation because we were so behind. Nobody knew that more than Coach did.

"Heads up, let's talk for a moment," he said. "We got one more day to go. We need to finish strong!" he said forcefully. "How's your leg, Cedric? You gonna be able to run?"

Ced injured himself in the long jump with a messed up landing. He'd been on the infield all day yesterday with an ice pack and a swollen knee. He gave Coach a reluctant thumbs up.

"Good man," Coach said. "This is what we've been gearing up for all season. You boys are the cream of the crop. Some of the best runners I've ever trained. But I'm not the one you need to prove that to. We gotta give the people in the stands a team they can root for. More than anything, I want you to make yourselves proud out there. If you've been doing well, keep it up. If you haven't, I want you to be inspired by your teammates around you. Am I gonna see gold?"

"Yes, Coach!" We clapped loudly to hype ourselves up. Having that energy was what moved us forward. Today was the day we showed our dedication to the sport we loved.

Coach followed the pep talk with a list of commands. "If you have an event in the next hour, I'll meet you on the field so we can warm up. The rest of you stay close. Let's bring it home for Morrison!"

It was gonna be a while before the 400 got going. I found an open section of the infield to watch the other events. I threw on my earbuds and cut on a track from Beanie Sigel. "We run everything!" he rapped ferociously. Beanie wasn't worrying about anybody else. Popping bottles and making money. That was it. Forget what other people said. The way he spat lyrics made me want to mob through the track right now.

The women's team from Morrison was out in full force. They had their own coach and they practiced separately from us. The only time we were in the same place was at a meet or on the bus. Every one of the girls had thighs thick enough to put a man in a headlock.

I always checked for this one girl named Ericka on the team. She was a distance runner and came to every meet with makeup on. I could never figure out how it didn't melt off. She was a mixed chick with rich, brown eyes and legs like lightning rods.

Her presence said "look, but don't touch." I never said anything to her because of April, but I always wanted to. Besides being beautiful, her talent in the 800- and 1500-meter blew the other girls away. I let Ericka put me under her spell until somebody announced that the 200-meter was set to begin.

Marshall was running in this and three other events. He strode onto the field, very aware that eyes were on him. He gave the people in the bleachers the spectacle they came to see. The gold chain with wings that he always wore dangled from his neck. I hated that thing. It was just like him. All shine, but fake as hell. Still, he was the one to beat.

Marshall got a good start out of the blocks, then sped past the other runners with a clear shot at first. The stadium was on edge waiting to see his time. Not only was it one of his personal bests, it was a record for our school. He high-fived everybody within reach as he grunted his way off the track. Deep down I didn't want to see him win, even if he was my teammate. It put points on the board for us. I had to be good with that.

I wanted to get a good warm up in before my first event. I started with stretches, then high knees and forward lunges. The calisthenics prepared me for the task at hand. I wanted to finish out the season knowing I posted the best times I could. If Marshall had his way, I woulda quit the team a long time ago. If I did that, I wouldn't be on the field ready to do damage. Quitting wasn't an option for me.

I was all set for the 400-meter race by the time Coach Jackson came over. He made sure to check on each of his runners before their events. "While you're out here, I want you to warm up your mind too," he said to me.

I stopped mid-lunge. I'd never heard that one before. "What was that?"

"It's not your body you have to worry about," Coach said. "You are fully capable of running this race, Cole. I've seen you do it successfully many times. Your battle is in not giving in when your mind tells you it's too much. If you don't plan on pushing yourself from the first step to the last, you shouldn't run at all. You only get one shot in the 400-meter, you hear me?"

"I'm on it, Coach." This time I meant it.

There was something about walking on a new track for the first time. It reminded of stepping onto the diving board at the community pool in South Philly. I wanted to jump in and join my friends below, but I was always scared. I told myself to forget about the nerves and make the leap. As soon as I did, that fear was behind me. Same thing with running. When the race was over, the nerves were gone. Afterward, I would always wonder why I was scared in the first place.

I joined the other sprinters stretching at the starting line. We nodded to each other without words. We were gladiators ready to fight until we were the last man standing. The announcer called out our lane assignments. "In lane five, Colin Hill." I tensed when he said my name. There were no wild cheers, just idle conversation from the stands. "Runners to your marks!"

I sucked in my last breath of oxygen before I positioned myself in the blocks. My fingers barely touched the rust-colored track beneath me. "Set."

This was it. My heart beat outta my chest. I listened for the gun. Boom! I bolted out of the blocks, pumping my arms fast to pick up speed. My body was an engine running on all cylinders. I let the crowd and the competition fade into the background. Nothing but the rapid pace of my feet flying over the track.

I sped like a bullet train until I got around the first turn, then I set a more controlled rhythm. I relaxed my arms. I kept the fast leg turnover pumping. Out of the corner of my eye, I spotted bruh from Cookman. He had a slight lead. I wasn't gonna worry about a runner who wasn't me. This was *my* race. In the straightaway, I cycled my arms faster until I hit maximum speed.

Sweat flew off my forehead before it could drip down to my eye. My legs burned from the lactic acid building in my system. My arms were on fire. I had to keep going! I was neck and neck with Cookman in the final stretch. My body shuddered as I powered my way over the finish line.

Slow down. Breathe. My lungs were weak from fighting for air. My legs were relieved to finally stop churning. Me and the seven other runners stood at the finish line. We waited impatiently for the news from the scoreboard.

There was my name in first! 47.26 seconds! That was a tenth of a second off my personal best *and* I scored five points for the team! I didn't think I'd place 'cause my times were so slow. I knew I could push it harder. There may not have been rings on my uniform, but no one could tell me I wasn't a star Olympian. Marshall glared at me from the finish line like the sore loser he was. That made me more satisfied than anything. I proved him wrong.

Coach jogged over with his arms spread wide in celebration. "Now that's the performance I needed from you, Cole! How do you feel?"

"Like I could run a marathon!" I exclaimed.

"If you can do 26 miles, 400 meters should be a cakewalk. Don't forget, it's not enough to be fast in this event, you and the team have to come together. Trust and teamwork, that's how you win medals."

"Fans and runners, this is the last event of this year's MEAC championship, the men's 4x400 relay," the announcer boomed. "After the individual events, Maryland-Eastern Shore is in third with 98 points, Morrison State moves into second with 102 and Bethune-Cookman maintains the lead with 105 points."

If we won the relay, that was it. We got the five points we needed to win the title. It was either that or zero points. We didn't come this far to go home empty-handed. Nick and Sergey would run the first and second leg in the relay and I was third. Marshall was the anchor. He was the one who would cross the finish line if we won. It didn't matter which of us held the baton when they got to the line. We had to be the first team to do it.

"Let's get a quick prayer in," Coach called to the four of us. "Marshall go ahead and give us a word."

We linked arms and bowed our heads. I cleared my mind of the noise on the field as Marshall prayed.

"Dear Heavenly Father," he began. "Thank you for bringing us here to glorify your name. Give us the strength we need, Lord. Help *all* of us pull through, including those who may be weak at this moment. We need your guidance to be men on that field and represent for our school."

I opened my eyes. Marshall looked directly at me as he spoke. "We ask these things in your son Jesus' name. Amen."

"Amen!" we shouted.

If he thought that dig was gonna throw me off, he'd better think again. I was in beast mode. I was running better than ever against the best schools in the MEAC. I followed Nick as he left for the line where the other teams stretched in preparation.

"Hey, congrats on the 400 meter," he shook my hand. "That was quite a feat. Let's do it again and bring it home."

I instinctively scanned the bleachers in the off-chance that April or my roommates came to the meet. They weren't there. It was confirmation that my leg of the race was on me. Nobody else. April was my crutch for way too long. Whether she or my roommates or my parents were here or not, I was gonna run my best in this relay. I wouldn't settle for anything but first place.

The eight runners on the first leg lowered into the set position. With one shot of the gun, the organized chaos began.

"And they're on their way in the 4x400 finals!" the announcer declared.

As Nick flew through the first lap, Sergey positioned himself for the hand off. He snatched the baton with ease. Sergey put distance between himself and the rest of the pack. I readied myself in the lane with my right hand stretched behind me. Seven other runners wanted this bad. I wanted it more. When Sergey was within a couple of meters, I took off. I matched his speed so we could get the clean pass. "Stick!"

The metal baton connected with my hand. I sped around the track giving the race everything I had. The thundering footsteps behind me got closer as we raced around the turn and into the straightaway. No way I was gonna lose this lead!

I fought against my aching legs and the pain taking over my teeth and arms. I gave it as much drive as I possibly could. Marshall was ahead of me. His arm was out, ready for me to make the handoff. I adjusted my speed until we were Siamese twins on the track. "Stick!"

I slammed the baton in his hand and held it for a beat. I wanted to make sure that he had a firm grip. I moved to the side of the track to catch my breath. Marshall disappeared down the lane. It was up to him.

Marshall had a solid lead. The seven other guys chased after him like junkyard dogs. The win was ours! Marshall slowed down as he approached the line and shot his fists in the air. The hell? The idiot was so into himself he didn't see the man from Cookman pull ahead of him to take first.

We had it in the bag! And we lost! Just like that it was over! Marshall's stunt put us in second place. No points. Not a single one. The Cookman fans went wild. They waved their maroon and gold flags and hugged each other. They were going home champs. Marshall talked that trash and still lost, even after we handed him the lead. He was the reason we were going home with silver.

Our team met at the finish line where Coach stood in disbelief. None of us would look Marshall in the eye. If the guys were pissed off like I was they wanted to strangle him too.

"What counts is you did your best," Coach said with heart. He didn't believe it, really. Neither did I. That wasn't *our* best. "You all go change into your warm-ups. After the medal ceremony is over, we'll go home but you're gonna do it with a winning attitude. You are Morrison men and we never show defeat."

I should've been mad, but I wasn't. I did what I set out to accomplish. They were gonna hand me a gold medal for the 400 and a silver for the team. We didn't win the MEAC title, but second place wasn't bad considering where we were earlier in the season. We'd be back next year. We'd go even harder. I would never be the dead weight again.

If somebody told me at the beginning of the semester I would celebrate a win at a gay club, the first thing I would've said was "where did I get a medal from?" Second would be "why would I be at a gay club?" But here I was with a gold and silver medal tucked in my pocket, waiting at the Alibi for Tyree to come through. It wasn't a celebration for me. It was to congratulate Ty on the student government election. That was my boy. He deserved it.

There were more people in the Alibi than there were last time. It was a Saturday night, which meant every club in Tampa was jumpin'. Tasha was by the bar recapping the election to Jason. She had on her turn-up outfit: black, knee-high boots and a yellow Morrison shirt tied in the front.

Tasha was here because she was in Tyree's good graces. She was the one who got him to run for SGA. I wished I could say that Tyree invited me and Jason 'cause we were back to being friends. It was more outta obligation to the people who lived with him.

After he finally came out of his bedroom, he didn't say much to us. He was a zombie drifting through the apartment. If me and him were in the same room, he'd run off to somewhere else — the bathroom, the kitchen, the street outside. Anywhere I wasn't. And he did it without a warning or an apology. I thought about how violently he took himself out — or tried to. I figured it was best to stay outta his way. I didn't want him attacking me. Or himself.

Tyree avoided me, but Jason got it worse. He shot Jason down with death stares and groans of disgust as he walked by. I wasn't talking to Jason either. I didn't want him to bring up Miami. Anytime he tried to, I stopped him or walked away. I wanted to get the ordeal out of my system. Seeing the mouth that swallowed my dick kept the memory alive.

Somebody hustled through dancers, coming our way. There was Tyree wearing a long-sleeve shirt tucked into a huge belt buckle. He strutted past me without a nod or a hello.

"Hey, Tasha!" Tyree kissed her on the cheek. He ignored Jason, who was in the same breathing space as Tasha.

"Excuse me, it's Student Government Association president Tasha Nichols, thank you!" she joked.

"Ooh excuse me, Miss President!" he stifled an earnest laugh. "Girl, we're gonna go in! The next school year is gonna be *ah*-mazing."

"It sure is, thanks to you and the new board."

Jason stepped forward to interrupt him. "Hi Tyree," he said.

"Hello," he said coldly. He looked Jason up and down. That was it. Tyree turned his attention back to Tasha. "So this is your first time at a gay bar? You're in for a treat! I'm so glad you could make it."

If he gave Jason the cold shoulder, I wasn't gonna do much better. Tyree had it in for us. He invited me to this thing. That was a good first step. I'd meet him halfway.

"Whatsup, Tyree," I said. He didn't shake my hand like a grown man would. He put his palm into mine and gripped it lightly. Tasha eyed us suspiciously wondering why we weren't talking. Were we ever gonna be boys again?

"Hi, I'm Cole," I said to her. Her eyes widened with surprise. "Hiiiiiiiiii! Tyree, is this your boyfriend? Pleasure to meet you! I'm Tasha."

"We met once before," I said. "And naw, I'm not gay. I'm his roommate." I didn't want to make too much of a deal out of it in front of Tyree. I kept my mouth shut. The next move was on him.

"Oh, I'm sorry! Roommate!" Tasha exclaimed. "I'm telling you now, I have a man at home so don't get fresh. So boys, do I look fabulous?"

"You look flawless, miss lady," Tyree said. "You betta watch out. One of these boys is gonna mop them boots of yours."

"I have my stun gun in my purse," she winked. "Your president has to look good!"

I wasn't gonna stand around looking stupid while Tyree pretended like I didn't exist. The only reason I didn't throw my hands in the air and walk out was Day Day. He swished toward us wearing a metallic silver swimsuit, matching high heels and a platinum blond wig. Derrick transformed himself into a fine-ass woman. The man was nothing to fuck with.

"Hey, darling!" Day Day gave Tasha an air kiss. She didn't recognize who it was. "Fancy seeing you in my neighborhood!"

"Derrick, is that you?!" She dropped her purse to throw her arms around him.

"Ooh hey, watch the body, baby! This is top of the line Home Depot! So what do you think?"

Tasha was freaked out seeing her friend in drag. She hadn't loosened her grip on his waist. "You don't understand guys; we work in the same office, but I've never seen him like this! You look incredible Derrick! You *have* to hook me up with makeup tips."

"In here it's Dayneisha Divine! And yes sweetie, whenever you like. We'll go the MAC counter and have us a nice shopping spree," he said. He politely moved her hands down to her sides. "Tyree, come gimme some sugar. I'm so proud of this one."

"Aw Day, you're the best friend a guy could ask for." He rolled his eyes at me and Jason.

"Baby, I'll move heaven and Earth for you if I need to," Day

Day gushed. "So listen kiddies, it's about time for me to begin my dragnificent duties. It's going to be a glorious show tonight."

Tasha bounced around like a kid in a toy store. She was more hyped than any of us. I couldn't say I was as eager as she was my first time here. I was on edge from the moment we set foot inside. I couldn't deny the experience was fascinating. The boys in the club weren't hiding out from anybody. They were coming together like a family. It was a second home.

Day Day instructed us to follow him. "Come here by the stage. Korey has seats for you."

Sure enough, Korey was settled at a black, round-top table. There was a card on it that read "Reserved" in cursive letters. "I'm glad you're back, guys," he purred. "Cole, you're looking smashing. You're not giving Mike Tyson tea tonight, are you?"

Not anymore. And smashing? In a T-shirt and jeans? I guess it was a compliment, but I didn't see it.

"What's your name, baby girl?" Korey asked our guest.

"It's Tasha, but tonight you can call me Madam President," she giggled.

"If that's the case, you can call me the Queen."

We settled into our seats just as Day Day appeared on the stage with a microphone. The silver outfit made her shimmer like a diamond in a coal mine. The blond wig was poofy enough to fill the club from the ceiling to the floor. "Yesssss divas and darlings! Thank you for gracing us with your presence at the Alibi tonight! Give yourself a round of applause for being alive and well! Also, I want to give special love to this hunk of beefcake in the front. Hey there!"

She pointed to a dude distractedly flipping cocktail napkins at the next table over. He jumped in surprise when she called him out. I would too if a six-foot tall drag queen came at me. His friends patted him on the back to congratulate him. He was the object of her affection.

"Excuse me, sir. What's your name?" Day Day asked. "Yes you, Tyson Beckford. Where you from?"

"Opa-Locka!" he shouted over the low rumble of the club.

"Opa-Locka, Florida? I think I got a cousin in jail there. He owes me money. He thinks he doesn't have to pay me back because he's behind bars. I'ma have them put me in there too so I can get my $3 from that bastard. Ole triflin' ass. They got him for breaking and entering... another man's booty in a public bathroom! That is nasty and might I add illegal in the state of Florida! Get you a room at the 'momo' like the other boys do. See, I'm a lady. You'd never catch me doing any mess like that. Unless you have a fat stack of cash. Then we can talk," she laughed.

Day Day climbed down into her target's lap. She caressed his head. He didn't flinch. "Do you wanna be my sugar daddy tonight, honey?" she asked. "Buy this lady a drink? Bartender! Bring me a bottle of Tanqueray. The new love of my life is going to pick up the tab. We getting hitched tomorrow, y'all."

He laughed nervously. None of us were sure if he was really on the hook for her liquor tonight.

"Chile, let me stop playing," Day Day smiled. "You don't know me from Adam. What's my name?"

"Um, I'm not sure," the guy said shyly into Day Day's mic.

"You can call me Dee, last name Licious. Just kidding! I am Dayneisha Divine and it is my pleasure to be your emcee and star performer tonight." She licked his ear and flounced back on the stage.

"If you haven't been to the Alibi before, you're in for a real treat. Before we start, I want to introduce to you a gem of a friend and the new vice president of the Morrison State University SGA, Mr. Tyree Iversen!"

"Woo-hoooooo! Go Tyree!" Tasha clapped. We joined her in a round of applause. He took a bow.

"Okay, I'm going to sing a special number for you," Day Day said. "And by sing I mean I'll mouth the words to another woman's track. But I need some help. Tyree, come here. Korey, get your ass to the stage too. You boys can be my backup singers."

I immediately recognized the song. It was "Heat Wave" by Martha and the Vandellas. One time, Tyree made me watch a bunch of YouTube videos of 60s girl groups for two long hours. I couldn't forget something like that.

Day Day swerved to the doo-wop tune, occasionally making eye contact and pointing to each of the boys watching her. Tyree and Korey mimicked her dance moves, toeing from side to side. None of them actually sang, but you'd never know it. Their lips hit every single word with precision as if the music was their own. They were larger than life. With those three together, I knew they were gonna tear it up.

It was good to see Tyree back to being his usual cheerful self again. After I found him bleeding on the bathroom floor, I thought that was it. He was dead. He tried to kill himself based on me being careless. It was my words and actions that stung him so bad he picked up that razor. I gave Tyree my word that I would always back him up. I fell through on my promise. I was a terrible roommate and a worse friend. He was right about me. I'd only thought about myself.

I didn't know he had a crush on me, but that wasn't a good enough reason for me to come down hard on him the way I did. When we rode back from Miami, I didn't wanna hear about Tyree's fantasies of us being a couple. I blocked him out. I thought it was over when we got out of the car. It wasn't. He was an emotional wreck. I didn't notice and I didn't care.

Finding Ty in a dark red pool of his own blood, angry stab wounds on his legs and arms, him knocked out cold — I thought somebody murdered my boy. I panicked. My first reaction was to tear through every corner of the apartment to see if the killer was there. Then I saw the razor in Tyree's hand.

I carried him as fast as I could to his car. I hauled ass to the hospital. I didn't know if I would hear him speak again. Or smile. Laugh. Crack jokes on me. I wanted all of that back.

No one would ever catch me crying, but damn if I wasn't letting it out here in the club. The only light in the room came from the stage. Where I sat in the audience, no one could see me tearing up. I couldn't go another day living with the distance between us. I didn't have to be gay to love him. He was my brother. I needed him back by my side. I wanted him to always have the same type of joy he had on that stage.

"What's going on, Cole? Are you okay?" Jason leaned over to me.

"I'm good. Just thinkin'." I lowered my head into my hands. The trio ended the song with a classic girl group pose. Shoulders back, arms up, hips jutted to the side. The three of 'em took a long bow as the people around us rooted them on.

"Ladies and gentlemen, give a hand to the incomparable Tyree Iversen and my good Judy, Korey!" Day Day hugged them both.

I didn't want everybody at the club to see me crying like a bitch. I needed to get myself together so I wouldn't spoil the night. There weren't many places to hide out, so I positioned myself by the bar. There was a familiar face at the other end.

I couldn't make out who it was. Was that Marshall?? I pushed past the guys lined up for drinks to get over to him. Wasn't that some shit! A dude who had his arm wrapped around my teammate grinned like they were in love.

I knew this man was gay! Marshall gave me hell about my roommates and here he was in the Alibi with another dude! His friend saw me scoping them out. He whispered in Marshall's ear. My teammate locked eyes with me. Without missing a beat, Marshall pulled dude out of the club. He stomped his way through a herd of people in a rush to get out.

Jason came up beside me with no clue what was going on. "Have you already ordered?" he asked.

"I'll be back." I took off before he could ask where I was going. I ran after Marshall and his mystery man. "Yo, Marshall!"

"What, Cole?" he said exasperated.

"What are you doin' here? You talkin' about me bein' gay and you're hugged up on this man. I oughta be callin' *you* out in front of the team." I was so pissed I could barely get my words out.

Marshall sighed heavily. "I'm not gay, Cole. This is my brother." Both of them looked like they wanted to crawl into a hole and disappear. "Ron, can you give us a minute to talk?"

Ron was shaking from getting called out. He nodded to Marshall and headed toward their ride.

"That's your brother? What you doin' with your family in a gay club?" I knew he didn't think I was gonna believe that story.

"I don't know okay!" he blurted out in frustration. "The other night Ron sat me down and told me he was gay. I didn't see it coming."

Marshall's words got caught in his throat. The bravado he always brought to the track was gone. Admitting the truth about his family was killing him.

"I thought Ron might be gay because he never had a girlfriend. It wasn't something we ever discussed," Marshall said tearfully. "He was the oldest of us brothers but in my family's eyes he could never be the man of the house. He ran away to California six years ago. I hadn't seen him since. He finally came back and every conversation we should've had a long time ago happened this week. Ron wanted me to come here with him and I said yes. I had to. He's my brother."

"That's a lot to handle," I said sympathetically. "I'm sorry. I didn't understand what was going on."

Marshall looked relieved to have said something. His frustration turned into regret. "Cole, I know I've been an asshole to you. I was scared that if my brother was a homo people might think I was gay too. I've been shifting the blame to guys like you who don't deserve it. I put so much of myself into track that I don't want to give people any reason to say I'm not the best out there. Do me a favor? Don't tell anybody about my brother or that I was here?"

"Why not?" I snapped. He got me angry all over again. "You haven't done anything but give me hell the whole season."

"I don't want Coach or the team thinking I'm a fag," he pleaded.

"Gay," I said. "Don't use that word. And tough shit if they do. If you come at me again, I will beat you down and tell everybody you've been sexing dudes under the bleachers. I'ma say you been on that crack rock too and that's how you got your wins."

"None of that is true!" Marshall yelped.

"It will be if I tell everybody it is."

"That's cold," he shook his head.

I had him beat. He had no choice but to leave me alone. "I'm your teammate, Marshall. You better start treating me like one."

"So wait, are you gay?" he asked.

"Bruh, not everybody here is gay. Some people come to have fun and support their friends. Are you?"

"Nope."

"So that's settled. Tell your brother I said good luck. I'll see you next time we're on the field."

"Alright Cole," Marshall shook my hand. He shuffled toward his car where Ron was waiting for him.

Marshall might not have come out as gay, but at least he recognized he was an ass. It was good to know he'd be off my back. Two medals from the MEAC championship and an apology from Marshall. It was a great way to end the season.

I turned to go inside. Big surprise. Tyree was standing behind me. Damn, this man knew how to sneak up on somebody.

"Doin' crack and havin' sex under the bleachers? *Really*, Cole?" Tyree eyed me in disbelief.

"I needed to tell him somethin' to shut him up. He's the one who's been givin' me static. Specifically about you."

"What do you mean me?" Tyree said with surprise.

"Marshall kept callin' me gay 'cause he saw me around you and Jason. I never said anything. It wasn't worth you stressin' over."

"Oh, I will go over there and tell him exactly who he should be messin' with!"

I stopped Tyree before he charged like an angry bull toward Marshall. "Listen, I wanted to say I'm sorry. For real. I don't ever want you to think I don't care about you because I do. I may not always see things from your perspective, but I promise I'll try to goin' forward. I might slip up sometimes, but know that you're still my boy."

Tyree came down from his anger. "I know you think you

let me down, Cole. That was half of it. My problem was that I allowed other people to get to me, including you. I didn't know how bad of a place mentally I was truly in. To make things worse, I let my expectations of our relationship overshadow how good a person you are. Looks like I'm gonna be here for a while longer, so I want us to work on getting our friendship back."

I wanted the same thing too. I never thought it would be possible again. We hugged for a long time, exchanging everything we couldn't say with our embrace. We had both laid the foundation for the brick wall between us. With every second we held each other, we tore it down piece by piece.

"So tell me something," Tyree said as we finally let go of each other. "Are you missin' April? That girl was the love of your life."

"Ha, not really," I said. "I could use more quality time with my roommates. We haven't kicked back at the apartment like we used to. Do you miss her?"

"I never cared for April that much," he said with a sly grin.

"Yeah and you didn't do a good job of hiding it," I laughed. "But just so we're on the same page, this doesn't mean I'm playin' for your team. I slipped up, I might be at this club again, but I'm still straight. I promise."

"Got it," Tyree said warily. "But if you were on our team you'd make for a great tight end! You like that sports reference?"

"Bruh…"

"I had to get it out of my system!"

"I'ma let you have that one. So we're cool?"

"Like Blue Bell ice cream."

JASON

I counted down the minutes until the probate show began. My line brothers and I huddled on a public basketball court to ready for our journey to campus. Our attire for the night was similar to what we donned for set but injected with Theta colors.

The blue camouflage pants and close-fitting navy tank tops we wore invoked a military presence. On our feet were brand new, coal-black combat boots tied together with orange shoelaces. The odorous clothing that swaddled us when we were on line was gone. Tonight we would start our lives anew.

Our prophytes — members of the fraternity who pledged before us — arrived for the show, including Thetas who already graduated from Morrison. The brothers wore either Theta windbreaker jackets or dress shirts with orange and blue bow ties. After our nine-week long struggle to make it to this momentous evening, we understood the endurance required to wear the colors.

Some of them carried flaming torches that would light our path to the show. Others hoisted wooden paddles over their heads like trophies. The sight of the instruments of misery gave me horrible flashbacks. They were symbols of the fraternity, beloved for generations, but I was glad we didn't have to be subjected to them anymore.

DP silently prepared the Thetas to make the two-block walk to campus. His Theta jacket draped over his shoulders like the cape of an opulent king. It was an arresting shade of orange with Theta Pi Chi emblazoned across the back in royal blue. The collar sported a number 1 in bold typography. "Genesis," his line name, was inscribed on both sleeves.

DP came over to us and pulled five orange ski masks over our faces. "You okay? You good?" he asked each of us with an encouraging slap on the back. "This is what you practiced for! You guys are Thetas. Go out there and let them know it!"

We nodded from under the masks. Vaughn would be my backbone tonight along with my four other line brothers. Before we gathered, he, Junior and Chima circulated tips on how to best outwardly convey the strength of the line. Rodney no longer trembled in the face of the unknown. As men of Theta, our nervousness was a mere hurdle toward greatness.

DP led the procession with one of the glowing torches in hand. "Follow me. Keep your eyes on the fire," he said.

We exhaled any doubt, then began our victory march toward the quad. Our arms were locked around the man in front of us. We were unbreakable. The clunk of our footsteps provided the rhythm as we assertively rocked from side to side. "Let 'em know!" DP barked. We proudly belted out the Theta chant with so much power the student body could've heard us a mile away.

"I said Ooh! Aah!
Smooooooth!
Like a Theta Man!"

The roar from the mob of students grew louder as we marched down the sidewalks of the quad. Flashes from camera phones strobed like fireworks against the night. I couldn't make out any faces as we edged through the throng of onlookers, but the fanatic yelling was unmistakable. We finally halted at the Theta plot in the northernmost area of the quad. The chanting from our colleagues buoyed every positive emotion that cycled through my mind. The collective honor was everything I could've prayed for.

"Go 'head Junior!"

"I see you, frat!"

"Do your thang, Ace!"

"Greetings!" DP yelled over the growing commotion.

We'd said the greetings for the brothers countless times before, but never with the same level of fanfare. Every greeting was more resounding, funnier and over-exaggerated than it was in the bubble of set. The crowd laughed along with us while we praised the virtues of our prophytes.

We paused briefly to catch our breath before Ace called to us: "Brothaaaaas! Are! You! Ready!" It was time to step!

We moved our hands and legs in unison to assert intricate movements with our bodies. Slap-stomp-stomp! Slap-stomp-stomp! The steps that were so challenging to master in the days prior became a faultless cadence. Black fraternities executed variations of this performance for more than a century. Yet our synchronicity exceeded anything I witnessed previously.

"Now break it down frat!" Ace yelled.

"If you're purple and gold, your steps are old!" we shouted to the dazzled spectators. "If you're red and white, your moves ain't tight! If you're gold and black, you best step back! If you ain't orange and blue, we can't see you!"

"And you don't want none of this!" Rodney finished.

We pulled our fists to our chests, keeping our arms up and our elbows out. The brothers shouted their reassurance of our success so far, which in turn imbued our vigor. Chima's deep baritone bellowed the opening lines of the fraternity song. The mass of people gathered around us lowered their chatter to a hush. They understood the importance of the moment.

"There are Thetas in this place!
Though hardships we may face,
We're brothers by and by,
Men of Theta Pi Chi!"

"You better sang Chima!" someone urged him on. We, his line brothers, joined him for the second verse. Our quintet sang from the depths of our souls, soaking in the lyrics of the century-old anthem.

"There are Thetas here right now!
Our heads will never bow,
Because no one can deny,
The brothers of Theta Pi Chi!"

After we concluded our song, we lined ourselves in a row

facing an infinite assemblage of our peers. DP thrust Master of Disaster above our heads as if it were a sword raised in salute. "These men have worked hard! More than any of you will ever know! It's time for us to share with you the five newest brothers of our great fraternity!"

DP rested the paddle on Rodney's shoulder. "The Ace of the Spring line! The head and the heart! You may know him as Rodney Jensen! We know him as... Brother Apocalypse!"

When DP lifted the orange ski mask from Rodney's head, an explosion of cheers erupted through campus. An unexpected number of female students chanted his name in jubilation. Rodney was an undercover ladies man! If this was the admiration he cultivated before pledging, he was sure to be an even bigger hit with the ladies going forward!

DP quieted everyone for the next introduction. It was my turn. Through the slits of the ski mask, I caught a glimpse of my future. It was my destiny to be a leader who united people for a common good. Be bold, I reminded myself. Even the most influential men and women were scared sometimes. It was how they responded to the adversity that truly defined them.

"The deuce!" DP yelled. "The number two of the Spring line! Mr. Jason Cooper A.K.A. Brother Sisyphus of Theta! Pi! Chi!"

He yanked off my mask to reveal the vortex of flashing lights around me. I was bursting with happiness and a sense of relief that the era of pledging had come to an end. Thank you, God, for carrying me through!

I wished my mother could see me. She'd be exceptionally proud. We were part of a legacy of incredible Black men who shared an unbreakable bond. Instead of crying, my face contorted into the most aggressive scowl I could manage. There was no weakness in our frat!

My baby Vaughn was next. He was likely as shaken as I was waiting for his debut. Everyone wanted to see who was under his mask. I already knew. It was the most brilliant and loving guy I'd ever met. "Our Number 3!" DP shouted. "Vaughn Ford also known as Brother Eternity!"

The mask flew off. Vaughn tilted his head back victoriously as he accepted his new title. I wanted to look over at my rock and congratulate him, but we were specifically instructed to face forward until the show was over. Thetas *never* bowed.

As DP moved on to Junior, the crowd showered him with adoration. There was a female voice among them whose fervor exceeded that everyone else. "I love you, Junior!" she screamed. That must have been his girlfriend! I was so pleased they would be reunited. Our line was deeply aware of how much he missed her. "Here he is, Morrison State! Jonathan! Martin! Junior! Better known to us as, Brotha Blue Light Special!"

The sonic boom of several dozen men voicing their support for our line brother drowned out the cheers from everyone else. The football team turned out in large numbers to root on their linebacker. Junior proved to the Thetas and his compatriots that he was a force to be reckoned with.

"Last but certainly not least!" DP shouted into the void. "The number 5, the Tail of the Spring line, the calm in the storm. Chima Eze! Also known as, Brotha Rosa Parks!"

The response was deafening as the final link in the line was inaugurated. We stood proudly in front of our classmates representing generations of Thetas that came before us. We strove valiantly for our place in the pantheon of Black Greek history.

"Morrison State University! I introduce to you! The spring line of Theta Pi Chi Fraternity, Incorporated! The Five! Facets! Of Fortitude!"

Our line flashed the Theta sign in celebration — our two hands cupped together with index fingers touching to form the Greek letter Theta. Once we'd soaked in every hurrah, we threw our arms around each other, jumping while we chanted "Theta, Theta! No one betta!"

Our prophytes joined the huddle, calling out the name of the fraternity we loved dearly. These men were my family! Nothing could tear our brotherhood apart.

"Theta Piiiii!" DP yelled.

"Chiiiiiii!" we cried in response. "YOU KNOW!"

The after party had just begun when we arrived at Brother Major Payne's house. My four brothers and I sported brand new line jackets with the Theta shield on our chest. "SISYPHUS" was embroidered on the back of mine in block letters just above a bold "2." I would forever be the deuce of the Spring line of the Morrison chapter of Theta Pi Chi.

The house was jammed almost to capacity with our classmates, friends and members of the other fraternities and sororities. When we stepped into the room, everyone inside stopped to commemorate our presence. "Look at them Theta boys!" someone boasted as the applause rang.

"Y'all give it up!" DP egged the guests on.

Our brothers pushed their way through the crowded space to welcome us to the post-probate bash. I greeted everyone I could, then split from the group to search for Tyree and Cole. I found them in the kitchen keeping watch over boxes of pizzas.

"There's the boss man," Cole pounded my fist. "You finally

got your letters! It's a good look, Jay."

"Cole was screaming for you," Tyree said with disinterest. "Did you hear him?"

"No, I couldn't hear anything, to be honest! It was so crazy!" I said. "Thank you guys for coming. I can't tell you how much it means to me to have you both here."

Tyree sucked his teeth. His glare shifted from me to a guy who walked into the kitchen clutching a can of Bud Light. I struggled to recognize the face. Was he a friend of his? Tyree reached past me to calmly select a banana from the fruit bowl on the counter. He delicately removed the peel, examined it, then eyeballed the stranger. Our roommate advanced toward him guided by malicious intent. The target looked around in confusion.

Tyree eyed the banana once more. "If you ever touch me again I will rip your dick off without breaking a sweat," he said.

In one chomp, Tyree did away with the tip of the curved fruit and spat it angrily at the guy. The masticated banana struck him directly in the crotch. Tyree's bosom buddy crashed into a group of sorority girls in his haste to leave the room. I'd never seen anyone look so terrified!

Cole laughed so uncontrollably he almost dropped to the kitchen floor. "What was that about?" he asked.

"Remember when I told you about that boy in my class who came at me in the hallway? That was him," Tyree said.

"What's he doing at this party?" I peered over everyone's heads to get another look at him, but he had vanished.

Cole straightened himself and shook off the laughter. "Tyree, I think he got the message you were sendin', fam. We can chase him down and karate chop him if you need us to."

"I can protect myself," Tyree said defiantly. "The only reason he'll ever step to me again is if he wants to end up like that banana. Jason, come with me outside. We'll be back. Cole, stay here."

Being sequestered with Tyree frightened me more than our line's calamitous summit at the beach. He came to the probate show at Cole's suggestion, but we hadn't yet had a meeting of the minds after the tryst at the hotel. The raucous partying in the house deadened as we closed the door behind us. No sooner had we stepped into the backyard that Tyree lashed out, boiling with hostility.

"Jason, you're disgusting," he hissed. "I could never stab a friend in the back the way you did. Cole may not have known that he was the apple of my eye, but you were fully aware. Not only did I have to deal with being rejected by him, but you made it a thousand times worse. You slept with him when you thought I wasn't looking! Tell me now, what was going through your head?"

I looked away ashamed. "Vodka. Too much of it."

"Being drunk is not an excuse!" he peered at me angrily.

I prayed for God to send someone who could help pacify the confrontation. My line brothers, anyone. However, the party inside was insulated from our argument. The compacted rage was ours to share.

Tyree squinted at me bitterly. "I have listened to you talk about being in the closet and how pledging is hard and whine on and on about your mother. None of that bothered me because I thought I was talking with a friend. You played me like a piano, Jason."

"Tyree, this past year I lost sight of who I am to the point that my judgment was clouded. Everything you've said about me is true. What I did was horrible and I don't expect to receive your forgiveness."

My admission of guilt would be returned with a slap across the face from the Tyree I knew. Instead, he stood silently with the manic expression of a tortured soul.

"Surprise, Jason, I am going to forgive you," he scoffed. "If I told you that we should go our separate ways that would be letting you off the hook. So guess what, we're gonna stay friends. That's your punishment. You'll have to relive your sins every time I'm in your presence. I've learned where my strength lies and I won't let you hurt me again."

I was taken aback by his proclamation. Yes, I wanted us to remain friends but surely we would need a conciliation period. Our emotions were too raw to reunite so quickly. Perhaps that was his intention. We would heal together.

"Listen up, boy," Tyree said firmly. "I have a great life ahead of me and you're not gonna get in the way of me accomplishing what I've set out for myself. What you need to do is get yourself a hobby. One that doesn't involve having sex with your roommate."

A hint of a smile unfurled at the corner of my mouth. It was a natural response to what I knew was an intentional joke Tyree layered over his aggravation. There was an unexpected passivity in his words as if he'd considered his speech to me many times over.

Tyree scanned my face with a deep stare. "I've got somethin' for you," he said. He handed me a tiki, a necklace with the Theta letters carved out of wood, threaded with a thin rope and two beads tacked on the end.

"I've been holding on to this since you told me that you made the Theta line. When they picked you, I had no doubts you'd see it 'til the end. Even if we both weren't meant to be Thetas, I'm glad one of us could carry it through. So, we'll consider this a peace-offering?"

I gave Tyree the biggest squeeze I could in appreciation of the gift, but more so to kindle the reformation of our friendship. "Thank you, Tyree!"

"Don't think anything of it," he said soberly. "And I appreciate you comin' to the hospital. I was in a terrible place mentally. I blamed you for my troubles. Truth be told I was glad you were one of the first people I saw when I woke up. I love you and I hate you, but that's part of being a family. We'll always have our ups and downs."

I clutched the gift in my hand. "Tyree, let me make it up to you. Next year if you want to pledge, I'll put in a good word on your behalf. You have the tenacity to handle everything we endured during the pledging process and more."

"Aw, thanks hun," he sighed. We embraced one more time as an act of love. I would always carry the regret from the mistakes I made in our friendship. We would never forget, but I'm glad he found it in his heart to forgive me. We both needed second chances at life.

Cole came bounding out of the house with Vaughn trailing behind him. "Hey, frat! You guys enjoying the party?" Vaughn asked.

"Yes, we needed a moment that was just for us two," I said. "By the way, Cole and Tyree, I want to introduce you to somebody."

My roommates exchanged confused glances. Cole cocked his head, assuming I was playing an ill-conceived prank. "Who, Vaughn?" he asked incredulously. "We were choppin' it up inside the house a minute ago. Jason, we know who this is."

"Okay, let me rephrase that," I said. "I want to *re*-introduce you to somebody. This is Vaughn. My boyfriend."

Tyree couldn't contain the jubilance that was his trademark.

"Your boyfriend?" he exclaimed. "Y'all better do the damn thang! Go on wit' it!"

"Double congrats, man!" Cole said.

My roommates were thrilled that I had an upstanding partner to devote my attention to. Tyree didn't have to worry about me being distracted by Cole. He was out of the picture.

Vaughn grinned from ear to ear. He'd been waiting for me to say those words for the longest time. I was glad to speak them. We'd faced many challenges as a duo and had more to come. I would stand by his side as we soldiered on.

"So this is the real deal?" Vaughn said with joy. "I don't have to creep around with you anymore?"

"Let's give it time before we make an announcement, but yes." I took his hand. "I want us to spend time in each other's company without reservation. And I want you to visit me at the apartment anytime, day or night."

Tyree and Cole watched our interaction like they were sharing a tub of popcorn at a romantic movie.

"That's cool and all but don't be makin' a bunch a noise when you're in the room," Cole teased.

"Please don't mind him," Tyree pushed Cole to the side. "Jason, you pay rent like everybody else. You can do whatever you want."

"We'll be respectful, guys," Vaughn said. "In the meantime, let's go inside before the brothers launch a search party for us."

The celebration was in full swing with students dancing in every available space in the house. My line brothers were at the center of the room, taking in praise from the coterie of Greeks that surrounded them. DP — Brother Genesis — signaled for Vaughn and I to join the reception.

"There's my neos!" DP said as we entered the living room.

Vaughn and I huddled with Rodney, Junior and Chima while the guests encircled us. "I'm such a proud prophyte. It was an honor to lead these men into our fraternity. Let's toast to the Five Facets of Fortitude! Your hard work paid off. I know you're gonna represent Theta to the fullest."

"Thetas!" DP shouted over our heads. "Let me hear y'all!"

"Theta Pi Chi! Alright, alright, alright! Theta Pi Chi 'til the day we die!!!"

JASON

It was much hotter in Miami than it was when we were here in the spring. It was now July, the dead of summer. The sun gifted us with a healthy dose of Florida heat. Not that I minded. I had a can of sunscreen and my companion Vaughn to protect me.

The last time my roommates and I were in the city, it was an absolute disaster. Cutting everything short because of an indiscretion between Cole and I was not how I envisioned the trip would play out. That was why we were having a do-over. Our goal was to bury the troubling memories we desperately wanted to forget.

We were underneath the sprawling umbrellas of the Carlyle Hotel, a white, art deco building with an unrivaled view of

Ocean Drive. Across the street, palm trees swayed above a crew of bronzed volleyball players engaged in a high-spirited match. Tyree and Cole were here and so was the latest addition to our group, Cole's new girlfriend Ericka.

I liked his new companion far more than April, a tragedy of a woman in every sense of the word. Ericka was more endearing and much less abrasive. So far Cole and his sweetheart were inseparable. They were both on the track team and always cheered each other on at meets. The pair frequently jogged through the neighborhood side by side, inspiring each other to go beyond their limits. When the four of us spent time together, it was always a pleasant gathering.

Cole and I hadn't discussed our carnal indulgence since the last time we were in Miami. I hadn't stopped wondering since then if he was bisexual or gay. He had only shown interest in women in the time that I knew him. Also, Ericka had obviously assumed a primary role in his life.

I didn't understand how someone could engross himself in homosexuality and then continue on as if he were only sampling free food at Costco. Cole attributed it to a moment of weakness. Our friendship crossed a line that he hadn't anticipated, but he maintained that he wasn't attracted to men. His stance was befuddling, however I accepted it rather than belabor the issue. One mistake on both of our parts would not be the end of our trio.

The school year ended last week so there was no more studying or exams for us until the fall. Without the workload, we'd all become more mellow versions of our previous selves. Tyree breathed easier after he was voted into the student government association. The board wouldn't meet for school business until September, but he was buoyed by the coming change he'd affect at Morrison. The time away from campus also meant Tyree was distanced from his past aggressors. He reset himself and found greater peace of mind.

My GPA took a hit because of pledging, which I expected. With fewer extracurricular interruptions in my future, I had every intention of bouncing back. I also had the Thetas to help me in my endeavors. Our brotherhood exceeded my expectations. Normally, I would return home to Athens for the summer, but other than my mom, I didn't have a reason to go back. My new life was in Florida. I had built my own version of a family here.

My independence didn't mean I loved my mother any less. I set forth to be the man she always wanted me to be. Of course, Vaughn wasn't the mate she had in mind, but it was something we both would have to come to terms with one day in the future. I wasn't yet ready to disclose our intimacy to her.

My friends sat around the table sipping on peach daiquiris while Tyree and I enjoyed virgin piña coladas. I hadn't given up drinking completely, but I abstained every so often to maintain a greater balance in my life. It was a vice that I learned I could live without occasionally.

Tyree eyed Cole, who diligently gulped his daiquiri. "I see somebody's broadening their horizons," he said. "I thought that drink would be too girly for a member of the Hennessey fan club."

"Nah, it's sweet, like my sugar," Cole said. Ericka smiled like she'd won the lottery. They exchanged fleeting glances as if they were communicating a private joke that no one else could hear.

"Cole, you'll be a senior next semester," I said. "What do you have planned for your last year at Morrison?"

"I wanna do an internship at a law firm or maybe study abroad. Somewhere like South Africa."

"If you go, you have to take me with you," Ericka cooed.

"Baby, I wouldn't think about leavin' without you." He planted a kiss on her cheek.

"I traveled to South Africa in high school," Vaughn volunteered. "My family has connections down there. If you want, I can hook you up with a place to stay."

"That's wassup! My man." Cole fist bumped Vaughn across the table. My guy was always so resourceful.

The beep from the Grindr app on Tyree's phone rattled the table. We waited patiently for him to finish browsing. "I wanna see what this city has to offer!" he explained without regret. "I'm not gonna let anybody stop me from findin' my dream guy. If at first you don't succeed, try many, *many* times."

"Can't argue with that," Ericka said. I could. Cole and I looked at Tyree disapprovingly. We would not allow him to fall down the same rabbit hole again.

"Don't get me wrong. I'm not lookin' for a husband, y'all," Tyree said as if he'd read our minds. "The way I see it, I can come to Miami and have me a vacation boo. Any foolishness I can leave on South Beach."

"Do you see any contenders for the title?" I asked.

He showed me his phone. It was a screenful of shirtless torsos with bulging muscles. The amount of baby oil and cocoa butter in the pictures was staggering. "Okay! May the best man win!" I winked. "It's beautiful out here, guys. What are we doing next?"

"I wanna go to Lincoln Road and go shoppin'," Tyree said without hesitation.

"Isn't that the neighborhood with the fancy stores?" Cole asked. "Tyree, you ballin' like that?"

"You know good and well I'm not purchasing anything, but if I decide to cop a Fendi bag that's nobody's business but me and Jesus's."

"Amen," Vaughn said.

"See, I like you Vaughn. You understand me."

Tyree passed a smile around the table that acknowledged we were back in his good graces. I was ecstatic that I no longer had to distance myself from him. I couldn't think of anything worse than turning away someone I loved in their darkest hour. I would never do it again.

Vaughn set two $20 bills on the table. "Guys, here's some money to cover our drinks. Jason and I are gonna head to the beach. We'll be back soon."

Vaughn and I strolled under the palm trees toward the aquamarine twinkle of the ocean. After we crossed Theta, I never thought about the beach the same way. The serene waves lapping at the shore were forever a reminder of how Vaughn and I worked as one to overcome the greatest hardship of our lives.

A lifeguard's whistle warned a group of frolicking children away from the treacherous waters they neared. I surveyed the beachgoers around us. A sense of anxiety overwhelmed me. Vaughn was aware from our experience with one another that I was uneasy about our closeness in public view.

"Can I be candid with you?" I said. He nodded. "We've come a long way since we first met, but this is still new to me. I don't want to lose you because of my insecurities. You deserve all of me, not restrictions and complications."

He took my hand in his and brought it to his lips. "We can take things as fast or as slow as you want. There's no rush. I love you, Jason."

"I love you too, Vaughn." My first instinct was to give him a quick peck on the cheek as a thank you. Screw it. I leaned in for a real kiss that would set my soul ablaze. The sweetness from the daiquiri lingered on his lips and blended with the salty ocean air. The involuntary tremors that coursed through my body reverberated so deeply I had to steady myself.

His warm hands gripped the curve of my backside to pull me closer to him. Vaughn persuaded me with his tender kiss, relieving my apprehension with every brush of his hands against my flushed skin. I released myself into the arms that kept me safe all those weeks. At that moment, I didn't care if I was surrounded by the entire population of Florida. Vaughn was mine.

The man who brought me so much joy swept his arm around me. "Jason, know that we're in this together. I'll be here for you as long as you'll have me."

I silently vowed to do the same for him. I let the sun-drenched shore wash away my doubts. Vaughn and I embraced so closely not even a grain of sand could pass between us. The ground I stood on was stronger than ever.